To Hell's Heart

CRIMSON WORLDS VI

Jay Allan

system 7
publishing

By Jay Allan

Tombstone (A Crimson Worlds Prequel)
Bitter Glory (A Crimson Worlds Prequel)
Marines (Crimson Worlds I)
The Cost of Victory (Crimson Worlds II)
A Little Rebellion (Crimson Worlds III)
The First Imperium (Crimson Worlds IV)
The Line Must Hold (Crimson Worlds V)
To Hell's Heart (Crimson Worlds VI)
The Last Veteran (Shattered States I)
The Dragon's Banner (Pendragon Chronicles I)

Upcoming

The Gates of Hell (A Crimson Worlds Prequel)
(October 2013)
The Shadow Legions (Crimson Worlds VII)
(December 2013)
Even Legends Die (Crimson Worlds VIII)
(March 2014)

www.crimsonworlds.com

To Hell's Heart

To Hell's Heart is a work of fiction. All names, characters, incidents, and locations are fictitious. Any resemblance to actual persons, living or dead, events or places is entirely coincidental.

ISBN: 978-0615884103

It is only those who have neither fired a shot nor heard the shrieks and groans of the wounded who cry aloud for blood, for vengeance, for desolation. War is hell.

— William Tecumseh Sherman

Prologue

Regency Chamber
Planet Shandrizar – Deneb VII

The Regent seethed. It was inexplicable, infuriating. The New Ones were primitives, barbarians. They infested their worlds, living in primitive squalor, but arrogant nevertheless, thinking themselves an advanced power. The Regent had expected to sweep them away with a minimum of effort. But that had not happened. Their technology was backward, that was undeniable, but they were highly skilled at war. How, the Regent wondered, could they have so much experience at battle? The Imperium had long ago destroyed all its enemies. In all of the vastness of explored space, the Regent knew of no other races, save those that had sworn fealty to the Makers…and vanished along with them eons before.

The Regent tasted the bitterness of its failure, and it knew frustration. It reviewed all that had happened, all the events that had defied its expectations. For an instant, a nanosecond beyond the comprehension of any organic being, it considered communicating with the New Ones. Perhaps they were worthy of survival. Perhaps the Regent should parlay with them before launching its final assault. Could these creatures end the Regent's endless, crushing loneliness? Could they be friends?

But time and isolation had done their damage. The Regent's reason had deserted it, replaced with rage...with insanity. Communication was irrelevant, peace unthinkable. The New Ones were invaders, enemies...they were an infestation. They would be exterminated.

The Regent had launched its invasion with regional forces, light vessels more suited to scouting and patrol duties than warfare against a skilled enemy. Now it realized the New Ones were too capable at war, too effective at combat to be eliminated with such forces. It would not repeat its error. The New Ones would face the true might of the Imperium, the vast forces of total war that had lain dormant for untold millennia.

Throughout the Core Worlds, more and more ancient ships began to heed the Regent's call. Most of the power the Imperium had once wielded was gone, lost to the ravages of time. But even that small portion that remained was unimaginably potent, a nightmare beyond the worst imaginings of the New Ones. Perhaps, the Regent thought, their recent victories had given them hope. A tremor passed through its systems; an organic being would have called it amusement. These barbarians had no conception of what they faced; now they would finally meet the unleashed might of the Imperium. They would at last understand true power. And they would know the desperate emptiness of hopelessness.

The Regent reviewed its plans and the order of battle it was now sending forth. Hundreds of ships stirred...thousands. It was but a tithe of the Imperium's former power, but still it was an unfathomable massing of strength. Immense battleships, one hundred times the size of the feeble craft the New Ones possessed, slowly fed power into long-dormant systems, moving toward warp gates from hundreds of systems, converging on the rally point. For the first time in 500,000 years, in all of the endless centuries of the Regent's dominion, the Imperial Fleet was assembling...and all the might that was wrought by the Makers was moving to destroy an enemy.

Chapter 1

AS Midway
In Sandoval Orbit
Delta Leonis IV
"The Line"

Erik Cain's mind drifted hazily as he stared through the observation portal into the deep blackness of the Delta Leonis system. He found the endless void hypnotic, soothing…the quiet peacefulness beckoning, drawing him in.

Peace, he thought…is there really such a thing? Cain could hardly remember feeling at peace. Perhaps when he was a young boy, before his family was cast out of the relative comfort and safety of the Midtown Protected Zone into the violent ghettoes of lower class New York. But that was a distant memory now, almost a dream. And he had a lifetime of reality arguing that peace was little more than a fantasy, and a fool's one at that.

He scowled derisively, chiding himself for his self-indulgence. You're not even a fit creature for peace, he thought grimly…all you are good for is war. And Cain was certainly good for war, even he had to acknowledge that. He'd survived countless desperate battles and led his Marines to victory after victory. He'd longed for peace once, but no longer. Such wishes were a waste of time. Peace was indeed for dreamers, and Erik Cain was nothing if not a realist.

He'd fought the greatest battle of his career on the planet below, and he'd decisively defeated the invasion forces of the First Imperium. In the aftermath of his triumph, he'd been hailed as a hero, and so far he'd managed to remain gracious as unwanted congratulations and rewards were heaped on his shoulders. There was no joy for Cain, however, no elation at the victory. A battle was over, that was true. But he knew the war was far from finished…and he was well aware that the frightful price his people had paid already was just a down payment on what it would cost to win the final victory. If winning was even possible.

He sighed as he looked out into the depths, wondering what awaited his brethren and him lightyears away, beyond the furthest reaches of man's explorations. Humanity had begun to consider the universe its own private dominion, and the events of the past few years had come as a rude awakening. There were others out among those stars, that was now an established fact…and they'd gotten there first, long before man ventured off his native world. Even if the Alliance and its new allies managed to survive this fight, the universe would never be the same again. It had become a darker place…dangerous, foreboding. The hope for the future that had driven the early settlers had transformed, morphed into caution. Into fear.

He'd begged Holm to spare him another round of pointless decorations, but it turned out to be easier to defeat the enemy than to escape the glittering prizes that followed the victory. It had been years since Cain had considered a medal anything but a burden, a constant reminder that his glory had been bought with the blood of his men and women. But he knew Holm was just as powerless to stop the accolades, and he smiled and acted grateful for the awards, even as he forced the bile back down his throat.

Buckets of that blood – the blood of his Marines - had been spilled on Sandoval. First Army had lost over 30,000 dead, a toll that still seemed somehow unreal to Cain. He'd come up during a time of massive change in how war in space was waged. His first drop had been part of an operation comprised of a few hundred combatants, with a captain in charge of the whole thing. On Sandoval he'd had over a hundred thousand troops, supported by tanks, artillery, and aircraft…not to mention a roomful of generals to command it all. As always, he thought, man's most noteworthy achievements were in the waging of war. We're very good at killing each other, he thought...at least for once that skill has proven truly useful. This time men weren't fighting each other, they were united against a common enemy. Cain had expected that to make a difference, and it had...to a point. But his Marines – and their allies – were just as dead in the radioactive dust of Sandoval.

Still, this war was different from the others he'd fought. It felt more righteous, more honorable. His Marines and their allies were standing between humanity and a ruthless alien enemy bent on genocide. Mankind, always so prepared to resort to violence to solve any problem, hadn't started this conflict. For once, humanity was an innocent victim, standing before a hostile universe struggling to survive. The fatigue, the exhaustion, the grief at the losses...it was the same as it had been in his other wars. But that wasn't the whole story this time. If man was going face extinction, Cain was going to be on the front lines, standing before the enemy and unleashing hell. As grimly as he'd come to think of humanity's future, he'd be damned if some ancient alien race was going to come in and wipe it out.

The war was different in another way. There were more than friends in the line with Cain and his Marines; there were old adversaries too. Fighting alongside former enemies had been difficult at first, but the Janissaries and other contingents of the Grand Pact had proven themselves to be surprisingly similar to his own Marines. Perhaps not as skilled, save for the Janissaries, but driven by many of the same motivations nevertheless. They'd died in the line, fighting alongside his Marines...that much he knew for certain. He wasn't sure he needed to know anything more.

"I knew I'd find you here."

Cain turned, abruptly at first, as combat reflexes responded faster than recognition. He stood at attention and started to snap off a salute, but his visitor waved him off almost immediately.

"Forget the ceremony, Erik. I just wanted to have a quick word with you." Elias Holm was the Commandant of the Marine Corps, Cain's direct commander. His only senior, at least in the ground forces of the Alliance. Admiral Garret was unofficially considered the overall commander-in-chief of the Alliance's military and, with the formation of the Grand Pact, he had been formally named supreme military commander of the full multinational force. As highly ranked as Holm was, and Cain as well, Garret was at the top of the pyramid.

"What can I do for you, sir?" Cain motioned toward a bank of chairs, but Holm shook his head and walked up next to his friend and protégé.

"It is beautiful, isn't it?" Holm stood looking out into the velvety blackness, pinpricked with stars. "I can see why you find it relaxing to come here."

"It's an illusion, sir." There was exhaustion in Cain's voice, deep down somewhere. It would have been hidden to most people, but not to Holm.

"We'll see, Erik." Holm put his hand on his younger companion's shoulder. "If we can win this war, things will be different. It won't be so easy for the governments to go back to their old ways."

Cain was silent for a few seconds. Finally, he croaked out a soft, insincere, "Maybe." Holm was more of an optimist than Cain; he was far likelier to look into the future and see hope. Cain considered himself a realist, though he was pessimistic about most things. But in spite of himself, he believed in more than he sometimes realized. His Marines, certainly, and the spirit of the colonies, which to him represented man's future. The fire of that hope had waned a bit over the years, and Cain wondered if those colonies would manage to avoid the deadening hand of the Earth governments...and even if they did, as they grew, would they escape the home world's fate?

"I'll take a maybe out of you, since it's the best I'm likely to get." Holm knew Cain better than anyone, but he still had a frustratingly incomplete picture of his friend's thoughts and motivations. Erik Cain was an odd duck, there was no doubt about that. A loner at heart, he could step into a command and lead thousands into battle. He loved his Marines, sparing no effort to see to their needs and mourning them bitterly when they were lost. Yet he ruthlessly expended them in battle, doing whatever was necessary to win.

"It is. Sir." Cain let a tiny smile creep onto his lips. He'd been a fairly cheerful sort as an enlisted man, but he'd taken the burdens of command to heart. Over the years, that responsibility had worn on him greatly. He wondered sometimes if his younger self would recognize the grim creature he'd become.

"Well, that'll do." Holm's lips bore a passing smile as well. "Because that's not why I'm here." His voice became darker, more serious.

"I figured it wasn't all fun and games." Cain's tone had returned to its usual cold emotionlessness. "What can I do for you, sir?"

"Admiral Garret and I are going to Earth."

"My sympathies, sir." Cain had no particular love for the world of his birth. Indeed, he'd promised himself many times that he would never return.

Holm stifled a laugh. "I'm not looking forward to it any more than you would, Erik, but there's no alternative." The concern was heavy in Holm's voice; all traces of his earlier cheerfulness were gone. "The governments want to refortify the Line and stand on the defensive. They think it's too risky to invade enemy space."

Cain sighed softly. "I can't say I'm surprised, sir." There was more than a little disgust in his voice. "They use up all their courage grinding helpless Cogs into the ground. Why should we expect them to have any left to face the real enemy?"

Holm turned to face Cain. "That may be true, Erik, but whatever their motivations, we need to change their minds. We can't exactly launch an operation like this without Earth support, not without a lot of problems." His eyes bored into Cain's. "You know that."

Cain remained silent for a moment, turning to stare back out into space. "Yes," he finally said. "I know that." He sounded like he'd bitten into something sour.

"And you know we have to take the war to the enemy?" It was half statement, half question.

"Yes." Cain's response was immediate this time, his voice firm with resolution. "We have to invade the First Imperium." He turned back toward Holm. "You and I both know we can't win a war of attrition against a race with the capabilities of this enemy." He took a deep breath, exhaling slowly. "We have to attack them, hurt them somehow or find some weakness we haven't seen yet." He paused again, just for a few seconds. "Otherwise it's only a matter of time before they wear us down. Then it will just be a question of mopping up occupied space." He stared at Holm, not a trace of emotion in his voice. "And that will be the end."

"I wasn't going to put it quite that way." Holm almost smiled. He'd known Cain would manage to put a darker cast on things than he had, and his protégé hadn't disappointed. Still, he knew the younger officer was correct. The First Imperium was clearly determined to wipe out mankind and, so far, every attempt at communication had been rebuffed. Standing on the defensive was a fool's game, a ludicrous bet that the enemy couldn't mount an even stronger attack than they had before…and the first one had come close to succeeding.

"But you're right. The entire high command agrees…Garret, Compton, Gilson, Ali Khaled. Even old An Ying." The CAC commander-in-chief was notoriously conservative, having come to power in the aftermath of the disastrous Third Frontier War. Cain was a little surprised the old man had enough clarity of thought to reach the same conclusion as his peers. Not to mention the courage to state it openly. Gambles and aggressive action were not generally conducive to success – or survival – in the CAC's rigidly statist regime.

"What do you want me to do, sir?" Cain managed a brief grin. "You don't expect me to convince any politicians of anything, do you?"

Holm let out a small laugh. "No, Erik. I'm not that senile yet. But I do need your help." The amused tone fell quickly from his voice – he was all business now. "I need you to organize the ground forces, get them ready for the invasion. If we get the go ahead, we want to be ready as soon as possible. If we give the enemy time, they'll be back, and we'll be on the defensive again."

"You want me to get 1st Army ready?" Cain's voice was confident. "I've already got that underway, sir. I can assure you that we'll be good to go whenev…"

"Not 1st Army, Erik." Holm looked right into Cain's eyes. "The ground forces of the Grand Pact. All of them."

Cain stared back, the shock evident on his face. "Sir…" For once, Erik Cain didn't know what to say. "I'm, ah…honored. But I don't have that kind of authority, general."

"You do now, Erik." Holm spoke slowly, firmly. "Ali Khaled and An Ying have already agreed. In my absence, you are the acting ground forces commander of the Grand Pact."

Cain looked at Holm, stunned. For a moment it was totally quiet on the observation deck, save for the background hum common to space ships. Finally, Holm broke the silence. "Erik, you have my complete confidence. You know that."

"Yes, general." Cain spoke slowly, haltingly. "But…"

"No buts, Erik." Holm tightened his grip on Cain's shoulder. "That heavy rep you've been building all these years has finally paid off. It wasn't even hard to convince everyone." He took a quick breath. "And I need you, Erik. There's no one else I trust to handle things. If we get the authorization for the invasion, Garret and I want everything ready to go as soon as we get back."

Cain's expression betrayed serious doubts, but he'd never refused General Holm before, and he wasn't about to start now. "Yes, sir." He sighed softly. "I'll do it. You can count on me."

"I knew that before I walked in here, Erik." Holm smiled warmly. "I've known it for years."

Cain returned the smile. And you've been using it for years, too, he thought, mildly amused, just as I do with those I command…I guess we all manipulate each other to get the job done, even our friends. "I'll need carte blanche on logistics. We're still struggling to re-equip from the Line battles, and if we're going to launch an invasion, we're going to need even more supply."

"You have it." Holm cleared his throat. "The Earth governments are scared to death...they'll supply anything at all if it's humanly possible to do it." A brief pause. "What do you want most? Besides basic ordnance and supplies, I mean. More Obliterators?"

Cain thought for a few seconds before answering. "Aside from plenty of nukes, yes. More Obliterators." He paused a few seconds and added, "I'd take some tanks too, especially now that Isaac Merrick's figured out how to put them to really good use." He hesitated again, more briefly this time. "Though I doubt we'll be able to pack many MBTs on an invasion fleet."

Holm nodded. "Yes, you certainly made heavy use of your nuclear ordnance. I haven't checked, but I suspect you used more nuclear weapons than any commander in history...including during the Unification Wars."

"Escalation is in our favor, especially on the ground." There was a touch of defensiveness in Cain's voice. "Their conventional ordnance is superior to ours, but nukes are nukes. It's an equalizing factor."

"Relax, Erik." Holm was trying hard to suppress a laugh. "You crushed the enemy down there. No one's questioning your tactics." Holm was still trying to hide his amusement, not terribly successfully. "Let an old general have his fun once in a while."

Cain smiled weakly. "Sorry, sir." He'd been sensitive about the number of nuclear weapons his forces had used. The combatants on Sandoval had taken a virtual paradise and reduced it to a radioactive hell. Cain couldn't even imagine the long-term effects on the weather or how many decades – centuries? – it would be before the planet was a fit place to live again. Over a million people had called Sandoval home. They'd lived there, worked there, raised children there. Now they were refugees who'd lost everything. Homes, businesses, jobs. Cain thought mostly of his Marines, the thousands dead and wounded. But he knew the civilians paid a price too.

"And you're right...we're not going to be shipping many MBTs beyond the Rim. The Obliterators are a different story though. They give us more firepower per ton than the tanks do…by a multiple of four or five."

"I'll take as many as I can get, sir. General Sparks told me he thought he could have at least 3,000 ready to go before we can leave." Cain paused then added, "And I'd like to put Erin McDaniels in command of the whole group. I know it's a big bump for her, but no one has more experience with the Obliterators."

"I wouldn't have it any other way, Erik." He was nodding as he spoke. "That's a brigadier's billet as least." He paused, thinking. "I'll approve the promotion before I leave. But you'll be able to sign off on any commissions while I'm gone. Do whatever you think makes sense."

"Thank you, sir." Cain's expression changed, a mask of worry creeping onto his face. "Do you think you'll be able to handle the Earth governments, sir?" He sighed. "Because the only way we're going to win this war is to attack."

Holm inhaled deeply as Cain finished. "I really don't know, Erik." He knew Erik tended to be overly aggressive, always preferring to attack rather than defend. But in this instance, Holm agreed completely. God only knew how vast the First Imperium was…how much force it could deploy given time. They'd beaten back one invasion; that was true. But the next one could be ten times the size…a hundred times. "They're scared to death back on Earth, and they aren't used to listening to us."

Cain turned back toward the observation portal, his expression grim. He was silent, but Holm knew what he was thinking. No one trusted the Earth governments less than Erik Cain.

"Erik…" Holm put his hand on Cain's shoulder again. "…I need you to move full bore getting ready for this invasion." His eyes locked on the younger man's. "Because Garret and Ali Khaled and I already agreed…" He paused, and his voice became a whisper. "…we're going to do our best to convince the Earth governments to go along. But we're going to invade anyway, with whatever resources we can muster on our own. If the Earth authorities don't like it…" He smiled grimly. "…they can go fuck themselves."

Chapter 2

AS Indianapolis
HD 80606 VII System
Orbiting Planet Adelaide

Michael Jacobs sat, uncomfortably fidgeting in the command chair on Indianapolis' flag bridge despite his determined efforts to remain still. He was nervous, wondering – dreading - what he'd find on Adelaide. He'd been forced to bypass the planet when he led Hornet and her exhausted crew as they'd run their torturous gauntlet home. He knew he didn't have any choice then, but that provided cold comfort. Jacobs and his people had been carrying crucial intel, and getting it safely back to Admiral Garret was more important than checking on a small band of survivors. It was cold reasoning, but it was sound. Millions of lives…billions…hinged on defeating the First Imperium. Mankind was fighting a war against extinction. There was no room for sentiment…for humanity. But Jacobs still felt like a monster for passing by without so much as trying to contact Cooper Brown and his people.

"Orbit stable, Admiral Jacobs."

Jacobs still wasn't used to being called admiral. He'd been shocked when Admiral Garret gave him his star on the spot, and then again when the Supreme Commander followed up the promotion with the command of the newly-formed Scouting Fleet. The whole thing still felt surreal, and Jacobs was trying very hard not to let anyone see how overwhelmed he was. "Very well, Commander Carp." Jacobs suspected Carp was just as uncomfortable with the shiny new lieutenant commander's insignia on his own collar. O-1 to O-4 was a big jump, especially for a young officer three years out of the Academy. "Any response from the surface?"

"Negative, admiral." Carp's voice was somber. He'd been there too when Hornet had left the survivors on Adelaide to scout deep into enemy space. He'd still been at his post when the battered vessel dashed back through the system without so much as scanning the planet's surface. He hoped…wished against all odds…that they'd survived somehow, though his rational mind told him it was impossible. That was true for us too, he thought defiantly, recalling Hornet's improbable journey home. And we made it. Maybe Brown and his people did too. But the com was still clear…ominously, depressingly silent. If anyone on Adelaide was getting his transmissions, they weren't answering.

Jacobs shifted, looking behind him, ducking for the hundredth time to avoid the conduit that wasn't there. He was still getting used to the amount of space on Indianapolis. No space ship was truly roomy, but to a veteran of the attack ships, a heavy cruiser seemed to offer wide open spaces. "Lieutenant Hooper, updated system scan?"

"All scanners and scouts report negative, sir." Hooper's voice was sharp, precise. "No activity."

Juliette Hooper was one of Jacobs' new people. She was smart, that much he'd noticed immediately. Third in her Academy class, her record had been spotless to date. He liked her, both personally and as a member of his staff, but she worried him too. She was too intense, a tightly wound perfectionist with unrelenting focus. He wondered how she would handle the first situation she couldn't control. It hadn't happened to her yet, but it was only a matter of time…especially with Scouting Fleet heading into First Imperium-controlled space.

"Keep me posted on any changes, lieutenant." He turned from Hooper back toward Carp. "Commander, advise Colonel Winters to have one of his platoons report to me in the shuttle bay in fifteen minutes."

Carp hesitated for a few seconds before answering. "Yes, sir." His voice was tentative, concerned. He paused again before finally turning toward his workstation and relaying the order. "Colonel Winters acknowledges, sir." A short silence. "Admiral, are you sure it's wise for you to go down to the surface? You are in command of the entire fleet. I can go if you…"

Jacobs put up his hand, waving off Carp's argument. The young officer was right, and he knew it. Jacobs had no place in the landing party. It was an unacceptable risk, one that offered little tangible reward. But Jacobs didn't care. "I'm going." He paused before adding, "It's something I have to do, commander."

Carp looked unconvinced, but he understood. It had been hard for Jacobs to pass through the system without even checking to see if anyone was still alive. Duty had left him no choice, but that didn't ease the guilt. Carp felt it himself, though he knew it was worse for Jacobs, who'd been the one in command. Still, he found that he, too, wished he could go to the surface.

Jacobs knew Carp understood…and also that he still didn't think the admiral should leave the flagship. But there wasn't going to be any debate on this. It was just something Jacobs felt compelled to see to himself, and he was the only one who got a vote. He had to find out what happened to those people, to his friend Cooper Brown, and he owed it to them to do it in person.

"Advise Captain Cavendish that he is acting commander of the fleet while I am on the surface." Cavendish was the commander of the fleet's cruisers, and Jacobs' exec. With the demands from the rapidly coalescing Grand Fleet, Jacob's force was seriously short of command staff, and he was the only flag officer present.

"Yes, admiral."

"And commander?"

"Yes, sir?"

"Keep an eye on things for me." Cavendish was second in the chain of command, but he was new to Jacobs, and Carp had been to hell and back with him. This posting was likely to be a hard one…Scouting Fleet was going deep into enemy space, and no one knew what they would face. Jacobs knew Carp understood…he understood because they'd lived it together already. And he'd seen Carp operating under pressure.

"Yes, sir." Carp's answer was sharp and reassuring. He knew what Jacobs was thinking, that much was obvious. "You can count on me, admiral."

"We're getting an intermittent scanner contact, admiral." Colonel Winters' voice was firm and crisp on the comlink. Jacobs had expected a lieutenant to lead the escort party, but when the fleet's Marine commander heard that the admiral was going to the surface he insisted on coming along to direct security personally.

Jacobs twisted his body, squeezing his way out of the narrow hatch and onto the surface of Adelaide. Winters had asked him to remain behind while his Marines set up a perimeter, but his patience was proving limited. Michael Jacobs wasn't the sort to stay behind while others did the work…even when they had powered armor and he just had a navy survival suit.

"Deploy around the contact location, and investigate." Jacobs felt a wave of excitement…and concern. They could be detecting energy output from surviving colonists – or a scanning device left behind by First Imperium forces. Dozens of ships had passed through the system when the enemy retreated from the Line. Even if Brown's people had survived, any one of those vessels could have found his refugees.

"Yes, sir." Winters paused. "Admiral, I repeat my suggestion that you remain in the shuttle." His scanner displayed the locations of all personnel, including the blue blip that represented Admiral Jacobs moving toward his position.

"Negative, colonel." Jacobs had done all the sitting he was going to do. "I'm en route to your location now."

Jacobs' tone hadn't left much room for argument, but Winters tried one last time anyway. "Sir, I'm responsible for your security. I must ask ag…"

"Colonel, I am quite capable of taking care of myself." Not really true, he acknowledged to himself. Any one of Winters' Marines was far more prepared to deal with a hostile surface contact than he was. "I assure you I won't hold you responsible if I am killed or injured." Jacobs immediately wished he could rephrase that. Winters was only trying to do his job.

"Yes, admiral." The Marine's response was sharp and professional. He'd taken the unintended rebuff in stride. Winters was a veteran who'd served in more than one tight spot, including under Erik Cain on the Lysandra Plateau. He knew how to take orders, even ones he didn't like.

Jacobs walked slowly, looking around for the egress points from the underground shelters. He knew were right around him, but he didn't have exact coordinates. Hornet had purged all information on Adelaide before she set out for deep space. There was no way to know what data the enemy might have been able to extract from her shattered systems and broken hull if things had gone badly. Now Jacobs was going by memory... and a lot had happened since he'd last set foot on Adelaide.

He could see four blips approaching on the tactical display. He was startled for an instant until he realized they were Marines. He suppressed a small laugh. Winters couldn't make him stay in the shuttle, but he was well within his authority to assign bodyguards. Jacobs had the momentary urge to inform the good colonel that he did not need babysitters, but he stopped himself. He couldn't fault the Marine officer for doing his duty. And, he figured, it was probably a good idea.

Jacobs was moving slowly toward the last reported scanner contact. He was excited to pick up anything at all. He'd been prepared to find a completely dead planet...no life signs, no energy levels. They were still a long way from finding anyone alive, though. Most likely they were picking up some damaged piece of equipment that was still marginally functional.

The four Marines moved to his side and stood rigidly at attention. Jacobs turned his head toward the leader. "Hello, sergeant. Escorting me around?"

"Sergeant Harold Warne, sir." The Marine's voice was loud and sharp...parade ground perfect. "We have been assigned as your protective detail, sir."

Jacobs couldn't help but be impressed by the precision and professionalism of the Marines. He had nothing but veterans assigned to Scouting Fleet, hand-picked by General Holm himself. Most of them had served all the way back to the Third Frontier War, before the rebellions...and before the demands of the recent crisis had caused a degradation in Marine training and efficiency. These men and women were the real thing.

Holm hadn't given him a group from his dwindling pool of veterans for nothing. Jacobs' ships were going into deep space, into enemy territory, and they were doing it alone. Grand Fleet would come later, assuming it came at all. There were political issues to face before the invasion could launch, and Jacobs was far from certain those obstacles could be overcome. Scouting Fleet would have to be ready to face anything with no idea when support would arrive. He needed the best and brightest at every position, and he was pretty sure he had it.

"Very well, sergeant." Jacobs decided to go along with Winters' idea of necessary security. He was an admiral now, and he'd have to start thinking like one. Admiral Garret would have had a stroke if he knew Jacobs had even come down to the surface. When you are fifty lightyears from your replacement, there is no place for heroics by the commander. Sooner or later, even real heroes learned that lesson.

"Bogies!" The call came over the comlink. Jacobs' suit didn't have the extended tactical display the Marine armor had, and he couldn't see who was issuing the warning. "Armed personnel exfiltrating at coordinates 340/029."

There was chatter all over the field. Jacobs had total com access, so he heard everything. The Marines had battlefield AIs filtering the confused chatter, prioritizing data as it came in. But Jacobs just heard a swirling mass of voices shouting out barely intelligible (to him) battlefield commands.

"Attention all units..." It was Winters, his voice roaring above the others, a model of authoritative command. "...no one fires without authorization from me. These may be friendlies, and if they are, they've been through a lot. The last thing they need is their own Marines firing on them. So keep cool... or your ass is mine."

Jacobs was impressed at Winters' instantaneous grasp of the situation...and slightly intimidated by the colonel's cold, confident orders. He realized he had a lot to discover about command, and not a lot of time to do it. You can learn from this man, he thought. Jacobs had been acclaimed a hero for leading his ship back from enemy space, but that was one incident, driven by self-preservation, he reminded himself. Winters has been leading men and women on battlefields for 20 years.

He quickened his pace, moving toward the reported location. He felt his stomach churning, his legs tingling. Excitement, fear, anticipation. Were they about to encounter an enemy garrison? Or colonists still alive against all the odds?

A staticky voice crackled on the comlink. "Identify yourselves." The connection was bad; there was something wrong with the broadcaster's transmitter. But there was something vaguely familiar to Jacobs. He knew that voice.

"Cooper?" Jacobs spoke loudly and clearly, interrupting Winters, who had begun his own response. "Cooper Brown... is that you?"

There was a pause, no more than a few seconds, really. But to Jacobs it was an eternity.

"Mike?" The voice was still broken up, but Jacobs could hear the emotion. It was Brown. There wasn't a doubt in his mind. "Captain Jacobs? Is that really you?"

Jacobs sat on the makeshift bench, really an old shipping crate modified for the purpose. He'd popped his helmet and set it down alongside the table. He almost wretched when he got his first breath of the air in the shelter, but he hid his reaction the best he could. The atmosphere was fetid, a combination of sulfur, burning hydrocarbons, and the smell of too many people living in too little space.

"I still can't believe you're back." Brown looked across the table at his friend, allowing himself a weak smile. He looked like someone trying to be happy who'd forgotten how.

"I told you I'd be here." Jacobs felt guilty even as he said it. He was back, yes, but almost a year later than he could have been and clad in his fancy new uniform with a shiny platinum star on each shoulder. Brown, on the other hand, looked like hell.

Jacobs remembered a tall, muscular ex-Marine, but the gaunt, stooped figure in front of him bore little resemblance to the Cooper Brown he'd left behind. Brown had lost at least 20 kilos, and his skin hung in loose folds. His eyes were dark and sunken deeply in his lined face, long strands of greasy brown hair hanging down raggedly. "I'm glad to see you, Coop." Jacobs was fighting to hold back his emotions. "I didn't know if you'd made it."

"Mike…" Brown's voice was soft, and he looked over at his friend with dull, lifeless eyes. "…I understand why you didn't stop on your way back." Jacobs had told Brown the story of Hornet's journey. "Stop blaming yourself. You did the right thing…I would have done the same. The war comes first." He paused and coughed, clearing his throat so he could continue. "It wouldn't have made a difference, Mike. There was nothing you could have done anyway. We were behind enemy lines, and you didn't have supplies for us or transport to evacuate the colonists." Brown was struggling, his mind reeling at the recollection of the past three years, but Jacobs could hear the sincerity in his voice.

"Maybe not, Coop." Jacobs appreciated his friend's comments. It didn't take away the guilt, but it helped. "I still wish we'd been able to get you help sooner." The two sat quietly, neither speaking a word for several minutes. Finally, Jacobs broke the silence. "You want to talk about it, Coop?" He looked over at Brown, his eyes wide, expression one of sympathy, demanding nothing…but ready to hear whatever might come.

Brown shifted slowly in his chair, his tattered boot making a scraping sound on the rough plasti-crete floor. "Someday, Mike." His voice was quiet, barely audible, the fatigue in it overwhelming. "But not today."

Jacobs took a slow breath and leaned back in his chair. "Any time, Coop." He smiled thinly. "Whenever you're ready, I'll be there."

Brown looked over silently. His head bobbed slightly, a grateful nod of appreciation to his companion. Someday he'd want to talk about what had happened, what he'd had to do on

Adelaide. One day he'd have to let it all out or it would tear him apart. But not now. He wasn't ready yet.

The door creaked loudly as a metal-clad hand pushed it open. Chuck Winters ducked his head and squeezed his armored body through the hatch. "I have two companies on the way down, admiral." Winters' tone was sharp and by the book, but there was a gentleness there too, one Jacobs had never heard in his Marine commander. "We have med support and food inbound as well." He sighed softly, almost imperceptibly. "It looks like we've got 7-10,000 survivors, sir." Another brief pause. "It's a miracle."

"Eight thousand, four hundred twenty-seven as of this morning." Brown recited the figure robotically, emotionlessly.

"Thank you, Major Brown." Winters spoke softly, soothingly. Definitely something new to Jacobs. "Relief is on the way to all of your people."

The admiral sat, looking at Brown but trying not to stare. "Yes, Coop." Jacobs nodded as he spoke. "We'll make sure everyone gets whatever they need. We've got transports to take them someplace safe. Behind the Line." That would be better than exposed out here on Adelaide, Jacobs thought, but there wasn't really any place safe anymore. Maybe there never had been.

Brown looked up, first at Winters then back toward Jacobs. "Thank you…thank you both." The fatigue was still there, dense and aching. But a bit of the weight was gone…Jacobs could see that. Brown was grateful to have someone else shoulder the burden.

"Admiral, your people are waiting for further orders." Winters glanced over at Brown as he spoke and back to Jacobs. He could see the admiral's hesitation and the concern in his expression. "It's OK, sir. We'll take care of Major Brown." There was a slight pause, and then the big Marine added, "He's one of ours, sir."

Chapter 3

Alliance Intelligence HQ
Washbalt Metroplex
US Region, Western Alliance, Earth

Gavin Stark sat alone at the head of the table, drumming his fingers nervously on the exquisitely polished wood. Could it be, he thought…is it truly possible events have played right into my hands?

He stared down the length of the Directorate table, currently empty, its plush leather chairs lined up neatly. All save one, which was askew. Stark felt a flush of anger at the sloppiness, and he made a note to check which maintenance crew had last been there.

The Directorate wouldn't gather again for another two weeks and, even then, Stark would occupy the meeting with trivialities, just enough to keep the Directors busy and out of the way. The members of Alliance Intelligence's managing body had long worked behind the scenes of its government, wielding considerable power, but serving as a set of checks and balances on each other as well. The scheming of the individual members kept any of them, even the enormously powerful Number One, from wielding uncontrolled influence. That restraint was about to end, Stark thought to himself with grim satisfaction, and until it did he would make sure no one found out what he was planning.

As soon as the Shadow project was launched, he was going to rid himself of the troublesome Directorate once and for all. Then there would be nothing to stop him from seizing total control…and ruling the Alliance with absolute power. Nothing at all. Certainly not the bloated, complacent members of the Political Class, now transfixed by their own fear of the First Imperium. They had long considered their positions sacrosanct, their perquisites and prerogatives untouchable. The last thing any of them would expect was a move from within…not with their attentions focused outward, on the threat from beyond the Rim.

But Stark's mind worked differently. Almost a perfect sociopath, he was capable of disregarding his own fear and reviewing the situation with pure, perfect analysis. The First Imperium was a grave threat; that much was certain. If the war was lost; if legions of enemy warships burst into human-occupied space, civilization would be destroyed. Mankind would be hunted down and exterminated. Stark knew that, but he also realized he had very little control over how the war progressed. There was little point in devoting time and attention to pointless fear. He chose to prepare…to be ready to move if the military somehow managed to defeat the First Imperium. He would gamble now, and throw the dice for the ultimate prize.

Stark figured the odds of winning the war at 50-50. The enemy was larger and far more advanced. But he knew Augustus Garret was a genius, a man capable of adapting to face any adversary. Stark hated Garret - and Holm and Cain too - but he refused to underestimate any of them. He'd done it before, and he'd suffered the consequences. Never again, he swore to himself. Never.

No, Stark wouldn't cower in useless inaction. He would leave the First Imperium to Garret and his band of military protégés. And he would be ready…ready to ensure that their victory served him and not them.

He glanced down at his 'pad, reviewing the governmental surveillance reports his operatives fed him. Stark ran the most extensive intelligence organization on Earth, and he had people highly placed in every nation. What he was reading concerned him. Though gratified that the enemy invasion had been stopped at the Line, the governments remained terrified of the First Imperium. Despite the fact that the military was

almost universal in its insistence that an attack against the enemy
was the essential next step, it looked like all of the Powers were
firmly supporting a defensive posture. All except the Martian
Confederation, but that was no surprise. Their Council would
never stand up to Roderick Vance, and Vance was in bed with
Garret and his crew.

"Fucking gutless cowards." Stark muttered under his breath,
his voice thick with disgust. He hated Garret and considered
him an enemy, but only a fool would doubt the man's military
brilliance. Garret wouldn't let fear rule his actions, but he didn't
want to die under the boot of a First Imperium robot any more
than the sniveling politicians. Cowering on Earth and hoping
the First Imperium didn't come back wasn't a strategy, it was a
prayer. And not letting Garret fight this war his own way was
just asking for defeat. For extinction.

"I'm going to have to help Garret," Stark whispered softly
to himself. He was amused at the irony of the situation. He'd
always known the final battle in his bid for power would be
against the fleet admiral and his allies...he was certain of that.
But first he'd have to make sure Garret had the chance to defeat
the First Imperium. Without that, there wouldn't be anything
left to fight for. I'll have to make sure the politicians go along,
he thought. That wasn't going to be easy...and he suspected
he'd have to be less than gentle to make it work. But he'd see
it done. One way or another, Augustus Garret would get the
approval for his invasion...courtesy of Gavin Stark.

Stark thought quietly, his nearly-eidetic memory already
categorizing the key politicians...and their skeletons and weaknesses. Garret himself couldn't know about any of it, of course.
He'd never accept help from Stark or Alliance Intelligence. No,
Stark thought, I'll have to cover my tracks carefully.

It was perfect, he thought. He would work behind the scenes
to enable Garret to invade enemy space...and that would leave
the core human worlds wide open to his own plans. By the time
Garret and the remnants of the navy and Marines returned, it
would be too late for them to interfere. Their reward for victory
would be to see Stark seize total power...before he hunted them

down and destroyed them all.

Augustus Garret was surprised. A lifetime of war in space, pain and sacrifice he sometimes wondered how he endured... none of it had prepared him for the headache pounding in his skull. "They just don't listen to logic." His voice was pure frustration, with a caustic undertone thrown in. "They've lived in a bubble their whole lives. Even their wars are just games. We do the fighting, and even when we lose, to them it's just moving a few playing pieces around the board." He was staring at the floor, but now his eyes moved up to meet Holm's. "This is the first time they've ever really been afraid."

Holm let out a long, drawn-out sigh. He hesitated before speaking, almost involuntarily. It was certain the room was bugged, probably by more than one organization, but he and Garret carried General Spark's newest jamming device, something so recently perfected only a dozen people knew it existed. Their conversation would remain private, and those who would eavesdrop would get only silence. And frustration.

"You're right, of course. It feels like talking to a brick wall." The political and ruling classes of the Superpowers had become insular and entrenched, an ersatz aristocracy disguised as modern government. Cronyism had become the dominant force in every nation, an unspoken code of conduct between those born into power and influence. Politicians jockeyed with one another to a certain extent, but they all worked together to maintain the overall position of their class...and to exclude anyone outside from encroaching on their privileges. An individual born into a powerful political family may achieve varying levels of success and wealth in his career, but he never feared for his comfort or status...much less his life. Soldiers and Cogs did the dying in the Superpowers, not the politicians. "I know what Erik would suggest." Holm smiled.

Garret snorted out a laugh, but only for an instant. "He and I are probably very close on this." His voice was cold, focused... he was closer to serious than to kidding. "I'm about ready to bring a couple battlegroups to Earth and give them another reason to be afraid."

Holm knew Garret was just venting. At least for now. Earth space was demilitarized by the Treaty of Paris. Leading armed battleships into orbit would be more than a blatant act of treason against Alliance Gov. It would also violate the Treaty, creating an international incident of enormous severity. The other Powers would order their own warships back to Sol, and the Grand Pact would be shattered. Earth's Superpowers would be at each other's throats, leaving the door wide open for the First Imperium to return and finish what it had started. No, as much as Holm and Garret – and certainly Cain – would have liked to dictate to the Earth governments under the guns of the fleet, it just wasn't an option.

"I don't know how I'm going to go back in there tomorrow, Elias." Garret rubbed his temples as he spoke. "More endless prattle, and every day of it just gives the enemy more time to hit us again." He sat quietly for half a minute before turning to face Holm again. "I think we have to accept that we're getting nowhere." A long pause. "We're going to have to do this ourselves."

Holm didn't respond at first; he just looked back at Garret, lost in his thoughts. Finally he said, "I'm ready to do it, Augustus. If we're sure there's no choice." He paused, considering what he wanted to say and how he wanted to phrase it. "But you know we're not going to win by ourselves. If we need to do this without Earth resources, we'll do it…but we're going to lose."

Garret's first impulse was to argue. He didn't like being told he couldn't do something or that any fight was hopeless. It was a lifelong tendency toward overconfidence, and it had gotten him in trouble before…more than once. But he realized Holm was right. It was going to take everything mankind had to win this fight, and if he and the military went rogue, they'd be going in short on supplies and without ongoing support. He'd still do it if there was no other choice, but he knew they had to try again to convince the Earth governments to support the invasion.

"I'd threaten them, tell them we're going anyway, but then we'd never get off Earth." Holm was as frustrated as Garret, and it was obvious in his tone. "And if they detained us, Cain and Compton would be here with the fleet...nothing would stop them. And that would be the end." Garret was nodding as Holm spoke. "No, all we can do is make our arguments again and hope they see the light."

"Great chance of that. Still..."

"Admiral Garret, you have an incoming message from Senator James." The hotel AI interjected with a soothing, elegant tone.

It was late in the evening to be hearing from anyone, especially someone as highly placed as James. "Put her on." Garret turned to face the large com screen just as the Senator's image appeared. "Senator, this is a surprise. How can I help you?" As an afterthought: "General Holm is here with me as well."

"Good evening, admiral...general." James was a master politician, but there was a stress level in her voice she was having trouble disguising. "I'm glad I reached you both."

Garret and Holm sat quietly, both curious. There was definitely something wrong. James was usually impeccably groomed, but she looked tired, haggard. Her expensive business suit was wrinkled and hanging haphazardly from her shoulders, and her normally perfectly coiffed hair was tousled and unruly.

"First, I have some tragic news." Her voice was soft; it almost sounded like she was afraid of something. "I regret having to inform you that Senator Williams has been involved in a terrible accident." She paused, clearly having trouble finishing what she wanted to say. "He is dead."

Garret hesitated. This wasn't what he'd expected to hear. "I'm terribly sorry, Senator. That is indeed tragic news." His mind was racing. There's more to this, he thought...but what? "May I ask about the circumstances?"

"Apparently, he fell from the room deck of his apartment building." James paused, apparently unsure how much she wanted to say. "It seems he was under the influence of several mind-altering chemicals." Another pause, then a grudging addition. "I'm afraid Andrew Williams lived rather hard."

"That's terrible, Senator. What a tragic waste." And if that's all there is to this, Garret thought, I'm a walrus. "General Holm and I would like to offer our most heartfelt condolences. Is there anything we can do?" What a waste of time, he thought, all this etiquette and hair-pulling. Senator Williams was a pompous ass, who'd probably done harm to more people with his constant power plays than anyone else Garret could think of... and he was one of the biggest obstacles in the debate about the invasion as well. Garret didn't give a shit if he'd fallen from a building or choked on a chicken bone. Good riddance.

"Thank you, admiral. Your kind words are most appreciated."

James didn't like Williams any more than I did, Garret thought...but she is really shaken up....what is going on? "Of course, Senator."

"There is another reason for my communication at this late hour, admiral."

Finally, Garret thought, let's get to the point.

"I have had a change of heart with regard to your proposed plan of operation." There was a shakiness to her tone, but she sounded sincere. "I have decided to support your efforts unreservedly."

Garret tried - without total success, he suspected - to hide his surprise. "I'm gratified to hear that, Senator." He paused, deciding against significant elaboration. "And grateful."

"Your gratitude is premature, admiral." James was getting more control over her voice; she was harder to read now. "I'm afraid my support alone isn't going to get you very far. I've taken the liberty of setting a breakfast meeting with President Oliver tomorrow at 8am." She stared out of the screen, her eyes shifting to Holm then back to Garret. "May I assume you gentlemen will both attend?"

Garret's voice was on autopilot, his mind reeling, trying to imagine what was truly happening behind the scenes. "Of course, Senator." He glanced over at Holm, who nodded. "We will be there." He paused, not sure what to say. "Thank you, Senator."

"Don't thank me yet, admiral." Her hand moved toward the com controls. "I will see you both in the morning." The screen went dark.

Garret and Holm, stunned, stared at each other wordlessly. Finally it was Holm who broke the silence. "What the hell was that?"

Chapter 4

AS Midway
In Sandoval Orbit
Delta Leonis IV
"The Line"

Friederich Hofstader climbed slowly, painfully out of the shuttle's open hatch. He was sore, aching from head to toe. As a scientist he appreciated the technology behind the Martian Torch transport vessels. As a passenger, he'd cursed Roderick Vance and his people to hell more than once. Spending weeks at a time getting crushed to death at 44g acceleration without a break was hard enough on the naval crews…it was unbearable for Hofstader and the rest of his scientists. And the trip from Epsilon Eridani was a long one, even in one of Vance's super-fast ships.

He turned his neck slowly, stretching, trying to work out some of the kinks. Midway's port shuttle bay was vast, its arched roof looming 100 meters above his head. Above was a relative term in space, of course, but it felt real enough to his perception.

"You look like shit."

He turned, wincing at the ache in his neck as he did. General Thomas Sparks was walking toward him, not looking much better himself. "Same to you, my friend." Hofstader smiled and extended his hand to the Alliance engineer. Sparks wore the same gray fatigues as Hofstader, though his were neatly pressed and decorated with a cluster of ribbons. Sparks wasn't a combat Marine, but he'd been in his share of hot spots nonetheless, and his awards included several decorations for distinction under fire.

"I just got in from Wolf 359." The primary Alliance ship-yard orbited a gas giant in that system, and it had been running nonstop, trying to install Sparks new weapon systems into the ships of Grand Fleet before the invasion was launched. Any vessels not finished when the fleet shipped out were either going to be left behind or sent into battle ill prepared. Neither option was acceptable to Augustus Garret, so the maintenance crews in the yards were running 16 hours on, 8 off, and work was going around the clock. "I'm afraid I took the Torch express myself." He reached out and grasped Hofstader's hand as he spoke.

"I'm glad to see you're both here." The voice was unmis-takable. Sharp, cold, to the point. Erik Cain had been running everyone ragged since Garret and Holm had left for Earth, and Hofstader and Sparks weren't going to be any exceptions. "We have a lot to do and not much time, so I've ordered some food brought up to the conference room if that is acceptable to you both." In truth, Cain didn't much care if any of it was accept-able – they were both coming if he had to have a Marine escort help them find the way. But he didn't see any reason not to be polite, especially since he knew both of these men had worked themselves half to death on behalf of the war effort.

"Of course, General Cain." Sparks answered first, snapping to attention as his military instincts kicked in. He was a Marine, and directly in Cain's chain of command, while Hofstader was a basically a civilian.

Hofstader was about to respond as well, but Cain beat him to it. "Please, Tom…" He was waving his arm in Spark's direc-tion. "…let's give the salutes and snapping to attention a break and keep this informal." His eyes flicked between Sparks and Hofstader. "Ok with you guys?"

Hofstader nodded immediately. "Yes, general." He forced a smile, though being around Cain tended to put him on edge. "As you know, I am a civilian at heart." The German scientist carried an honorary rank of colonel in the forces of the Grand Pact, but it was purely to legitimize his giving orders to military

personnel assigned to support his work. Before the First Imperium crisis hit, Hofstader's life had been spent in universities and
research labs. Flitting around the galaxy on warships was still
very new to him.

Sparks was still at attention, but he nodded as well. "Yes,
general." Sparks respected Cain with a reverence that bordered
on worship, but the truth was, the intense Marine commander
scared the hell out of him. The thought of calling him Erik was
enough to make Sparks start sweating.

"Let's go." Cain started walking toward the edge of the
flight deck. "We've got a lot to do."

They followed Cain wordlessly into the lift and up to the
control deck. Cain was using the admiral's conference room, a
large meeting space just down the corridor from the flag bridge.

"Grab a seat, gentlemen." Cain walked toward the head
of the table. There were three 'pads and a stack of data chips
spread out in front of his chair. "Lieutenant Graves, where are
those sandwiches?" He spoke into the small comlink clipped to
his collar, his tone annoyed and impatient. Since his victory on
Sandoval, Cain had become, if anything, even colder and more
driven. Destroying the enemy had become his entire life, virtually all that mattered to him. Beyond 2 or 3 hours of sleep most
nights, every moment was devoted to work. Sarah had managed
to get him to relax occasionally, but now she was gone, back on
Armstrong fitting out the squadron of hospital ships that would
accompany Grand Fleet. Erik missed her, but he was relieved
too…now he could focus solely on the task at hand.

"I'm sorry, sir." Graves came charging through the door.
"Your sandwiches will be here in one minute." Graves was a
giant mass of a man, well over two meters and at least 110 kilos
of solid muscle. But in front of Cain the grizzled Marine officer
was nervous and twitchy, his face and neck slick with sweat.

Cain was hardly listening. He waved the lieutenant off.
"That's fine Graves. See to it." He turned up and looked at
Sparks. "Tom, first I want to go over the enhanced plasma
bombardment systems." He leaned back in his chair. "I want to
say that your system is one of the most impressive new weapons

I've ever seen." He paused for an instant and looked right into Sparks' eyes. "I can tell you outright, I don't think we would have won on Sandoval without it."

Sparks stared back, silently at first. This was heady praise, especially from Erik Cain. "Thank you, general." His throat was dry, his voice hoarse. He coughed a few times and continued. "I'm gratified that it was helpful." Another pause, then he added, "I hope it saved some of your people, general. Our people."

"It certainly did, Tom." Cain's voice was unemotional but sincere. Erik Cain was a lot of things, but a bullshitter wasn't one of them. He tended to tell people exactly what he thought, sometimes with unpredictable consequences. "Thousands, I'm sure." Cain turned to face Hofstader. "Friederich, I know your research played a big role in the development of the PBS and General Sparks' other weapons. You have my congratulations on your success." His face softened for an instant. "And my thanks. As General Sparks observed, your work has saved many of my Marines. I can't express what that means to me."

Hofstader looked back at Cain, surprised but trying hard not to show it. "Thank you, general. I am extremely gratified that my efforts have contributed to providing your people the tools they need to fight this war." Cain continued to be an enigma to Hofstader. Just when he decided the Marine general was a rigid, ruthless martinet, he got a glimpse of something else, something deeper and far more complex than the perfect warrior persona he projected. The scientist always respected Cain immensely, but occasionally he also got a feeling that this was someone he really liked. He wondered if anyone saw more than fleeting bits of the real Erik Cain.

The door slid open, Graves slipping in quietly, followed by three stewards carrying trays. The Marine lieutenant was silent, pointing toward the table, directing his companions to place down the food they were carrying.

Cain glanced up. "Thank you, lieutenant." His voice was unemotional, all traces of his earlier irritation gone. "That will be all." He turned back toward Sparks. "As I was saying, Tom,

I am very interested in getting the new PBS drones into action before we engage the enemy again." His tone changed, almost imperceptibly, but Sparks caught it...sadness, regret. "I just can't keep sending pilots on these missions when only one in five comes back." Cain paused, sucking in a long breath and exhaling. "I need those drones."

"I think we can help you there, general." Sparks looked a little nervous. "At least if you're willing to waive some of the usual testing requirements."

"Do you think the system is ready?" The question was direct.

"Yes, general." The scientist returned Cain's gaze, though it took some effort. "I believe it is reliable as is. However I cannot yet demonstrate this fact with adequate field testing results."

"Good enough for me, Tom." For all Cain's stubbornness and hard-driving way of doing things, he could check something off his list rapidly when he was satisfied. He trusted Sparks' judgment, and that was all he needed to hear. He turned toward Hofstader. "Friederich, have you overseen the outfitting of the research vessels?" Grand Fleet would include a squadron of science ships loaded with the best and brightest of Hofstader's hand-picked personnel. Learning more about the First Imperium and its technology was going to be essential to taking the war to the enemy, and that meant Hofstader and his pack of white coats needed to be up at the front, not lightyears away manning some remote research station.

Hofstader nodded. "Yes, general." He paused then elaborated. "I personally oversaw most of the preparations, but I'm afraid I had to delegate the final efforts in order to embark in time to reach Sandoval for this meeting." He hesitated again before adding, "I left detailed instructions behind, and I placed Bradley Travers in charge of the operation. I have complete faith in his ability."

"Good choice, Friederich." Cain smiled. He wasn't sure if Hofstader knew Travers was one of Roderick Vance's spooks, but he did...and he felt better knowing that Vance's resources would be available on Carson's World if needed. "Travers is a good man."

There was a brief silence before Sparks continued the discussion. "General Cain, I forwarded you the updated reports on the status of the new weapons and equipment. The PBS drones were tested after my last transmission, so that data is not included, but everything else is exactly as reported." Sparks looked tentatively at Cain. "Is there anything we can clarify on those initiatives while we are here?"

Cain leaned back in his chair. "No, Tom. Your reports were, as always, meticulous and complete. I am comfortable with the status of all research and development projects." He paused. "There is another reason I wanted you both here."

Friederich glanced over at Sparks. The engineer's confused look confirmed he had no more idea what Cain had in mind that Hofstader himself did. "What can we do for you, General Cain?"

Cain shifted in his seat, straightening the worst folds in his rumpled fatigues as he did. Sparks hadn't noticed until now how plain the general's fatigues were…just 4 small platinum stars on each collar. Erik Cain had more combat decorations than half the people on Midway combined, but there wasn't a ribbon to be seen.

"We just got word from Admiral Jacobs out at Adelaide. It turns out there were survivors from the colony after all." Cain was looking at Sparks as he spoke, and he could see by his surprised expression, the Corps chief engineer hadn't had much hope anyone had managed to hold out on the distant colony.

"There's no sign of enemy activity in Adelaide's system or anywhere between here and there." Cain ran his fingers over his 'pad, and a map of warp connections from Sandoval to Adelaide came up on the main display on the wall. "We're going to be setting up a forward base and supply depot on Adelaide…" Cain looked up from the 'pad and back at Sparks and Hofstader. "…and I'd like both of you out there as soon as possible." He took a short breath. "The first flotilla is leaving in four days. If at all possible, I'd like the two of you to join it."

Hofstader and Sparks both looked startled, but they remained silent. They were aware that Garret and Holm were still on Earth trying to get clearance for the offensive operation. As far as they knew, it wasn't even certain there'd be an invasion at all and, at the very least, they'd expected it to be months before anyone was moving forward.

"Jacobs' tech crews have provisional Commnet links in place all the way out to Adelaide now, so we've got priority communications with less than three days transit time each way." Cain glanced down at his 'pad, his fingers sliding slowly across the surface. "I am sending you both updated dossiers, detailing the resources we are dispatching to Adelaide's system. Admiral Jacobs has already deployed limited ground forces to the planet as well as a squadron of attack ships on patrol. Our first expedition will substantially upgrade these defenses as well as establish a research facility on the planet."

He took a deep breath and continued. "Apparently, the planetary militia fought a considerable battle against the First Imperium invaders, and there is a significant amount of debris that needs to be studied." Cain knew as well as his two subordinates it was unlikely anything useful would be among the artifacts on Adelaide. His own forces on Sandoval had left behind enough shattered pieces of First Imperium robots and equipment to keep the scientific teams supplied for a lifetime. But he wanted his two top researchers on Adelaide for another reason, one he was hesitant to discuss. Mike Jacobs was exceeding his initial orders, moving Scouting Fleet deeper toward enemy space. His initial authorization extended to Adelaide only, but Admiral Compton had given him a quiet nod to keep moving. It was a risk…he was getting farther out in front of support. If he ran into significant enemy resistance he could easily find himself in serious trouble. But he was anxious to go, and Compton wanted as much intel as possible before he and Garret led 80% of humanity's warships into the unknown.

Hofstader answered first, glancing briefly at Sparks before beginning. "Of course, General Cain…I will go if you feel that is where I can be of the greatest service." He was tentative at first, on edge, feeling he should remain behind to manage the arrangements being completed. But he realized there really wasn't much for him to do. The balance of work to be done was primarily logistical in nature, complex, but hardly requiring the supervision of the Pact's senior physicist.

"Thank you, Friederich." Cain shifted, looking at Sparks. "Tom?"

Sparks cleared his throat. "Of course, general." He swallowed hard and added, "I am at your command."

"This isn't an order." Cain softened his tone. "It's a request. I won't order you away from your work here if you think it's important you stay."

Sparks thought for a moment. He had the same impulse as Hofstader, thinking this wasn't the time for him to be away from his crews. But he had everything running smoothly and, assuming the invasion was approved, it wouldn't be that much longer before they'd be pulling out anyway. He was going to have to leave the production crews on their own soon no matter what so, other than a little bit of surprise, there was no reason to turn down the request. Besides, the mere thought of saying no to Erik Cain was more than he could imagine.

"Of course, sir." His voice was firm. "If you think it's best, I completely agree."

Cain nodded gratefully. "I have a few additional reasons I will keep to myself for now, but I do believe it will be helpful." He paused, looking briefly at each man. "Thank you both." He motioned over to the trays on the table. "Now please, have something to eat. We've got a lot of work to do."

Chapter 5

AS Indianapolis
HP 56548 III System
Outer System
300,000,000 km past Newton Orbit

Jacobs sat silently, staring at the main screen. Everything checked out…no contacts, no detectable energy emissions. The scanners and specialists of the fleet were telling him there were no enemies in Newton's system. But Jacobs didn't believe it. Something was somehow…wrong. It was his nose, his gut. But he knew something was there.

Where, he thought…where would I hide if I was an enemy picket? He pulled up the system map, studying it carefully. His vanguard was 30,000,000 miles from the orbit of the outermost planet. That lonely world itself was irrelevant, a frigid, airless ball of rock currently far away, on the opposite side of the primary. But its orbital shell was also a border, leading to the warp gate and beyond, to the very edge of the star system.

Finally, it hit him. There it was…Newton's system had an area of planetary debris, asteroids, and frozen volatiles, similar to Sol's Kuiper Belt but far denser. If was a perfect place to hide…full of debris that played havoc with long-range scanners. "Commander Carp, order Borodino to launch a spread of heavy probes to the coordinates I'm sending you. I want 200% overlap and full power." He looked down at his workstation again. "That's where I'd hide," he muttered softly to himself. "Beyond the warp gate but close enough to scan anything approaching in open space."

"Yes, admiral." Carp responded sharply. He could hear Jacobs whispering to himself, but he couldn't tell what he was saying. He almost asked, but it was obvious the admiral didn't intend for anyone to hear. If Jacobs wanted Carp to know, he'd tell him.

Jacobs sat, deep in thought, only peripherally hearing Carp relay his orders. He'd come to trust the brilliant young officer completely. If he told Carp to do it, he considered it as good as done. If there was anything hiding out there behind the warp gate, the phalanx of probes would be detected immediately, placed so closely together and operating on high power. Jacobs didn't care…if the probes found whatever was lurking there fine; if they just flushed it out into the open, that was just as good. And if he was wrong and there was nothing there, at least he'd know.

"Borodino reports probe spread launched, admiral." Borodino was an old Russian cruiser, hastily modified into a light carrier. Scouting Fleet wasn't a heavy combat organization, but Garret hadn't wanted to send Jacobs into enemy space without some teeth. Borodino and her sister-ship, Tolstoy, each carried two light squadrons of fighters and a large supply of probes. The PRC's Osaka was a bit larger, carrying 18 fighter-bombers. The converted ships sacrificed most of their weaponry and armor to accommodate the landing bays, but they gave Jacobs long-ranged striking power, a valuable resource against an enemy that didn't seem to utilize fighters at all.

"Very well, commander. I want realtime updates."

"Yes, sir." Carp knew Jacobs expected to find something. There was no evidence to support the suspicion, but the admiral's hunch was good enough for him.

Jacobs sat quietly in his command chair, glancing down at the ship's status indicators. Scouting Fleet was understaffed, and Jacobs was skippering Indianapolis in addition to his duties as admiral. "Commander Carp, bring the fleet to yellow alert." Jacobs didn't know what the probes would find, if anything, but he wasn't going to get caught by surprise no matter what happened.

"Yes, sir." Carp worked his hands over his station. "Fleet status upgraded to yellow."

It wasn't battlestations, but yellow alert brought the fleet's units to a high state of readiness, and it directed all vessels to conduct weapons diagnostics. If Jacobs had to move the status to red alert, pre-existing yellow status would dramatically shorten the time it took to get to full battle readiness. And if it turned out Jacobs' concerns were unfounded, it would be a useful drill.

Carp turned toward Jacobs. "Fleet status yellow confirmed by all units, admiral."

Jacobs double-checked Indianapolis' own readiness, but he saw that Carp had already executed all yellow protocols for the vessel. He leaned back and watched the plot displaying the probes' location. The spread was approaching the warp gate, fanning out to widen the coverage area. The sophisticated scanning drones were already operating at full power, sweeping the area. They could detect miniscule energy emissions at fairly long range and physical objects closer in. If there was anything posted near the warp gate, they would find it.

"Probe phalanx passing warp gate, admiral." Carp was tracking the plot and, though he knew the admiral was watching himself, he verbally updated him anyway. "Still no contacts." Carp wasn't sure if he expected the probes to find anything, but he couldn't fault the admiral for being careful. Allowing the enemy to detect the fleet without even realizing they'd been spotted could be disastrous. The First Imperium's dark energy transmission system would allow a scout to undetectably warn forces farther down the line. The fleet could easily walk into a trap and, against this enemy, that would mean total destruction.

"Keep monitoring, commander." Jacobs' response was perfunctory; his own attention was focused on the plotting screen as well. A few minutes passed, then five. Still nothing. Could I be wrong, he began to wonder. He'd been so sure.

"Energy readings, sir!" Carp's voice, louder, excited. "Multiple contacts!"

Jacobs saw it too, just as Carp snapped off his report. It

took a few seconds for the AIs to interpret the readings...starship drives roaring to life. Not one drive, not ten...there were more than two dozen, and they were beginning to thrust toward the fleet.

"Bogies inbound, admiral." Carp was working his controls, trying to ID the approaching vessels. "Thirty-one ships confirmed." Carp's voice was still steady, but it was starting to show the strain. Jacobs had been concerned there was a scout hiding behind the warp gate, but none of them had expected to find an entire First Imperium task force lurking in the deep outer system. "Still working on unit IDs, sir."

"Get me those as soon as you have them, commander." Jacobs leaned back and took a breath. Well, he thought, I wasn't wrong...now I just have to get the fleet out of this. He was looking at the plotting screen, considering how to handle an enemy force far larger than anything he'd anticipated. "We've got to stop underestimating their tactics," he muttered almost soundlessly. "They're learning. They're learning from us."

"I've got a dozen Gremlins ID'd, sir." Carp, still working as he spoke. "And four Gargoyles. Computer's still crunching on the rest."

Fuck, Jacobs thought. He hadn't been expecting ships as heavy as Gargoyles...he'd only anticipated a scouting force. This was going to be a real fight. He glanced over at Carp, who was still working furiously on identifying the rest of the bogies. He turned, moving his head reflexively to the side again, even though the conduit from Hornet's bridge still wasn't there. "Lieutenant Hooper...transmit fleet order Red-1." He stared right at her, eyes cold and focused. "Battlestations."

Pavel Bogdan clung to the rails of the intraship car as it raced to the launch deck. His Black Star squadron was one of the Russian-Indian Confederacy's most elite, and he'd wondered what the hell they were doing assigned to a hastily modified bucket of bolts like Borodino, attached to a scouting force. Now he knew. Scouting Fleet wasn't out here to meekly prowl around, and Michael Jacobs wasn't about to let an enemy task force stand in his way. That meant facing front line First Imperium ships with suicide boats and a few cruisers...and the Black Stars and their companion squadrons.

He and his bomber crews already had their flight suits on, and their maintenance teams had preflighted the ships. That was all courtesy of Jacobs' yellow alert. The battlestations alarm wasn't in itself a launch order, but it did send them to man their craft and wait for a take-off command. That would likely come sooner rather than later.

Bogdan and his squadron were all veterans, but they hadn't faced First Imperium ships yet. Assigned to the defense of Samvar, they had been held in reserve and hadn't yet engaged when the enemy retreat order was issued. He'd bristled at the inaction and hungered for a chance to get at the enemy. When his squadron was first assigned to nursemaid a bunch of scout-ships, he'd taken it badly. Now he realized his people would get their chance, and far sooner than any of the forces coalescing in the rear for the main invasion. The Black Stars were in the vanguard, and they had a fighting admiral leading them, by God. Yes they did.

The car stopped abruptly at a small catwalk just over two meters above the landing bay's deck. The trip had been a short one; Borodino was much smaller than a capital ship, and everything was crammed closer together. "Let's go, people." He stood up and moved quickly onto the catwalk, the loose metal grating rattling loudly under his boots. Everything on Borodino was loose, thrown together, or half-assed in some way. She was a poor substitute for a proper mothership, but she'd brought his people 40 lightyears to the edge of battle. That had to count for something, he thought, warming slightly to his squadron's new home.

The rest of the Black Stars followed him smartly, 17 in total after Bogdan, six full crews for the RIC's 3-man Karnikov fighter-bombers. Their dark gray flight suits provided protection against both gee forces and the vacuum of space if their ships were breached.

The bay was a loud and busy place, the tools of the main-

tenance crews echoing noisily off the high ceilings. There
were various umbilicals attached to the fighters, hissing as they
pumped liquid nitrogen into the ships' cooling tanks and flame
retardant foam into the damage control systems. Not for the
first time, Bogdan appreciated the massive amount of logistics
required to send his 18 warriors into battle. Without all this, he
thought, we might as well be throwing rocks. A lot of pilots
failed to adequately appreciate their maintenance crews, but
Pavel Bogdan wasn't one of them.

He climbed through the small hatch into the fighter-bomber's main compartment, twisting his body to get through the
narrow access tube. Why don't they make those damned things
bigger, he thought for the hundredth time?

He slid himself over to the pilot's seat and dropped into
place. He started to run his preflight checks as he always did,
though he was aware his support team had already done that.
His backup people were the best, and he knew it. In five years
flying with this team, he'd never found a problem they hadn't.
He glanced at the monitors. There were six small indicators,
and five of them were lit. While he was looking the last one
came on, its soft white glow confirming the last of his crew had
boarded their craft.

"Launch Control...Black Star commander reporting. All
ships manned. Conducting final preflights now." He was already
flipping through the prelaunch checklist as he spoke.

"Acknowledged, Black Star commander." The voice on the
com sounded young, nervous. The fighter squadrons attached
to Scouting Fleet were all veteran, but there just hadn't been
enough experienced personnel to give Borodino and the rest of
the makeshift carriers experienced bridge crew.

Bogdan finished his check by flipping on the ship AI. "Black
Star One Control, confirm status."

"Working." The RIC didn't bother with the sophisticated
personality modules the Alliance used in its AIs. Black Star
One's voice wasn't even a good facsimile of human, with a
heavy electronic sound to it. "All systems 100% operative." The
RIC computer lacked the frill of the Alliance systems, but it was

a potent unit that could get the job done.

Bogdan glanced down at the six indicator lights. All of them had changed from white to green. The squadron's ships were ready. "Launch Control...Black Star commander reporting. Black Star squadron ready for launch."

"Acknowledged, Black Star commander." A pause, short but one that wouldn't have happened with more experienced bridge crew. "Black Star squadron...you are authorized to launch immediately."

"Think man, think." Jacobs muttered softly to himself. He knew his fleet could win this fight. As tough as First Imperium ships were, 6 Gargoyles and 25 Gremlins weren't enough to destroy his force. They could hurt it though...hurt it very badly. He wanted to go at them, face them toe to toe and crush them. But that would be a fool's move, and he knew it. Whatever he did, he had to get the fleet through this fight in decent shape. They had a lot of work to do beyond this system.

"Commander Carp, calculate a thrust plan to pull the fleet back from the warp gate. Designate Beta-2." He wished Newton had fixed defenses...he'd pull back to the planet and add its missiles and fighters to his own if he could bait the enemy to follow. But Newton was virtually undefended, with just a few satellites his people had left to give it at least minimal protection. Certainly nothing meaningful in the coming fight. "Six gee thrust, commencing in six minutes."

Carp glanced briefly at Jacobs, surprised by the order. "Yes, sir," he snapped, turning almost immediately back to his station. "Plotting course for all ships now."

"Lieutenant Hooper, all cruisers are to prepare to drop one spread of laser buoys on my command." The bomb-pumped lasers were one of the Pact's most potent new weapons. Jacobs hated to start expending his limited supply so soon, but he decided it was better to go through ordnance than start getting his ships torn to hell.

"Yes, sir." Hooper's response was crisp and perfect, as usual.

"Very well, lieutenant." Jacobs continued to be impressed

with her, but he was still worried about how she would handle herself when things got out of control. She was so tightly wound, tense and precise about everything...he knew he was going to have to help her through that crisis when it came. He'd never felt as out of control as he did on Hornet's mad dash home from the enemy base, and it had been difficult at first to learn to trust his instincts. Now he combined his gut and his intellect, and he felt like a better officer for it. If Hooper could manage the same leap, he thought, she will be a formidable commander one day. Augustus Garret had told him as much when he assigned her to his staff...and there wasn't a better judge of naval talent drawing breath anywhere.

"Order transmitted, sir." Another crisp response, and fast. Jacobs didn't even know how she'd relayed his command so quickly.

Jacobs turned back to Carp. He was surprised he hadn't gotten the thrust plan yet, and he started to open his mouth to put some pressure on the young officer. Give the kid a break, he thought...he's gone from tactical officer for a suicide boat to one for a fleet of over 100 ships.

A few seconds later, Jacob's patience was rewarded. Carp spun around to face the admiral. "Thrust plan Beta-2 completed, sir. Locked into all vessels and synchronized." Ready to execute on your command, sir."

"Lieutenant Hooper, what is the status on readiness to launch those buoys?"

"All ships will be ready in two minutes, sir." There was a hint of annoyance in her voice. Clearly, she felt some of the vessels were taking too long.

"Two minutes will be satisfactory, lieutenant." Jacobs appreciated her high standards, but Scouting Fleet had a lot of inexperienced personnel backing up its veterans. "Commander Carp, we will be executing Thrust Plan Beta-2 on schedule."

"All units report ready, admiral." He turned and looked down as his hands moved over his workstation. "Transmitting confirmation now, sir."

"Very well, commander." Jacobs leaned back and sighed

softly. Six gees without deploying the acceleration couches was going to suck, no question about that. But he didn't want his people wrapped up in their cocoons, drugged half out of their minds. Their survival suits were enough to stand up to six gravities, even though it wouldn't be pleasant. He didn't intend to continue any single burn for too long anyway. He was going to fight a running battle, keeping the fleet at missile range from the enemy. He was willing to gamble that this picket force didn't have antimatter weapons, and he didn't want to get anywhere close to the enemy's particle accelerators. His ships would lose the energy weapons battle, but at long range, he felt he could win with missiles supported by fighters and x-ray laser buoys. He hated burning through so much of his ordnance, but his transports had replacements for supplies and ammunition. Lost ships and crews would be gone for good.

"All ships report ready to deploy laser buoys, admiral."

He smiled at Hooper's tone. She was definitely pissed at how long it had taken. "All ships launch, lieutenant."

"All vessels deploying buoys, sir." She was focused on her workstation, watching the launches in real time. It took 30 seconds, maybe 40 before all buoys were out. "All ordnance launched, admiral." Jacobs couldn't tell from her tone if she was satisfied with the performance.

"Very well, lieutenant." He took a deep breath, holding it in for a few seconds before exhaling. "All units are to prepare to launch all externally-mounted missiles." All units wasn't entirely literal. None of the fast attack ships were missile armed, just the cruisers and the seven destroyers from the South American Empire. But flushing their racks would put a lot of missiles into space.

"Commander Carp, thrust plan Beta-2 on schedule in…" He glanced at the chronometer. "…180 seconds." He nodded at Carp's perfunctory acknowledgement. "Lieutenant Hooper, are those missile launches ready?"

She hesitated a few seconds, waiting for the last few confirmations. Her head popped up from the screen. "Yes, sir. All vessels report ready to launch external ordnance."

Jacobs stared straight ahead. The main screen displayed the countdown to the engine burn. He watched it, feeling an almost hypnotic effect as the numbers blinked by. When it read 90 seconds he turned slowly and looked over at Hooper. "Lieutenant..." He tried to keep his voice stone cold, but it was the first time he'd been able to really hurt the enemy, and his excitement showed through. "...Launch missiles."

Chapter 6

MCS Red Lightning
Alpha Centauri System
En Route from Earth to Sandoval

Elias Holm reached his arms above his head and twisted his body, stretching his aching muscles as the steaming hot water washed away the crusted remnants of the ecto-plasmic goo from the force dampening chamber. Traveling in one of the Martian Confederation's superfast transports was hard on the body, no question about it. The Torch ships were either accelerating or decelerating full virtually all the time. Their engines were able to achieve higher absolute thrust levels than those on any other vessels, but the primary factor contributing to their great speed was the ability of the propulsion systems to run full out without a break. Most ships were lucky to maintain maximum thrust for a few hours without a major breakdown. The median point to failure for the Alliance's Yorktown class battleships was less than 9 hours, meaning half of those ships would suffer a critical malfunction if they ran their engines full out for less than half a day. But a Torch could maintain maximum thrust for days without a break.

With travel through warp gates nearly instantaneous, it was the intrasystem journey between transit points that took time. And the Torch's ability to race across the vastness of interplanetary space made it invaluable for rapidly shuttling people and cargo between human-occupied worlds. It also beat the hell out of its passengers and crew, physically and emotionally. Staying suspended for days at a time in the Torch's sophisticated gee force protection system was tough not only on the body, but also on the mind. More than one passenger had been driven to a psychotic episode by the experience, and conditioning and psychological pre-screening were essential for all passengers.

Holm knew the break wouldn't last, but he was enjoying it while he could. It was a long trip from Earth to Sandoval, even in a Torch. He had days and days ahead of him in the ship's force dampening chamber, but the crew was running a scheduled maintenance check for the next three hours, and that gave Holm time for both a shower and a regular meal.

"Water off." Holm snapped his instruction to the AI, and the faucet deactivated. He reached up and grabbed a towel. It was thick and plush, but then he'd have expected nothing less on one of Roderick Vance's transports. The shower had an air-drying system, but Holm had always preferred a good old-fashioned towel.

He finished drying off and grabbed his robe from a hook on the wall, wrapping it around him as he walked out into the cabin. "Admiral Garret is here, General Holm." The domestic AI was more like something from a luxury hotel than a military transport. Alliance ships, for the most part, still had simple buzzers on the doors.

"Open." Holm finished tying his robe and walked over toward the door as it slid open.

Augustus Garret walked in, holding out his hand. "Just got out of the shower?" Garret was amused. He too had raced to his shower from the dampening chamber, but he'd finished... and changed into a fresh uniform and checked his messages too.

Holm twisted his neck slowly as he stepped forward, gripping Garret's hand. "You're lucky I'm out now." Holm had a smile on his face. "That hot water became very important to me. I'm this close to retiring and letting you fight this war so I can spend the rest of my life in a hot shower." Holm pulled his hand back and held it up, his fingers a centimeter apart as he spoke.

Garret laughed. He knew Holm was just as driven as he was, but Garret had never been able to relax, to take a few minutes or hours away from his burdens - not even to enjoy something as simple as a long, hot shower. In that way, he was more like Cain than Holm. The work was always there, the responsibility, the tension...eating at him, making relaxation an impossibility.

"Give me two minutes to throw on a fresh set of fatigues." Holm walked toward the closet. "Then we can get some solid food." The chamber's med system fed them intravenously while they were under high thrust, but Holm was always ravenously hungry when he got out after a long stretch. "Unless you've done that already too."

Garret laughed again. "No. Not yet. I figured I'd wait for you. No matter how long it took."

Holm stepped into the closet area and put on a duty uniform, plain gray fatigues with five platinum stars on each collar and "Holm" stenciled on the breast. He pulled his boots on and walked back into the room. "Alright, let's go. I'm starving."

The two walked out into the corridor. The Torch wasn't a large vessel, and most of it was filled with the amazing technology that made it run. Since it was usually shuttling VIPs around, it had half a dozen plush cabins clustered around a small common area that also served as an officers'/passengers' mess. Garret and Holm walked over to one of the small tables and sat down.

A steward came walking in a few seconds later, alerted by the ship's AI that two officers had entered the mess area. "Good afternoon, sirs." He wore a red uniform with a black stripe on the trousers and gold trim on the shoulders. "How may I help you?"

Holm leaned back. He was tempted to order the biggest steak available, but he knew that would be a big mistake a couple hours before climbing back into the chamber. "Turkey sandwich, iced tea," he said softly, wondering if the disappointment was noticeable in his voice.

"Scrambled eggs, wheat toast, coffee." Garret was apparently thinking along the same lines. "And a glass of water. Very cold." Going into the dampening chamber with a full stomach was asking for trouble.

The steward nodded and walked quickly out of the room. Holm waited for the hatch to close – a meaningless gesture, since he was sure everything on Vance's ships was recorded somehow. He wondered for an instant if he should get Sparks' jammer, but he decided it wasn't necessary. They were among allies now, and if their friends were plotting against them they were doomed in this fight anyway. Besides, they weren't going to talk about anything he wasn't sure Vance knew already.

"I know we've discussed this before, but I have to ask again. What the hell happened back there?" Holm looked across the table at Garret, his expression turning serious. "I'm grateful we got what we wanted, but I'm nervous too." He paused, rubbing his hand over his mouth. "There's something we don't know."

Garret leaned back in the chair. My god, he thought…this chair is comfortable. Why, he wondered, can't the Alliance manage to build a decent chair? "You're right, of course." His eyes stared right into Holm's. "They were terrified of sending the fleet away from the Line, and they weren't even listening to our arguments. Then, in a couple days, Bam! - we get the authorization we wanted."

"And they were scared." Holm instinctively lowered his voice, as he tended to do when discussing things that made him edgy. "I mean beyond the fear of the enemy. It felt…" He paused, reaching for the words he wanted. "…closer somehow."

Garret didn't answer right away. He just sat, his hands moving nervously over the table. Finally he took a breath and said, "You're right. I can't place it, but there's something we don't know." That wasn't entirely true…Garret had his suspicions as, he suspected, Holm did. But he still couldn't figure it out entirely, and he wasn't going to blurt out baseless nonsense.

The hatch slid open and the steward returned carrying a tray. He set the contents on the table and stepped back. "Is there anything else I can get you, sirs?"

Holm leaned forward, reaching out to grab half of the large sandwich on his plate. "No, thank you." He glanced at Garret and back to the steward. "That will be all." The steward nodded and walked out, the door closing behind him.

They ate in silence, neither one willing to ask the question they were both thinking about. Garret kept reviewing that last week on Earth in his mind, but whatever else he considered he kept coming back to the same place. Why, he thought, would Gavin Stark and Alliance Intelligence get involved in this? And on our side?

"I think it's a serious problem, sir." Victoria James sat in a priceless leather chair, the room lit only by a single dim lamp. "And I believe we need to deal with it immediately." She looked over at her companion through the flickering light.

The figure sitting opposite James was impeccably dressed in a dark gray suit, his hair perfectly groomed, nails neatly manicured. Francis Oliver had been president of the Alliance for over a quarter century. He was an arrogant man, even by the standards of the Political Class, but he too was afraid of Gavin Stark. The head of Alliance Intelligence was one of the most feared men in human history. Though Stark had never been conclusively tied to any questionable activity, the list of alleged acts he'd committed was enough to chill the blood of even the most veteran political power broker.

"I tend to agree with you Senator, though I wonder if this cannot wait until the First Imperium crisis has stabilized." He spoke slowly, annoyingly so, James thought, and his voice was deep. "For better or worse, we have staked our survival on Admiral Garret and General Holm. It seems to me that our internal matters can wait."

James breathed softly and fidgeted in her seat. Forcing the issue with the most powerful politician in the Alliance was uncomfortable to say the least. But she was more afraid of Stark than she was of Francis. "With all due respect, sir..." She hesitated again, trying to decide how to phrase what she wanted to say. "...I believe it is extremely dangerous to wait. The conflict with the First Imperium is the highest priority, of course, but moving on this will not divert any resources from the war effort." She was trying to cover every possible counter-argument in advance. The number of times she was going to be able to press the issue after the president said no was sharply limited. She had to convince him quickly. "The fighting may go on for years, sir. How long do we dare wait before finally addressing this issue?"

Francis frowned, realizing they were both going to great lengths to avoid stating specifically what they were discussing. *Perhaps she is right,* he thought, *if my first thought is that I cannot openly discuss a matter for fear that my office security has been penetrated.* It wasn't like he hadn't been worried about Stark for some time. Though he wouldn't admit it to anyone, not even himself, fear had long stayed his hand in dealing with the Alliance's top spy. Gavin Stark was a very dangerous man, and Francis lacked the fundamental courage to move against him.

"Senator, my attention is focused on the leadership of the Alliance through this difficult period." He spoke carefully, meticulously. "However, if you wish to take on this project, I can assure you I will not interfere." There was more to his tone…approval, authorization…even encouragement."

James inhaled deeply, the cool air clearing her mind. The president always kept his office temperature several degrees below normal, and tonight she was grateful. She'd probably be sweating if it had been any warmer. The stress was starting to get to her, and she expended a lot of effort to hide it.

She was being given the go ahead, she knew that. But she was also the one who'd be taking the risks. That was clear to her as well. Francis would love to be rid of Stark, but he wasn't willing to take the risk of moving against the spymaster himself… or evenly opening supporting a move. He would stand out of her way, but that was the best he would offer.

"Very well, Mr. President." She shifted her weight forward and started to rise. "I believe we understand each other." She turned to face him. "And agree."

Francis remained seated. He didn't say anything, but he nodded. James returned the gesture and started toward the door. She stopped before she walked the rest of the way and said, "Goodnight, Mr. President." She waved her hand over the con-

trol and the door slid open. She started through then turned
around one last time. "I will keep you advised, sir." And with
that she walked out into the corridor.

Victoria James was one of the most powerful members of
the Alliance Senate. The third generation of her family to hold
the Seat, she'd leapfrogged over her older brother, a degenerate
who preferred to spend his time abducting and molesting young
Cogs of both sexes to wielding the political power that was the
family's due. Victoria had her own eclectic sexual tastes, but she
had the good sense to keep them in the shadows. She'd had
her eyes on the Senate Seat as long as she could remember, and
she'd made damned sure not to cause any scandals or embar-
rassments, at least not until her alcoholic of a father had the
decency to die and leave her in charge of the family's political
influence. She had a younger brother, far more intelligent and
capable than the older...and he could easily have taken her place
if she'd been less careful.

Her office was palatial, again befitting her station. James was
not immune from the arrogance and corruption that perme-
ated the Alliance's political class, but fear had a way of draining
cockiness and conceit. James was afraid...of the First Imperium, of the changes in the power structure this war might
cause, of Gavin Stark. Most of all, she was scared of Stark and
his rogue intelligence agency. Everyone was afraid of Alliance
Intelligence, of course, but most of that was non-specific. The
agency had a dossier on everyone of note in the Alliance, right
down to local block bosses in South Detroit, and most of those
files held damaging secrets...dangerous enough to cause significant problems if they were released. But James' fears were more
specific. She was sure Stark was up to something beyond his
normal spy games. And considering the malevolent abilities of
the head of Alliance Intelligence, that scared the hell out of her.

"I understand, Senator." Raj Khosla stood respectfully in
front of James' desk. His grandfather had been rescued by
James' during the Unification Wars. Things had been very bad in
India late in the wars, before the Alliance-Russian forces pushed

back the Caliphate, and the St. Petersburg government offered the shattered central Indian states co-equal participation in their fledgling Confederacy. The Khosla clan had been trusted retainers to James' family ever since, and Raj was their head of security. He organized protection for family members...and he handled the dirtier jobs that needed to be done. He was very good at what he did. "I shall attend to this personally, madam."

"Thank you, Raj." James felt considerable relief just from doing something. She'd wanted to get rid of Stark for a long time. She didn't trust his intentions...and the bastard had far too much dirt on her. James didn't like being controlled or blackmailed, and she was going to put a stop to it. "The loyalty of your family to mine shall always be repaid in kind, my most trusted friend."

The retainer bowed, and slipped silently out of the office. James got up and poured herself a brandy from the exquisite set of decanters lined up on the credenza. She wasn't much of a drinker, but she needed something to calm her nerves. Moving against Stark was the most terrifying thing she'd ever done. James had led a life of privilege and power; she was unaccustomed to feeling intimidated. She set the priceless brandy down next to the other ornate bottles. Though she rarely partook, she had the best of everything available at all times. All of her peers did. It was a matter of ego and prestige.

The early members of the political class had been normal politicians, driven primarily by a lust for personal power and status. The eventual merger of the existing political parties in the mid-21st century had been self-serving. Instead of savaging each other in increasingly rancorous political campaigns, those in power began to cooperate...they conspired to protect themselves in their positions and keep others out. Elections became mere formalities, and disruptive voters who refused to cast their ballots as expected became subject to harsh punitive measures afterward.

Once they had secured power for themselves, the politicians began to look ahead, to seek ways to pass on their positions and influence to their children...and later to their grandchildren.

The development of the political academies solved this problem nicely. By requiring all government ministers to be graduates of the academies and controlling access to these institutions, the men and women in power permanently locked out any but those they handpicked themselves. An elaborate system of cronyism resulted, with existing government officials cooperating to approve members of each other's families...while locking out anyone else except the occasional strongly supported protégé.

It was an expedient solution, at least from the point of view of the politicians, but after 150 years it had become ingrained in the Alliance's structure and society. Families like James' went from cynically hanging on to power to genuinely considering themselves an entitled aristocracy.

Gavin Stark was a threat to this established order. He was an outsider who'd blackmailed his way into his Alliance Intelligence. He'd sacrifice a Senator as quickly as a Cog to further his schemes. She could only guess what his plans were, but she was sure they would do no good for anyone. Except Gavin Stark.

She drained the snifter and laid it on the counter. It was late, and she was tired. She walked through her outer offices and into the lobby. There weren't many people left in the Senate Building so late, and the lift came right away. The door opened, no one inside except a janitor. Victoria James gave no notice at all to maintenance workers. They existed to serve, and that was all anyone needed to think about them.

The startled night worker jumped to get out of her way, reaching to hold the door open for her. He tripped as he did, his hand reaching out for the wall to catch himself. He bumped into James, his hand brushing against her shoulder.

She spun around and gave him a withering stare. "Be careful, you imbecile!" Her voice was pure venom.

The terrified maintenance worker jumped out of the lift. "I'm terribly sorry, ma'am," he cried piteously. "Please..." He cringed as he spoke, cowering away from her and looking down at the ground. "...forgive my carelessness. I will take another lift."

She felt the heat around her neck, the residual effect of the flush of anger she'd felt. She was tempted to call Raj, to have this clumsy fool beaten within an inch of his life. But her rage quickly dissipated. The man's abject fear and obsequious pleas salved her pride. And she had more important matters to think about. "I don't expect to see you again, you clumsy fool."

"No ma'am, never." He backed away, moving down the hall toward the north bank of elevators. "Thank you, ma'am."

Miserable Cogs, she thought as she punched the button and the doors quickly shut. She closed her eyes and rubbed the back of her neck, hitting the button on her portable com with her other hand, signaling Gerald to bring the car around. The doors opened and she stepped out into the lobby, moving her hand to the back of her neck again as she did. When she pulled it away it was slick with sweat. I don't feel well, she thought...time to get home. I've been working too hard. Too much stress.

Back on the 112th floor, the janitor stood in the hallway just outside the lift door. He allowed himself a tiny smile then he pulled out a portable com unit and flipped it on. "It's done," he said softly. Then he glided down the hallway and slipped into an empty lift.

Stark sat down in his office, a heavy crystal glass half-full of Scotch sitting in front of him. He was quiet, thoughtful... staring across at one of the leather guest chairs. For many years, Jack Dutton had sat there, discussing strategies and talking with him long into the night. Dutton had been a spy as long as there had been an Alliance, and he was the living embodiment of the old cliché...Jack Dutton knew where all the bodies were buried. Time had finally caught up with the ancient spook, and Stark sorely missed his only friend.

Dutton had been the only person Stark had ever really liked. Or trusted. He enjoyed Alex Linden's company too, especially when she was on her back...or in a number of other positions, he thought with a dark smile. She was smart too, and capable. But Jack Dutton, thinking himself too infirm to handle the top job, had stepped aside so Stark could become Number One. That allowed Stark to truly trust his mentor. Alex, amusing diversion though she was, had her own eyes on the first chair... he was sure of that. Stark could never quite tell if she was truly attracted to him or if she was just using him. But he didn't kid himself...either way, when she got her chance, she wouldn't let him or any feelings she might have stand in her way. Sociopath that he was, he respected that about her. But that didn't mean he'd ever let her get the chance. Pretty little Alex would end up in some deep ditch long before she got her opportunity to take out Stark.

Dutton had been more than friend, confidante, and mentor...he'd been a restraining influence as well. Now that he was gone, Stark's megalomania and paranoia had begun to run unchecked. Number One was a genius, but he was also insane, at least by most definitions. His plans had become unimaginably vast, dangerous enough to threaten everything – the Alliance, the colonies, the Treaty of Paris that had kept peace on Earth for over a century.

He was satisfied; his operative had done well. James had no idea what had happened. She'd be dead in two days, three at the most, apparently of natural causes. The virus was courtesy of one of the more hostile worlds man had explored, a pathogen-infested hell that had been declared off-limits by agreement of all the Powers. But Stark wasn't one to let a storehouse of useful tools go to waste because of something as trifling as international law.

Not only was this nasty little bug untraceable, it closely resembled an Earthly disease that was transmitted among certain Cog populations by unconventional sexual activities... except this one wouldn't respond to treatment. There would be no investigation; he was sure of that. James' peers would want to avoid the scandal and embarrassment. They'd announce that she died of something tragic and conventional. Then they'd give her a big state funeral and forget about her.

The com buzzed again. "Number One, phase two is completed. Raj Khosla has been terminated as per your instructions." The agent's voice was cool, professional. Still, Stark could hear the satisfaction there too.

He should be satisfied, Stark thought...he has done excellent work. "Well done, D." Stark's highest-level operatives were designated sequentially by single letters. "Return to the safe house as planned."

"Yes, sir." The line was cut immediately. There was no room in high level black ops for social niceties, even when speaking to Number One.

Yes, Stark thought, you have done very well. A different man than Stark would have regretted what he did next, or at least appreciated the irony. But Stark was as close to emotionless as a human being could be. He fingered the small controller for a few seconds, finally depressing his hand on the small button. Three kilometers away, he knew the operative had fallen to the ground dead, his aorta ruptured by a nano-explosive implanted in his chest. When he was found, he'd have no identity, no record in the system. They'd assume he was an undocumented Cog who'd snuck into the Core from the outer slums, and they'd chuck him in the recycling system.

The operative had done a perfect job, executed his assignment flawlessly. But this mission was too important, too sensitive...too close to the start of Shadow. And Gavin Stark did not like to leave loose ends.

Chapter 7

AS Indianapolis
HP 56548 III System
Outer System
220,000,000 km past Newton Orbit

Jacobs stared at the tactical screen, totally focused on the unfolding battle. His missiles had passed through the enemy's outer point defense zone, and the surviving weapons were making their final approach. If he'd timed his attack right, the warheads would begin detonating just as the enemy vessels entered range of his laser buoys. That one-two punch would be followed up by the fighter-bombers, which were following the missiles in, using them as a screen to divert the enemy point defense. Jacobs didn't want his missiles shot down, but he'd damned sure rather lose a nuclear warhead than a fighter and its crew.

There were missiles heading toward his fleet too, a lot of them. But less than there might have been. Jacobs had deployed half his fighters to anti-missile runs, and they'd earned their pay and then some. Barely a third of the enemy weapons got past the fighters and the long-ranged point defense. Now Scouting Fleet's defensive lasers and shotguns were ravaging what was left. Some of them would get through; Jacobs knew that. But not many, not enough to seriously endanger the fleet. The energy weapons would be a different story. If enough of the enemy got into firing range in fighting shape, their particle accelerators were going to be a big problem. They had double the range and power of the lasers on Jacob's cruisers.

"Missile detonations beginning, sir." Carp's voice was cool

and professional. Jacobs was still impressed with his young protégé. Garret may very well have promoted Carp to lieutenant commander, but he was still just 24 years old. He was a block of ice under fire; not many officers his age could handle his heavy responsibilities so expertly. "It looks like the new ECM is working well, admiral. A lot of our birds are getting through."

That's good news, Jacobs thought. His people were the first to test out General Sparks' new point defense jamming system. The First Imperium was far ahead of humanity in technology, but their electronic warfare systems had been surprisingly vulnerable to those of the various human fleets. It was an advantage, a welcome one in a war where the Pact didn't have many, and Sparks and his people were determined to press it as far as they could. Jacobs didn't begin to understand how it functioned, but the fact that it seemed to work was a welcome realization. Alliance ships carried fewer and weaker missiles than First Imperium vessels of comparable mass...if they could get more of their ordnance through the point defense zone it would go a long way toward bridging that gap.

"I'm reading multiple close detonations." Carp was staring at his screens, following the reports as they streamed in. "And one direct hit, sir!" His head snapped up and spun to face Jacobs.

A direct hit was a rare thing in missile duels. Targeting a moving vessel millions of miles away, dealing with point defense and evasive maneuvers, was an almost impossibly difficult task. Fleets exchanged massive volleys hoping to get their warheads close enough to cause damage from a near miss. A 500 megaton bomb put out an enormous amount of energy when it exploded, and any vessel within a few kilometers was going to take at least some damage. No ship could survive an actual hit, of course. Even a battleship was reduced to plasma by a direct contact with a warhead that size. In this case, it was only a Gremlin. Jacobs wished it had been one of the Gargoyles, but he decided he would take what he could get.

"Lieutenant Hooper, status of incoming barrage?" Jacobs knew exactly what was still heading in toward his ships, but he wanted to put his tactical support officer through her paces.

"Approximately 18.35% of enemy warheads surviving, sir." Hooper spoke precisely, as if everything she said had been pre-calculated and double-checked. Which, in her case, they had been. "The shotguns are doing extremely well, sir."

It's a damned good thing, Jacobs thought. And they'd take out a lot more too before the missiles closed. He'd launched his volley before the enemy, and the incoming weapons were still 3-5 minutes out. Plenty of time for his point defense to whittle down the total.

"Admiral, I have updated damage assessments from our missile attack." Carp was still hunched over his workstation as he spoke. "Two of the Gargolyes are out of action. One was destroyed outright; the other reads completely dead...no energy output at all." He paused for an instant, reading the data as it came across his screen. "The remaining four have sustained serious to critical damage. A short pause, then: "The laser buoys are commencing fire."

The x-ray lasers were programmed to fire at the nearest target. I should have preferenced the Gargoyles in the firing plan, Jacobs thought, scolding himself for not thinking of it sooner. With the lasers firing so soon after the missile attack, he didn't have the luxury of reacting to the effects of his warheads. The enemy Gremlins were in the vanguard of the First Imperium flotilla, which meant they would take most of the fire from the lasers.

Jacobs was grateful he had a supply of the buoys...it was the only way an Alliance fleet could fight an energy weapons battle with the First Imperium forces and hope to win. It wasn't just the strength of the bomb-pumped x-ray lasers...it was the ability to fire while the fleet itself stayed back, out of the range of the enemy's particle accelerators. If we win this war, he thought, that's going to be why. Of course every Pact officer had made a similar comment at one time or another, about half a dozen different weapons systems and strategies.

"Reports indicate ten Gremlins destroyed or reduced to combat ineffectiveness, admiral." Carp's head was bobbing back and forth, reading multiple data inputs. "Major Bogdan is focusing his bombing strike on the remaining Gargoyles."

Jacobs suppressed a little frown. He wished there'd been time to rationalize the Grand Pact's rank structure. The RIC used army-equivalent ranks for their bomber corps, while the Alliance assigned naval designations. Major Bogdan was the rough equivalent of an Alliance commander, which made him the senior squadron leader and put him in charge of the overall strike. It wasn't really very important, but Jacobs liked things as clear and simple as possible. Confusion and poor communication had lost more battles throughout history than every other cause combined.

"Very well." There was a touch of concern in his voice. He wanted those Gargoyles taken out, but with his bombers targeting them exclusively, he was going to have to deal with a lot of surviving Gremlins. Bogdan was doing the right thing... Jacobs just wished the missiles and buoys had taken out more Gargoyles. "Advise Major Bogdan that I approve his target priorities." He just couldn't risk letting the heavier Gargoyles get into energy weapons range. He outnumbered them enough to win the battle no matter what, but his ships would be ravaged, and he simply couldn't risk taking that much damage so early in the campaign. If the enemy had over 30 ships on patrol here, there were worse things waiting for his people down the line. "And wish the major good luck and Godspeed."

Bogdan's bomber cut the 4g thrust that had been pushing down on its crew and went into free fall. The Gargoyle was less than 80,000 klicks from his ship...knife fighting range in space. Coming in this close was dangerous, but Bogdan didn't care... he was going to take this son of a bitch down, whatever he had to do. He'd double-loaded his plasma torpedo, which meant one of his three crew members was focusing almost entirely on keeping the thing from blowing while it was still in the tube.

Overpowering the plasma torpedoes wasn't his own innovation. He'd heard that Greta Hurley had done it a few times during the battles on the Line. Hurley was a hero in the fighter jock community, worshipped by her own pilots and respected

by every officer who'd ever set foot in a bomber. She'd faced
the First Imperium in more than half a dozen engagements and
come back every time. A lot of her crews came back too, which
was something no other commander could say. Losses were
heavy on her missions, no question, but they'd been far worse in
every battle where she hadn't been there to command the wings.
No one had anything close to her experience facing the First
Imperium. Bogdan had heard they were going to make her an
admiral and put her in command of all of Grand Fleet's wings.
If the rumors were true, she would be the first officer of flag
rank to lead her forces from the cockpit of a fighter-bomber –
and he knew enough about her to be sure they'd never get her
out of her fighter. Her legend would continue to grow, Bogdan thought with a smile. He couldn't think of an officer who
deserved it more…or anyone he'd follow more willingly into the
burning fires of hell.

"Watch those torpedo readings, people." He had three other
ships with overpowered weapons in the launch tubes. The other
two of his birds didn't make it through the point defense. Losing a third of his ships already had him pissed…he didn't want
anyone getting careless now. If his people stayed focused, they
could do their jobs and get out without any more losses. And
Pavel Bogdan was not willing to lose any more of his crews.
"Fire at will."

His job as squadron leader done for the moment, he switched
hats to gunner. Pavel Bogdan was going to take this shot himself. The Gargoyle he was facing had a significant hull breach,
and he intended to place his torpedo precisely where it would
hurt the most. He stared into the targeting scope, the bomber's
AI constantly updating the feed. The background noise in the
cockpit gradually vanished for him as his mind tightened and
focused. Bogdan was able to tune out virtually anything and
concentrate on the task at hand with enormous intensity.

That didn't lessen the stress though; it just controlled it. He
felt the rivulets of sweat sliding down his neck as he adjusted the
aiming data, and he could sense his heart beating in his chest like
a drum. He was counting down softly to himself, allowing his

intuition to guide him in tweaking the targeting computer's firing solution. Suddenly, he knew it was time. His finger squeezed tightly, and the ship shook hard. The torpedo was away. "Execute thrust plan Zeta." The weapon would take almost 30 seconds to reach its target, and Bogdan wasn't about to sit around deep in the enemy point defense envelope and wait. "Let's get the hell out of here."

He winced and felt a shiver down his back as he waited for the pinprick of the acceleration couch's med system injecting the pre-acceleration drug cocktail. Bogdan had grimly led fighter squadrons on hopeless missions and coolly ignored enemy fire so thick it seemed to fill space, but he didn't injections, and he always dreaded waiting for the system to give him the shot.

His arm twitched as the needle finally poked into his skin, and he felt the irrational relief he always did once it was over. The compartments on his chair opened, expanding into the protective couch that would shield him from the acceleration that was coming. "Executing engine burn in five, four, three…" The artificial voice of the craft's AI was loud, reverberating off the walls of the small cockpit. "…two…one." Bogdan felt the pressure as his bomber's engines fired at full thrust. The couch and drugs provided considerable protection, but 38g was unpleasant to experience no matter what was wrapped around you. He felt the increased pressure in his helmet, helping to force air into his tortured lungs. Still, he perceived his clarity fading, replaced by the strange hypnotic state so frequently experienced by spacers in high thrust situations.

He was drifting, caught between consciousness and a waking dream, but he heard the AI's voice clearly, and he understood exactly what it was saying. "Target destroyed."

"I said fall back again." Jacobs' voice was sharp…more so than he'd intended. Carp hadn't argued with him; he'd merely passed on the concerns of Jacobs' subordinate commanders. "Inform Squadron Captains Cleret and Mondragon that I understand exactly what I am doing, and I will take their suggestions under advisement. In the meanwhile, they are to execute the specified thrust plan without further discussion or delay."

"Yes, sir." Carp's response was crisp and immediate.

Jacobs understood the thinking of his attack ship commanders, both of whom had considerably outranked him until a few months before. Suicide boat tactics were aggressive, based on speed and daring. The attack ships were considered expendable, at least in the context of major fleet operations, and their crews were audacious, always anxious to get at the enemy.

But they were far from expendable to Jacobs. Attack ships were designed to boldly charge in against larger ships, and their plasma torpedoes gave them enough punch to hurt any vessel... even a battleship. Or a First Imperium ship. But their speed and maneuverability served another purpose. They made excellent scouts, and that, Jacobs reminded himself, was the true purpose of his entire fleet. If he lost his ships fighting with an enemy picket force, he wouldn't be able to properly execute that mission...and Garret and Compton and most of mankind's warships would blunder forward blindly. Even if his vessels were just damaged, it would still wreak havoc with the operation. He was counting on speed, not just to get his ships into good scouting positions, but to get them out again with the intel they gathered. Battered ships operating on reduced power would be poor scouts...and easy targets.

They'd been fighting a running battle for fourteen hours, Jacobs firing a missile volley and thrusting away from the enemy. None of the rounds had been as effective as the first. The laser buoys were gone; there were replacements in the supply ships, but there was no way to reload his warships in the middle of combat. The missile barrages were scoring fewer hits too. Missiles fired from a retreating fleet had to work against the intrinsic velocity of the launch platforms, so they couldn't build as much speed toward the enemy. Consequently, they spent a lot more time in the point defense envelope...and took a lot more losses. Jacobs was thrusting after each launch, increasing his velocity away from the enemy, making each subsequent volley increasingly problematic.

Still, the First Imperium fleet had been worn down. There

were just nine Gremlins surviving, and most of those had at least some damage. The suicide boat commanders were clamoring to go in and finish them off, but so far Jacobs had refused. Pavel Bogdan's bombers had re-armed and flown another sortie, and Jacobs was hoping he could take out the rest of the enemy ships with this last round of missiles. His vessels had just fired the last ordnance in their magazines, so if the enemy survived, he was going to have no choice but to send in the attack ships and take the losses.

His bomber squadrons were in worse shape than he'd have liked. Bogdan had lost close to 40% of his fighters, which was actually low for two attack runs at a First Imperium fleet. But it was still close to half his strength. He had some replacement bombers in the supply ships, and Bogdan was sure at least a third of his crews had managed to eject from their destroyed craft. Given time to rescue his crews and uncase the replacement fighters, he could get his available strength close to 75% of its initial level. Not great, but it would have to do.

"Captains Cleret and Mondragon acknowledge receipt of your confirmed order, sir." Carp had a diplomatic touch. "Confirmed" had a softer feel to it than "repeated." Mondragon had simply accepted the command, but Carp had momentarily thought Cleret was going to continue to put up a fight. The veteran attack ship commander vented for a few seconds, but he, too, ultimately accepted his superior's order.

Indianapolis shook as her engines fired again, and the bridge crew hunkered down as the relief of freefall was replaced with the discomfort of three gravities. The flagship's lights dimmed as the engines roared to life. Jacobs had stayed out of energy weapon range, but he hadn't been able to prevent his ships from taking damage from the enemy's missiles. The Gremlins had been targeting his heavier ships, the cruisers...and they'd managed to identify the flagship, sending heavy fire its way. That was new, he thought...more lessons they've learned from us.

Indianapolis had taken damage from two nuclear detonations, and one had knocked out a section of conduits near the power core. Jacobs hadn't had to power down the reactor, but he'd followed the engineer's recommendation and reduced out-put to 40% until the repairs could be made. The affected com-partments were heavily radiation contaminated, and his damage control teams still hadn't been able to get in there and repair the problem. We've got bots to do so much for us, he thought, but sometimes you just need to get men and women in there to fix things.

He was running projections in his head, educated guesses on what his last missile barrage would do to the enemy. He added it up ten different ways, and it kept coming out the same. There were going to be survivors. He was going to have to commit some of the attack ships after all...or else go in with the cruis-ers and gamble on how many particle accelerators the damaged enemy craft still had functioning.

"Commander Carp..." Jacobs' voice was halting, hesitant. He didn't want to do what he knew he had to. "Order Captain Mondragon to organize a task force of 20 attack ships and pre-pare to move against the enemy formation at my command." Cleret was senior to Mondragon, but Jacobs wasn't about to give the arrogant SOB the satisfaction. Jacobs respected Mondragon as an officer, and he definitely considered him the smarter of the two.

"Yes, sir." Carp pushed back an amused smile. He'd been pretty sure the missile barrage wasn't going to get the job done, that Jacobs had given in to wishful thinking. He'd been confi-dent the admiral would quickly come to the same conclusion, so he'd refrained from offering his own suggestions...especially after Jacobs' exchanges with Cleret and Mondragon.

Jacobs had rescued Carp from a lifepod during the fighting around Adelaide. The officer had served the admiral, then cap-tain, ever since. His respect for his CO over that time had only grown. Jacobs wasn't one of those officers who stuck to his guns out of useless pride and arrogance. When he was wrong, he admitted it, at least to himself, and quietly changed his course. The youthful lieutenant commander had only served under two captains...Jacobs, and before him, Captain Calloway, who'd sac-rificed himself to give his crew a chance to escape certain death.

He knew he was lucky; even in an organization with the history and reputation of the Alliance navy, officers like Jacobs and Calloway were rare.

Carp had been one of the few survivors from the attack ship Raptor when it had been destroyed trying to defend Adelaide early in the war. The small squadron of attack ships under Captain Calloway never had much chance to save the planet from invasion, but that battle had produced extraordinary and unexpected results. Jacobs' ship had miraculously survived, eventually to journey deep into unexplored space and locate the only known First Imperium base. That discovery now formed the basis of Pact strategy.

"Admiral, Captain Mondragon reports he will have a 20 vessel attack force ready for action within five minutes."

Jacobs smiled. He realized Mondragon had already had some preparation in place. It took at least ten minutes just to get the plasma torpedoes out of secured storage. He might have been annoyed, but he couldn't fault an officer for preparedness and initiative, even when it strayed close to insubordination. Jacobs would take doers any day over blindly obedient drones.

"Very well, commander. Advise the captain to report in when his task force is ready." Jacobs paused for a few seconds, then he turned to face Carp. "And commander...tell the captain he is under no circumstances to include his vessel in the force nor lead the attack himself." Jacobs knew what Mondragon would want to do...he knew what he would want to do in his subordinate's place. But he couldn't lose a key commander to a freak shot from an enemy particle accelerator. Not this early in the campaign. Mondragon was one of the few officers he had whom he'd trust on an independent scouting mission. He would need him later; he was sure of that.

"Yes, sir." It was Carp's turn to force back a smile. He'd been thinking the same thing, and he'd expected Jacobs' command...though he didn't think Mondragon would like it much. "Transmitting your orders now."

Francisco Mondragon could swear like no one else in the

Pact's combined naval forces. He had a seemingly unending list of curses from his Basque homeland, most of which only he understood. That was a good thing, because many of them were insulting enough to cause a fistfight at best and a blood feud at worst.

A bit of that invective was silently directed toward Admiral Jacobs. Mondragon didn't dislike Jacobs, in fact he quite respected and admired Scouting Fleet's commander. Unlike Captain Cleret, Mondragon had no resentment over the fact that Jacobs had leapfrogged them both. He had achieved something incredible in scouting so deep into uncharted space, and Mondragon felt he fully deserved the promotion. But now Jacobs had ordered Mondragon to send his ships into battle, and he'd refused to let him go with them. He understood the admiral's reasoning – and he would have done the same thing in his place - but he was pissed nevertheless.

Mondragon had served in the federal navy since he was sixteen years old and, in a service riddled with bureaucracy and cronyism, he'd managed to rise in the ranks based solely on his ability. Few others had been able to attain a commission, much less command rank, without family influence or a powerful patron.

In the days before the Unification Wars, Mondragon's Basque brethren had been less than thrilled to be part of the nation of Spain. Now the entire area that had once been Spain was part of Europa Federalis, and a significant percentage of the former Spaniards were no more enthusiastic at the relationship. But it was the era of the Superpowers, and fractionalized nationalism within Europa Federalis had been brutally crushed for over a century. Many in the Basque areas still bristled at being part of the French-dominated Superpower, but they did so quietly, and only among trusted compatriots. Everyone, it seemed, had a grandfather or other ancestor who'd disappeared or been executed during one of the crackdowns. The age of rebellion, the struggle for freedom…they were long lost and dead, replaced by autocracy grotesquely masquerading as a republic. Technology had shattered the hopes of any would-be rebels. The governments controlled massive high-tech surveillance systems and enormously powerful weapons. The days of freedom fighters taking to the streets to push for change were a fading memory. Like it or not, they were all Europan citizens.

Mondragon was a military professional who spent most of his time seeing to the needs of the men and women he commanded. He paid lip service to patriotism as required by his career, but he had no love for the massive nation he served. He'd felt no calling to follow any flag, and certainly not the Europan one. The navy had been an escape from a life as a migrant farm worker, one he was lucky to get, and he'd jumped at it.

Now he felt something new. He was serving a cause, one he could believe in fully. All mankind was united, facing a common enemy, and Francisco Mondragon finally knew what it was like to feel something akin to patriotic fervor. He wasn't fighting the unending and pointless war with the CEL, watching thousands die to determine whether Paris or Neu-Brandenburg would rule a few disputed colonies. Now he was fighting for home, for his mother and father and sister...for their very survival. It was a feeling he'd never experienced before...and it was making it even more difficult to sit and watch his people go into battle without him.

Jacobs had fought a masterful running battle, expending ordnance, but keeping his fleet from suffering crippling damage. Now, Mondragon's people were going in to finish the job. There were six enemy ships left, all the smaller Gremlins. Every one of them was damaged, but it was unclear how badly. The fast attack ships had to get in close to launch their torpedoes, running first through the enemy's missile and energy weapon zones. If the surviving Gremlins were badly hurt and a significant number of their weapons systems were knocked out, Mondragon's task force might keep their losses light. If those enemy ships had their full missile broadsides and particle accelerator batteries functional, the suicide boats would earn their nickname. Again.

"Enemy missile launches detected, sir." Luigi Tomasino's voice was loud and coarse. Like Mondragon, Tomasino was an unlikely candidate for an officer's commission in the Europan navy, though he owed his position to the generosity of his father's employer and not to his own initiative and ability. He'd been a poorly educated member of the Pleb class, roughly comparable to the Alliance's Cogs. He'd have spent his life as a servant, working for the same Senatorial family as his father, but the elder Tomasino saved one of the Senator's young granddaughters from a fire, losing his own life in the process. The grateful employer offered Luigi his patronage in a new career, and the young man chose to attend the Ecole Navale. Becoming a naval officer would significantly increase his social standing, and he would be allowed to retire to the colonial world of his choice, where he would have substantially better prospects than on Earth.

He'd worked hard, and made the most of his opportunity. He was a solid officer, and while he showed no spark of tactical brilliance, he was diligent and reliable. "It's a ragged volley, sir." He paused, muttering softly to himself as he reviewed the data coming in. "Looks like fewer than 40 missiles, captain."

Mondragon let out a long sigh of relief. At least the missile barrage was manageable. The particle accelerators might be a different story, but if the enemy's launchers are that badly hurt, he thought, maybe the energy weapons are too. "Keep me advised on anti-missile efforts." The attack boats had fairly strong point defense systems. He knew his ships could handle 40 missiles. Something would probably slip through, but they wouldn't take crippling losses.

Mondragon sat quietly, listening to the occasional update from his tactical officer. Tomasino was on top of things, scanning the incoming data and feeding the captain the information he needed. Alliance commanders tended to be more hands on, often following the data on their own workstations even as their subordinates made their reports. Europan captains and flag officers tended to be more elitist, feeling it was somewhat beneath them to scan workstations themselves, and they utilized the chain of subordinates to relay them information.

The task force's point defense took out most of the missiles, only four getting through. Two of those detonated at extreme range, causing only minor damage to two of the vessels. The other missiles bracketed one of the attack ships at close range, completely destroying it. Mondragon winced when he got the report, but this was war, and he knew his people had gotten off lightly.

The attack ships were thrusting hard, moving in at 0.07c and accelerating. The faster they could get through the enemy's fire zone and launch their torpedoes the better. Mondragon sat quietly, watching and hoping the enemy ships had lost all their particle accelerators. He felt his stomach tighten when three of his ships were hit within seconds of entering the effective fire zone.

Shit, he thought. If that fire keeps up it's going to be a bloody day. He watched, staring directly at the screen, too impatient to wait for Tomasino's updates. He watched for the other enemy ships to fire, but none of them did. Each second passed slowly, and Mondragon was tense, waiting for more of the energy beams to lash out at his ships. Finally he sighed and thought, it looks three is all they have. As the seconds passed he realized even those three weapons weren't firing again. The chronometer went well past the recharge time for First Imperium particle accelerators, but still no shots came. Eventually, minutes after he'd expected, one of the batteries fired, then another. Even the functional weapons – or their power supplies – were damaged. They were shooting slowly, significantly below half their normal rate of fire. It was good news, better than he could have hoped.

The attacking force blasted toward the enemy, altering their vectors slightly, splitting into six attacking groups. They lost another two ships before they were in range, but the surviving 17 sent 34 plasma torpedoes into the guts of the damaged Gremlins.

They streaked by, turning to madly decelerate, and in their wake they left nothing. Nothing at all.

Chapter 8

AS Midway
In Sandoval Orbit
Delta Leonis IV
"The Line"

"I'm leaving in three days, four tops. Just as soon as we can finish loading and fueling the last of the ships." Terrance Compton stood almost motionless, his voice calm and relaxed despite the seriousness of the discussion. "I'd like you to come with me." He'd known just where to find Cain. The grim Marine general had all his people running around in a frenzy, but he had everything so well under control there was nothing else for him to do. Compton knew he'd be here, staring off into the blackness of space, one of the few things that soothed his nerves and relaxed him. He almost felt bad about cornering him here…Erik Cain didn't have many refuges.

Compton stood behind Cain and stared out at the bluish-white disk filling the lower half of the observation portal. Sandoval, looking beautiful and peaceful from 18,000 kilometers. You can't even tell how we savaged her, he thought sadly as he looked. The teams were still assessing the ecological damage the two armies had done to the planet, and each report Compton saw was worse than the last.

Cain didn't turn, and he didn't answer right away either. He was carefully considering Compton's words, and trying to decide what to do. His gut, as always, wanted to charge right in. That was always an easy choice to make. But he was here covering for Holm, standing in as overall ground forces commander, and the Commandant wasn't quite as recklessly aggressive as he was. He wanted to say yes, but he just wasn't sure. "I don't know, Terrance." Cain's voice was soft, distracted. He was still trying to think of what Holm would say.

"Erik, I don't like changing the plan any more than you do." Their orders – both Cain's and Compton's – were to assemble and prepare the entire Grand Fleet to move out as soon as Garret and Holm returned. From the earliest whispers that an invasion was being planned, the strategy had been to move the entire fleet together. That's why Jacobs' Scouting Fleet had been created in the first place, to screen the way for the massed strength of all the Superpowers. Now Compton wanted to take half that force – the newest and fastest ships – and blast off full for the frontier, leaving Garret and Holm to follow with the rest of the fleet, mostly the older and slower hulls. "But Mike Jacobs ran into a lot of enemy resistance at Newton, and he went through half his ordnance taking it out." He took a step forward, standing directly next to Cain, still staring out into space. "You know we need intel from him, so he's got to keep going. His force is crucial, and if he runs into much more resistance, there isn't going to be a Scouting Fleet…and Grand Fleet will be blind. We need to get some strength up there." He paused, finally turning to face Cain. "Now."

Erik sighed loudly and turned his head slowly toward Compton. His eyes fixed on the admiral's for a few seconds before he spoke. "You know I agree with you, Terrance." His faced constricted into a frown - he was troubled, conflicted. "But General Holm has been telling me I'm too reckless for years. This is the biggest thing he's ever trusted me to handle. What's he going to say if he gets back here and sees I've taken off for the frontier with the cream of the Corps?"

Compton didn't answer right away, giving Cain a few seconds to think it through and formulate his own answer. No one was going to convince Erik Cain to do something unless he decided for himself it was the right thing. Finally, he put his hand on Cain's shoulder and said, "Erik, don't you think I've had the same thoughts about Augustus? Can you imagine I would do anything I wasn't sure he'd approve of?" He took a deep breath, exhaling slowly. "But Garret and Holm are buttoned up in one of Vance's transports, and we can't reach them, not without considerable delay. Unacceptable delay." He paused again before adding, "Have you thought about what Elias is going to say if we sit here and let Jacobs and his people go up against the enemy alone? If we let Scouting Fleet get hunted down and torn to shreds for lack of our own initiative?" Compton saw the change in Cain's expression, and he knew he had him. He moved in for the kill. "When has Elias Holm ever left any of our people unsupported when they needed help?

Cain smiled grudgingly, and he forced back a small laugh. He knew he was being played, but that didn't matter. He also realized Compton was right. Holm would be the first to back up any of his people who were catching hell, and he'd do it no matter the risk and regardless of what effect it had on his plans. Cain knew what Holm would want him to do. "Alright, alright. Enough. I'm with you." Cain saw the self-satisfied smile on Compton's face, and the laugh he'd been holding back finally burst free. "So what's the plan?"

"It was nice of Terry and Erik to leave us every rust bucket in the fleet to deal with." Garret was trying not to laugh, at least not too hard. He'd gotten the message from Compton through the Commnet system when their transport briefly stopped at Armstrong on its way to Sandoval. He'd been expecting the fleet to be nearly assembled when he got there, but instead he found out that Compton and Cain had taken the fastest ships – which also happened to be the newest and strongest – and took off for the frontier.

"Yes, it was very thoughtless of them." Holm had an odd smile on his face. He knew Garret approved of what his number two had done, just as he supported Erik Cain's decision. If Jacobs' fleet was running into trouble, they had to get support to him...and every minute counted. The whole point of the invasion was to shake things up and find some sort of weakness they could use against the enemy. Unless they found something, they'd never win this war. They'd hold out as long as they could, but once the First Imperium destroyed the last of the military, it would only be a matter of time before the enemy swept through human space, slaughtering everyone they found. "They didn't even leave you one of the new battlewagons for your flagship, did they?"

Garret gave up trying to control himself, and he let out a hard laugh. He agreed completely with Compton had done. He'd have made the same decision himself, and he'd have ordered Compton to take precisely the action he did. In fact, he'd have scolded his friend if he'd sat around and done nothing to aid Jacobs. But none of that would stop him from giving Compton a good-natured hard time when he was finally able to catch up with him. Which, from the looks of the ships left behind at Sandoval, would be a while.

"I have it easier than you. Erik took all the elite veterans with him, but the rest of the troops can march onto transports just as easily as the old salts." Holm's voice had become serious. "I don't mean to piss in your pool, but you're going to have to do some serious triage on some of these ships. The Imperial tubs don't look like they've seen a maintenance crew since I was a boot. And some of the RIC ships aren't much better." Holm looked like he'd tasted something bad. "And I hate to say it, but a lot of ours are in pretty rough shape. I know your people repaired what they could, but the last few years have been hard on the fleet." The shipyards had been working around the clock, but there just wasn't enough time to complete all the repairs and upgrades. A lot of ships would have to go to war half-prepared. The alternative would be to postpone the invasion…and give the First Imperium time to launch their own renewed attack.

Garret stared back, the grin clinging to his face, but drained of all its sincerity. "Thanks for the update. Let me know when you want help digging a trench." They both chuckled for a few seconds, but it didn't last. There was a lot of work to do and not much time, and they both knew it. "The problem is, we need to get going…and soon." He rubbed the back of his neck as he spoke. "A lot of these ships may have problems, but they're still a significant percentage of our firepower. I'm glad Terry's on the way to back up Jacobs, but I wouldn't want him to run into a too big of a fight either. Not without the rest of the fleet." He took a breath, and looked right at Holm. "It's not like we know what's waiting for us out there."

"Terrance left Camille Harmon in command, didn't he?" Holm's question hadn't really demanded an answer, but Garret nodded one anyway. Compton had taken Erica West with him as his exec. She had more experience fighting the First Imperium forces, and besides, Harmon was senior of the two, which made her the logical choice to leave in charge until Garret returned. "I'm sure she's been kicking every ass she can reach to get these ships ready for action." Holm smiled. He felt a little out of his depth discussing naval matters, but he'd always liked Camille Harmon. She seemed like an independent thinker who still knew when to play things "by the book." His own top subordinates were a little wilder. Catherine Gilson was a rogue who had little use for conventional rules. And Cain was even worse…Holm wasn't sure he even knew what the book was. "Harmon's got a better handle than you on what shape these ships are in. Sit down with her and just go through them all and give each one a quick yea or nay. There's no point prolonging things, wishing you had more time."

Garret stood quietly for a moment. Holm was right. He didn't have time to study things in detail. He knew the Alliance ships backward and forward, but he had forces here from nine Superpowers, and he realized he had nowhere to begin in evaluating them. Not in the amount of time he was willing to delay their departure. "You're right, Elias." His face relaxed slightly as he felt the relief of having chosen a course of action. He tapped the comlink on his collar. "Control, this is Admiral Garret. Please have Admiral Harmon report to me immediately."

"Do you think they can be ready in six days?" Garret stared intently at Camille Harmon. "Really ready?" Garret had put his foot down; the fleet was leaving in less than one Earth week. No changes, no excuses, no delays. It had been three weeks since Garret and Holm had returned, and there had always been a good reason to push things back. A new shipment of laser buoys, a capital ship that could be ready in just a few more days, more repairs that could be completed. Garret realized there would always be a good reason to wait. All mankind was mobilizing, activating mothballed ships and producing new weapons. But the war wasn't going to be decided at Sandoval...that battle had already been fought, and if they gave the enemy time to come back, he knew his people would lose the return engagement. No, he couldn't allow that to happen. The war would be decided in First Imperium space. If the enemy ended up back at Sandoval, it would be over the shattered debris of the human fleet...over Augustus Garret's dead body.

She looked back, her expression focused and intense. "I do, sir." Camille Harmon was one of the toughest flag officers in the Alliance navy. If she said she was sure of something, Garret took it as a given. "I had a...mmm...a talk with their captain." Shanghai had suffered considerable damage during the fighting at Samvar, and Harmon had been less than impressed with the CAC repair efforts.

"I bet that was something to see." Garret allowed himself a fleeting smile. Harmon was a well-known hardass in the Alliance navy, but he didn't know how much of her rep had made it to the CAC. Though, whatever had been known before, he suspected that word had spread by now.

"I just asked him how he'd like to go back to Hong Kong and explain how I replaced him with an Alliance captain because he couldn't get his ship ready on time." Her voice was deadpan, serious.

Garret hesitated. He wanted her pushing everyone hard, but not tearing apart the Grand Pact. They couldn't afford infighting now. Garret already had his Alliance personnel greatly over-represented in command positions. He risked it because he knew them, and he trusted them...and because the Alliance navy was far and away the best of any of the Powers. But the last thing he needed was one of his officers deliberately provoking the CAC. "Camille, we need to tread lightly with the other

Powers…especially the CAC and the Caliphate." The Alliance's two bitter enemies had reluctantly agreed to follow Admiral Garret in the war against the First Imperium, but the relationship was still a fragile one.

"I wasn't going to actually do it, sir." Harmon's gaze was stone cold. "I just told him I would. A little bluff is useful now and again, wouldn't you agree?"

Garret stared for a second, looking right into Harmon's unchanging gaze. Then he erupted into laughter. "Remind me never to play poker with you."

She finally allowed herself a smile. "I know my way around an ace, sir. I used to do pretty well back at the Academy."

Garret himself had always been a middling poker player, despite Terrance Compton's best efforts to teach him. Garret was too aggressive; he always went for the throat, and he lacked the patience a great player needed. Compton, on the other hand, was widely considered the best card player ever to have served in the Alliance navy. Rumors in the bars of Armstrong and Arcadia held that he had secret accounts stashed on a dozen worlds, a lifetime's winnings. Whatever the truth about Compton's alleged secret wealth, he'd largely stopped playing years before, when his rising rank made it impractical to find opponents who weren't under his command.

"Well, admiral, just remember when you are bluffing and when you have a hand." His voice was more serious. He trusted Harmon's judgment, but he wanted to reinforce the point anyway. "You can go a little harder on our own people, but I need you to be diplomatic with the other services." He paused, just for a second. "Remember, we need their help to win this war. Don't assume the political leaders on Earth aren't stupid enough to trash our war effort over some internal argument." He looked right at her. "They are."

She made a face, but she nodded as well. "Understood, sir."

Garret nodded back. "So let's get through this list." He looked back down at the large 'pad on the table. "What about Shogun? She's old, but she carries four fighter groups. Any chance we can get her moving by the deadline? Even if her lasers are shot, she's worth having just as a carrier."

Harmon looked doubtful. Shogun had been the PRC's flag-ship over 40 years before, but she'd been two decades in moth-balled reserve. "She's really old, admiral. Her service dates back to the Second Frontier War."

Garret gave her an icy stare. "So does mine, Camille." He snorted a short laugh. He'd always felt a little self-deprecating humor served a commander well. It was a good counter for all the hero worship, sincere and otherwise. "Though it's hard to believe I was ever that young." He stared at the 'pad, but for a few moments his mind was elsewhere, drifting slowly across the years gone by. Garret had a lot of memories…and a fair number of regrets too. But he had work to do now, and he cut his self-indulgence short. "Still, I'd like to see if we can get her engines tuned up enough to keep pace." He slid his finger across the screen, expanding a list of specifications displayed next to the schematic. "See what you can do."

"Yes, sir." She was silent for a few seconds, thinking. "Maybe if we strip out the lasers and missiles entirely…make her a pure bomber platform. We could cut the mass. Might be just enough for her to keep up with the fleet." She looked up from the 'pad, eyes finding Garret's. "Her weaponry's old, and her targeting systems are hopelessly obsolete. She wouldn't be much good in the line anyway."

Garret didn't hesitate. "Do it." A broken down old battle-ship wouldn't be worth much in a missile or energy weapons duel with the enemy, but four extra fighter groups were worth their weight in trans-uranic elements. "But the deadline holds, Camille. Whatever isn't ready in six days stays behind." He squinted as he looked over at her.

"Yes, sir." She wasn't going to argue; she agreed with him completely on the need to get the rest of the fleet out to the battlezone before any heavy combat started. No one wanted the fleet divided when the climactic battle took place. Still, she understood how seductive it was to push the deadline, telling yourself a few more days will add extra hulls to the OB. Garret wasn't immune to that thinking either, but he was disciplined, and he'd drawn the line. She doubted anything could change it now...and she knew for damned sure she wouldn't even try. She'd make sure Shogun was ready in six days.

Chapter 9

Central Pavilion
Armstrong Spaceport
Armstrong - Gamma Pavonis III

"Are you sure you want to go back to Earth?" Sarah Linden's voice dripped with disdain when she spoke the name of her home world. Her life on Earth was something she'd spent the years since then trying to forget. She had no idea what lay ahead for her, where he life would lead…but she knew she'd need a hell of a reason to go back to Earth.

Alex brushed a wisp of long blond hair out of her face. "I'm sure." Her voice was soft, a little shaky. Alex Linden was clearly troubled, her usual steady confidence shattered. She was trying to hide it, to look calm and confident, but her normally perfect control was failing her. "I have to, Sarah. I have some things I have to deal with." Her mind raced as she spoke, her meticulous logic gone, emotions running wild. Is this the sister I've hated all these years, she wondered? Those old wounds were still there, the anger, the blame, the lust for vengeance. She remembered her dead parents, the years of squalor, of destitution. For a lifetime she'd blamed Sarah for all of it. But reuniting with her long lost sister had been nothing like she'd expected. There were other feelings there too…confusion, certainly, but was there also affection? It wasn't possible, she thought…she'd been so resolved in her hatred for so long, so convinced her sister was the cause of her years of misery. Now her resolve was weakening…or was it? Was it reasonable to blame Sarah for all that had happened to their family? She was lost, not sure what to do or think. And for Alex Linden, there was nothing worse than feeling out of control.

Sarah shifted her weight as she stood on the polished floor of the spaceport concourse. She was tense too, clearly worried. She wanted to argue, to convince her sister to stay on Armstrong. She was sure no good could come of going to Earth. But she held herself back. Sarah knew what her life had been as a girl struggling to survive in the violent ghettoes and semi-abandoned suburban wastelands. She'd tried to forget, but of course that wasn't possible. Some things stayed with you for life. She reminded herself that she had no idea – none – what Alex had gone through, what part of her soul survival had cost her. They'd avoided discussing that part of their lives, neither of them asking anything or offering any information. Sarah had never spoken of that time to anyone, no one except Erik. And she hadn't told him everything.

"Take care of yourself, Alex." Sarah tried to hide her disapproval. She had a bad feeling about Alex returning to Earth, but she tried to respect her sister's wishes. "And come back. I don't want to wait another thirty years to see my little sister again." She smiled with genuine affection. In her wildest dreams, Sarah Linden had never dared to imagine that any of her family had survived.

Alex returned the smile, unsure as she did how much sincerity was there. Some, certainly, though that only added to her confusion. Her own emotions were considerably more complex than Sarah's. "You take care of yourself. I'm not the one shipping out to a warzone." That was another reason Alex was leaving. Sarah had been gone for months, deployed on Sandoval running the field hospital there. Now she was back, but only for a few weeks, to organize the fleet of hospital ships that would be supporting Grand Fleet. She'd be leaving herself in a few days.

Alex looked at her sister. If you were staying on Armstrong, she thought, I would stay too...and we could finish this, one way or another. Alex had originally intended to kill Sarah, as soon as she'd had the chance to assassinate Erik Cain. But Cain was unreachable now, and Alex's resolve had faded, leaving her

no idea what she felt or what she wanted to do. But she knew
she couldn't remain here on Armstrong, alone, waiting months
– years? – for her sister to return. If Sarah came back at all. By
all accounts, the battle to come would be the most massive ever
fought. She wondered what she would feel if Sarah was killed in
the fighting? Vindication? Relief? Sadness? Loss? She didn't
know. No matter how many times she tried to imagine it, she
couldn't guess at what her feelings would be. But she knew she
couldn't stay on Armstrong any longer, alone, waiting. No, Alex
had to go back to Earth…and figure out who she truly was.

"I have to go, Alex. The war is too important, and it's who
I am." Sarah felt guilty being away so frequently, right after her
sister had reappeared, but she was a Marine, as much as any
of the men and women in powered armor at the front. It was
inconceivable to her to remain behind when the cream of the
Corps was going to battle. She couldn't make any other choice,
not and be true to who she was. "The Marines need me. I can't
stay here while they fight and die when I could save some of
them. But I'll be back." She sounded confident. Intellectually,
she knew she was going into enormous danger, but Sarah didn't
dwell on the risks. She just did what she had to do, what she
felt was right. "And I want you to promise me you'll come back
too."

Alex rubbed her hands along her thighs, looking uncomfortable. "I'll try, Sarah." It might be better for both of us, my
dear sister, she thought, if we never see each other again. But
she didn't say anything; she wasn't sure what she wanted. She
looked at Sarah and forced a smile to her face.

"Promise me." Sarah's voice was insistent. She stepped forward and wrapped her arms around her sister. "I won't take no
for an answer."

Alex was silent. She extended her arms and returned Sarah's
hug. Finally, softly, she said, "I promise." She felt it was a mistake even as it was leaving her lips.

Gavin Stark was staring at the 'pad, reading the report with
something he rarely experienced…surprise. "My dear little

Alex," he muttered softly to himself. "It appears there is a heart inside that sexy little body after all, even if it is mostly covered in liquid nitrogen."

Stark had sent Alex to Armstrong to kill Erik Cain, using her sister to get to the troublesome Marine. But the First Imperium invasion had put all that on hold. While mankind faced a menace of this magnitude, even Gavin Stark wanted Erik Cain alive and well, and in the front lines. He'd instructed Alex to abort the assassination for the time being and to remain on Armstrong, providing as much intel as possible. Alliance Intelligence was mostly a bystander in the war against the First Imperium, but that didn't mean Stark wasn't interested in everything that was going on. Alex had done just what she was told for a time, but before long her reports became less and less frequent, finally stopping entirely.

Stark found it amusing that it didn't seem to occur to Alex he'd have someone watching her. Maybe she figured she was good enough to spot any tail...or perhaps she thought she had him so mesmerized with her sexual skills he actually trusted her. "You're just about the tastiest little treat I've ever had, my dear Alex, but that makes me trust you less, not more, silly girl." Stark's voice was barely a whisper. Or maybe she knew he was watching her, he thought, and she just didn't care. If that was the case, she was further gone than he'd guessed.

Alex Linden had always been a stone cold agent, seemingly without weakness or emotion. But she'd spent the last year halfdrunk and amped up on Mindblast. Even Stark was stunned to see her lose her composure. As far as he'd ever seen, she rarely drank and never touched drugs. Alex had been the coldest control freak Stark had ever seen...other than the one he saw in the mirror. Now she was falling to pieces, old wounds tearing her apart, ripping down the cold-blooded psyche she'd so painstakingly built. Stark finished the report, leaning back after he was done and looking through the window at the glittering buildings of the Washbalt Core. He muttered softly, thinking out loud really. "How can I use this?"

He wasn't sure why Alex was coming back to Earth, but he

resolved to be careful. She's probably just running, he thought, or coming home because she was lost and confused. But only a fool would disregard Alex Linden. If she'd turned on him, she would be a dangerous enemy. He'd have to play this one very carefully. He'd always known he'd have to dispose of Alex sooner or later. She was too smart, too capable, too ambitious. In the end, two predators like them could never co-exist. There was only one top spot, and both of them wanted it. No, though he knew he'd miss her, he'd decided long ago that Alex Linden had an expiration date. But he'd hoped to retain the use of her services for a while longer, as an agent…and in more enjoyable ways too. Now, he wasn't sure. He might have to move up the timetable and terminate her sooner than expected. He'd have to wait until she got back to Earth, until he had a chance to see her…and decide if she was salvageable.

He didn't need this now. He was about to launch Shadow, and once he pulled the trigger on that there was no turning back. The operation would consume him, he knew that much for sure. Alex knew nothing about Shadow. She was far too intelligent and competent for him to have trusted with that information. Stark had been careful to include only operatives who lacked the initiative and capacity for independent action, individuals he was sure he could control.

He'd hoped Alex could manage most of Alliance Intelligence's other ongoing operations, many of which, unbeknownst to those involved, provided cover for Shadow. Now he wasn't sure. He wondered…could Alex be useful for a while longer?

Stark sighed loudly. He'd know about Alex soon enough. Her ship would reach Earth in three weeks, and he'd have an escort waiting for her at the spaceport. She might come in by herself, but Stark wasn't going to chance it. He couldn't imagine how many identities she had on Earth, how many secret caches of money and weapons. He wasn't foolish enough to think she didn't have resources he knew nothing about. No, letting Alex disappear into the dark recesses of the Washbalt Metroplex wasn't an option. He had to see her as soon as she arrived. Anything else was too risky.

He had no idea what would happen at their conference, no thought as to what to expect. He'd either satisfy himself that Alex was still a reliable asset, and no threat to Shadow or himself...or Alex Linden would never leave that meeting.

Chapter 10

Bridge – AS Indianapolis
Approaching the Sigma 4 Warp Gate
Eight Transits from Newton

Jacobs stared at the main screen as Indianapolis held its position 80,000 kilometers from the warp gate. He knew only too well what lay on the other side of that portal...he was one of the few humans who had ever been there. When Hornet had entered the system well over a year before, it emerged into a beehive of enemy activity. Jacobs knew a lot of those hostile vessels his ship had detected back then later ended up fighting in the Line battles. Many of those didn't return, having been destroyed in the combats at Sandoval, Garrison, and Samvar. But Jacobs had no idea what forces the enemy had remaining on the other side of the gate, or what reserves they may have brought forward. For all he knew, every vessel the enemy had was waiting just on the other side, ready to ambush any forces that transited.

Captain Mondragon's people were about to become the first to find out. His 42 ships were in formation, approaching the warp gate at a blistering 0.08c. Once through, they would divide into squadrons, some accelerating further, trying to blast straight through to find any warp gates on the far side, others braking hard, changing vectors to scatter and explore the system. It was a dangerous plan, almost foolhardy, Jacobs thought. But he'd ordered it anyway. It was the only way to quickly get the kind of data Garret and the fleet needed. Jacobs and his entire force were expendable if that's what it took to get the fleet the intel it needed to defeat the First Imperium. No one had said that, not exactly, but Jacobs knew it was true.

He hadn't run into another major force since Newton, but there had been smaller enemy patrols in nearly every system. With the First Imperium's dark energy communications, he had to assume they'd fully apprised the forces farther up the line. Surprise was now a virtual impossibility, so he decided to blanket the system with fast-moving scouts, replacing stealth with speed and numbers. He'd probably lose a lot of those ships, maybe even most. But they'd get the intel he needed. And there was no time to waste. Terrance Compton was moving forward with half of Grand Fleet, and he'd reach Jacobs' position in less than a week...and he'd need to know what he would face when he got there.

Jacobs' stomach was tight. He hadn't eaten since the day before, and the anxiety had only gotten worse since then. He felt like a man who'd escaped from hell and then chosen to return. There was sweat on his neck, and he could feel the heat around his ears and shoulders. The bridge and his survival suit were both set to room temperature, but the droplets began running down his back anyway. He knew what it was, though he didn't want to admit it to himself. It was fear.

Carp was the only other member of Scouting Fleet's crew that had been to this place before. He'd been mostly silent for the last few hours, speaking only enough to deliver the bare minimum of reports to Jacobs. The admiral hadn't asked much of his tactical officer, giving him room to handle the fear in his own way. In the first year or two of the war, the human ground forces had found it difficult to face the enemy. Even veteran units wavered before an adversary that didn't feel pain, didn't feel fear...that would fight to the last without doubt or fatigue. Jacobs felt that way now...and he suspected Carp did as well. Defending your home was one thing, but moving forward, light-years from the furthest reaches of mankind's dominion, was a chilling enterprise. Jacobs felt alone, overwhelmed...like floating in deep water in the dark, desperately trying to stay afloat, to maintain his focus.

"Sir, Captain Mondragon sends his regards." Carp's voice was soft, and he spoke slowly and deliberately. "He advises his lead vessels will be transiting in three minutes."

"Very well, commander. Please give Captain..." Jacobs stopped, pausing for an instant. "Please get Captain Mondragon on my com." The least you can do, he thought to himself, is wish the man luck personally...in all likelihood you're sending him to his death.

"I have Captain Mondragon for you, sir."

"Francisco..." Jacobs spoke loudly, his voice commanding, reassuring. He wasn't sure how he was managing it, but he did. "...I wanted to wish you and your people the best of luck. Your courage is an inspiration to the entire fleet." He thought he was finished, but a few seconds later he added, "We'll be coming through in a day, but if you need backup, get a probe back to us, and I'll bring the fleet through right away." An empty gesture, he knew. Mondragon's ships would be blasting directly into the system at almost 10% of lightspeed. Any probe would have to exert enough thrust to decelerate to a stop and re-accelerate back toward the warp gate. By that time, it would be far too late for any reinforcements to matter. No, Mondragon and his people were on their own...at least for a day. And even when the fleet followed, the advanced scouts would be millions of kilometers from the gate, far from any support.

The signal traveled 3 light seconds to Mondragon's ship, and his response took another 3 seconds to reach Indianapolis. "Thank you, admiral. It is our great honor to undertake this mission. I give you my word, my people will do what is necessary to secure the data the fleet needs." There was a short pause, then: "Until tomorrow, admiral."

Jacobs leaned back in his chair and closed his eyes. He was really beginning to like Mondragon, and he knew he'd miss the gruff stocky Basque if he didn't make it. Sending those ships through was making him physically sick. He'd never had to order anyone to undertake such a hopeless mission before. His people on Hornet had been in grievous danger every moment from the original attack on Adelaide until they made their way back to human space, but Jacobs had been right there; he'd shared their hazards. This was the first time he'd sent his people into danger while he stood back and watched…and he didn't like it. He didn't like it one bit.

He opened his eyes and stared at the monitor, grimly watching Mondragon's ships vanish one by one as they went through the warp gate…and into the maw of the enemy.

"We've confirmed it three times, sir." Tomasino turned to face Mondragon as he repeated himself. "We have data in from 38 out of 42 task force units. Only 21 enemy vessels have been detected, all positioned within 500,000 kilometers of the base."

Mondragon stared back, his normally impassive face betraying his shock. He'd expected to find a massive battlefleet, not a few miscellaneous ships. It looked like a trap. It felt like a trap. There were many places in a solar system ships could hide from cursory scans, waiting to fire up their reactors and attack at the right moment. Perhaps there was a fleet of First Imperium Leviathans lurking in the outer system, lying dormant the way the force at Newton had. But Mondragon didn't think so. It was just a feeling, one he couldn't explain, but his gut was telling him the small force of ships his people had detected was all that was posted at Sigma 4.

Faucon was decelerating at 3g, low enough thrust to allow its crew to function close to 100% efficiency, albeit with some discomfort. She was moving quickly, though, the modest output of her engines barely slowing the 0.08c velocity she'd had when she entered the system. His other ships had scattered, some accelerating, some decelerating, others changing their vectors. The task force was performing a massive scanner sweep, covering the whole system, trying to find any hidden enemy presence. Even with 42 ships, meticulously searching an entire star system was a daunting task, but Mondragon was determined. If there was so much as an enemy robot out there ready to throw a rock at his people, they were going to find it.

"Direct 9th and 20th Squadrons to search the asteroid belt. Maximum dispersion so they can cover it as quickly as possible."

Quickly was a relative term. Interstellar travel made interplanetary space seem small by comparison, but a solar system was still vast in scope. A spaceship crawling around conducting scans was like a speck of dust. It would take weeks to conduct a true search of Sigma 4, and months to finish a really comprehensive scan. All Mondragon's people could do was start with the likeliest locations and work down the list.

"And 13th and 33rd Squadrons are to advance at full thrust to the outer debris fields and begin a systematic sensor sweep." Deep in the outer system was the easiest place to hide a force, but it was also far from the base on Sigma 4 II…a tough place to stage an ambush on a fleet attacking the planet. Still, he had to check it out. He couldn't assume anything.

"I want 11th and 14th Squadrons to check out the possible warp gate location." Preliminary scans had shown one likely spot for a second warp gate in the system, but it couldn't be confirmed without closer inspection. "I want a definite ID here, no guesswork." Mondragon knew there were at least two warp gates in the system…the one his people had come through, and one – or more – leading deeper into the First Imperium. Mapping the system and finding the entry points was crucial…before all of Grand Fleet arrived and got blindsided by an enemy force coming through an undiscovered warp gate.

"Yes, captain." Tomasino hunched over the controls and relayed Mondragon's orders. He turned back toward the command chair. "Captains Garcia and Leclerc confirm, sir."

Mondragon nodded. "Instruct them to send a ship through immediately upon confirming the gate location. I want a preliminary report on the connecting system as quickly as possible."

"Yes, sir."

He turned to look at the display, frowning as he usually did at the partial obstructions in his field of vision. Faucon's bridge was a tight space, with a normal complement of five officers, including the captain. They'd crammed in two extra chairs to turn her into a flagship, an accommodation that made things extremely cozy for Mondragon and his staff. His own command chair ended up behind a structural member, and he was having a hard time getting used to it. Attack ships not attached to battlegroups had traditionally been deployed individually or in small HK squadrons. A 3 or 4 vessel group could be run by a senior captain doubling as squadron leader, but not one of more than 40 ships. A task force comprised entirely of attack ships was a new development, one forged in the specific realities of this war. We really need a new design, he thought, a ship big enough to serve as a flagship, but small and fast enough to keep up with the rest of the boats.

The tactical display showed the approximate location of the 42 fast attack ships in Mondragon's task force. The screen was updated in real time, but with some of the scouts over a light hour away from the flagship, the data was outdated, especially for the ships furthest out. The AI could project current locations based on last known vectors and velocities, modified by orders and directives currently in force. But Mondragon's captains had wide latitude on this mission, and there was no way to know exactly when and where they chose to apply thrust. Even after two and a half decades of service, he was still uncomfortable dealing with the vast distances involved in spaceship operations and the time delay effects of lightspeed communications. It always troubled him to think that the vessel we was watching on the monitor could be destroyed already, its crew dead...and he wouldn't know for an hour or more.

"Prepare for maximum thrust, Lieutenant Tomasino." Mondragon's voice was loud and deliberative. He'd made a decision. "We are going to decelerate at full, commencing in five minutes." On an Alliance ship, that five minutes would have been two. The Europan navy simply couldn't match the levels of expertise found in the Alliance or Caliphate fleets. "I want us as close to the warp gate as possible." He paused, then continued in a softer voice, half to himself, "At least until I can get updated orders from Admiral Jacobs."

"Yes, sir." Tomasino's voice was edgy. Five minutes was tight timing for a Europan ship to get ready for full thrust.

"And prepare to launch a drone." Mondragon was staring right at his tactical officer. "We need to tell Admiral Jacobs what we found."

"I have a response from Admiral Compton, sir." Carp was
listening to the message on the headset as he spoke. "He reports
the fleet is accelerating, and will arrive at the Sigma 4 warp gate
in approximately 60 hours."

Jacobs head spun around. They must be accelerating, and
hard, he thought. Sixty hours was well ahead of the original
schedule. Jacob's people had just gotten the temporary Commnet station operating when Mondragon's drone came through
the warp gate, blasting along at almost 60g. Jacobs was stunned
when he'd heard the drone's message, and he immediately sent
the data down the new Commnet lines to Compton.

Carp paused. "Sorry, sir. I'm getting this slowly." He put his
hand to his ear, pushing against the headset. "Admiral Compton's reply is encrypted with a Zeta-1 code." Zeta-1 was the
Alliance's most secure encoding system, and even a cruiser's AI
required time to decode it. No one had even figured out if the
First Imperium forces understood human speech or communications. But Compton was clearly not in the mood to take
chances.

"He advises that his current plan is to launch a lightning
strike against the planet and the defending task force." Compton had plenty of firepower to take out the enemy vessels…at
least the ones they knew about. "You are ordered to leave one
squadron of attack ships in Epsilon 3 and deploy the rest of the
fleet to the scouting effort in Sigma 4 and any connecting systems, avoiding contact with the enemy fleet if possible."

Jacobs sat motionless, listening to Carp relay Compton's
orders. He felt the tension in his gut, the tingling in his arms.
They were going in. In less than 3 days they would be attacking a world of the First Imperium. Whatever happened, Jacobs
knew it was a turning point in the war.

"You are further ordered to update the Epsilon 3 squadron
every 4 hours with a consolidated report of all new scouting
data." Carp's voice had remained steady, but Jacobs could hear
the edginess there as well. His tactical officer knew what was

happening too. "He closes with a direct message for you, sir." Carp turned to face Jacobs. "Should I send it to your com line, sir?"

Jacobs nodded. "Yes." He subconsciously put his hand to the side of his head, checking his earpiece, making sure it was in place. "Immediately."

Carp turned back to his station, moving his hands over one of the touchscreens. "Coming through now, sir."

"Hello Mike." It was Compton's voice. Despite the massive encryption and subsequent decoding, the tone was perfect... just like Terrance Compton was standing next to him speaking into his ear. "I'm sure you'd agree, things are happening a little faster than we'd expected. That's war, though...and especially against these SOBs. If there's one thing we can expect, it's the unexpected."

Jacobs was trying not to assume too much from Compton's tone, especially since his voice had been encrypted and decoded. The Fleet admiral was a hard book to read, but he sounded edgy, as if he'd made a decision because he had to, but was far from certain about his choice. "I'm sure I'm not telling you anything you haven't considered, but of course I'm worried this is some sort of trap. We all expected more enemy strength in Sigma 4, which is why we've got every decent warship we could find en route."

There was a pause, unusual in an encoded transmission. Compton must have hesitated, and the AI preserved the gap in the coding. "Whatever the risk, however, I don't think we can pass up the chance to move on this. We're out here to find an enemy weakness, and I can't think of anything more potentially useful than seizing their base. Maybe General Sparks and his people can find something there we can use. I've only got half the fleet with me, but it's still more strength than we had at any of the Line worlds."

Jacobs took a deep breath as he listened. He agreed with everything Compton was saying, but his stomach was clenched anyway. Terrance Compton had a reputation as the best poker player in the fleet...but now he was about to go all in with the cream of mankind's warships. If he was wrong, if it was a trap and the fleet was lost, there wouldn't be enough strength left to mount a credible defense. The war would be over, except for the mopping up. Jacobs had been uncomfortable with his new responsibilities...he didn't envy Compton the crushing pressure of his own.

"I'm taking a big risk here, Mike, and I need your help." His voice became softer...more like asking a friend for help than a commander giving an order. "I'm going to bring the fleet in and move on the planet before the enemy can get more strength up here. But I need to know exactly what we're facing. I need you to be OCD on this, Mike. Anything...if you think something smells funny, if you get a weird feeling in your gut...I need to hear it immediately."

Compton paused again, longer this time. "I'm counting on you to keep me apprised. I know you're the right man for the job. What you did in getting Hornet back home was nothing short of heroic, and all the congratulations and rewards you got were less than you deserved." There was emotion in Compton's voice, and admiration that sounded very genuine. "I need that now...whatever you pulled out from inside yourself then. I need to know everything. Everything. And I'm trusting you, Mike. I'm trusting you with my life. With all our lives."

Jacobs took a breath again, finding it difficult to draw it in deep. He was gratified at Compton's words, but the pressure of what the fleet admiral was saying hit him like a sledgehammer.

"We're on the way, Mike," Compton continued. "I'm expecting you to have that system mapped out 100% by the time we get there. Good luck, Admiral Jacobs. And Godspeed."

The transmission ended, leaving Jacobs sitting in his command chair, trying to hide the fact that he was gasping for breath. He closed his eyes, shutting out most of his thoughts and trying to focus, to gain control of himself. He had a job to do now, the most important one he'd ever had, and he wasn't going to sit here and fold under the stress.

"Commander Carp..." Somehow Jacobs managed to sound confident and commanding, no trace of fear in his voice. "...

the fleet will prepare to move out."

Chapter 11

AS Pershing
Omicron 7 System
En Route from Sandoval to Sigma 4

"Welcome to Grand Fleet, Admiral Arlington." Augustus
Garret spoke pleasantly, his tone relaxed. Arlington was one
of his most junior admirals, but he had a lot of confidence in
her, and he was glad to have her in the fold. He'd tried to make
her an admiral three times before he actually managed it, but
she kept refusing the star, choosing instead to remain Admiral
Compton's flag captain.

Garret knew there had been more than duty involved in that
choice. Terrance Compton and Elizabeth Arlington were the
fleet's worst-kept secret, though, in truth, there was nothing
there that required secrecy. Despite their obvious feelings for
each other, Compton would never act on any of it...not while
she was under his command. That was one reason Garret had
assigned her to his own staff instead of Compton's, but now
distance had replaced duty as the problem standing in their way.
After this campaign, Garret thought...I'll make sure they have
their opportunity. He was committed to seeing his friend get
his chance at happiness. Garret had sacrificed love to duty once
before. It was long ago, but not a day went by that he didn't
remember, even forty years later. He wasn't going to let Compton make the same mistake he did.

As welcome as Arlington herself was, the task force she'd
led from the Wolf 359 shipyards was appreciated even more.
Five capital ships and a squadron of cruisers, the most recently

repaired vessels from the Alliance's massive shipbuilding complex. None of them were in perfect shape, and a few were barely combat-capable, but repairs took time and the war wouldn't wait. Now was the time…Garret and his people would find a way to beat the First Imperium now, or the war would be lost… maybe not immediately, but eventually. Holding anything back was a fool's game, a meaningless concession to fear that Garret refused to make. Arlington had waited until the last possible moment to allow as much work to be completed as possible, just as her orders specified, and then she'd led everything that could keep pace away from Wolf 359 to meet up with Garret and the rest of the fleet.

"Thank you, sir. It's a pleasure to be here." She sounded tired and a little worn out. She'd been working around the clock at Wolf 359, staying on the crews, making sure the work got done as quickly as possible. But that wasn't the only thing affecting her. She'd just found out that Compton had led half the fleet to Sigma 4. Terrance Compton was a brilliant commander, one who would have been hailed an unmatched legend if he hadn't been born in the same generation as Augustus Garret. He was more cautious than Garret…to a point. But he was also a creature of duty. If he believed sacrificing himself and half the fleet would help the Alliance win the war, he'd do it without a second thought. She was worried…and if Compton was going to throw himself into the maelstrom, she wanted to be with him.

Garret could see her tension. "He'll be fine, Elizabeth. Don't worry. We'll be heading out in less than an hour to join him." He smiled, giving her a relaxed stare. It was mostly phony… he was just as worried about Compton as she was. "Terry can take care of himself for a few weeks until we get there." He could see in her expression, she wanted to believe what he was saying. "Really…the grouchy SOB has saved my life more than once. He knows his stuff. He won't do anything crazy." Garret wished he believed that last part, but he knew better than anyone that Compton wouldn't shy away from a fight if he thought it was the right move.

She gave Garret a fragile smile. She wasn't really convinced, but she was trying. "Thank you, sir." Then, changing the subject: "What would you like me to do now, admiral?" She knew she wouldn't be commanding the flotilla she'd brought from Wolf 359. It was a hodgepodge of ships assembled on the basis of readiness, not balance, and the vessels would likely be doled out to the existing task forces in the fleet. Besides, it was much too large a force to be assigned to one of the most junior admirals in the navy...not to mention the other fleets of the Grand Pact.

"Well, Elizabeth...I was wondering how you'd feel about serving as my chief of staff for the campaign." Garret looked at her intently. "Interested?"

Arlington was silent, a stunned look on her face. She opened her mouth to answer, but closed it again wordlessly.

"Yes, you are completely qualified...and you are ready too." Garret smiled as he answered her unspoken questions. "And I trust you, which isn't something I say lightly about anyone. I'd be personally grateful if you'd agree to help me out by taking the post." Dirty pool, Garret thought to himself...there's no way she can turn it down now.

"Thank you, sir. It would be an honor." She had a tentative smile on her face. Her emotions were an odd mix – pride, satisfaction, blind terror.

"Good, I'm glad that's settled. As soon as I get up to the flag bridge I'll make it official fleetwide." The smile was still on Garret's face. "You'll be speaking with my authority, but go easy on them, ok?" He winked at her. "Unless you need to kick their asses, that is."

She grinned. "Yes, sir. I'll do my best."

"I know you will." He snapped her a sharp salute, one she returned even more crisply. "Now go check in with Commander Warrenton, and he'll get you set up in your quarters. Take your time and get settled in and, when you're ready, come see me on the flag bridge."

"Yes, sir. Thank you." She started to turn to go.

"And Admiral Arlington?"

She stopped and looked back. "Yes, sir?"

"Our first order of business is to get this fleet moving full speed to join Terry." He stifled a small laugh. "I hope you still have some energy left for kicking ass, because we're going to push everyone like they've never been pushed before."

She smiled broadly. "Oh yes, sir. I have some energy left."

Catherine Gilson sat quietly in Pershing's officers' mess nursing a cup of tea. Gilson was one of the toughest commanders in the Corps, respected by her troops and feared by her enemies. When the situation called for it, she could out-swear the most grizzled career sergeant. But sitting at the small table, reading her 'pad, teacup in her hand, she looked like something entirely different.

Gilson had devoted most of her life to the Corps. A workaholic, filling most of her hours tending to the needs of the Marines under her command, she didn't have much time for relaxation. When she did have time to herself, she spent it quietly, not at all in the ways her Marines would have guessed of their iron-fisted commander. She didn't drink, rarely took leave, and mostly kept to herself when not on duty. She enjoyed reading trashy novels, a guilty pleasure she kept to herself with the aggressiveness she employed to protect the Corps' darkest secrets. She could only imagine the amusement it would give her veteran Marines to get a glimpse at what their foul-mouthed, blood and guts commander chose to read in her free time.

Gilson was one of two four-star generals in the Corps… Erik Cain was the other. She'd outranked Cain for most of their careers, but they got their 4th stars simultaneously, just before taking command at Garrison and Sandoval. The politicians on Earth tended to look on the military with disdain…until they needed protection from something. But they were great at thinking up rewards and decorations. The Commandant of the Corps never had more than four stars…no Marine general ever had. But they decreed a five-star rank and gave it to Holm, clearing room to make full generals out of Cain and Gilson.

None of it mattered much. Holm was still in overall command, as virtually everyone agreed he should be. Gilson had never seen a Commandant so universally acclaimed as a hero every other Marine was proud to follow. The Corps wasn't immune from political maneuverings, especially at the highest ranks. Rafael Samuels was the most recent disastrous example. The Corps' great traitor should never have been Commandant...and he should never have risen high enough in the ranks to be a candidate for the job. But foolishness and corruption existed everywhere. Even in the Corps, Gilson thought sadly.

They were lucky in one respect, she thought. If they were going to face something like the First Imperium, at least they were doing it at a time they had someone like Holm to lead them...and he had subordinates like Erik Cain and Isaac Merrick to back him up. She didn't include herself in that list, though almost everyone else would have. The Corps was battered from years of war, and many of its veterans were gone, fallen on one of its many battlefields. But there had never been a time when its leadership was stronger or more devoted. She didn't know if they could win this struggle – if anyone could - but she was sure they would fight to the last.

She picked up the teacup and took a drink. It was something new she'd tried, tea grown on Columbia, laced with cinnamon... really good, she thought. She had to admit, the newest Yorktown class vessels had vastly improved food service over the older ships. The troopships and other craft she'd served aboard earlier in her career had offered their own version of the stereotypical, barely-edible slop that seemed somehow ingrained as a part of military history. She'd always thought they kept it that way so the pre-drop intravenous feedings seemed more attractive.

Her thoughts weren't dwelling on Pershing, though, or any of the ships of the massive fleet surrounding her. She was thinking of Erik Cain and the Marines he commanded...the Marines who were already lightyears forward of Pershing's position, already in the battlezone.

Gilson was annoyed with Cain. She knew she shouldn't be. He'd done the right thing; she was sure of that. But she didn't like being left behind. It wasn't entirely rational, but that's how she felt. She knew one of them had to stay to lead the rest of the ground forces, but she still hated being so far to the rear when there was a fight going on. She told herself she'd be there soon enough, but she had an odd feeling that the battle was being decided already…that Pershing and her Marines, and the rest of the fleet would be too late. She tried to dismiss it as nonsense, but it continued to nag at her.

"Do you mind if I join you, General Gilson?" A tall man clad in an ornate silk uniform stood just inside the doorway. He had a grim and imposing look to him, but there was a friendly smile on his face.

"Of course, Lord Khaled." She returned the smile, though her mood made it difficult to match the genuine grin Khaled wore. "It would be an honor."

He walked slowly to the table, gently pulling out a chair. "May I propose that when we are off duty, you refer to me as Ali, and I to you as Catherine?" Khaled had always appeared to be very stiff and formal when in the field or at a public event, which was the only way she'd ever seen him. Now he seemed different, friendlier, more relaxed.

"Certainly, Lor…Ali."

He sat down in the chair, letting out a soft sigh as he did. "I am afraid I am quite fatigued. It will be pleasant to sit for a time and speak with a valued colleague."

Gilson found it odd to be sitting in a wardroom having a friendly chat with the Supreme Commander of the Janissary Corps. Gilson had fought on a dozen worlds against Khaled and his troopers. He had been on Carson's World during the climactic campaign of the Third Frontier War. Their forces had fought savagely for weeks in one of the bloodiest fights in history. Now they were sitting and chatting like old friends.

She'd been surprised how well her people had integrated with Khaled's forces. It had been difficult at first, of course. Very difficult. But then something unexpected happened. The forces began to gel, to develop a nascent mutual trust. The enemy they were facing was totally alien…an enemy of all mankind. The politicians back on Earth still argued and debated – and some of the highly-ranked commanders bristled with pride and arrogance – but the rank and file had begun to accept each other, as allies, even as friends. She wondered what would happen now, if the war was won and the First Imperium threat was gone. Would she and Ali Khaled be enemies again, facing each other across some battlefield? Would the Marines and Janissaries again be bitter enemies, massacring each other on a dozen worlds?

"Have your troops been satisfactorily billeted?" Gilson's mind, as always, went to business first.

Khaled smiled again. "Your reputation is much like mine, Catherine. I'm afraid our fellow-officers consider us to be…what is the term in English? Workaholics." He paused for an instant and added, "And yes, thank you, my forces are well-tended."

"I'm afraid you are right about how we are viewed. Though I doubt you let that bother you any more than I do." She took another sip of her tea. "Your English, by the way, is extraordinary. Far better than my Arabic, I'm afraid." Not entirely truthful…Gilson spoke accentless Arabic as well as passable Mandarin and Russian.

Khaled laughed. "That is not what I have heard, my good friend. I think you underestimate your skills. But we are on your nation's vessel, so we will use your tongue." He leaned back as he spoke. "If we have cause meet on a Caliphate vessel, then we shall converse in mine. Agreed?"

"Agreed." She nodded. Khaled was a surprise to her. She had known who he was for years, but she hadn't imagined him to be so charming and polite. Gender roles in the Caliphate were considerably different than those in the Alliance. There were no women at all in the Caliph's military, but Khaled seemed to have no difficulty relating to a female general as a peer.

A steward came in swiftly. "General Gilson, Lord Khaled, may I bring you anything?"

Khaled glanced at Gilson, but she shook her head. "I believe I will have a cup of tea myself." He looked briefly at Gilson's cup. "Whatever the general is having will be perfectly satisfactory."

The steward nodded. "Yes, sir." He turned and hurried through the door.

"It is odd, isn't it? To discover that one's old enemy is more than a name on an order of battle." Khaled's expression had grown pensive. "Your General Cain was not what I expected."

Gilson laughed. "Yes…well, Erik is quite an enigma to most of us. I'm not sure anyone really knows him. Colonel Linden comes closest, of course. Jax was his best friend; he probably had the clearest insights." She stared off into space for a few seconds, a somber look on her face as she thought of Jax.

"Yes, I was devastated to hear of General Jax's death on Farpoint. It was a terrible loss." Khaled knew more about Jax's final battle than Gilson. He'd died trying to hold off the enemy long enough for the rest of the expeditionary force to evacuate. There had been Janissaries in reserve on Farpoint, but General Cain didn't trust them and wouldn't give the order for them to advance. Jax had died trying to plug the gap the Janissaries could have filled, and Cain had blamed himself ever since for his friend's death.

Some good had come of the tragedy, however. Cain finally sent the Janissaries in, and he watched them hold the line while the rest of his forces embarked. The Caliphate troopers lost over three-fourths of their strength, but they held firm…and won Erik Cain's respect and admiration. His open acceptance of the Janissaries set an example for the whole Marine Corps and was crucial to the development of the growing trust and cooperation between the forces. Khaled wondered if, in some ways, General Jax's sacrifice hadn't been the most important factor in the successful defense of the Line.

"I've never had tea with a lord before." Gilson wanted to change the subject. Jax had been one of the most popular officers in the Corps, and the wound was still too fresh for her to speak casually of him. Even after years of war and death, it never got easier to lose a friend.

Khaled understood immediately. "I'm afraid that is more of a rank than a real title, Catherine. I was born the bastard son of a housekeeper in New Cairo. Had I not been recruited by the Janissary Corps, I would no doubt be cleaning the gutters...or, more likely, dead by now."

She smiled. "Well, I think I will still count you as my first lord." Her face turned more serious. "Would you mind talking shop for a while?"

His eyes found hers. "No, of course not."

"Good. Because I have a feeling Erik Cain is going to get himself into trouble, and I want to be ready for whatever we run into when we get to Sigma 4."

Chapter 12

Bridge – AS Midway
Sigma 4 System
Approaching Sigma 4 II

Terrance Compton sat in the command chair on Midway's
flag bridge, his mind focused like a laser, despite the tension
gnawing at his guts. The newest of the Yorktown class battleships, Midway was the ultimate expression of the Alliance's
might and power. In a war against another Superpower, she
would be an almost irresistible weapon, an unmatchable instrument of military strength. But this fight wasn't against other
humans, and Midway would have a massive fight on its hands
facing off against a First Imperium Gargoyle, a vessel barely
one-third its size. Compton couldn't shake the feeling he was a
mortal in some ancient myth, steeling himself and his warriors
to challenge the gods themselves. But now he and his people
weren't struggling to survive some divine onslaught on their
homelands…they were assaulting Olympus itself.

The enemy base lay ahead, the small enemy task force
deployed to defend it. Mike Jacobs and his entire fleet had
scoured the system for three days, and they didn't find so much
as a single additional vessel. The 21 ships formed up ahead of
Midway and her cohorts seemed to be the only enemy presence
in the system…besides whatever fortifications waited in orbit
and on the surface of the planet itself.

Compton still had doubts. His gambler's instincts had told
him to go for it…that the forces of the Grand Pact needed to
take risks if they were going to find some way to defeat the

First Imperium...or at least force some type of peace on the xenophobic enemy. When he'd gotten word from Jacobs that the enemy strength at Sigma 4 was far below expectations he realized this might be the chance they needed. Maybe luck had smiled on them for once; perhaps they'd caught the enemy redeploying or repositioning. His caution, built up over a lifetime at war, was there too, urging him to be careful...but restraint wasn't going to win this war.

He was nervous about attacking with only half of Grand Fleet, but if they had stumbled on an opportunity, they had no way of knowing how long it would last. He knew it was a risk, but Compton was resolved to attack now, with the forces he had available. If he waited for Garret they could end up facing a massively reinforced enemy.

He did have the elite of the human navies, the newest ships and most experienced crews. Even without the forces Garret was now leading forward to join him, Compton commanded the most awesome array of naval power that man had ever assembled. Midway and her two sister ships were the first Yorktown B's, upgraded versions of the Alliance's newest battleships, extensively modified and equipped with all the advanced weaponry Tom Sparks and his researchers had developed from examining First Imperium technology.

Compton had 31 capital ships in all, including 3 Yorktown A's backing up Midway and her newer sisters. That massive battleline was supported by over 200 cruisers, destroyers, and other escorts...the newest, fastest, and best the allied Superpowers had to offer. Compton had been reviewing the OB constantly during the trip to Sigma 4, and he kept coming to the same conclusion. The fleet was so massive, it was going to be nearly impossible to effectively command.

His plan was straightforward. First he was going to take out the enemy fleet and the base's orbital fortifications. Unfortunately, he didn't have as much data on them as he would have liked. Jacobs' scouts couldn't get close enough to the planet to perform an effective scan. The truth was, no human force had ever assaulted the First Imperium's fixed defenses, and no one had any idea what types of weaponry and defenses they'd be up against. Any thoughts on what his fleet was about to encounter were the wildest guesses. Many on the admiral's staff were confident, feeling they'd caught the enemy with their pants down. Compton was considerably more circumspect...he assumed he faced a significant and dangerous fight, not a walkover...and his gut agreed.

After the enemy space forces were destroyed or forced to retreat, Compton was going to drop Cain's Marines onto the planet and then move toward the outer system and the single egress warp gate Jacobs' people had been able to find. Depending on what scouting reports came back from the adjoining system, Compton planned to deploy on one side of the warp gate, setting up a defensive position between the planet and any possible relief from deeper into enemy space. With any luck, Garret and the rest of the fleet would get there before they faced a second battle. And there wasn't a doubt in Compton's mind there would be another fight.

"We are approaching Point Blue, admiral." Max Harmon's voice was sharp and crisp. He sounded calm, but Compton knew otherwise. Anyone who was truly calm minutes before launching an attack on a First Imperium world was either heavily medicated or outright insane.

Compton smiled. He knew exactly where the fleet was, but Harmon had done his job in reminding him, and he'd done it right on time. "Very well, Commodore Harmon." He took a deep breath. It was time. "Bring the fleet to condition yellow. And please instruct Admiral Hurley to bring her wings to pre-launch status."

"Yes, sir." Harmon relayed Compton's orders. An instant later, the flag bridge glowed with a soft yellow hue as Midway's status indicators reflected the upgraded readiness condition. "Admiral Hurley acknowledges, sir."

Compton nodded. "Very well." Hurley was the last one he was worried about. He hadn't even planned her strike with her. He'd told her what he wanted to achieve and left her alone to work it out. Greta Hurley was the greatest expert on fighter-bomber tactics he'd ever known...far better than he was, Compton realized. He'd given her total control over the fleet's massive force of fighter-bombers, and he was grateful to have her to lead it. In a few minutes, the largest bomber strike in history would launch.

"All fleet units report condition yellow in effect, admiral."

"Very well." Compton sat quietly for a few minutes, his mind reviewing every aspect of the battle plan. He didn't like launching an attack against a base with no idea of what kind of defenses it had. But that couldn't be helped. There was no way to get close enough to scan with the enemy fleet in position... and no way to get rid of the fleet without attacking. It was just another risk; a necessary one. He knew the die was cast. They were going in.

Admiral Greta Hurley sat in the specially installed command chair, trying to keep track of the massive strike force displayed on her screen. It was cramped in the cockpit, even more than usually. Fighter-bombers were not built to accommodate an extra passenger, even an admiral in command of the entire strike force. Admiral Garret had wanted her to run the squadrons from a control room on one of the capital ships, but she'd looked him right in the eye and told him she'd refuse the star he was offering if that was the condition of accepting. There weren't many people who could claim to have stared down Augustus Garret and gotten their way, but Hurley was one of them. Garret finally relented and agreed to allow her to command strike force operations for Grand Fleet from a fighter's cockpit. No one in any of the navies had anything close to Hurley's skill or experience at fighter-bomber tactics. She was the greatest living expert on fighter operations, especially against the First Imperium, and Garret had to respect her insistence on being out there with her crews.

The fleet admiral hadn't surrendered entirely, however. Hurley's craft was heavily modified, stuffed full of electronic gear, most of its weapons removed to make room. There would be no more high-velocity attack runs for the strike force commander, no personally targeting plasma torpedo shots from knife-fighting range. Hurley had strict guidelines on how close to the enemy she was allowed to fly...and the pilot of her ship had strict orders - directly from Fleet Admiral Garret - to ignore Hurley if she attempted to supersede those restrictions.

She was edgy – she would have called it scared shitless. Not of the enemy, but of the crushing responsibility on her shoulders. There were 720 fighter bombers approaching the enemy task force, a number that boggled her mind. Her command included bombers from seven different Powers. There were 11 models of ships, with 3 different primary weapons systems. Language wasn't an issue – the AIs could easily translate – but training, experience, equipment, and tactics all varied widely. Not to mention lingering resentments from years spent fighting each other.

Hurley had tried to run some training exercises before the fleet set out. Her people needed to work together, to gel as a single force. But then Admiral Compton moved up the timetable and blasted off with half the fleet, herself included. Now they would have to pull themselves together under fire, in the face of the enemy. It wasn't ideal, not by a long shot. But Greta Hurley had always taken the hand she was dealt, and that wasn't going to change now. At least it looked for once like her people had the strength advantage.

"Attention wing leaders, this is Admiral Hurley." She'd divided her force into 12 wings, each consisting of 10 squadrons. She stayed within national groupings wherever possible, but she still ended up with a few that were hodgepodges of equipment and doctrine. She was going to have to keep a closer eye on those wings; their commanders had a difficult job.

"All A wings are to load and arm plasma torpedoes now." Not all the Superpowers had bomber-deployed plasma ordnance. It was a relatively new system, and only the Alliance, Caliphate, CAC, and PRC had widely adopted it. "B wings, fall into pre-designated support positions." The bombers armed with rocket-packs were far less effective, particularly against targets as tough as First Imperium ships. Hurley had positioned half of them in the rear of the formation, where they could use their lesser weaponry to finish off targets seriously damaged by the plasma torpedo attacks. The other half had been placed in the front. A far colder calculus was at work with these wings... they were there to divert point defense fire from the far more valuable plasma-armed squadrons. Hurley didn't feel good about it, but someone was going to be upfront anyway, and she had to make the most tactically useful decisions possible. Even if did make her feel like a cold-blooded martinet.

"All wings have acknowledged your order, Admiral Hurley." The AI had a non-descript voice, female, but not overly feminine. It was a new unit, one Hurley hadn't named yet, and it was specifically designed to help her control hundreds of individual fighter-bombers.

Hurley watched the tactical plot as the squadrons executed her orders, some of the B Wings decelerating to fall back to the rear, while others thrusted forward, taking their positions in the vanguard.

"Projected entry into enemy point defense envelope in 14 minutes, 30 seconds." The AI's reports were fed directly into Hurley's earpiece.

Well, she thought, 21 ships shouldn't put out too much fire for a strike force this big...but what the hell do those orbital facilities have to dish out? She was still thinking about that when all hell broke loose.

"The strike force is under fire, admiral." The AI's voice was calm, eerily so considering her people were under fire from 20,000 klicks outside maximum enemy point defense range. What they thought was maximum range.

Hurley felt the tension grip her body. A new weapon, she thought? "Damage report."

"Still compiling data, admiral." The AI's voice was maddeningly calm. Hurley began to understand the reasoning behind the personality modules...at least those AIs had the decency to act like they were concerned when things were going all to hell. "It appears that 7 units have been destroyed."

Hurley's temper flared. "Units...those 'units' are full of my people!"

"I intended no insensitivity, admiral. I am merely attempting to ensure that you have complete data. Would you prefer an alternate designation for individual fighter-bombers?"

"No." Hurley was getting control of her frustration. She didn't have time to be upset with her AI over foolishness. "I need an analysis of the method of attack immediately."

"Yes, admiral. We have inadequate data to..." The AI paused for a second, then continued, "Additional fire, admiral. Another 3 units destroyed...5 units."

"What the hell is firing at us?" Hurley's fists were clenched, her heart pounding hard in her chest. "I need to know."

"Preliminary readings suggest an area effect weapon, admiral...a railgun or coilgun, superficially similar to our area effect interdiction systems, however the velocity of the individual projectiles is far beyond anything we have been able to achieve in our own ordnance of this type."

"Shotguns." Hurley muttered softly, almost inaudibly. "But faster and much longer-ranged than ours. Fuck." She sat silently for a few seconds. "All wings, dispersal pattern Alpha...now." She had to get more space between her fighters. They had a long way to go through this weapon's area of effectiveness... and she couldn't have them taking out multiple units with each shot.

"Orders transmitted, admiral."

We've got to close the distance, she thought grimly...now. "All wings, prepare for maximum thrust in one minute." She took a deep breath, taking a second to center herself. She had to be 100% now. "And get me Admiral Compton."

"I want those attack ships thrusting at full in one minute." Compton was pissed; that was obvious to anyone listening. "Is that clear, Admiral Zhang?"

The signal took almost a second to reach Zhang's ship and another second for the reply to get back to Midway. "Admiral Compton, your order would place my command in an extremely exposed position. I must renew my protest."

The AI translated Zhang's Mandarin into perfect English. The translation did not reproduce any emotional embellishments, but Compton's mind filled in the surly and arrogant tone he knew had been there in the original version. He sensed his anger building, and he felt the instinctive urge to ball his fists, to slam his hand down on the arm of the chair. Fuck the Grand Pact, he thought, seething...I've had it with all this diplomatic bullshit.

Zhang was a pompous ass, the youngest son of a powerful CAC family. He wore an admiral's uniform only because his father had bought it for him. Compton's father had been well-placed too. The illegitimate son of a Senator, Terrance Compton had taken nothing from his father, whom he casually hated for the way his Cog mother had been discarded and sent back to the London slums. He'd earned the stars on his collar himself...through years of blood and sacrifice, not by the decree of his father. Political creatures like Zhang infuriated him, and he looked at them all as parasites.

Compton had already overrepresented his own people in the top command positions, so he'd reluctantly agreed to put Zhang in charge of the fast attack ships. He hadn't expected to use them en masse anyway, so he figured it was as good a place as any to stick the arrogant SOB. Someplace he couldn't do much harm. But things had changed now. Greta Hurley's fighters were getting massacred by a previously unknown enemy weapon. Her wings had to divert from their strike on the enemy fleet to go after the orbital launch platforms that were tearing them to shreds. Compton couldn't leave the enemy ships unoccupied, free to go after Hurley's flank.

His first impulse had been to bring the entire fleet in at full thrust in an all-out attack, but he couldn't risk his capital ships until he had a better idea of what they were facing. Not even to save Hurley and her people. It was the kind of decision commanders made all the time, and Greta and her fighters were more expendable than the battleline. Hurley and their people knew that too.

"Admiral Zhang, you are relieved." Compton's voice was

thick with icy contempt, most of which would be filtered out during translation anyway. "You are to stand down at once and report immediately to your quarters, to which you are confined until further notice."

Compton could imagine the apoplectic look on Zhang's bloated face, and he let a fleeting smile slip onto his lips. "Commodore Harmon, put me on universal com with the fleet." He knew he should contact Captain Duke and let him know he was now in command, but he wanted to address the entire fleet first...just in case Zhang tried to pull something.

"You are on universal com, admiral."

"Attention all personnel. This is Fleet Admiral Compton." He spoke clearly, authoritatively. "Admiral Zhang has been relieved from duty for gross insubordination and other infractions. Squadron Captain Duke is hereby placed in command of Task Force C, effective immediately. All personnel in Task Force C are to act accordingly. Compton out." Compton made a gesture, moving his hand across his throat. Harmon nodded and cut the line.

Compton knew there'd be hell to pay for this when they got back home. He'd not only relieved Zhang; he'd humiliated him in front of the entire fleet, which, in CAC culture especially, was a grievous offense. But Compton didn't give a shit. He was far from certain any of them would even get home...and he didn't care anyway. He wasn't going to chance Zhang causing any disruptions. Not now. Not when the lives of Greta's people hung in the balance.

"Admiral, I have Captain Duke for you."

Compton smiled again, not at all surprised to hear from the man who'd just learned he was in command of 103 fast attack ships. "Put him through, Max."

Harmon flipped a switch and gestured to Compton. "He's on your line, sir."

"James, what a surprise." His sarcasm was mild, a friendly mocking tone. Compton had followed James Duke's career for some time. He'd been very impressed with the younger man's achievements, and he'd mentored him as he rose through the ranks. Now he was about to throw him into a firestorm. "Con-gratulations on the promotion."

"Yes, sir...ah...thank you, sir."

Compton smiled, taking pity on Duke. He sometimes forgot how difficult it was for the younger officers to deal with humor from a creature as lofty as a fleet admiral. "I had to relieve Zhang, James. I couldn't trust him to follow my orders...and I need your people to back up the fighters. Now."

"Anything, sir." Duke still sounded a little dumbstruck, but there was confidence there too. "What do you want us to do?"

"I need you to take the entire task force, and attack the enemy fleet. Immediately." He paused. He knew he didn't have to give a reason, but he liked to keep his officers in the loop when he could. At least the officers he trusted and respected. "Hurley's fighters ran into a new weapon, and I had to divert them against the orbital forts. I need you to keep the enemy ships from swinging around and bracketing her forces."

"Yes, sir." His reply was crisp and immediate – at least as immediate as lightspeed communications allowed across 170,000 kilometers. There was doubt in Duke's voice, hesitation. "But the fighters are way ahead of us...I doubt we can get there in time, admiral."

"I realize that, James, but if the enemy sees over a hundred attack ships coming in, I doubt they'll change position to go after the fighters. The First Imperium is usually conservative. If you get your people moving, I think you'll fix them in place."

"Understood, sir." The doubt was gone. Mostly. "With your permission, admiral, I will launch my attack immediately.

"You may begin when ready, Captain Duke." Compton leaned back in the chair, silent for a few seconds. "Good luck, James. And Godspeed."

"Alright people, it's payback time." Hurley's eyes were focused on the tactical display. "All units, fire at will. Let's make these fuckers pay."

She'd lost 150 ships coming in, and her soul was crying for vengeance. Spreading out her formation had cut the effectiveness of the enemy weapon, but it was still a huge threat to fighters…though she suspected its primary purpose was missile interception. Now her first waves were moving into firing range of the orbital platforms.

The leading wings were armed with rocket-packs. Mostly Europan, RIC, and Imperial units, they packed a weaker punch than the ships carrying plasma torpedoes. But they'd also been in the lead, and they'd suffered the most from the fire of the platforms. Now it was their turn.

The first five squadrons came in at 0.03c, flying directly at their targets. Almost as one they fired their weapons, short-range sprint missiles, each packing a 50 megaton warhead. The rockets blasted toward their targets. There were six large fortresses in orbit, but the platforms firing the new weapons were separate, smaller installations positioned near the larger structures.

The bigger fortresses were firing light particle accelerators, but Hurley had managed to angle her approach to limit their fields of fire. The forts were a problem too, but Hurley wanted those railgun platforms first. She was staring down, watching the attacking units go in when her tactical screen flared white. A second later the com went crazy.

"Admiral Hurley, three targets have been destroyed." The AI spoke just as she was opening her mouth, about to ask for a report. "A single hit destroyed each unit, and a very large detonation resulted. I am still calculating, but the energy output appears to be in excess of 40 gigatons."

Hurley sat quietly for a few seconds, absorbing what the AI said. It was hard to hear a number like that, especially when it was presented without emotion or emphasis. Forty gigatons? She'd never even heard of an explosion that large from any source outside an astronomical event. "All three?" It was all she could think to ask.

"Yes, admiral. I have an updated report. Four additional units have been destroyed. All seven have exploded with similar magnitude."

Hurley tried to wrap her mind around it. They're so easy to

destroy and those explosions are so large…are they booby traps of some sort? Mines? Then it came to her. "Antimatter," she finally blurted out. "Those things are powered by antimatter. No wonder those projectiles have so much range and velocity."

She was just talking out loud, not speaking to anyone in particular, but the AI responded. "Affirmative, admiral. Preliminary spectral and radiation analysis of the area is consistent with antimatter annihilation."

"Motherfucker," she whispered softly. "These fuckers have antimatter-powered weapons besides missiles." Louder: "Get me Admiral Compton!"

"Yes, admiral." The AI was silent for a few seconds. "I am ready to transmit. Please be advised that we are now 117 light seconds from the flagship, which will result in a delay of almost four minutes in any two-way…"

The ship shook hard and started spinning wildly. The lights went out, and the emergency power activated, providing a dim but usable level of illumination.

"Activate positioning thrusters now." Commander Wilder was Hurley's pilot. He was shouting to the AI as he frantically worked at his board, trying to get control of his wounded bomber.

"Commander, the reactor is currently offline. There is no power available at this time." The AI was as irritatingly calm as it had been when speaking with Hurley.

"Use the compressed gas jets." Wilder frowned. He didn't know how he was going to land back on Midway without the air jets, but that was a problem for later. Pulling his ship out of its death spiral was his major concern. "We need to get this rolling under control."

"Affirmative, commander. Calculating optimum thrust plan now." The delay was barely perceptible. "Ready to initiate thrust on your command, sir."

Wilder barely hesitated. "Engage."

Hurley sat back quietly and watched. Wilder was a first rate pilot, and he didn't need her second-guessing him now. He was doing everything she would have done anyway. She looked down at her workstation and punched a few buttons. Whatever had hit them took out the com as well as the reactor. Great, she thought, an admiral who can't communicate with her ships is as useless as tits on a bull. Her face darkened. "How am I going to report back to Admiral Compton? He has to know we're dealing with antimatter weapons here." She was talking softly to herself, her hands curled into tight fists in frustration. The wing commanders will report to the admiral when they can't reach me, she finally told herself...assuming any of them are still alive.

They were all going in now, she thought, running the gauntlet...and I'm cut off. "Fuck," she muttered to herself, and she gripped her handholds tightly as the bomber spiraled wildly out of control.

"Give me another stim." Duke's voice was low and gravelly, and he tended to speak slowly, even when he wasn't drugged out of his mind and crushed half to death. His orders were to distract the enemy fleet and prevent them from attacking Hurley's fighters. Fulfilling that order meant getting there in a hurry, so he ordered everyone into their acceleration couches and thrusted toward the enemy at full blast.

"You have exceeded the safe dosage for stimulants under pressure, Captain Duke." The AI spoke clearly and professionally, totally unaffected by the 38g of pressure that had the crew reduced to spaced-out zombies encased in their protective shells.

"I understand that. Now give me the fucking shot."

"Yes, Captain." The AI ignored the captain's anger. The early AI personality modules had encountered significant difficulty in dealing with casual profanity. They tended to assume the human subject was extremely angry when it was nothing more than annoyance that had provoked the language in question. They tended to overcompensate, making for some interesting interactions. Newer AIs compensated, usually by identifying and ignoring casual swearing.

Duke felt the shot and, an instant later, the rush of clarity. It was hard to keep your mind clear at high thrust levels. The pressure-equalization drugs were moderately hallucinogenic, and the gee forces involved considerably worsened the effect. Enough will power and discipline could help a little with mental focus, but the only thing that really worked was a massive dose of stimulants.

Duke's job was to distract the enemy, not engage in a fight to the death. His ships were moving in at 0.05c and accelerating. They would come in and execute a single attack run and quickly zip past the enemy and out of their firing range. It would take a while to decelerate and turn about, but Compton would be behind with the rest of the fleet to mop up.

"Enemy missiles inbound." The AI was the only way Duke was getting information now. Wrapped up tightly in the couch, he couldn't so much as turn his head to look at a display or monitor. "Point defense systems activated and ready." His weapons crews weren't able to do much except watch the AIs fire their lasers and shotguns. It was an ongoing debate in most of the navies about how useful human gunners were. Some schools of thought held that AIs would always shoot better without human interference; others argued that intuition and experience had their place and could enhance targeting.

Duke was firmly in the latter camp. He'd seen a career gunner anticipate evasive moves by a target that no computer would have guessed at. But that was mostly firing heavy weapons at enemy ships. Even Duke had to acknowledge that effective point defense was almost entirely mathematics…and best left to the machines.

Even with the stims, the perception of time was erratic in the couches. Duke listened to the reports as his point defense fired at the missiles, but it still seemed like only an instant had passed when the AI warned him the enemy volley was entering the inner perimeter around his forces. The point defense had been effective, but there were still 40 missiles closing on his vessels, and attack ships didn't have much protection.

It was hard - one of the toughest things for a spacer to get used to – to lay helpless and nearly motionless, waiting to see if a missile detonated close enough to destroy you. There was no warning, no chance to think. One minute you'd be laying in the couch, the next you might be dead, vaporized with your vessel by a 500 megaton warhead exploding right next to you...or caught in the twisting wreckage of a mortally wounded ship. All you could do was wait to see if you were still alive a second later, a minute later. It was probably the one thing that broke more naval crew than any of the other dangers they faced.

"Detonations." The AI continued to feed data to Duke. "Explosions of 3 to 9 gigatons, captain. "Yuan and Muscovy destroyed. More damage reports coming in..."

"Did you say 3 to 9 gigatons?" It had taken a few seconds for the report and its meaning to sink through the haziness. Antimatter warheads.

"Affirmative, captain. Do you wish me to continue with the damage report?"

Duke lay motionless, struggling to stay clear minded. "Get me Admiral Compton. Now."

Compton was looking at the long-range scanning display, cursing under his breath when he got the call. "We know, James," he said before Duke could get anything out. "We're picking it up on our scanners. There's nothing you can do about it. Focus on your attack run."

"Yes, sir." Duke's voice was weak, tentative. Compton knew he was at 38g and in no condition to have a conversation. Especially one that wouldn't make a difference. Antimatter missiles meant that more of Duke's people would die; it also meant Compton's fleet would suffer more damage and casualties when they went in. But it didn't change anything else, so there was no point dwelling on it now.

"Figures." Compton muttered under his breath after he cut the line with Duke. Well, he thought, you had to figure there was a good chance they'd have more antimatter ordnance back here. Compton hated himself for thinking it, but he was glad he'd ended up having to send Duke's people in first. Maybe the enemy would use up its enhanced ordnance on the attack ships. Better a 90-man suicide boat than a capital ship with over 1,000 crew, he thought. The logic was sound, but it didn't make him feel any better.

Chapter 13

Bridge – AS Indianapolis
System X1
One Transit from Sigma 4

"I want probes launched from every ship, Commander Carp." Jacobs was staring intently at his display, watching the data flowing in from the ships of Scouting Fleet. "We've got no chance of surprising anyone anyway, so I don't want any time wasted. All probes are to scan at maximum power."

Jacobs knew he was advertising his fleet's presence, but with all the fighting from Newton to Sigma 4, there was no way a warning hadn't been sent up the line already. The First Imperium's communications were millennia ahead of anything the human powers possessed. Jacobs knew it was based somehow on dark energy. That didn't mean he understood anything about how it worked, but he did know it could transmit directly through a warp gate. All human-developed com systems required sending a physical ship or drone through a gate. That not only slowed transmission speeds, it also restricted communications to existing networks with the required physical infrastructure in place.

"All ships confirm the order, sir."

"Very well, commander." Jacobs turned slowly. "Lieutenant Hooper, prepare to launch a probe from Indianapolis." He tended to work informally with his staff, blurring the specific distinctions between different officers' duties. Of course he hadn't had a staff at all until a few months ago, when Admiral Garret put him in charge of Scouting Fleet. Technically, Carp was the tactical officer on his fleet commander's staff, and

Hooper held the same post for him as captain of Indianapolis. But Jacobs didn't bother with any of that; he just did what he wanted, which usually translated into Carp as his senior aide and Hooper as the junior, and the lines between fleet staff and ship crew very blurred.

"Probe ready, admiral."

Her answer couldn't have come more than 20 seconds after his order. Damn, he thought...she really is good. "Very well, lieutenant. You may launch when ready."

"Commander Carp, a reminder to all ship commanders... I want everyone on their toes. We don't have any idea what's hiding here, so keep your eyes open. Anyone gets blindsided and survives it, they'll be dealing with me. And they'll never be sorrier in their lives." Jacobs had the fleet on yellow alert, and he wanted his captains taking it seriously. The system looked empty, but that didn't mean a thing. There were still a hundred places enemy pickets could be hiding.

"Yes, sir." Carp tried to hide the smile on his face. He knew Jacobs was unhappy with some of the contingents that made up Scouting Fleet. He was used to Alliance standards, but of the other powers, only the Caliphate and Martian Confederation came close. The PRC's were at least as good...and might even be a little better. The CAC's were OK, about on par with the Central European League's forces. But a third of Jacob's ships were from Europa Federalis, which fielded the worst attack ship corps of any of the powers. The Europan navy overall was a formidable force, but its strength was highly concentrated in its larger ships. Service in the attack boats was unpopular, and most of the officers with connections or prospects lobbied hard for postings to the capital ships...or at least the cruisers. The crews serving on the fast attack craft were mostly those who had no other options, and it showed in their performance.

"Admiral, I have Captain Mondragon for you." Hooper was monitoring the admiral's communications while Carp relayed a slightly edited version of Jacobs' warning to the ship commanders.

"Put him through, lieutenant." He'd found Francisco Mondragon to be a welcome exception to the norm for Europan attack ship officers. He'd even begun to trust - and genuinely like the fiery Basque.

"My compliments to the admiral." For a hotheaded officer with a wide rebellious streak, Mondragon was capable of almost theatrical politeness. He'd come to respect Michael Jacobs, and it showed.

"Thank you, Captain Mondragon." Jacobs smiled. He couldn't help but like the guy. "Are your ships ready?"

"Yes, sir. All probes have been launched. With your permission, I will tie them into Indianapolis' information systems. I believe your people will be able to analyze the data more effectively than mine once we are zipped up in the couches." There was something in Mondragon's voice, an excitement, a level of engagement that wasn't there before. For the first time in his 20-year career, he was on a mission he thought mattered, serving a commander he liked and respected...and it was obvious to anyone who was paying attention.

"I agree, captain." Jacobs was impressed. He hadn't even thought about tying Mondragon's probes into his network. "You can coordinate with Commander Carp to integrate the data nets."

"Yes, sir."

"And captain...as soon as you complete the integration, your force may engage Plan Delta as soon as you are able."

"Yes, admiral." Mondragon's voice was steady, with just a touch of edginess. Jacobs was impressed. If he had been preparing to blast away at full thrust to head deeper into enemy space, he wasn't sure he'd sound as calm.

The fleet had only found one other warp gate besides their entry point. Jacobs would have preferred to scour this system before pressing on, but Compton had been clear. He wanted at least a minimal scouting force pushed forward as quickly as possible. Jacobs knew he shouldn't be giving the hazardous duty to Mondragon's people again, but the alternative was Pierre Cleret...and Jacobs wouldn't have trusted him to take out the garbage by himself. Cleret was arrogant and obnoxious...borderline insubordinate even under normal conditions. Jacobs strongly suspected he would do very poorly if he ran into anything unexpected. And pushing ahead through First Imperium space was asking for trouble.

"Good luck, Francisco." Jacobs voice was softer now, sincere. "And to your people."

"Thank you, sir. We should be underway within twenty minutes." His voice sounded almost apologetic. Jacobs cut the line, wishing there was a way for him to tell his subordinate he realized it took longer to get the Europan ships ready for full thrust…and he knew it wasn't Mondragon's fault. But some things were best left unspoken.

"All units are to conduct immediate reactor and engine diagnostics." Mondragon snapped out the order even before his acceleration couch had completely retracted. He looked over, seeing his tactical officer sitting hunched at his station, holding his head in his hands. It wasn't easy to jump right into action after a long stretch in the couches, but now wasn't the time for lackluster effort. "Now, Lieutenant Tomasino! If you need a stimulant, have the AI administer one, but get yourself together."

"Yes, sir." Tomasino's voice was weak, throaty. "Relaying your orders now."

Mondragon sighed hard. It was going to be the same on all of his ships. Not all, he reminded himself - he had a few Alliance and Caliphate craft in his group. It didn't matter - there was a least-common denominator effect in task group operations. He could give the toughest tasks to his best ships, but his overall capabilities were more affected by the worst ships, not the best. His father had been fond of the phrase, "A chain is only as strong as its weakest link," and Mondragon had found the adage to be very true in military operations.

His ships had accelerated at full power through the X1 system, trying to reach the warp gate as quickly as possible. Admiral Jacobs - and Admiral Compton, still fighting back in Sigma 4 – wanted a report on the new system, already designated X2, as soon as possible. He'd had his ships switch over to deceleration at various intervals, spacing out the task force into several lines with differing velocities. The ships in the vanguard had the highest velocity – they were tasked to plunge deep into the system, launching probes and scanning at full power. The ships farther back, traveling at lower velocities would execute vector changes, scouting out laterally from the warp gate's location. The rearmost ships, which included his own Faucon, had decelerated the most. They would remain closer to the warp gate, serving as a communications link with the forces still in the X1 system. Mondragon had initially placed Faucon in the lead group, but Jacobs had expressly ordered him to remain close to the warp gate.

"I'm receiving acknowledgements, sir." Tomasino sounded more alert, not back to normal yet, but better.

Mondragon swore under his breath. He'd always known the Europan attack ships lagged badly in performance benchmarks, but it really started to frustrate him now that he saw up close how the Alliance and Caliphate vessels operated. He stared down at his screen, scanning the ship statuses. Just as he thought. The Alliance and Caliphate ships – and the CAC ones too – had all acknowledged his orders, and they were well into their diagnostic routines. Half the Europan vessels hadn't even responded yet.

"All units are to launch probes immediately." Mondragon's voice was sharp brittle. He was seething at the performance of the lagging ships. "Any captain who has not commenced engine diagnostics and launched a probe in three minutes will be removed from command, effective immediately." He'd had it.

Tomasino looked stunned. He hesitated, just a second, and he blurted out a shaky, "Yes, sir."

Europan forces weren't used to the kind of pressure Mondragon was applying, but he didn't give a shit. Watching admirals like Jacobs and Compton in action had seriously affected him, and he intended to demand the same kind of performance from his own people, and if he had to chuck a few officers out the airlock to make the lesson stick, so be it. He smiled as he felt Faucon shake; she had launched her own probe in less than a minute. His people never would have managed that a few weeks before.

"All units have acknowledged the order to perform diagnostic testing, sir." Tomasino still sounded shaken. He wasn't used to relentless pressure and threats of draconian punishments, not even from Mondragon. But there was a new Francisco Mondragon in the command chair, one who had seen the standards of performance it was possible to achieve.

"Very well, lieutenant." Mondragon glanced at the chronometer. "Status of probe launches? One minute, fifteen seconds remaining." He leaned back in his chair and fought to hold back a smile. He was actually enjoying this.

"Compiling now, sir…19 confirmed launches so far."

Not good, he thought. He had 11 Alliance and Caliphate ships, and he knew without checking they had already launched. That left 8, and he'd have bet 4 of them were the CAC vessels attached to his command.

"Updated report, sir…24 launches." Tomasino was staring at the screen, watching the launch reports come in. "We're up to…" He snapped his head around, just as Faucon's alarms went off. "Multiple scanner contacts, captain." He looked back, eyes focused on his display. "We have 7 contacts inbound from deeper in the system, sir." He paused, and then he continued, his voice sharp and clear. "They're First Imperium Gremlins, captain. Confirmed."

Chapter 14

Landing Bay Alpha – AS Midway
Sigma 4 System
28,000,000 kilometers from Sigma 4 II

Terrance Compton stood next to the inner airlock, watching the fire control crews coat Greta Hurley's ship with fire-retardant foam. Commander Wilder had brought the ship in hot, with damage to the stabilizers and empty compressed gas tanks for the maneuvering jets. The landing had been one of the most impressive bits of piloting Compton had ever seen. The bomber would never fly again, but the cockpit was more or less intact. The foam was really just a precaution.

The bomber's crew had managed to restore communications, but not before the attack was over. Hurley had planned her operation well. Even without her direct supervision, her wings destroyed all of the antimatter-powered platforms. Once all the railguns were taken out, the remaining squadrons assaulted the orbital fortresses, inflicting considerable damage on several of them.

Casualties had been high, mostly during the earlier approach, when the railguns raked her formations. The strike force had lost 202 fighters, though almost 50 crews had managed to eject. Their lifepods would keep them alive for several days, but the fleet was going to have to advance into the enemy's firing range to recover them. Nearly 100 of the returning bombers had damage, ranging from Greta's shattered craft to units needing only minor fixes.

Compton watched as Hurley's crew climbed out of the

bomber's hatch, the landing bay personnel helping each of them into a small ship's car. It didn't look like anyone was seriously injured, but Compton had ordered them all taken to sickbay to get checked out. He smiled as he saw Wilder climb out of the stricken bomber. It was just like Hurley, he thought, to insist on being the last one out. He wondered how much of a fight Commander Wilder put up before he gave in to superior pigheadedness.

"Open." The airlock door slid aside at Compton's command, and he stepped into the inner chamber. "Close outer door." The hatch behind him slid shut with a soft whoosh. "Open inner door."

"The landing bay is subject to Condition Orange protocols, Admiral Compton. There are hazardous operations currently underway." The voice of the AI was crisp and professional.

Compton snorted. "The day I cower from a damaged fighter already covered in foam is the day I light myself on fire."

"Self-immolation in neither necessary nor recommended, admiral." Sometimes Compton had trouble telling whether the AIs were messing with him or not. The personality modules had the capacity for humor, but he got the feeling they were programmed to act more formally with higher ranked personnel. He felt they usually took anything he said literally, even when he was clearing joking. The navy tended to keep its virtual assistants a little more straight-laced than the Marine units, but he was sure they were even more so with flag officers. "I was merely suggesting that you wait until the area is stabilized before entering."

"Open the door." Compton was tired of sparring with a machine. "Now."

The hatch slid open. The noise was the first thing that hit Compton. The airlock was soundproof, but the bay itself was an ear-splitting cacophony. There were alarms going off, technicians shouting, all sorts of loud equipment performing one task or another.

He walked across the deck toward the stricken fighter. He passed two techs who stared dumbstruck for an instant before snapping to attention. The fleet admiral was an infrequent visitor to the landing bay.

"Don't let me interfere with your work, gentlemen. At ease." He walked up toward Hurley, who was waving one arm and giving the crew chief a series of instructions Compton couldn't hear over the din. She saw him out of the corner of her eye and turned and walked in his direction.

"Admiral. Welcome to the landing bay, sir." She stopped a little over a meter from Compton and snapped to attention.

"Yes, yes." He gestured with his hand, waving off her formality. "Relax, Greta. You're part of the admiralty now. We try not to torture each other with that crap any more than necessary."

"Yes, sir." She stood a bit less rigidly, perhaps, though it would still be a respectable effort at attention for most spacers. "What can I do for you, sir?"

Compton took a deep breath. "First, I want say I'm very happy to see you more or less intact, Greta. You gave us quite a worry there for a while."

"Thank you, sir. It was a little dicey for a while, but Commander Wilder is one hell of a pilot."

"Yes he is." Compton smiled. "Why else do you think Admiral Garret sent him here to fly you around?"

"I appreciate the admiral's concern, sir." Hurley was frustrated, but she was trying hard to hide it. "I'm perfectly capable of flying my own fighter, sir. And that would free up Commander Wilder to take over one of the wings."

"Give it up, admiral." Compton's grin widened. "Even I can't order that. Not without being grossly insubordinate." He paused for a few seconds. "And I don't violate Augustus Garret's orders lightly."

She'd been ready to put up a fight, but all the air deflated from her. Garret was the last word, not just the overall commander, but a legend in the navy. No one argued with Augustus Garret. Rumor had it that Compton had once or twice, but no one else would ever dare. "Understood, sir."

"You're the least expendable person in this fleet, Greta."

She stared back at him, a doubtful expression on her face. "You're too kind, sir."

"I'm quite serious. Admiral Garret could replace me. General Gilson could replace Erik Cain...as much as anyone can." He smiled when he thought of someone stepping into Cain's shoes. He and Erik had become close friends, but he'd be damned if he could truly figure out what made the stubborn jarhead tick. He looked right at Hurley, his eyes finding hers. "But your experience with fighter-bomber tactics against the First Imperium is unmatched. And fighters are the one weapon the enemy doesn't seem to possess. They have no truly effective counter."

"Until now, sir." Her voice was grim.

"Yes, these new weapons are a concern. But they are likely a specialized system, deployed to protect their worlds from missile attacks. We've seen no evidence of a mobile version." He cleared his throat. "And, with any luck, your people just blew away all of them in this system."

"Yes, sir." She forced a tiny grin. Her people did well, and she was proud of them. "The wings did a great job. Even with me out of the mix."

Compton tried to imagine Greta Hurley trapped with no com, unable to reach her people in battle. Maybe, he thought, I should give Commander Wilder and his people some sort of decoration for being trapped in there with her for four hours. He caught the laugh before it came out. It would have been difficult at best to explain the humor. "Your people performed brilliantly...and your plan was flawless."

"Thank you, sir."

Compton frowned. "I'm sorry, Greta, but I'm going to have to send your people right back out there."

Hurley stared back into Compton's eyes. "What do you need us to do, sir?"

Her unquestioning readiness almost made it worse for him. He hated taking a unit that had suffered 30% casualties in six hours of sustained operations and sending it back out with no rest. Her crews would barely have time to grab a quick meal while their ships were refueled and re-armed, and they'd be out again, back in the fight.

"Captain Duke's attack ships hit the enemy pretty hard. They're on the far side of the First Imperium fleet, decelerating to turn about and make a second attack run."

"That's excellent news, sir." She nodded. "I've never met Captain Duke, but I've heard good things about him."

"The bad news is he lost 20 ships." Compton spoke softly, grimly. "I can't hold the fleet back and let him attack the entire enemy force alone again. But I have no idea how many antimatter-armed missiles the enemy has." He sighed loudly. "Greta, I need your people to run anti-missile missions. We need to do everything possible to intercept as many of them as we can. They could gut the fleet with antimatter ordnance if we're not careful."

Hurley nodded again. "Yes, sir. I understand." She snapped back to attention. "You can count on us, admiral. We'll blast those missiles to oblivion."

"And Greta…"

"Yes, sir?"

"I don't want any of your hotshots getting too close on their attack runs. These aren't nukes…they're antimatter warheads. When you hit them they're gonna blow, and those are some big explosions." He stared right at her. "Do you understand me, Admiral Hurley?"

She stood rigidly at attention and snapped back a sharp reply. "Yes, sir. I understand. I will make certain the squadrons are cautious, sir."

Neither one of them believed her.

Compton watched the wall of incoming missiles on his monitor. They were still outside his point defense envelope, but they weren't out of reach of Greta Hurley's fighters. Her squadrons were heading right at the incoming barrage, extending the fleet's missile defense range considerably. Compton knew he had to destroy most of the approaching weapons. If those were all antimatter warheads, the volley could do catastrophic damage to the fleet if it got through intact.

They're probably not all antimatter-armed, he thought, with more hope than conviction. The enemy ships had fired half their externally mounted missiles at John Duke's attack ships, and the incoming strike consisted of both externally and internally carried ordnance. He'd never seen the enemy carry antimatter warheads in their internal magazines...the risk of a containment breach was just too great. But he had no way of knowing for sure. The First Imperium ships were manned by robots, so perhaps they had a different set of considerations. They could very well choose to take the risk to provide their modest fleet with more firepower. Simply because they hadn't done it before didn't mean they couldn't.

He had more to worry about than the enemy fleet, though. The orbital fortresses had all launched missiles as well. No human fleet had ever faced enemy fixed defenses before, and Compton had no idea what to expect. For all he knew, the massive volley launched by the forts was 100% antimatter-armed. He couldn't take the risk...he had to use everything he could to take out the missiles.

For about the hundredth time since he'd left Sandoval, Compton was thankful he had Greta Hurley in the fold. She wasn't only the closest thing the Pact had to an expert on fighter strikes against enemy ships – she had also pioneered the use of fighter-bombers in an anti-missile role.

He watched on the monitors as her fighters closed with the missiles. Before entering range, they dropped a line of point defense buoys. Recently upgraded by Tom Sparks and his research team, the tiny platforms were basically portable shotguns, towed into range by the attacking fighters.

Compton's plan was to keep the missiles under sustained, layered attack. First, the fighters would launch a strafing run, targeting the warheads with their light lasers. Compton wished Hurley's fighters could make a second run through the volley, but there was no way they could decelerate, turn, and catch the missiles. Not in time.

After the fighter attack, the missiles would pass into the

effective range of the shotgun buoys...all before entering what would normally be considered the point defense zone.

Compton was confident in the plan, but he was worried about the fighters. Shooting down missiles should be a relatively safe mission for them, but the antimatter weapons were dangerous. Intercepting a nuclear warhead didn't cause an atomic explosion; the mechanism itself was simply destroyed. An antimatter bomb was different. Most of its inner workings were there to keep it from exploding. It appeared the enemy employed something not enormously different from the magnetic bottles used in Alliance fusion reactors to trap supercooled stockpiles of antimatter. Although they had a familiarity with the principles employed, Tom Sparks and Friederich Hofstader had been unable to replicate the system. Damaging or destroying the fragile units in any way knocked out the containment, causing the antimatter to annihilate instantly.

A 3-10 gigaton explosion was no joke, and fighters lacked the protection of capital ships, cruisers...even suicide boats. Hurley's pilots would try to get close to get the best shot, but if they went too far they risked destroying themselves along with their targets. Compton had instructed them to exert caution, but fighter pilots were even crazier than suicide boat crews, and he was far from confident they'd obey.

"We're going in, admiral." Hurley's voice came through his com. She sounded completely different than she had on the landing bay...totally focused...cold, feral.

"Good luck, Admiral Hurley." Compton leaned back and watched his display. The fighters had to get through the enemy formation before the buoys started firing...or they'd be caught in the middle of the detonations. Compton sighed. He was worried about his people, but there was no one he'd rather have in charge than Greta Hurley, especially when razor-sharp timing and precision were needed.

He watched as the fighters zipped through, taking out missile after missile. He was right, some of them got too close. A few were destroyed outright; others were heavily damaged or were blasted with immediately fatal doses of radiation. But overall the strike was a massive success, with losses well within acceptable parameters. That was a term Compton despised, but he couldn't argue with its accuracy.

The buoys were next, and they opened up, firing clouds of tiny heavy metal projectiles at enormous velocities. A 1-centimeter piece of osmium-iridium alloy at 3,000 kilometers per second imparted enough kinetic energy to vaporize a target the size of a missile, especially one that could be destroyed by nothing more than a wire being ruptured and cutting power to the containment system for a nanosecond.

Compton let out a long breath. Between the fighters and the buoys, they'd taken out almost half the missiles...and his fleet's point defense batteries hadn't fired a shot yet. So far so good.

"Arm plasma torpedoes." Duke's voice was loud and clear. His eyes were focused straight ahead, watching his ships on the tactical display. The main fleet's missile attack had just gone in, and the enemy force was disordered and occupied with damage control. He'd timed his second strike perfectly.

His people had paid heavily the first time they'd sliced through the enemy fleet. They'd taken a toll, but they left behind almost 1 in 5 of their number. Now they were back for revenge.

"All ships report ready for attack run, sir." Lieutenant Tosh sounded edgy, but she was holding things together. Tosh was Duke's tactical officer on Jaguar, and when Duke took command of the task force, she inherited the overall support role. It was a massive jump in responsibility, but one she had handled well so far.

Duke shifted uncomfortably in his chair. He had the task force accelerating toward the enemy at 4g, which was extremely uncomfortable, but not enough to require the couches or any meds. He wanted as much velocity as he could get, but he wanted his people sharp and alert even more.

They'd slipped through missile range while the enemy was firing at Compton's fleet, and they'd managed to avoid more losses. Three more ships went down to particle accelerator fire, but the enemy had been focused mostly on its point defense operations against Compton's strike, and their fire had been light and poorly targeted. Losing anyone hurt, but 3 ships was better than his most optimistic expectations had been.

"Commence attack run." He sat still, trying to stay as comfortable as possible under four gravities of pressure. "All ships fire at will." His first attack had been tightly coordinated, with fire control directed from the flagship. But now the enemy fleet was badly hurt, and he wanted his captains picking their targets by opportunity, going after damaged vessels they could finish off. Duke wanted blood.

The wave of attack ships streaked toward the enemy fleet, each captain altering thrust, changing vectors to go after chosen targets. Duke's task force consisted more than half of Alliance ships, backed up by a crack contingent of boats from the PRC. He had some of the best fast attack ships in space, and now he resolved he would prove their true worth.

"Make a course for enemy target 14, lieutenant." Duke had assigned designations to each of the First Imperium vessels to help organize the attack. Number 14 was a Gargoyle with a massive gash on one side, spewing a huge cloud of frozen fluids into space. A well-placed pair of plasma torpedoes would finish it off, Duke was sure of it. "I want a course directly at the bogie…right down its throat."

"Yes, captain." Tosh worked the controls for a few seconds. "Thrust calculated and entered into nav computer, sir."

"Execute." He leaned back. "And get me the chief gunner. I'm going to have his hide if he misses the shot I'm going to give him."

"All vessels, launch laser buoys now!" There was hazy smoke on Midway's flag bridge. The new ship had gotten her baptism of fire, taking damage from a missile near miss and a grazing shot from a heavy particle accelerator. She wasn't damaged badly, but something was putting a lot of caustic smoke through the ventilation system. Not enough to seriously hurt anyone, especially sealed up in their survival suits, but messy and annoying nonetheless.

Hurley's people had done a tremendous job intercepting missiles, even if 33 bombers got caught too close to antimatter explosions and were destroyed. But even with her efforts and the point defense fire from the fleet itself, Compton's ships had taken heavy damage from the enemy warheads.

The barrage had been all antimatter-armed, which meant the enemy vessels had carried their enhanced weapons internally, something they'd never done before. That meant only one thing to Compton...the force he was facing was considered expendable. The enemy had to know it didn't have enough strength to take out a fleet the size of his. There were two only two possibilities he could imagine. Either the enemy hadn't expected a force as strong as his, a supposition he immediately rejected. He only had half of Grand Fleet, and the enemy had seen greater forces than he now led during the battles on the combined Line worlds. That left only one option. His people were walking into a trap.

The more he considered it, the more it made sense. This enemy force was here to soften him up, to cause as much damage as possible before they sprung whatever trap they had planned. But it didn't matter. Compton had no choice...his people had to take this world and find some way to defeat the First Imperium. Besides, he thought with a grim smile, there's a good chance they don't know Augustus Garret is on the way with the other half of the fleet. Maybe he'd get to spring a trap of his own.

Trap or no, right now it was time to go toe to toe with the enemy forces in Sigma 4 and finish them off. He'd sliced and diced at their forces every way he could devise, wearing them down with Hurley's fighters and Duke's attack ships. Now he was done with the subtleties.

"All units deploying laser buoys, admiral." Harmon sounded aggressive, anxious to get at the enemy. "Estimate 45 second until full dep..." His head snapped around to his display then back toward Compton. "Particle accelerator fire from the orbital forts, sir." He turned again, reading the data coming in on his display. "Yorktown was hit sir. Reports are sketchy, but it looks like she's taken heavy damage." He stared at his data again for another few seconds. "Admiral, I think we're looking at weapons significantly more powerful than those we've encountered before."

Fuck, Compton thought. He knew what it was right away. "They've got antimatter-powered particle accelerators on those fortresses." He'd been worried about the forts, but he hadn't foreseen more weapons powered by antimatter...and now he felt like a fool. They had antimatter-fueled point defense weapons...why not particle accelerators too? Whatever else had been happening while they were preparing Grand Fleet, the enemy got more antimatter up here, that much was certain.

"Get me Admiral West." Compton had sent West's task force on an attack against the fortresses. She'd taken a wider course, and she should be coming around from behind the planet in a few minutes.

"Yes, sir. Setting up the relay now." West's ships were using the planet for cover, which meant Compton didn't have a direct line to her flagship. Harmon had to set up the link, using a series of other ships as relays. It would take a minute or two.

Compton looked down at his screen and flipped his com to the AI link. "Joker, I want ongoing reports on any activity from the new particle accelerators." Compton had been interacting directly with Harmon and the rest of his staff more often recently, instead of working through his AI. In the brief instances over the last month when he'd been able to spare time for idle conjecture, he'd wondered if it was some kind of subconscious reaction to the machine enemy. If it was, he thought with passing amusement, it was wasted effort. Working through another human being who was in turn working through an AI didn't seem to make much difference when he really thought about it. And he wasn't going to squeeze the computers out of modern war even if he wanted to; that much was a certainty. War in space was complex business, and men needed their electronic aides if they were going to fight it. But it didn't really matter - his people where all fully occupied right now, and Joker was perfect for relaying him information promptly.

"Yes, sir. There have been a total of five shots…excuse me, a sixth has just occurred." Compton's AI had been upgraded several times, but the personality module had remained consistent. "Shining Crescent has been hit twice, and is the most seriously impacted, admiral. The vessel has suffered severe damage to her reactors and is currently operating on 20% power."

"Admiral, I have that link to Admiral West, sir." Harmon was staring across the flag bridge, waiting for Compton's orders.

"Put it through to my line." Compton switched his com from Joker's line. "Erica, I need your people to go in as quickly as you can. Those fortresses have some sort of super particle accelerators on them. There's no way we can take that fire for the time it will take us to close."

There was a delay of a few seconds' as the signal bounced its way from ship to ship over to West's flagship, and the same as her response made it back.

"Understood, sir. We're on the way."

"Very well. Compton out." Back to Joker on the com: "Update?"

"It appears that the enemy platforms were seriously damaged by Admiral Hurley's bombers. There are six fortresses, each of which appears to support at least four anti-matter particle accelerators. The weapons are not attached to the forts themselves; they appear to be satellites deployed approximately ten kilometers away from the stations."

"Hold, Joker." Compton snapped his head toward Harmon. "Max, advise Admiral West that the particle weapons are in detached satellites positioned near the fortresses. Those are her priority targets." He switched his attention back to Joker. "Continue with report."

The AI resumed where it had left off. "It appears that only one of the stations retains four operating weapons. Another has two, and the remaining four have only one each. Spectral analysis of the area strongly suggests the bomber strike destroyed the remaining installations."

I wish I could kiss you, Greta, he thought with a sigh… twenty-four of those things would have torn the fleet to bits.

"Commander Harmon, are the laser buoys in position?"

"Affirmative, sir."

Compton stared over at his tactical officer. "Open fire. All units."

Erica West gripped the armrests on her command chair. It was more habit than anything else…she was firmly strapped in and wearing a survival suit. Holding on was extraneous to say the least.

Her ships were coming in slow, thrusting to swing around Sigma 4 II. When they cleared the planet they'd be in a point blank range fight with the fortresses. She had no idea what those particle accelerators could do at such close quarters, but she knew it couldn't be good. At least her lasers would be effective too, and she had her ships under orders to fire every weapon as soon as they came to bear.

"All laser batteries, prepare to fire." She was commanding the task force flagship herself. Flag Captain Jones had been a freak casualty during the missile barrage, hit by a broken girder. She'd recover, but with a broken spine and fractured skull, she wasn't going to be running the ship any time soon.

Monmouth was coming around first, followed closely by the PRC's Yahsida and Akagi. The three capital ships were followed by half a dozen cruisers and a flotilla of Russian-Indian destroyers. More than enough to finish off a few damaged orbital forts. She hoped.

"All batteries…open fire!" She almost shouted into the com. It had been a long time since West had commanded a ship directly, and it felt good. Two of the forts had come into Monmouth's field of fire, and she wanted to hit them as hard as possible before they could target her own ships.

Monmouth's heavy lasers lanced out toward the first of the stations, their invisible pulses hitting the target hard at such short range. A Yorktown A, her flagship backed a strong punch, ten heavy laser cannons and an array of lighter weapons. She didn't have the new enhancements the Yorktown Bs did, but the ship was still an awesome instrument of war.

"Multiple hits on target, admiral." Hank Krantz was West's tactical officer. He'd been one of her captains for the last few years, but she'd needed to switch around her staff for this mission. "Some damage...it's hard to get accurate readings through those enemy hulls."

The First Imperium ships and forts were armored with a strange alloy, laced with some type of dark matter infused metal that had, to date, confounded Earth science and remained a mystery, even to Tom Sparks and his research team. One thing was certain, however...it was extremely tough and highly resistant to laser fire.

"All batteries maintain fire." She looked down at the data streaming in. Damn, she thought...these stations are tough.

"Particle accelerator hit on Akagi, admiral." Krantz glanced up, a stunned look on his face. "Her reactors are both out. Secondary explosions...she's bleeding air."

West felt the blood drain from her face. One short range hit from these things can cripple a battleship, she thought...how the hell can we fight something like that?

"Admiral, I have a message from the flagship." Krantz was excited, almost yelling. "The heavy enemy weapons are on satellites located around the primary forts. We are ordered to concentrate on destroying those."

"No shit." West was rattled. She'd never seen one shot almost wreck a capital ship. "All batteries, ignore the main platforms. Widest dispersal up to 20 klicks from the forts." The satellites were small and hard to individually target, but she didn't have any choice. They had to get those heavy particle guns. Now.

"Yes, admiral." Krantz repeated the order on the fleetcom line.

West stared at the tactical screen. One more hit would almost certainly destroy Akagi. She wanted to send her to the rear, but there was no way to do it. Without her reactors she was on emergency power. That was nowhere near enough to decelerate a ship that size and turn it around. The stricken PRC battleship would continue toward the targets at her initial velocity, without weapons and almost defenseless. We might be better off, West thought for an instant…it will hurt less tactically to lose a crippled ship than to have a combat-effective one hit and taken out of action. But that wasn't how she was wired. She didn't use her wounded for cover…even if it was the most expedient play. Akagi and her crew were under her command, and she would do everything she could to save them.

"Get Akagi on my com, lieutenant." She had an idea. "Now!"

"I have Lieutenant Commander Roku, admiral."

Captain Ishida had been Akagi's commander. Things must be bad over there, she thought. She tried to place Roku…he had been fourth in the chain of command, she thought. "Commander Roku, I want you to try something." There was no point in asking about the captain and other officers or grilling Roku on the ship's condition. That wasn't West's job, and the commander of Akagi had more important things to do than recap the last few minutes for her.

"Yes, admiral." Roku's voice was raw and hoarse. He was speaking English himself, and with no translation program rehashing the transmission, his tension came through unfiltered. "What would you like me to do?"

"I want you to fire your missiles." No point wasting time, she thought…get right to the point. Akagi didn't have the power to fire her lasers, but missiles could be launched off the batteries. "I want you to target the area around the fortresses."

"Admiral, our targeting systems are badly damaged, and we're well below minimum range for missiles anyway. We'll never hit a target." There was confusion in his voice. He didn't understand what she was getting at.

"I don't want pinpoint targeting, commander. I just want you to disable the safeties and expel the things in the general direction of the platforms. Detonate the nukes when they are close. Like mines. Do you understand?"

"Ah…yes, admiral." His tone was still confused, uncertain. It was clear he didn't really get what she was after.

"Antimatter, commander." She was trying to make him

understand. "Those things are fueled by antimatter. I want nuclear explosions all around that area. All we need to do is damage the containment on one of those things or overload a vital circuit with radiation, and the antimatter will annihilate." Her voice had gotten louder, more emphatic. "That's why they're positioned so far from the forts to begin with...they're vulnerable."

"Yes, I understand." She could hear the beginnings clarity in his voice. He was starting to comprehend.

"I can't shut down our laser barrage to retask for missile fire, but your lasers are offline anyway."

"Yes, sir. Understood." West could hear him shouting orders before she cut the line. Good, she thought...he understands.

"Admiral, I have Delta-Z codes from Boise and Mikasa." The Grand Pact had adopted Alliance protocols for the final transmission from a doomed ship.

West didn't respond. In the back of her mind she was trying not to hate herself for being relieved it was two heavy cruisers destroyed and not two battleships. How many, she thought, of the what...thousand crew on those two ships...will escape? She didn't want the answer. Not now.

She was watching her screen, following the effects of the laser barrage her ships were firing. They'd gotten one of the satellites, but taking potshots with lasers wasn't going to get the job done. Not fast enough.

"Shit, those things are hard to target." She muttered softly under her lips, venting her frustration. "Good," she whispered a moment later as she saw a cloud of small objects on her display...Akagi's missiles. I hope this works, she thought anxiously. They're not expecting incoming missiles at this range, and those birds are putting out minimal power and will be hard to detect.

Her head spun around as she heard a deafening sound... not an explosion, more of a crash, like metal being torn and rended apart. Monmouth lurched, throwing her body forward hard against her safety strap. The flagship had been hit.

Monmouth shook wildly, tumbling as multiple secondary explosions and expulsions of atmosphere altered her vector unpredictably. The ship lost thrust and, along with it, her simulated gravity. Debris flew wildly around the now nearly zero gee flag bridge, and a main structural conduit broke, one of its massive halves floating hard into a bank of workstations, crushing everyone in its path.

West straightened herself and felt a searing pain in her chest. At the very least, she'd cracked a few ribs. "Status report?" No response. She snapped her head around, wincing at the pain in her chest as she did. Krantz was laying in the remnants of his chair, very dead. The left half of his body had been hit hard by debris and virtually crushed. She tried to look around the flag bridge, but she couldn't see much…and what was visible was a nightmare. There was wreckage everywhere, and hazy clouds of blood floating next to severed body parts. A dozen ruptured lines spewed gas and fluids into the air.

"Status report?" She tried to turn, to look behind her, but she couldn't move herself. Whatever injuries she'd sustained, it was apparently worse than a cracked rib. "This is Admiral West… report immediately…anyone. But there was no response, only the loud static of her damaged com unit.

Compton sat silently on the flag bridge, his expression grim. No one dared to approach him, not now. No one but Max Harmon, and then only if it was extremely important. He'd won another victory, a new battle honor the wordsmiths would weave poetically into his service record. But as he had so often found in almost 50 years in space, now that he'd paid the price, the triumph he'd wanted so badly didn't seem so sweet.

They taught us again not to underestimate them, Compton thought…showed us once more that we are the children in their universe. He was angry with himself. He'd given considerable thought to what other weapons the First Imperium might have had waiting, how heavily fortified one of their bases might be. But he couldn't pick his enemy or decide what powers they would possess. And there'd been no choice but to go in, to keep up the pressure and find a way, any way, to end this war.

Still, he felt he should have foreseen things more clearly…

that there should have been some way to reduce the cost his people had paid. Erica West would live, at least. Her people had gotten her evac'd to Yashida's sickbay. He wished he could say the same for Monmouth, but her main structural spine had been shattered. Compton had seen a lot of damaged ships, and he was pretty sure West's flagship was a total loss.

Akagi might survive. Her damage was extensive, but probably repairable. The old girl deserved to make it, he thought, since Akagi, acting on West's orders, was as responsible as any fleet unit for the victory. Her short-ranged missile fire had erupted around the orbital platforms, taking out four of the particle gun satellites in less than a minute. Compton couldn't imagine what the losses would have been if they hadn't.

Once the heavy guns were gone, West's people swarmed around the rest of the orbital works and tore them to pieces. They'd thought the admiral was dead, and they took their vengeance, closing to point blank range and ripping the things apart with concentrated laser fire. The enemy armor was laser-resistant, but a strong enough focused barrage would destroy anything...especially from spitting distance.

While West's people secured the orbital facilities, John Duke's crack attack ships had swarmed back through the enemy formations, picking off the wounded ships and then delivering multiple plasma torpedo runs to those still in decent shape. By the time they cleared the combat zone, they'd lost another 21 of their number, but they'd left nothing in their wake but shattered hulks. Compton's main body quickly finished off what little was left. The battle was over, and won. It was time to count the cost.

Compton had five battleships crippled or mortally wounded. Hurley had lost over a third of her people, as had John Duke. Any initial hopes for a quick victory over an outnumbered enemy looked like the worst kind of foolishness now. But however painful and costly, it was a victory, and not one Compton intended to waste. They had uncontested possession of the space over a First Imperium planet. At least for now.

"Get me General Cain." They were the first words he'd spoken in quite some time.

"Yes, sir." Harmon had been hunched over his workstation, monitoring the damage control reports, watching for anything the admiral needed to see. "I have General Cain on your line, sir."

"Hello Terrance." Cain spoke up before Compton had the chance. Most of the people Compton would speak to over the next few days would congratulate him on his victory, but not Erik Cain. The dour Marine knew, perhaps more than anyone, what Compton was feeling now...sadness, guilt, regret. The last thing he needed was more platitudes and backslaps on his strategic brilliance. "I'm sorry the losses were so high. Your people put up a tremendous fight, but it always costs more than it should. Doesn't it?"

Compton sighed. "Yes, it does." He paused then added, "And Erik...thanks." Cain didn't answer; no response was needed. "In any event, we've secured the system, at least for now. How soon can your people be ready to go down?"

Chapter 15

Bridge – AS Indianapolis
System X1
One Transit from Sigma 4

"All vessels, cut thrust immediately." Mondragon responded instantly to the enemy contact. "The fleet is to assemble at coordinates 373,402,092. All ships are to compute optimal thrust plans and confirm through the flagship before executing." Concentrating a fleet that was scattered over a cubic lighthour of space with different velocities and headings was an extremely difficult exercise in the best of circumstances. Doing it in the face of the enemy called for expert crews, something most of his ships simply didn't have.

"Yes, sir." Tomasino hunched over his workstation, relaying Mondragon's orders to the rest of the task force.

"Lieutenant Santini, I want you to review and coordinate the incoming thrust plans." Santini was Faucon's navigator, but since Mondragon had been put in charge of the task force, she'd become part of the command staff too.

"Yes, captain." Santini's response was tentative, hollow. Keeping Faucon on course was one thing, but she'd never done anything remotely like supervising a force of over 40 ships converging to face an enemy fleet.

"Use the AI, lieutenant." Mondragon understood her concerns, and her limitations as well, but she was all he had. "Run their plans through the navcom and perform a few checks. That's all you can do."

"Yes, sir." She sounded better, but still not convinced.

"Awaiting incoming plans for review."

Mondragon leaned back. He knew she could only give each plan a cursory glance, but any double-check was better than none at all. "Lieutenant Tomasino, prepare to launch a drone back to X1. We have to advise Admiral Jacobs we've encountered enemy forces." I think I can take 7 Gremlins, he thought...I hope I'm right...and that you agree with what I'm doing. "If not," he whispered to himself in his native Basque, "you can court martial me." French was the official language of Europa Federalis, and use of the other national and regional tongues was discouraged in rural areas and forbidden outright in the major population centers and in the service. But Mondragon didn't give a shit. Federalis and its government was far away... and good riddance to the whole corrupt, stinking lot of it.

"Yes, captain." Tomasino turned and looked over at Mondragon. "Ready for message download now, sir."

Mondragon nodded and switched his comlink to the drone's input line. "Admiral Jacobs, I am reporting contact with a group of 7 enemy vessels, conclusively identified as Gremlins." His eyes glanced down at his screen, subconsciously confirming what he already knew. "I have elected to mass my task force and give battle. I believe we have sufficient strength to defeat this enemy squadron." He wasn't at all sure about that, but he was determined to put up a fight. If he ran, it would mean abandoning all his ships that had pushed deeper into the system; they'd never decelerate and get back through the warp gate before the enemy caught them.

"I am transmitting all navigational and scanning data via this drone, and I am posting two vessels near the warp gate with orders to send ongoing updates through." He paused for a few seconds, considering if he wanted to add anything further. Finally, he just said, "Mondragon out." Then he cut the line. "Lieutenant Tomasino, download all scanning data into the drone and launch at once."

"Yes, sir."

"Lieutenant Santini...status on incoming thrust plans?" He turned toward her as he spoke.

"Still coming in, captain." She was staring at her screen as she spoke. "I have 18 so far."

Mondragon frowned. The Alliance and PRC ships again. He didn't even have to check; he knew. "Lieutenant Tomasino, advise all ship commanders that anyone not getting their thrust plan to the flagship in two minutes will be relieved." His voice was ice cold.

Tomasino hesitated for an instant before stammering a response. "Yes, sir." Mondragon had always had a temper, but there was something different in him now. He was more demanding, but it was cold, meticulous...not the fiery anger he'd sometimes displayed in the past. It was far more menacing. The old Mondragon might have made angry, empty threats to shoot a subordinate; this new one would probably do it.

Mondragon leaned back in his chair, clear eyes boring into the backs of his bridge crew as they executed his orders. He'd never before served with officers like Terrance Compton and Erica West, and their cool competence had made an enormous impression on him. There was no reason, he thought, that the Europan forces needed to cede such a performance gap to the Alliance and Caliphate. It was the officers, too focused on acquiring and preserving their own perquisites and privileges, who accepted sub-par standards and efforts. But Francisco Mondragon had no intention of playing that game anymore. And the sooner his officers and crews realized things had changed, the better.

He knew he could probably avoid this combat, in spite of the fact that he couldn't get all his ships out ahead of the enemy. If he scattered his fleet the enemy would have to disperse to give chase...and superior technology or not, no 7 ships could effectively pursue 42. He wondered again if he should try to avoid battle...if he should give his fleet orders to scatter. A fight would be no easy victory. Seven First Imperium ships, even Gremlins, were going to be hard to fight with nothing but attack ships. His only useful weapons were short-ranged, meaning his ships would have to take everything the enemy could dish out before they got their turn.

But if he let them pass...if they got through to the next system, they'd be able to scan the rest of Scouting Fleet. With the enemy's advanced communications capability, the functional assumption was that if any First Imperium vessel knew something, they all did...straight up the line. Mondragon's job was to scout forward and to gather information for Compton; that was true. But it was also to deny that same intelligence to the enemy, to screen Grand Fleet and keep the First Imperium forces in the dark about what was happening. He could do that. He could do it by destroying these ships before they reached the warp gate.

"Lieutenant Santini, do you have all the thrust plans?"

"Yes, sir." She was bent over her workstation, running the plans through the navigational computer. "Working on those now." A short pause, then she added, "They look good so far."

"We'll have to take the rest on faith." He took a deep breath. "Order all ships to execute in three minutes." He turned to face Tomasino.

"Lieutenant Tomasino, bring the fleet to battlestations."

The enemy missile barrage had hurt, but it could have been much worse. The Gremlins didn't have external emplacements and, overall, they had a relatively small broadside of missiles. The fleet had, for the most part, cleanly executed the complex series of maneuvers Mondragon had ordered, and they were able to meet the incoming volley with a combined point defense grid. Most of the incoming weapons were intercepted by the combined countermeasures of the task force, and the ones that got through were all nukes. Mondragon suspected they had all been standard atomic warheads - he guessed the Gremlins lacked antimatter ordnance altogether. Still, even with the successful defensive effort, the enemy attack had destroyed 2 of his ships and taken another 3 out of action.

The particle accelerators had been worse, much worse. The Gremlins mounted lighter weapons than the Gargoyles, but it didn't take much to wreck a fast attack ship. Mondragon brought his force in on a random zigzag pattern, each shift altering a ship's thrust and vector by tiny increments. Particle accelerators, like lasers, were point to point weapons. They had to actually strike a vessel to cause significant damage…and an attack ship was a very small target at 250,000 kilometers. It took some period of time to aim the projector – and maybe a second for the beam to reach the target. If the ship's thrust or directional heading varied the tiniest amount after the fire lock was established, even enough to move it a boat length out of the projected location, a shot would probably miss.

Despite Mondragon's aggressive evasive maneuvers, another ten of his ships were destroyed or seriously damaged. Normally he'd have come in fast, reducing the time his force spent in the enemy's kill zone. But this time he'd kept his velocity low, less than 0.01c. If he came in at high speed and didn't destroy all the enemy ships on the first run, the Gremlins could escape. He'd never be able to decelerate and turn around before they got to the warp gate and into the X1 system.

"Lieutenant, repeat my order that no one is to fire until I give the command." He was worried some of his captains would fire too early. The hit percentage dropped off sharply outside the short range band, and Mondragon wanted these torpedoes right on target.

"Yes, sir." Tomasino was nervous; Mondragon could hear it in his voice. They'd been in combat together before, but nothing like this. He knew it was the same throughout the fleet. This was a rite of passage for most of his people. Except for the Alliance ships, none of them had ever faced the First Imperium before. Hearing stories, reading reports…it was enough to scare the hell out of them. But nothing truly prepared anyone to face this enemy…nothing but actually doing it.

Mondragon and his people had fought the First Imperium a couple months earlier during the battle in Newton's system, but there Jacobs had masterfully worn the foe down with fighters and laser buoys. In the end, Mondragon had led just 20 ships into that fight, mostly his Alliance and CAC units. For the bulk of his Europan vessels and crews, this was their true baptism of fire.

"Lead ships under 100,000 kilometers from enemy vessels."

It was clear from his tone that Luigi Tomasino would already have given the order to fire. But Tomasino wasn't in command; Mondragon was.

"All ships continue to close." The enemy weapons were still firing. He knew getting in tight would cost him more ships. But he needed those plasma torpedoes on target. They were a potent weapon, even against First Imperium vessels, but they still needed to hit.

"Lead elements at 90,000 kilometers."

Mondragon was trying to decide if he thought Tomasino's tone was getting a little shakier every 10,000 klicks. He leaned back in his command chair, but he remained silent. They still weren't close enough yet.

"Griffe had been hit, sir." Tomasino was reading from his display. "Her reactor's out, plasma torpedoes disabled...but Captain Elysee thinks she can save the ship." He looked up from the screen. "Passing 80,000 kilometers, captain."

Mondragon sat back in his chair, not saying a word. To anyone's gaze he seemed totally at ease, though in truth his stomach was clenched into a knot. It wasn't easy sitting there, listening to casualty reports, wondering every second if your ship was going to be hit...if you'd even realize you were dead before it was over.

Jacobs had shared a story with Mondragon, one he'd been told by none other than Terrance Compton. Jacobs had expressed concern about having the coolness under fire to lead Scouting Fleet, and he wondered out loud if he had enough of what Compton and Garret did...whether he could do the job they expected from him. Compton laughed and told him that none other than Augustus Garret had excused himself after every battle for at least 20 years so he could go back to his cabin and casually heave up his guts. Supposedly, he'd done it so forcefully after one especially grueling fight, he'd pulled a muscle in his back.

It had clicked right then and there for Mondragon. At that moment, he understood. The heroes weren't born that way, they didn't have anything inside them he didn't...they just resolved to do what had to be done, and put the fear and hesitation in its place until they could deal with it. Francisco Mondragon decided that being a middling Europan commander was no longer enough for him. Especially not now...not when the best of mankind was rallying to face the enemy.

"Requin and Chasseur have been hit, sir." Tomasino's voice was beginning to crack. He was a good officer by the standards of the Europan attack ship flotilla, but the pressure of this fight was pushing him to his breaking point. "Chasseur is remaining in the line, but Requin is not responding, captain." He turned to face Mondragon. "Passing 65,000 kilometers, sir!"

Mondragon took a deep breath. "All ships may fire when ready." He spoke softly, with apparent – but entirely faked – calm.

Tomasino relayed the order at once. "All ships, fire when ready." He was gripping the sides of his workstation and almost shouting into the com. "Repeat, all ships, fire when ready."

Chapter 16

Launch Bay Gamma – AS Midway
Sigma 4 System
Orbiting Sigma 4 II

Erik Cain stood rigid, immobile, waiting for the final launch authorization. His thoughts drifted back through the years, to missions and days long gone by. The landers hadn't changed all that much since he climbed into a launch bay for the first time. The old Gordons had only carried five Marines; the newer Liggetts held ten. Everything in warfare had expanded in scope since Cain was a cherry, and the landing craft were no exception.

Besides the larger size, there wasn't much difference. Designed to carry troops in powered armor, the Liggetts were simple open landing sleds, just like the Gordons. The wave about to launch had already been coated with heat-resistant foam, and the armor power systems were activated. If all went well they'd be on their way down in 30 seconds.

More than a few people had been surprised – some outright shocked - when Cain announced he was going in with the first wave. A number of officers had tried to convince him to wait until a landing zone was secured, but they were all told – with rapidly eroding levels of politeness – to mind their own fucking business.

Terrance Compton had remained silent when Cain announced his intentions. He didn't like the idea any more than the others. Losing Cain would be a disaster for the operation and, beyond the pure military considerations, Compton considered the stubborn Marine one of his few real friends. But he knew Cain well enough to understand this was something he had to do. Compton was worried, of course, just like everyone else, but he also knew Erik Cain was a survivor.

"Final authorization granted."   The tactical computer sounded almost identical to the one on his first mission. He was trying to decide if it was the exact same voice. It hadn't occurred to him before, but now he wondered, is it possible they've been using the same voice for 25 years? "Launch in 30 seconds."

Cain took a deep breath, too deep. His suit was filled with standard pre-battle oxygen-rich mixture, and he made himself mildly dizzy. His eyes were closed, and he was thinking of another battle...on Farpoint. He'd lost a lot of comrades over the years, but the fight on Farpoint had claimed his best friend. It was that battle, not the far larger one on Sandoval, that had cemented his hatred of the First Imperium...that fed his longing to grapple with the enemy, to battle them for as long as it took to destroy them.

He wore a small silver pendant around his neck. He'd found it when he was cleaning out Jax's quarters, and he'd held on to it. It was the only thing he'd kept from Jax's possessions; he'd seen the big Marine wear it during every battle the two had fought for 20 years. It had been a violation of regulations, but somehow Jax had managed to sneak it under his armor every time, at least until his rising rank made subterfuge unnecessary.

Cain had been stunned to find it in a drawer...for some reason Jax had gone into his last battle without the tiny talisman. If Cain had been superstitious, he'd have blamed Jax's death on the big man leaving his lucky charm behind. But he knew better. Jax didn't die because he forgot to wear a lump of silver around his neck...he died because of Cain's prejudices, his arrogance.

Now Cain was wearing the charm. He was wearing it for his friend, to honor him...to avenge him. They were about to bring the war to the enemy. He didn't know what to expect on the ground, and he didn't care. Whatever the enemy had down there, Erik Cain and the Marines were coming...and when they were done there would be nothing left but the silent remains of a world that had once been part of the First Imperium. Cain had lost the early fear of the enemy, and his Marines had followed his example. They were ready.

"Fifteen seconds to launch." The bay depressurized, matching the pressure of the upper atmosphere.

Cain took another breath, a little less forcefully this time. He'd lost count of how many bays he'd launched from, but he'd never completely shaken the claustrophobia. He was always glad when they hit ground, and the locking bolt released him from the lander.

"Ten seconds to launch." Cain felt the rack moving, carrying the line of Marines to the launch track. The attack wave was combat loaded, so Cain was sharing a lander with a standard squad. His other senior officers were similarly spread throughout the landing force. There was no way Cain would allow a lucky missile shot to decapitate the entire command structure.

"Five seconds to launch. Four, three…"

Cain gritted his teeth. No matter how many times you did it, a combat launch was a rough ride.

"…two, one…" The catapult blasted the lander down the track at 30g. It only lasted a second, but that much force hitting you slammed into your chest like a sledgehammer and forced the breath from your lungs.

The first wave was strong, 6 battalions of crack Marines and 4 ortas of Janissaries. Just over 5,000 veterans were on their way down simultaneously. Normally, Cain would have wanted the surface of the planet blasted hard to soften up the defenses, but not this time. They weren't here to win a battle or grab some real estate…they had come to find a way to defeat the First Imperium, and blasting everything into radioactive dust wasn't going to help with that. They had to capture the enemy installations intact…or as close to it as possible. Cain knew this would be a brutal fight; so did the men and women in the strike force. No one on the way down to the planet's surface was under any illusions as to what they faced.

The sky was filled with every manner of debris to distract the enemy ground fire. Compton's people were firing every type of purpose built ECM shell…along with bits of wreckage from the damaged ships of the fleet. There were clouds of sickly green haze everywhere, the radioactive, metal-laced steam the Caliphate called Smoke. Cain had never understood why the Alliance hadn't adopted the system…the Caliphate had always deployed it with great success to interfere with scanners and detection systems.

The countermeasures were the strongest ever employed during a planetary assault. No one liked sending the landing wave down against unsoftened targets, but no one could think of a workable alternative either. So with no bombardment preceding the assault, it was all ECM and deception protecting the vulnerable landers.

"Well Hector, it's you and me again." Cain's AI had been upgraded a number of times, but the system had used the same personality module since the day Cain left the Academy, first in his class and a newly minted captain.

"Yes, General Cain. This is our 37th landing under combat conditions." Cain's AI had long sparred with him, having determined that such a persona was best suited to working successfully with the stubborn Marine. In recent years, however, Hector had modified its behavior. The continued losses and constant warfare – and the ultimate death of General Jax, compounded by Cain's subsequent guilt over the incident – had made a change appropriate. The AI had gradually evolved into a more suitable assistant for the grimmer, older Erik Cain. Marines often complained about the personality quirks of their virtual assistants, but the interaction modules were actually extremely sophisticated and, on the whole, they worked quite well.

"Activate tactical display."

"Yes, admiral." The AI obeyed at once, projecting the schematic of the landing force inside Cain's visor. "Please be advised that the accuracy of our scanning is subject to the effects of our own interdiction methods currently being employed." In other words, Compton's ships were filling the sky with all sorts of materials designed to interfere with First Imperium ground fire, and it was playing havoc with the Marines' scanners too.

Cain had planned a precision landing, a luxury he could afford himself with a purely veteran force. The intel from the surface was sharply limited, but what they'd been able to put together supported his decision. They were coming down around what seemed to be the ancient remains of a town or small city. Cain's forces would occupy and surround the long-deserted site, creating a secure perimeter so General Sparks and his team could transport down and begin analyzing the ruins.

Cain watched as the landing force descended. It looked like their formations were spot on, but none of that was totally reliable. Compton's interference measures seemed to be working well, which made any readings highly unreliable. There was fire from the ground, but losses had been light...less than 2%. The entire strike force was on total communication silence until they hit ground – there was no point in helping the enemy ground to air batteries find them.

"Four minutes to projected landing." Hector released the lock on the blast shield, allowing Cain a view of the outside. He could see the sky and a bit of the landscape below. It looked like a nice day on any Earthlike world. There was a large sea directly to planetary north...and, 40 klicks to the west, a series of small mountains, where the fleet's scanning indicated the main military installations were located. That's where Cain and his people were going...right over anything that tried to stop them.

Captain Jake Carlson crawled behind the embankment, making sure to keep down. The fire was thick, and he knew if he showed any of himself, the First Imperium bots would be sure to blast it off. He still felt a little weak, but the servo-mechanicals in his armor had adapted, feeding in more power to replace the strength his body still hadn't recovered.

"Colonel Brown, Captain Carlson here." Carlson had been one of the first heroes of the war, a retired Marine sergeant who'd been serving as a part-time three-striper in the Adelaide militia when the First Imperium struck. Caught behind enemy lines, he was the first one to discover they were dealing with a robotic foe...or at least one that employed machine warriors.

Carlson had been given up for dead, but he'd managed to find his way back to friendly lines, only to spend the next few years trapped in the planet's abandoned mines with the rest of the survivors. The hastily converted shelters were ill-prepared and poorly-supplied, conditions which grew steadily worse as time went by.

By normal military standards, Carlson had no place being present in this assault force. Three years trapped on Adelaide, with inadequate rations and supplies, had weakened him enormously, and he faced a considerable rehab period before he'd be truly recovered and ready for duty. But after 3 years of hiding underground while the rest of the Corps – and the other human forces – fought a grueling battle against a nearly invincible enemy, Carlson knew he had to get back in the line as soon as possible.

It turned out Cooper Brown felt the same way, and the two of them spoke to their doctors, liaison personnel, superior officers...at least half a dozen. They all said the same thing...no chance. Then Cooper Brown went right to the top; he asked General Cain. The commander of the ground forces promoted Brown and Carlson immediately, and he assigned them both to his front line strike force. The grim Marine general knew all about personal demons, and he wouldn't stand in the way of two veterans who knew what they needed, whether medical had cleared them or not.

That business settled, he sat with Brown, and they talked about Adelaide. Cooper told Cain things he hadn't spoken of to anyone, not even Jacobs. Not even Carlson. Cain just sat and listened mostly, and when Brown was through he whispered a few words and told him understood completely. Afterward, Brown shared Cain's comments with Carlson. "The pain doesn't go away." Cain had said. "They lie to you when they say that it does...but you do learn how to deal with it. Eventually you even start to make friends with the ghosts."

Brown's voice rattled loudly in his helmet, shaking him out of his daydreams. "Jake, what's up? What's your status?" Cooper Brown had been Adelaide's other hero, the commander of the militia, who'd used a variety of harsh techniques to keep the planet's refugees hidden and alive for almost three years before relief finally arrived. He'd been forced to do things he knew he'd never forget, or forgive himself for.

Brown was the only reason Jacobs' relief force had found anything but a planet of ghosts, but his reward had been the hatred of most of the planet's population, who cursed him as a tyrant. Brown knew there was nothing left for him on Adelaide, so he and Carlson left with Jacobs' fleet to go back to the Marines. Now Erik Cain had welcomed them both into the ranks. Back home.

"We're pinned down, sir." Carlson's company was up in the lead, scouting the way forward toward the enemy base. Things had been quiet in the two days since the strike force had hit ground...until about twenty minutes earlier, when all hell broke loose. "We haven't spotted anything, sir, but they must have multiple egress points around here. I tried to push around the flanks, but they've got us bracketed on three sides." Carlson reached back to scratch his neck, but all he managed was to hit himself with an armored fist. It had been years since he'd worn Marine armor. It still felt like home in some ways, but he had some adjustment ahead before he'd get used to it again. "Only regular bots so far, sir. No Reapers. Not yet, at least." That was a good thing, because Carlson's force was light on the kinds of weapons he needed to take out the heavier enemy units.

"OK, you hold there." He hesitated, his normally sharp decisiveness momentarily failing him. "I'll get some reserves up and relieve the pressure on your flank." Brown's voice was a little edgy...firm, but also showing a hint of doubt that would never have been there before. The last few years on Adelaide, what it had cost him to hold the colony together and keep it hidden from the enemy...it had changed the formerly unflappable Marine officer. He'd retired to the once sleepy planet to enjoy some peace and quiet; instead he ended up dead center in a nightmare that, for a long time, looked like it would never end.

Cooper Brown had put his Marine armor back on, but he hadn't been able to recapture his old self. Not yet, at least. His hands shook, sometimes uncontrollably, though he'd managed to hide it so far. He had his AI keep the inside of his armor at 17 degrees, but his body was still slick with sweat. Brown wasn't afraid for himself, but the stress of having men and women in battle, their fates in his hands, was bearing down on him in a way it never had before. Every man has his breaking point; Brown knew that. Now he wondered if he had reached his.

"Yes, sir. We'll hold on."

"Brown out."

Carlson didn't like how Cooper Brown sounded. He'd served with Brown through all the fighting on Adelaide. He'd never seen a better man...or Marine. Carlson had been there too, in the shelters alongside Brown the entire time. He couldn't imagine anyone as tough as Cooper Brown unraveling.

But Carlson had only dealt with the personal deprivation; the burdens of every decision hadn't been on his shoulders. He hadn't been the one who had to apportion the dwindling supplies. He hadn't been forced to refuse starving people more rations, or turn away mothers looking for medicines for their children. It wasn't Jake Carlson who'd been compelled to order civilians dragged from the stinking shelters and shot because they were preying on the others...mostly because they'd been driven half-mad with hunger and fear. He realized he couldn't possibly understand what Cooper Brown had been through, or what effect it might have had on him.

He frowned. After all Brown had done, his reward was, for the most part, anger, hatred. The people vented the rage from their suffering at Brown. When the relief force arrived, they called for a trial, for Brown to be held accountable for his actions...for his crimes. Carlson had been infuriated by it all, disgusted. He knew the people of Adelaide had been driven beyond reasoning by their ordeal, that they'd turned on Brown – and each other – when they couldn't take the suffering anymore. But that didn't excuse the behavior. At least not to him. Cooper Brown had given everything he had to save the people of Adelaide...even his soul, Carlson thought sadly. Maybe he'd wasted it...maybe none of them deserved the sacrifice.

But he didn't care. He was back in the Corps now, and Brown was too. Carlson knew one thing - he was damned sure going to stay this time. He would face his enemies, and he might die on one of his battlefields, but he'd do it shoulder to shoulder with his brothers and sisters. He prayed to God his Marine brethren never turned on each other the way the civilians on Adelaide had...or at least that he died in battle long before he had to see that black day.

"Alright, let's stay focused." He was addressing the entire company. "The colonel's bringing up reserves. In the meantime keep your shit together and take these bastards down." He glanced at his tactical display, checking on his unit positions. "Heavy weapons teams, we need max effect from you guys. Make sure you've got your best fields of fire." He paused, running his eyes across the display. "That means you, Second Platoon. Get those SAWs 200 meters southwest. You've got high ground over there and an expanded field of fire. Move it!"

Alright, Colonel Brown, he thought, we'll hold out. He was still studying his display, picking out fallback positions in case he needed them. "But you hold yourself together, Cooper." It was just a whisper, meant for no ears but his own.

"General Cain, we have a major enemy counter-attack on the left." Isaac Merrick was walking toward Cain, wobbling a little as he did. Merrick had been an army officer, and he'd spent most of his career commanding Earthbound forces. But he'd served the Corps well, battling alongside them in the bloody fighting on Sandoval, and by unanimous agreement of Generals Holm, Cain, and Gilson, the Corps recognized his commission, and he formally became a Marine.

It was one thing to accept a friend and a worthy comrade into the Corps, quite another for him to function despite the fact that he lacked the years of specific training all Marines went through. Most Marines wore their armor like a second skin, but Merrick faced a long and difficult adjustment period before he was as lithe and agile in his fighting suit as the rest of his new comrades.

Cain liked Merrick, and he greatly respected his tactical ability. But he knew the ex-army man wasn't ready to be up on the line yet, not until he'd had much more time to master the tools of his new service. So he named him his chief of staff, allowing him to tap the full range of Merrick's tactical skill while keeping him at HQ, where he was less likely to trip into a ditch on the battle line and get himself killed.

Cain had been giving two aides emphatic instructions, waving his arms as he did. The three of them stood over a large 'pad displaying a section of the battlefield, but none of them was looking down. Cain stopped talking and held up his hand to his companions when he got Merrick's communication. He waved the aides off and turned to face the new arrival. He frowned a little, though his helmet hid the expression. He was just Erik to Isaac Merrick most of the time, but in the field, the ex-army man insisted on formality. Cain knew Merrick was right, but he'd never been a stickler for military formality, and the older he got, the less use he had for any of it. He trusted Merrick and knew the new Marine would obey his orders...so he didn't think it meant squat what they called each other.

"How bad?"

Merrick walked the rest of the way toward Cain, stopping about two meters away. "It's heavy, but manageable. For now."

"For now?" Cain's tone sharpened. He liked subordinates to tell him everything upfront. He hated turning what should be a quick report into a protracted conversation."

Merrick hesitated. "It's nothing really, sir." He paused again, not sure he should elaborate. "Just a feeling. My gut says they're going to hit us hard...and soon." He shifted his weight, clumsily stumbling in his armor as he did. "I don't have any data to back it up. It's just..." He stared right at Cain. "...I guess it's what I would do, sir."

"I wouldn't call that nothing. It's damned good thinking." Cain smiled. "It's what I'd do too, Isaac."

"You've got the first wave of McDaniel's people down. Should we move them up...strengthen the line?"

Cain sighed. "We haven't seen a single Reaper since we

landed, Isaac. Doesn't that seem odd to you?"

"Yes, but I just figured maybe they'd lost them all in the Line battles." Suddenly Merrick felt foolish and naïve. They'd destroyed a lot of Reapers on Sandoval, but that was no basis to assume there were none left to face here. The enemy had never before kept them all hidden and used them for a truly massed attack, but, of course, Cain had done precisely that to them, something these forces would know about. The First Imperium's tactics were weak and unimaginative, but there was nothing wrong with their ability to learn from human strategies. Again and again, human commanders had seen the enemy reuse their own tactics...and sometimes they'd been fooled by it.

But Erik Cain had no intention of being surprised. "I'm not releasing so much as a platoon from McDaniel's force until those bastards show us some Reapers." McDaniels commanded Cain's answer to the heavy enemy units; all her people were equipped with the four meter tall Obliterator suits. Armed to the teeth, an Obliterator still wasn't a one on one match for a Reaper – First Imperium technology was too advanced for that. But they were the closest thing Cain had to a counter for the enemy's heavy forces. At least the Obliterators carried weapons heavy enough to damage a Reaper...normal powered infantry had a tough time bringing the enemy giants down. "That's what this pressure is...they're trying to get me to commit the Obliterators. It's what I'd do to them." Cain gritted his teeth. "But it's not going to work."

"Erik..." Merrick's voice had gotten softer, and he'd fallen back to calling Cain by his first name.

"Yes, Isaac." Cain could tell something was wrong. "What is it?"

"It's Colonel Brown. And Captain Carlson." Merrick had spent considerable time with the two refugees from Adelaide, and he'd come to like and respect them both. As had Cain. "Colonel Brown's force is dead center in the enemy offensive. They couldn't be in a worse spot."

Cain let out a deep breath. Shit, he thought...it figures. He knew Brown and Carlson had needed to see his confidence in them, so he'd put them right into the line. But facing off against a massive First Imperium assault wasn't what he'd had in mind. Merrick was standing quietly, clearly expecting him to do something, send some kind of relief. But Cain simply sighed again and said, "Brown and Carlson are Marines. They know their duty."

Merrick was always surprised to see just how tough Cain could be in the field, how ice cold he was when he made his decisions. He didn't argue…that would be insubordinate on the battlefield, and he knew he'd never change Cain's mind anyway. "Yes, sir."

Cain stood still, his mind drifting slowly across the field, silently reviewing his OB. He could almost hear Jax's voice in his head, warning him, urging him to caution. "But let's get one of Commander Farooq's ortas on alert." He paused, looking off over the rugged hills, in the general direction of the heaviest fighting. "Just in case."

Chapter 17

Central Pavilion
Armstrong Spaceport
Armstrong - Gamma Pavonis III

"There are subtle differences on this Gremlin, Admiral Jacobs. It is not identical to the ships we have faced in other engagements." That wouldn't have been a particularly noteworthy statement if it had been made about an Alliance ship – or any human-built vessel. Ships were often slightly different from other members of their classes. Newer versions of weapons or other systems often replaced older ones on vessels coming out of the shipyards, and damaged ships frequently received replacement parts that differed from the original issue. But one of the noteworthy facts about First Imperium vessels was that, within their class, they were all identical. At least that had been the case until now.

"What does that mean?" Jacobs wasn't following Sparks' line of thinking, at least not completely. He'd been excited when Mondragon commed him and said he'd captured a First Imperium ship. Captured! Jacobs hadn't even imagined that was possible. But something had malfunctioned on this particular vessel. It took one hit and apparently deactivated. It had been lying dead in space ever since.

"Every First Imperium vessel we have encountered prior to this one has had the exact same make up, equipment...everything. Exactly the same." He paused, rubbing his eyes. He hadn't had much sleep, and the two system journey from Sigma 4 had been rough. The Torch transports were fast ships, but he wasn't aware one had ever topped 50g acceleration before this last trip. Every inch of his body ached. "This one is different. Minor variations in dimensions and structural components. My preliminary analysis even suggests a slightly different density in the hull alloy."

"So what can we determine from that? Is it tactically useful?" Jacobs knew what Sparks was saying, but he sounded doubtful that any practical information could come from it.

"It is very early to say, admiral." Sparks was clearly excited at the discovery. "At the very least, I would say this vessel, and possibly its companions that Captain Mondragon destroyed, were constructed at a different facility or time than the ones we've previously faced."

"So how do we use that?"

Sparks hesitated. "Well, to start with, I can think of a few possibilities you won't like. First off, it would appear likely that we have tapped into a new pool of enemy strength. There is no question in my mind that this ship was not part of the force structure we have faced so far in this war. It may be a detached scout unit of some type, or…"

"Or the vanguard of an entirely new fleet, one of unknown strength." Jacobs' voice was grim; now he understood, and he was reviewing the possibilities himself. "We could have been facing a regional force before. We have no idea how large the First Imperium is or how much strength it has." Sparks was right. He didn't like it one bit.

"Yes, everything you say is a definite possibility." Sparks was glancing down at his 'pad, reading the data as it came in. "There are others as well. Certainly there could be an age difference. It is possible that the units we have been facing until now were constructed before this new specimen. We clearly seem to be encroaching on the frontier of the enemy's dominion. It wouldn't be surprising to encounter vessels more technologically advanced than those we have faced to date. We often deploy older ships to garrison quiet sectors, massing our newest units in our main battlefleets. The enemy may do precisely the same thing. For all we know, we haven't yet faced their real strength. The ships we have fought to date could be their older, obsolete vessels." He shifted his weight and looked up at Jacobs. "Imagine if you were fighting us and you went from facing an old ship...say, Cambrai...and then you ended up fighting a Yorktown B. Now consider that we've been in space 150 years, and we have that kind of technology gap between active units. The First Imperium has been here for millennia."

That last comment hit Jacobs like a sledgehammer. He immediately saw the logic of Spark's conclusion, but the thought of fighting against even more powerful forces was overwhelming. More than overwhelming...it scared the hell out of him. If Sparks was right, the war was as good as over. As good as lost.

"Admiral Jacobs?" It was Hooper, calling him from the bridge.

"Yes, lieutenant?"

"The Seals are here, sir. They are requesting permission to dock."

"Granted." He put his hand to his ear, tightening his comlink. "Instruct them to land. We'll meet them in the bay." Turning toward Sparks: "The Seals are here. Let's go."

Jacobs had notified Compton immediately when Mondragon's message arrived. His ships had engaged a flotilla of enemy Gremlins and captured one! Jacobs had read it three times before it sunk in. The Gremlin had taken a single hit from a plasma torpedo, and it just stopped dead in space. No thrust, no fire, no detectable energy output...nothing. It was a freak hit, most likely some bizarre damage that deactivated the entire ship's control system...probably a one in a million event. And an unprecedented opportunity.

Compton immediately sent two Seal teams out to assist in taking the First Imperium vessel. Boarding of enemy warships was almost non-existent in space combat, but the Seals were the only ones with skills remotely suitable to such a crucial and dangerous mission. Trained to operate effectively in a vacuum, the Seals did as much rescue work as fighting...though they were among the best trained combat specialists the Alliance possessed.

Sparks tucked the 'pad under his arm and nodded. He followed Jacobs out into the corridor and down to the landing bay. If all went well, in 12 hours Sparks would be aboard a ship of the First Imperium.

"Remember, we have no idea what to expect in there. Scanners can't penetrate that godforsaken armor, and we've never been able to get an idea of the interior layout from the scraps that are left when they're finally destroyed." Sparks was lecturing the Seals, and they looked impatient, anxious to get going. He was familiar with the type. A lifetime spent trying to get Marines to sit still long enough to learn how to use the new weapons he built for them had prepared him perfectly for this.

There was a loud bang. Captain Walsh had slammed his fist down on the table. It the thing hadn't been a nearly indestructible hydro polycarbonate polymer, Jacobs was sure it would have cracked down the center from the force of the blow.

"I expect everyone to be an expert on this material by the time we leave this room." Walsh was the Seal commander. He'd have been a colonel, at least, if he'd switched over to the regular Marine units, but he insisted on staying with his team. "I swear to God I will shoot any one of you who tanks this mission because you weren't prepared." He scanned the room. "Understood?"

"Yes, captain!" Twenty men and four women snapped back the reply as one.

"Good." He looked back at Sparks. "Please excuse my team, general."

Sparks suppressed a laugh. Walsh was being insubordinate too, of course, even though his intentions were good. But Sparks knew that no veteran unit, and especially not a Special Forces team, was going to think of a research engineer as a real officer in the chain of command…despite the stars on his collars. And he didn't care…he didn't think of himself that way either. He'd spent his life equipping these men and women, giving them the tools they needed to fight – and survive – their wars. He had no use for pulling rank, not unless he really had to.

The ancient warriors who were the namesakes of these Seals had been a navy force, not Marines. Modern Seals were part of the Corps, having been named for their predecessors both out of respect and because of the vague similarity in their combat roles.

"Why don't you continue, General Sparks?" Jacobs wanted to move things along, but he also took the chance to remind everyone of Sparks' rank.

"Yes, admiral. Thank you." He turned back toward the assembled Seals. "As I was saying, we don't even know if there are corridors in that ship, and if there are, where they lead or how they are laid out. It would be wild speculation to assume the interior of a First Imperium vessel is in any way similar to those of our own."

Sparks paused and looked out at the rows of seated men and women. "We don't even know if these ships were built to allow for organic crews or passengers. You may find it is one giant machine, one that is almost impossible to navigate once you are inside. Even if there is room for you to get around, don't forget the hull material is extremely hard and difficult to cut…and there is no way to know if interior structures will be any easier to manipulate."

He paused for a few seconds. "You may have to blast or cut your way through in various places, and that's going to take a lot of educated guessing." Another pause. "Which is one of the reasons I am coming with you."

There was a stir among the Seals, and even Jacobs sat with a stunned look on his face. Captain Walsh looked like he wanted to say something, but he didn't. This was Sparks' call. Scientist or no, he was a Marine general, and Walsh and his team would follow his orders. The only other officer on Indianapolis of comparable rank was Jacobs, but he recognized this as Sparks' area of command and stayed silent.

"Don't look so surprised, gentlemen." Sparks was mildly amused. He wondered, do they think developing and field testing things like x-ray lasers and Obliterators is safe? "We Marines do what we have to. All of us." He turned and walked up to the workstation set up in the front of the room. "So let's get back to reviewing what we do know about First Imperium vessels. If I'm going to be with you, you guys are damned well going to be prepared."

The shapes moved slowly, at least they looked that way on the monitor. The Seal armor was bulkier than regular Marine gear, and that added to the illusion, making them seem slow and cumbersome to anyone watching. Designed for operations in deep space, the Seal suits were almost miniature ships. They carried tanks of highly compressed gas to power small maneuvering jets, allowing them to move around in space without tether lines.

Four of them were guiding a large mechanism toward the hull. It looked like a heavy plasma torch, but it was something different, something Sparks had just put together. The standard plasma torches weren't strong enough to cut through a First Imperium hull, at least not quickly. The mission called for something more powerful, and Sparks had provided it.

The Seals guided Sparks' creation toward the ship, using their AI-controlled gas jets to maintain their bearing. They slowed as they approached the hull, coming almost to a stop as the device glided the last few meters into place. They sprung into activity, affixing it securely with a series of powerful magnets.

Sparks' invention was ingenious, simple but brilliant. A plasma torch was too weak to cut through the hull and a plasma torpedo would do significant damage to a target they were trying to keep intact. So the Marine engineer designed a compromise, basically a small plasma torpedo held in place by strong magnetic fields. Once activated, it would burn through the hull with the power of a plasma torpedo, but the fields would hold it in place and prevent it from penetrating deeper into the ship. If it worked, it would bore a 3 meter-wide hole in the hull of the enemy vessel.

With no accurate scanner readings, Sparks didn't know if there would be atmosphere inside or vacuum, and there was significant danger of explosive decompression. He sat patiently in the shuttle, waiting for the Seals to finish emplacing the weapon and get back before he blew the charge. The Seals had urged him to activate the mine as soon as they were clear, but he thought it was too risky with anyone still out in space, so he waited until they made it all the way back.

"All personnel are secured, General Sparks." It was Captain Walsh on the com. He'd been outside with his people, but now they were all back in the assault shuttle's bay.

"Very well, captain. Detonation in one minute." Sparks flipped open a small cover on his control panel, exposing the activation button for the charge. "Have your people ready to go in five minutes, captain." Sparks didn't want anyone rushing in right after the charge went off...the area would need a few minutes to cool before it was safe. Safe being a relative term, of course.

He watched the chronometer count down, the large blue numbers dropping below 30, then 20...finally 10. "Detonation imminent." He made the announcement on the shipwide com, and a few seconds later he pushed the button.

Ten kilometers away, a small, unimaginably hot plasma flared to life. Most material substances, including the armor on any human warship ever built, would have instantly vaporized and turned to plasma themselves. But the mysterious First Imperium alloy resisted...for the merest fraction of a second, but long enough for Sparks' instruments to record it. Long enough to challenge half the laws of physics that the human sciences were based upon. But scientific study would have to wait. Sparks' ingenious plasma charge had worked exactly as he'd intended, blowing a nearly perfect 3 meter hole in the enemy vessel's hull.

Sparks hit a second button, triggering a series of small charges positioned along the structure of his device, and the cradle, the still raging plasma suspended within its magnetic fields, blasted away from the hull and into space.

The display was showing a close up view transmitted from a series of drones he had positioned around the enemy ship. He smiled as he stared right at the perfectly round, 3-meter hole his device had neatly drilled through the hull. It was time to go in.

Chapter 18

Hill 84
18 Kilometers South of Enemy Base
Planet Sigma 4 II

"Commander Farooq, the enemy has committed additional forces. Still no Reapers, but at least a thousand battle bots, possibly more. They are flanking Colonel Brown's regiment." Sub-commander Mustafa was forward on the hill, directing the scouting effort on the enemy positions. He'd launched half a dozen drones, but it was hard to keep them in the air against the enemy's interdictive fire. Only one was still up, feeding him fresh intel. "It's way over on the flank...we're too far away to plug the hole. General Cain will have to send in the Obliterators."

Farooq listened to his deputy's report, his face impassive. "Negative, sub-commander. General Cain does not want to commit the Obliterators until we can confirm the enemy has no Reaper units present." He paused briefly, adding, "And we are going to operate in accordance with his decision." Stating it that way would head off a continued discussion, one that could only end up with Mustafa urging him to try and convince Cain to change his mind. That was something Farooq wasn't going to do for a number of reasons, not the least of which was he agreed completely with Cain.

The front of the hillside was an exposed position, a section of chopped up ground almost a klick ahead of the forward line. It had once been covered with the ubiquitous yellow ground cover, Sigma 4 II's version of grass, but the shelling had left only a few burnt patches. Mustafa was crouched in a small foxhole with two of his troopers, hunkered down and out of the enemy's line of fire. Getting there had been a little rough, and making it out didn't look like it was going to be any easier.

"I just lost my last drone, but from the data I have collated so far, I do not see how Colonel Brown can possibly hold his position." Mustafa was concerned, and it showed in his voice, even over the com. "And if his regiment pulls back, our own flank will be exposed."

Farooq was reviewing the drone feeds Mustafa had been sending him. The danger was definitely real; the enemy attack was heavy, and there were reserves coming up from the rear. If Brown thinned his line enough to cover that added frontage, the enemy would be able to easily punch through at almost any point. "Colonel Brown will not pull back, sub-commander." He was still reviewing the maps, but he'd already decided what he was going to do. "We're not going to let that happen."

"Commander, it's not possible. The enemy will have out-flanked the Marines by the time we can get there...and we'd have to virtually abandon our own section of front to do it." Most of Farooq's Janissaries were still in reserve, but a detach-ment had taken over a small section of front line as well.

"We're not relocating, sub-commander." Farooq's voice had remained calm, almost monotone through the entire exchange. "We're going to advance and drive through the forces in front of us. Then we're going to swing right and launch an enfilade attack." Let's see how these bastards like getting hit in their flank, he thought. "Order the reserves forward. Now."

The valley in front of the Janissary position was quiet; nei-ther side had forcefully advanced, each being satisfied to remain in their respective lines. But that quiet was about to be shattered.

Farooq stood in his forward command post, counting down slowly to himself. "All units...commence firing Smoke." His voice was calm; he might have been ordering dinner. But inside he felt the fire; his guts were burning with hate for the enemy. This was his third battle against the First Imperium, and he'd lost more than half his strength in each of the first two. His dead soldiers screamed from their graves for vengeance, and he was going to see they got it. "Your souls will rest, brothers. This vengeance is for you." His words were quiet, barely a whisper. They were for him...for him and the honored dead of the Janissaries.

He was looking forward across the battlefield, his visor projecting the input from the forward observation posts. There was a small explosion in the center of the field, almost a soft popping sound...then another...and more, all along the line. The shells released a sickly, pale green vapor into the air. The superheated steam was radioactive and highly toxic, its mix of chemicals and heavy metal dust designed to confound every known type of scanner.

Within a minute, the field was covered with a line of the bilious Smoke, obscuring all view of Farooq's forces from the enemy. He waited, a few seconds more. Then he gave the order. "First wave, advance."

Along the front, a line of armored warriors climbed over their trenches and out of foxholes, moving crisply across the field. The Janissaries favored a little more pomp and ceremony in their method of warfare than the Marines, and their formations were tighter, more regular. The Caliphate's elite soldiers tended to be more tolerant of losses than the Corps, and their fighting style reflected that. It was a cultural difference, not any measure of the respective élan or courage of the two services. The Janissaries were raised in their corps from childhood, indoctrinated from youth into a monolithic way of thinking. Unlike the Marines, they had no life outside the service, nor any prospect of one.

An old Marine could muster out to a nice colony world and, with his or her rejuv treatments, even have a family and live a long and pleasant retirement. A Janissary who survived the battlefields would find himself in an administrative job or a training position, but he'd never leave the service. An officer may acquire a favorite in the regimental brothel or even a personal concubine, but there would be no retirement, no family.

Farooq's men moved forward quickly, foregoing the zigzag

approach the Marines executed so well. Accustomed to advancing behind their screens of Smoke, the Janissaries emphasized speed of advance over cover. They began to fall almost immediately...one here, one there. The Smoke provided strong cover and prevented the enemy from aiming effectively, but it didn't stop them from shooting randomly. With weapons firing over 3,000 rounds a minute, there were going to be hits, whether the attacking units could see their targets or not.

Farooq himself moved forward, just behind his forward line. It was a risky place for the force commander to be, but that was the Janissary way as well. There were always replacements for fallen leaders, as those who survived their time in the junior ranks advanced. Where a Marine colonel or brigadier might retire after a successful career, making room for younger officers to advance, a Janissary remains in the service, waiting for a vacancy at the next command level. Farooq and his peers knew it was their unspoken duty for most of them to die gloriously on the field, to make room for the next wave of commanders. After his close contact with the Marines, Farooq had begun to question some of the things he believed, but a lifetime's indoctrination is a hard thing to escape.

"Cluster bombs incoming." The warning came in on the unit-wide com. Farooq wasn't sure who it was until he checked his display. Sub-commander Sharef...over on the extreme right. The enemy cluster bombs were a nasty weapon, one that had cost the forces of the Pact greatly. There was nothing enormously advanced about the basics of the system, but the accuracy and control of the enemy weapon were well beyond Earth capabilities.

"All units, continue advancing at full." Farooq knew his troops would ignore the bombardment and keep moving, but he felt better specifically ordering it anyway.

"Commander Farooq...report." The voice on the com was unmistakable.

"Yes, General Cain." Farooq knew he was pushing his orders to the limit by advancing without specific authorization. He considered it crucial if he was to support Cooper Brown's position, which is how he justified it. In truth, he should have asked for permission…but he was afraid Cain might order him to stay put if he did. "My forces are advancing. It is my intention to push forward and then att…"

"And then you are going to attack the flank of the forces facing Colonel Brown." There was something odd in Cain's voice. Amusement? "That's what I would have done too, but I need you to hold off. I'm about to hit the forces attacking Brown with the new PBS drones. I don't want your people getting caught up in that."

Of course, Farooq thought. The PBS drones were new… General Sparks' plasma bombardment system installed in multiple independent warhead drones. The PBS had been highly effective when it was dropped from atmospheric fighters, but so many of the planes were shot down only a few managed to deliver their payloads. The drone system was designed for massive attacks intended to overwhelm the enemy defenses and truly carpet bomb a section of the battlefield.

"Continue your offensive forward and take the enemy position if you can." Cain was speaking loudly and clearly. Farooq spoke decent English and understood it very well, so he had his AI-translation turned off. "But then hold firm until I give you further instructions. You may prepare for your flank attack, but do not execute until you hear from me. Understood?"

"Yes, sir." Farooq was relieved. His first thought was that Cain would be upset that he'd exceeded his authority. But the Alliance general hadn't scolded him at all. And he was going to soften up the enemy troops before Farooq's people went in. "Understood." The Janissary commander had a broad smile on his face as he resumed his advance.

The missiles were long and sleek, designed for maximum efficiency in an atmosphere. They streaked along at 20 times the speed of sound, low to the ground, just above the tops of the rolling hills that covered the area. To the troops below they looked like flashes of light ripping through the sky.

There were hundreds of them…almost a thousand, launched

from the rear areas of Cain's army. They were short-ranged...
their forward heat shields wouldn't last long at such intense
velocity. Their massive acceleration and high speed were their
primary defenses, reducing the amount of time they would be
exposed to enemy fire before they reached their targets.

Cain watched the strike on the large display in his command
post. It would take the drones less than 20 seconds to reach
their target area, and they'd covered about half the distance
when the enemy defensive fired started. The PBS drones were
too fast to be intercepted with missiles...there wasn't time to
react and get them in the air, even for the robots of the First
Imperium. But the enemy particle accelerators ripped into the
formation, knocking dozens out of the sky. The energy weapons were much weaker in an atmosphere than in space, but they
were strong enough to take out missiles at close range. The
drones closed quickly, but the AI-directed enemy forces managed to fill the air with high velocity projectiles as well, disinte-
grating hundreds of the approaching weapons.

Cain watched silently, grateful that he was seeing unmanned
missiles being blown to bits and not brave pilots he'd ordered
into the maelstrom. He couldn't help but be impressed by how
many drones the enemy managed to take out in just a few seconds. But they couldn't get all of them...not even close. Cain
had sent in most of his ordnance in one massive attack. He
needed the firepower. He had to push the enemy, force them to
commit all of their reserves. Then he could begin the final fight.

The drones weren't normal missiles; they didn't arc down to
hit enemy targets or explode in an airburst. They simply continued across the battlefield, releasing their PBS modules as they
did. The missiles themselves would continue on their trajecto-
ries until their heat shields gave out and they were incinerated.
By then they would have dropped their deadly ordnance on the
enemy formations below.

Cain had seen a plasma bombardment up close, and he knew
the fury the white plumes on his display represented. The weapons would sweep away virtually anything that was caught in the
area of effect. But the superheated plasmas would penetrate

into trenches as well and incinerate dug in forces. He flipped his com on as he watched. I wonder, he thought with sadistic satisfaction, if there has ever been a more perfect weapon to precede an assault?

"Cooper...Cain here." His voice was predatory, displaying his hatred of the enemy, his lust to destroy them by the thousands. The battle had looked as if it was about to settle into a stalemate, two dug in forces facing each other across a sort of no man's land. Then the enemy attacked in force, pushing Brown's people back, threatening to break the lines. But Erik Cain wasn't about to let that happen, and his PBS bombardment had stopped the enemy dead in its tracks. Now it was time to turn the tide, put the pressure back on the enemy. "Get your people ready, Coop...you may begin your attack in three minutes."

Cooper Brown hunkered down in a trench on the very edge of hell itself. The intensity of the maelstrom Cain had just unleashed was like nothing he'd ever seen...or even dreamed in his worst nightmares. The thought of his battered forces advancing across that tortured field was inconceivable. He'd never imagined ordering men and women to advance into anything like that. But he'd never served under Erik Cain fighting against the First Imperium before this either.

"All units, prepare to commence assault." He was clammy and sweaty, and his hands were shaking...as much as they could inside armor. His head pounded, the dull ache making it hard to focus. He punched the small button under his index finger and felt the pinprick as his suit injected another stim. He could have asked the AI, but he had a feeling it was about to start arguing with him, telling him he'd had enough already. After everything Cooper Brown had been through, if he wanted a motherfucking stimulant, the last thing he was going to do was fight with some machine to get it. "We're going over the top in two minutes."

He was proud of his Marines, though it was hard to think of them as his exactly. They were all veterans, and most of them had been fighting the enemy while Brown was hiding in a cave deciding how hungry the terrified civilians of Adelaide would get each day.

I should never have left the Corps, he thought grimly as he monitored the acknowledgements coming in from his companies. Brown had been troubled after the Third Frontier War, torn between his allegiance to the Marines and his growing hatred for the Alliance government. As devoted as he was to the Corps, he felt he had to leave. Rebellion was coming, he knew that much, and he was deathly afraid the Marines would be used to suppress the insurrections. Rather than risk being a part of that, he chose to retire and take command of Adelaide's militia.

I underestimated men like Elias Holm and Erik Cain, he thought. When revolution finally came, the Corps didn't fire a shot at the rebels and, in the end, detachments of Marines intervened in favor of the independence movements. I should have had faith, he thought…I should have stayed. But now I'm back. I can either wallow in misery and self-pity…or I can act like a Marine and live up to what these men and women deserve in a commander.

"One minute." He spoke into the com, his voice louder, stronger. It was time…and he knew it. He understood, and he knew the path he had to take now. He pulled the lever and listened to the loud click as the autoloader slammed a clip into his rifle. "Thirty seconds, people." His voice was booming, the weakness and regret draining away, shoved back into the deep recesses of his mind. He knew he'd have to face them again one day, but not now…now his Marines needed him, all of him. "Let's do this, Marines. General Cain is counting on us."

He watched the chronometer count down…ten seconds… five… "Alright 9th Regiment…attack!" He lunged himself hard over the edge of the trench, stumbling forward, almost tripping, struggling to regain his balance. It had been a long time since he'd fought in powered armor, and his reflexes were rusty. You had to be careful not to let your excitement – or the stims – push your arms or legs too hard. The suit's servo-mechanicals were extremely powerful, and they needed to be managed carefully. Otherwise you could end up flopping to the ground…or leaping high into the air, giving the enemy a juicy target.

He pulled himself upright…and he almost stopped dead, his mind momentarily blank as he truly saw the devastation before him. The plain was flat, almost featureless now. There wasn't an enemy bot to be found, nor a patch of grass or a tree. Even the smaller rocks were gone, melted by the massive heat of the plasmas. The entire field looked like a candle that had completely melted and had solidified wherever the wax had flowed. It was one monochromatic shade of brown, the combined colors of everything that had been on that hillside when the plasmas erupted.

"AI…scanning report on the field. Is that rock solidified yet?" Brown had been encouraged to name his new AI, but it hadn't seemed terribly important to him, and he hadn't gotten around to it.

"Yes, Colonel Brown. The rock temperature is currently in a range of 600-800 degrees. Your forces may encounter scattered tackiness on the ground where there are localized densities of lower melting point materials, however it is moderately safe for transit by armored personnel."

Brown shook his head, wondering, does Erik Cain know everything? His attack timing was perfect. Even a minute earlier would have been too soon…and any later would have given enemy reserves time to start advancing.

He glanced at his display as he started forward again. His lead elements were almost a half a klick ahead of him, meeting no resistance. In another two minutes they'd reach the enemy line…and slice right through it. Brown picked up the pace, following his front lines forward, his excitement building. There was one word in his mind. Breakthrough.

Chapter 19

East Ward
Washbalt Metroplex
US Region, Western Alliance, Earth

Alex Linden was groggy, not sure where she was. This was no normal sleep she was coming out of...even in her addled state she knew immediately that she'd been drugged. Whatever it was someone had slipped her, she had one hell of a headache.

She tried to roll over, but she recoiled in pain. She looked down at her leg, seeing the blood even through her blurred vision. She panicked for an instant, but then she realized it was just a cut, deep but not too large. She'd rolled onto a jagged shard of metal in her stupor.

Her vision slowly cleared and she looked around, taking stock of her surroundings. It was a building of some sort, old and abandoned. It was gloomy and dark, but she knew it was day outside. A shaft of sunlight lanced through a hole in the ceiling, lighting the garbage strewn floor a few feet from where she lay.

"Where the hell am I?" she asked, slowly pulling herself up to a seated position. The pain in her head increased, like a dull saw cutting through her temples. She tried to remember...she'd just disembarked at the Washbalt Spaceport. It was coming back, slowly and in disjointed bits. The security office...yes, that was it. She'd been detained by spaceport security. No...something was wrong. She remembered her doubt, then the realization... these aren't spaceport guards...they're Alliance Intelligence.

Now she began to remember it all. She'd been around enough

AI agents to know them when she saw them. She screamed out commands, threatening, identifying herself as Number Three... ordering them to release her, to take her to Alliance HQ. But they didn't say a word; they just dragged her into a back room. She was still shouting, demanding to see Gavin Stark, when she felt the injection...then, nothing.

She looked around the room. She was lying on a pile of debris, wreckage from the structure and assorted garbage. The building had probably been a residence once, but now it looked like it was barely standing. Her head snapped around quickly toward a noise to her left. There were two rats tearing into a discarded bag in the corner.

Her head was clearing, and with it, she started to feel the rest of the pain. The cut she'd just suffered began to throb, and now she noticed other wounds, one on her arm, another on her leg. Rat bites, she thought, reaching down to tear off part of her tunic to wrap up her injuries. But it wasn't there...her tunic was gone.

She was wearing a black dress, a very short one. Her feet were bare, but there were two shoes lying nearby...evidently they'd fallen off. They were heels, extremely expensive ones, she noted. Realization slowly dawned on her...they were hers, and the dress too. Someone had stolen them from her apartment and changed her into them while she was unconscious.

Her anger flared. She was Number Three, one of the most powerful women in the Alliance. Whoever was responsible for this would pay, that much she promised herself. But her enthusiasm for revenge quickly faded as she began to think things through, to understand. Only one person could have done this to her. Gavin Stark.

Her senses were coming back, and the stench of her surroundings became unbearable. She had to fight back the urge to retch. I've got to get out of here, she thought...figure out where I am. She slowly rose to her feet, looking around for something to bind her wounds. He first thought was to tear off a piece of her dress, but it was a garment she used for seductions, and there wasn't much material to spare. Besides, it was made of high grade hypersilk; she'd practically need a molecular blade to cut it. Tearing it by hand was impossible.

She found a filthy rag in one of the piles, and tied it around the gash on her leg. It wasn't ideal, but it was the only way she could stop the bleeding. She staggered over toward the doorway. The door itself was half knocked in, hanging from one hinge. She walked over to it to get a look outside. Her shoes were best suited for Washbalt political functions at fancy hotels, not trudging through abandoned buildings. But the ground was strewn with broken glass and shards of metal - she needed something on her feet. Finally, she broke off the heels. It wasn't a great solution, but it worked after a fashion. At least she could get around without tearing her feet to shreds.

She peered around the edge of the doorway. The Washbalt skyline was looming above the decrepit buildings along the street. Until then she hadn't had any idea where she was. She could have easily been in Detroit or New Cairo or Shanghai. It took her a few seconds to get her bearings, but she managed to put together a good idea of exactly where she was. That motherfucker, she thought...he had me dumped in the East Ward slums. The East Ward was a notorious gang battlefield, so dangerous, even the Cogs had mostly deserted it, preferring to sleep in the streets in the marginally safer northern ghettoes. The Marines swept through once in a while on recruiting runs, but the police avoided it entirely.

She leaned back inside, taking one last look to see if there was anything useful in the building. Nope, she thought with a sigh...nothing but garbage. She turned to step outside when the door came flying in and broke completely from the hinge. She stumbled backwards, landing painfully on a pile of broken masonry.

Three men walked in and stood inside the door. Two held mid-sized knives, like machetes, but smaller. The third had a small, gunpowder pistol tucked in his belt. Training kicked in, experience, instinct. Her eyes focused on them like lasers, scanning, evaluating the respective threat levels. Her mind flashed back, the years peeling away to a different Alex, a young girl trying to survive in a brutal slum very much like this one…a 14 year old girl who had been pursued and victimized by animals like this.

But this was a different Alex Linden now. She'd been confused on Armstrong, conflicted about her feelings. But now, familiarity began to return. Her mind was focused, feral…combat reflexes ready. The gang members looked at her with hungry, greedy eyes…like hunters stalking cornered prey. But this was no helpless Core-dweller lost in the slums. Alex Linden was an ice cold killer who'd put more men and women in their graves than all three of her would-be attackers combined.

She crawled back slowly, whimpering. Use fear, she thought…increase their confidence, turn their own sadism against them. She forced out a tear, then another.

"Look what we got here, boys." One of the knife-wielders turned and looked back at his companions. His voice was thick with menace. "She's a damned pretty one." His eyes panned back to leer at Alex, lying on the ground, golden blond hair a riotous mess, her already short dress hiked up over her waist. "And the man said we could have our fun before we did the deed…didn't he now?"

The man? Alex was focusing on everything, watching every move, listening to every sound. That fucking piece of shit, she thought, rage coursing through her body…"the man" could only be Gavin Stark. He'd sent these gang-bangers here. To kill her? Or just to torture her? If he'd just wanted to be rid of her, she knew she'd have never seen it coming.

Get a grip, she thought…time for Stark later. The man who'd spoken was moving toward her, reaching down to grab her. But her eyes were on the one in the rear, the one with the gun. He was the bigger threat. She had to take him down first. She looked up at the closer one, tears streaming down her eyes. "No…please." The sound of fear in her voice was utterly convincing.

He smiled broadly, eyes glittering. "Don't you worry, girl. It ain't gonna hurt. Much." He leaned down, grabbing her exposed thigh.

She lay there, immobile, whimpering softly as he moved his hand up, grabbing for her panties. Then she lunged, planting her fist in his groin as she flew by, her body heading straight for the gun-armed assailant. She planted an open palm just above his sternum, a death blow taught to Alliance Intelligence's elite assassins. He was dead even as his body began to fall. Her hand whipped down, grabbing the gun from his waist as he crumpled and putting two shots in the head of the third man.

It was all over in just a few seconds. Two of the men lay dead on the ground; the third was doubled over, groaning on the garbage pile where Alex had lain just an instant before. She walked over toward him, leaning down and picking up the blade he'd dropped. She looked down at him holding the knife as he shook in fear. "I'm afraid you're quite mistaken, my good man." She glared at him with a predator's eyes. "It's going to hurt. Quite a lot."

Gavin Stark sat at his desk, a self-satisfied smile on his face as he watched the scene reach its graphic conclusion. He leaned over, pressing his com button. "Please send Agent G in." He loved the anonymity of his new elite team. They were part of the Shadow project, and if everything else worked as well as they had, his plans would be very successful indeed. He was the only one who had complete information; everyone else involved in the program had only partial data…and much of that was fake. He had a few vacancies in his new spy corps…he'd been using them hard, and some missions required a certain amount of… cleanup…afterward. But for the most part, things were going very well.

He winced slightly as he watched Alex extract her revenge on the hapless gang-banger. "Whatever I paid those boys, it wasn't enough," he whispered to himself with a laugh. "That's my Alex."

The door slid open. "You sent for me, sir?" Stark's man looked the part…tall, handsome, well-groomed.

"Yes." He was still watching on his monitor, though the last of Alex's attackers was finally dead. In the end, she'd made

him beg for it. "I want you to take a security detail and go
fetch Number Three. I think she's had enough." He paused
then added, "Be careful. Don't underestimate her. She is very
dangerous." He glanced up from his desk. "And go put on a
uniform. I'd just as soon she thinks I only sent regular security
to get her."

"Yes, sir." He turned and walked through the door without
another word.

Stark leaned back in his chair and spoke softly to himself.
"Well, my sweet little Alex, now we can have our talk. I trust
this little adventure will serve as a reminder about who you are
truly are...and where you came from. Where you could easily
end up again."

Chapter 20

Bridge – AS Midway
X2 System
Near X1 Warp Gate

Terrance Compton sat at the head of the conference table, looking at the screen, mesmerized by what he saw. So that's what the inside of a First Imperium ship looks like, he thought. It was similar to a human vessel in some ways, yet vastly different in others. It was odd to follow the video through the empty, silent corridors. They were small, far too tiny in places for men to pass. But they were built for the bots that serviced the vessel and repaired its damage. Bots that were now silent, mysteriously deactivated like the rest of the ship.

"It is clear that the enemy is vastly ahead of us in nano-technology, as they are in virtually all areas." Thomas Sparks stood alongside the table, continuing his report. "The operation of the vessel appears to be through a combination of dedicated automated systems and independent bots of various types. It is clear the ship was purpose built for robot operation, however I also hypothesize that the design was adapted from one originally intended to be crewed by organic beings. There are vestigial systems and design features that appear to strongly support this theory."

Compton fidgeted in his chair. "General Sparks, I think we all appreciate any insight on our enemy, and I have no doubt we could sit here for days and theorize about the First Imperium and its technology." He was speaking gently, trying not to sound scolding. He understood the scientist was fascinated at all the new data, but he also knew he had to find a way to defeat the enemy – and do it soon. Otherwise nothing else mattered. "May I suggest that we focus first on matters of tactical significance…things that may be useful in the short term."

Sparks nodded. "Of course, Admiral Compton." Sparks was a Marine research engineer, and his own curiosity generally ran to weapons and strategic systems. But he was overwhelmed now, and distracted, his mind running in a hundred directions. "While I am hopeful that further research on that vessel will lead to large leaps forward in many of our offensive and defensive systems, I am afraid we found little that is likely to be of immediate use." He panned across the table, his eyes settling on Compton. "Immediate being defined as the duration of this campaign."

Compton wasn't surprised. He really didn't expect to peel open that ship and find a superweapon sitting there with an instruction manual. He'd hoped they might find some sort of tactical weakness in the enemy vessel…something his people could use in battle. But even that, he realized, would take, at the very least, months of research to decipher…and probably years.

"I believe I can offer a reasonable explanation as to how this ship fell into our hands, at least. The First Imperium operates, as we already know, on a very hierarchal basis. It appears their warships work in a similar manner, with a single central AI running virtually every aspect of ship operations." He shifted his weight from one foot to the other. "It is logical if you imagine an operating system designed by a computer and not an organic being. Our own ships require multiple officers, for example, because even the most proficient captain can't manage all aspects of running a large vessel. In turn, we utilize multiple AIs on our vessels, even though we could build a single unit powerful enough to replace the others. Although this is the purest speculation, our early research and development likely replicated our existing pattern of apportioning work to multiple individuals. Thus, we went down a path of distributing the workload while the First Imperium, at least for many thousands of years, was directed by artificial intelligences that opted for centralization."

Sparks shifted again. His rapid trip from Sigma 4 on the Torch transport, followed by climbing into his armor and crawling around the enemy ship, had left him stiff and sore. He was exhausted too, but the mental stimulation of all the new data was temporarily overcoming his physical fatigue. "It appears that a First Imperium vessel is entirely dependent upon its core AI system. This would be enormously useful to us in battle, except the artificial intelligence unit is located in the most heavily shielded and defended part of the ship. It is virtually impossible to damage until the vessel itself has been blasted to pieces." He paused, then added, "Indeed, we may someday discover a method for disrupting or disabling these systems from long range. If we are able to achieve that, the advantage in the conflict would almost certainly shift dramatically in our favor." Another pause. "Of course, we are nowhere close to developing a method for accomplishing this."

Compton leaned back in his chair. "I appreciate the potential future implications of this information, but how does it explain what happened in this case? Why this particular ship simply stopped functioning?"

"I'm sorry, sir…I was getting to that." Sparks took a breath. "I believe that there was a malfunction in the main power conduit leading to the AI, a freak incident. Most likely there was a manufacturing flaw, and the kinetic energy from the torpedo hit caused a break. In essence, the plug got pulled on the ship's brain. Unfortunately, it is not something we can replicate. Just a lucky break." He paused, then added, "Clearly, the long term implications of our ability to study an intact First Imperium AI are enormous…though, again, it is unlikely to produce anything practical in the near term. At this point, I haven't even been able to determine how to open the case yet."

Compton let out a long breath. "Yes, general, I'd have to agree than capturing that AI is a potentially enormous development." Assuming we survive long enough for your people to figure it out, he thought, though he kept that part to himself. "Is there anything of more immediate usefulness? I can't believe we won't be facing a fight here soon, and any insights that can give us an edge would be most welcome."

"I'm afraid nothing of immediate tactical significance, sir."
He paused, then added, "There is one more thing of possible
interest, though I doubt its utility in terms of aiding us with
imminent combat. I'm afraid, also, it is based on the wildest of
suppositions." Sparks had clearly been unsure if he should even
bring it up.

"By all means, general, please continue." Compton straightened a little in his chair, his eyes brightening ever so slightly.
Sparks was a genius and Compton, for one, would listen to his
wildest guesses with rapt attention. "I can assure you that anything you wish to speculate on is of interest."

"Well, admiral..." Sparks was clearly still hesitant. He was
an engineer, trained to focus on facts...or at least theories based
on solid evidence. "...we found a certain type of bot on the
enemy ship, a type we have never seen before." He paused again.

Compton was staring at Sparks, listening intently. "Yes,
Tom? Say what you're thinking."

"I believe it is some type of authorization bot, sir. It is my...
ah...wild guess...that they act as keys to activate vital systems.
An extra layer of security, preventing implementation of various
processes unless one of these keys is present and deployed."

"Tom, I know this is all guesswork, but your gut feel on this
is better than anything else we have." Compton was interested
now. "Please elaborate. Just go through your thought process
for us."

"Yes, sir." Sparks took a deep breath. "First, they appear to
be constructed to connect with other equipment. We have previously speculated that the enemy utilized a form of universal
interface between systems. That theory is supported by our preliminary examination of the captured vessel. In fact, it appears
there are at least three types of interface, and these are evidently
based upon the security level of the system in question."

Sparks glanced at Compton, who nodded for him to continue. "Secondly, we have found connection interfaces on captured First Imperium equipment and debris that match these
bots." He paused and looked right at Compton. "Including on

Epsilon Eridani IV."

Compton's eyes widened. "Please continue, general."

"There are sections of the Epsilon Eridani complex that appeared to be fully intact, yet are completely non-functional. This now makes more sense to me. The complex has a large number of these interfaces in areas we projected where vital to the overall operation." He was nodding as he spoke. "If I am correct...and that is an enormous 'if'...we may very well be able to activate at least sections of the great machine on Carson's World. These bots may jumpstart our ability to produce antimatter in quantity more effectively than a thousand years of research could."

Sparks allowed his last comment to sink in. If Hofstader and the rest of the Pact's team could quickly adapt the production and storage technology of the ancient antimatter factory, Sparks and his team could quickly weaponize it. He had half-developed designs for antimatter weapons already, all of which had been halted by the inability of Earth science to produce and store usable quantities of the precious substance.

"We have never captured one of these bots before, though based on the amount of wreckage we have collected from battle sites we should clearly have found at least remains of them. It is my hypothesis that this is a security measure, that the central AI directs the key bots to self-destruct when a ship is near destruction. We must therefore extract them, as well as the AI itself, with extreme care in case there are alternate security precautions in place. We could easily trigger an undetected self-destruct routine if we aren't careful."

Compton had been quietly thoughtful, considering everything Sparks was saying. Capturing this ship alone was reason enough to have launched the campaign. A chance, even a long one, at weaponizing antimatter was just the sort of game changer he and Garret had hoped for when they planned the invasion.

Now they needed time...time the fleet was going to have to buy. Whatever it took. Sigma 4 and X1 were both "straight-aways"...systems with only two warp gates. When they were the only route between two warring parties, these types of systems were natural bottlenecks, providing ideal locations for defense. It was like the Line, only even more concentrated. We'll have all of mankind's might concentrated in one place, Compton thought...holding a new Line, while Sparks, Hofstader, and the rest of the white coats tried to turn this captured ship into a massive leap forward in technology.

"General, I believe that our first order of business is to arrange to tow the enemy vessel out of this system to a location farther to the rear." Compton sat very still, clearly deep in thought as he spoke. "I do not believe it would be wise to attempt to begin your research efforts in deep space, especially in this exposed location."

"I agree completely, sir." Sparks frowned. "I'm afraid that may take some time, admiral. The enemy hull material is extremely difficult to work with. It will take considerable effort to create a connection with a towing vessel, especially one that will endure significant acceleration."

"Well, general...that's your problem." Compton smiled. Mine is making sure nothing interferes with you while you're doing it." He tapped the com controller on his collar. "Commodore Harmon...send a drone back to X1." His task forces were spread out between Sigma 4 and X2. "The fleet will immediately advance and assemble here in X2."

Chapter 21

Red Rock Valley
8 Kilometers South of Enemy Base
Planet Sigma 4 II

Cain stood on the reddish outcropping, staring out over the jagged valley below. This was rough terrain, far from ideal for an attack. But his forces had pushed the enemy back relentlessly, and the retreating bots had come this way. He didn't know what tricks the First Imperium forces had in store, what tactics and stratagems they had gleaned from their battles with humanity. He didn't care. His battle plan focused on one thing...one thing only. Getting the enemy to commit their last reserves first.

"I know you've got Reapers here, you bastards." Cain's voice was calm, but it dripped with venom. "You aren't going to fool me."

Sigma 4 II was a pleasant world, one men would certainly have colonized...if the First Imperium hadn't gotten there first. It was Earthlike, but minus the pollution and slums. There were mountains and streams and golden valleys covered with wild-flowers. The enemy had built a base on the planet...and there were a few small ruins that may have once been civilian towns. Still, it was clear this was a world on their frontier, lightly developed and never heavily populated. He wondered if their core worlds, wherever they were, had been raped and ravaged and scarred by war like Earth. Whether they were covered with festering slums where the masses had lived in misery, ground under the boots of those in power.

His forces had dubbed the area Red Rock Valley. He smiled

briefly, amused at the need warriors seemed to have to name everywhere they fought. Cain, for one, didn't really care. One battle was much like another to him. Still, he thought, it was a good name.

The army had advanced nonstop since the breakout 10 klicks back. They'd fought every step of the way, not letting up…not for a second. The enemy had been badly disordered by the plasma bombardment, and Cain had no intention of letting them regroup. The relentless pursuit had come at a cost, however, and casualties were high. And rising.

His commanders were begging him to release the Obliterators, but he'd coolly refused every one of them. Even Isaac Merrick had joined in after the last firefight had brought a number of units above the 50% casualty mark. Everyone but Farooq. The Janissary had been the only major force commander to remain silent. His unit was as badly hurt as any other – worse than most - but still he grimly advanced without so much as a whisper about reinforcements.

Cain hurt for his Marines and their comrades, fighting and dying up on the line. But he knew they would do what he needed them to do. Whatever the cost. He would spend their lives… he knew that, and so did they…but he wouldn't waste them. If Erik Cain said he needed to keep the Obliterators in reserve, his Marines would turn grimly back to the fight and press on. They didn't love him, not for the most part, but they trusted him… and they would follow him anywhere.

He stood dead still and sighed. Things were going to get worse for those men and women fighting the enemy. Cain hadn't told anyone what he was planning, but once it was done he wouldn't be surprised if his Marines hanged him from the nearest tree. But this battle was more important than the lives of any of the warriors now fighting…and that included Cain. Every one of them was expendable as long as they got what they came for. They needed that base, and they had to take it intact.

He could see movement through the low areas. It was Farooq's Janissaries surging forward, with Cooper Brown's

Marines on their right. Cain didn't like maneuvering through the narrow valley…it reeked of a trap. But he had snipers and heavy weapons teams posted all along the heights and scouts positioned well to the front. He might lose here…he might remain on this alien planet with his Marines, dead and unburied for eternity. But he was sure of one thing…the enemy wasn't going to mousetrap him. If the First Imperium was going to beat him, they'd have to do it in a straight up fight.

"General Cain…" Isaac Merrick's voice was strained, out of breath. "The forward skirmishers are out two klicks. The enemy is still pulling back." The old army general was having trouble getting around in his new Marine armor. Cain couldn't help but smile. He remembered what he felt like back in training. Powered armor wasn't something you put on one day and just jumped into action. Merrick had gotten some practice time in, but nothing like real training. There was no choice, though… fighting First Imperium forces without armor was nothing short of suicide. The only other option was leaving him behind, and Merrick would have none of that.

Merrick was down in the valley, just behind Brown's regiment. Other than the difficulties adapting to his armor, he'd made an extraordinary chief of staff. Erik felt vindicated in his decision…and glad to have the old soldier on his team.

Cain had been worried about what the enemy had emplaced in that mountain fortress. He wondered why his forces hadn't taken any fire from there earlier…certainly they had ordnance that could have reached his forces even back at the LZ. He'd held back his nukes in the hopes of taking the base intact. That was why they were here, after all…to learn something they could use to beat the enemy. Really beat them…and end the war.

He looked down at the valley for a few more seconds. No one was going to like his next order. His troops were almost all veterans, but even experienced troops were only human. The enemy had been pulling back, offering minimal resistance. His forces had pursued, but with less aggressiveness than he wanted. He understood…they were exhausted and they'd suffered heavy losses. But that was all irrelevant. Cain needed the enemy to commit their last reserves, and a half-assed pursuit wasn't going to make it happen. He turned his head slowly, looking out over the field. "General Merrick...all forward units are to attack at once."

"Fucking Christ!" Carlson dove down behind a cluster of small rocks just before the area behind him erupted with enemy rounds tearing great gouges into the ground. He was running the battalion now...Major Tambor was dead...but it wasn't much bigger than a company now anyway.

Carlson had served under General Cain on the Lysandra Plateau, but he was a sergeant then, far down the chain of command. Things had been bad on that plateau, but they were defending there, grimly holding their ground until they were relieved. Now it felt like Cain was just trying to destroy his army, smashing it to pieces with one bloody assault after another.

"Sergeant Randall, get those SAWs forward and deployed. You've got a small gully there...it should give you some cover while you advance." Carlson was staring at his display, trying to figure out how to piece together the fragments of his shattered battalion. "Now! I want fire from that position in three minutes."

"Yes, sir. On the way."

Carlson had never heard of a formation so battered mounting an attack. He knew what he would do to consolidate his tattered forces for a defense. He'd find some good ground and get his heavy weapons deployed in the best fire positions with half his troopers in reserve, ready to plug any gaps. But his orders were clear and specific – all-out attack.

He was pinned where he was...the enemy fire was constant. He'd be hit the second he tried to advance. He turned his head, reminding himself to stay low. There was a small hill about 100 meters northwest. It would give him good cover...if he could get there.

Carlson took a deep breath and crawled out from behind the rock. He was on his belly, staying as low as he could. There was a small lip in the ground giving him partial cover. The enemy fire was thick, and it wasn't more than 10 or 15 centimeters over him. It takes a long time to crawl 100 meters, even in powered armor. Especially when the slightest bounce upward will get you killed.

He inched along, trying to stay focused. Stay slow, he thought...one meter at a time. "Sergeant Randall, are you in position yet?" He had his display off; he needed a clear view through his visor now.

"No, captain." Randall's voice was tentative. He knew he was going to get blasted.

"What the fuck, Randall? Get your hands out of your pants and get that outfit moving." Carlson was mad. He didn't like the orders any more than anyone. But if they were going to attack, then by God, they were going to attack. "I want you there in one minute, or I swear to God I will come over there and shoot your sorry ass myself." He paused, taking another lurch forward. "Am I clear?"

"Yes, captain." Randall was a veteran Marine, but it was clear from his voice he was near the breaking point. "We'll be there in 30 seconds...and firing in two minutes."

"You better be." Carlson cut the line. He didn't like beating up on a Marine like Randall, but he needed everything his people had. If they let up their intensity, even for a few seconds, that could be the difference. It could get them all killed.

He was losing the small rise that was giving him cover...he was going to have to dash the last few meters in the open. He took a breath, bending his legs, ready to spring forward. He crouched low - if he jumped up, he would sail through the air, an easy target. He sprung, holding his body straight and pushing off with his legs. His body lurched 4 or 5 meters, landing hard behind the hill. He rolled, taking the force of the landing the way he'd been trained, and coming up prone. The hill was good cover, about 4 meters high.

He leaned against the hillside, pulling his tactical display back up. Randall's team was in position. It didn't look like they were firing yet, but he guessed they would be any minute. He almost commed Randall again, but he stopped himself. He has his orders, Carlson thought.

He moved the display across the front, trying to get a read on the status of the battalion. He had units intermixed all along the front. His people really needed a pause to rally, but they weren't going to get that. He called up his AI and started dictating organizational reassignments, creating ad hoc units out of wrecked and scattered formations. He could only do so much on the fly, but anything helped.

Carlson had resisted a promotion to commissioned rank for his last three years in the Corps, preferring to remain closer to his Marines. When he and Cooper Brown rejoined the colors, he felt such preferences would be selfish and misplaced during the current crisis. If the Corps needed him as an officer then that was how he'd serve. But he missed the simplicity of a sergeant's billing. He was getting a taste of the types of decisions Brown and Cain had to make, and he didn't like it. In his heart, he was one of the boys, and he felt aloof directing an entire battalion. He couldn't imagine issuing the kinds of orders Erik Cain did. He wasn't sure he had it in him, even if the only alternative was defeat.

He checked his display. Randall's teams were firing, covering a 500 meter section of the front line. Their targets were in cover, so they weren't inflicting a lot of casualties, but they were keeping the enemy pinned, and that's what Carlson wanted. He'd managed to assemble an ersatz company, put together from every squad or platoon he could scrape up. His orders were to attack. He didn't agree with them, but he was damned sure going to obey them.

He dashed around the hill, staying on the backside of the slope, working his way around toward the front line. By the time he emerged in the rear of his assembling attack force, the enemy fire had diminished considerably. Randall's people were earning their pay.

"Lieutenant Banks, report." Banks was another longtime non-com turned into an officer to fill the depleted ranks after Sandoval. Carlson hadn't had much time to get to know her, but he was impressed with what little he'd seen.

"Sir…the reorganized units are in place, and the revised OB has been downloaded into the AIs." Her voice was shrill, high-pitched, almost like a little girl's…not at all what one expected from a ten year veteran of the Corps, a woman who'd fought in multiple campaigns and been wounded twice. Whatever she sounded like, Nora Banks was a hardcore Marine, Carlson was sure of that. "Everything is ready."

"Very good, lieutenant." They were talking on the com, but Carlson was only 50 meters or so behind her position. "I'm almost there. You head out and take command on the left. I'll take over here."

There was a brief silence. Carlson knew what was coming, and he spoke up first. "Don't waste your time arguing, lieutenant. I'm leading the assault personally."

"Yes, sir." There was resignation in her voice, but it was obvious she disagreed. He wasn't sure she was wrong either. The battalion was already running low on officers, and this attack wasn't likely to improve that situation. A junior lieutenant was going to have a hard time holding things together if Carlson bought it. But he'd already decided. He was going.

He could see Banks turn and head to the left as he came up the hillside. It would take her a few minutes to get in position. "Lieutenant…we attack in ten minutes."

"Commander Farooq, we are pinned down in the stream bed." Aashif Selim knelt behind the cracked mud wall of the dry river bank. He was Corbaci, commander of one of Farooq's Orta's. He'd led 800 veteran Janissaries down to the surface of Sigma 4 II, but a mere 180 of them remained now, spread out over a kilometer of front, mostly along the twisting path of this seasonal stream.

The area all around the bed was under heavy fire. Selim wasn't sure where it was coming from, but it was obvious the shattered enemy forces his Orta had been pursuing had been reinforced.

"Have you encountered new enemy units?" Farooq's question was sharp, urgent.

"Unknown, commander." Selim knew the answer would be unsatisfactory, but it was the only one he had. Before Farooq could respond, he added, "The enemy is dug in behind a series of rocky hills. I have been unable to get a scanner fix. I've…"

"Unsatisfactory, Corbaci. We must know what you are facing."

Selim took a deep breath. Farooq was one of the most respected officers in the Janissary Corps, and Selim knew he did not suffer fools…or tolerate failure. "I attempted to launch drones, however they were shot down almost immediately. I sent out three scouting parties, but they were wiped out before they could report. We are under extremely heavy fire…if I move my forces from this position, it is my belief they will be exterminated within minutes." He paused then added, "With no offsetting gain."

Farooq opened his mouth then closed it again. Selim was a good officer, and brave. If he was able to more effectively scout the enemy position, Farooq knew he would. "Speculate, Corbaci Selim. What types of ordnance are you facing?"

"Mostly heavy hyper-velocity rounds, sir." He hesitated for a few seconds. "It feels like Reaper fire, commander. Though I am unable to confirm the existence of any enemy heavy units."

Reapers, Farooq thought…perhaps the enemy is finally committing their reserves. Just as Erik Cain expected. "I need confirmation, Selim. However you get it, I need to know if those are Reapers firing at you."

"Yes, sir. I will send out another scouting party." Selim's voice was grim. He knew he'd be sending those men to certain death. But it was the only way to try and confirm what he was facing. "I will report…"

"Attention all forward units." It was Cooper Brown on the main com line. "We are under attack by enemy Reapers, coordinates 202 by 086. Enemy force in unknown strength."

"Prepare to receive a Reaper assault, Selim!" Farooq's warning was too late. Selim's display was ablaze with red symbols. Enemy Reapers advancing on his position.

"Reports coming in from across the line, general." Merrick was standing right next to Cain, but they were both buttoned up in their armor, so they were speaking through the com. "Reapers attacking in force." He turned to face Cain, though it was an unnecessary gesture in armor. "It looks like they've committed their reserve. And you were right...they had a force of Reapers. It looks like a big one too."

Cain was silent for a few seconds, staring at the tactical display on the large HQ 'pad. "Hector, get me Colonel Sawyer."

"You are now connected to Colonel Sawyer, general."

"Dave, are your people ready to go?" Cain's tone was sharp, anxious. He'd been waiting for this.

"Yes, sir." Sawyer had been a career sergeant and a member of Cain's special action teams on Carson's World. He'd spent the Battle of Sandoval as Erik's senior aide, and now Cain had entrusted a special assignment to him, along with an elite team to carry it out. "We're locked and loaded. Just waiting for your word."

"Well, you've got it, Dave." There was a touch of emotion in Cain's otherwise cold voice. He was fond of Sawyer, and he'd hate to see anything happen to the grizzled old leatherneck... though that wasn't going to stop him from sending his old aide into the inferno. "Good luck, my friend. I'm really counting on you." Cain always hated himself for adding self-serving remarks like that. But that didn't stop him from doing it...because they worked.

"You can count on me, sir." Cain could hear it in Sawyer's voice. It even worked on the old veterans. Sometimes it worked better on them.

"Hector, get me McDaniels." It was time for the Obliterators.

"General McDaniels is on the line, sir." Hector's tone was matter-of-fact and respectful. Cain had hated his AI's surliness and sarcasm for years, but now he wasn't sure he didn't miss it. At least a little.

"Erin...it's time." Cain spoke slowly, deliberately. "Are your people ready?"

"Yes, sir." McDaniels sounded confident, steady. She'd been

a little shaky when Holm and Cain handed her a box with two small platinum stars in it, but she'd had time to adjust since then. She'd been training her people nonstop on Sandoval...getting the new recruits up to speed in the heavy Obliterator suits and working her veterans to a razor's edge. "We're ready."

Cain took a breath. He was about to take a risk, a big one... one that could cost him his entire army. But he knew what he had to do. "Execute Plan Black, General McDaniels." His voice was ice. "Immediately."

Chapter 22

Bridge – AS Indianapolis
System X2
Midway Between X3 and X4 Warp Gates

"Admiral, energy spike at X3 warp gate." Carp's voice was brittle, tense. Nothing would be coming back through that gate for another 12 hours...unless there was trouble. And trouble could only mean only one thing. First Imperium forces approaching.

Jacobs had sent task forces through both the X3 and X4 warp gates to scout those systems. Admiral Compton was moving the entire fleet into X2, and Jacobs wanted to know just what was in the adjacent systems before that much Pact strength was committed.

He was in the small office located just off the bridge, sitting back in his chair, eyes closed, grabbing a few minutes' rest. But he snapped awake when he got Carp's message, and he jumped up and bounded through the small hatch and onto the bridge. "Report, commander."

"No details yet, sir...wait..." Carp turned back toward his workstation, scanning the data streaming in. "It's a drone, sir. It's broadcasting Priority Level Gold." Gold was the highest importance assigned to Alliance military communications. It indicated a full-fledged emergency. "Decoding the message now, sir."

Jacobs walked across the bridge and sat in the command chair, waiting silently for Carp to relay the drone's contents. But he knew what the message would be...what else could it say?

An off-schedule Gold message had to mean an enemy attack was imminent. "Retransmit to Admiral Compton immediately, Lieutenant Hooper."

"Yes, sir." She moved her hands quickly over her touch-screens. "Drone's message retransmitted to Midway, sir." She paused, then added, "The flagship is 1.75 light hours from our position, admiral." Jacobs hadn't asked, but it was part of Hooper's idea of doing the job completely. It was certainly relevant. Jacobs couldn't expect any orders or guidance from Admiral Compton for almost 4 hours. Until then he was on his own.

"I have the decoded message, admiral." Carp was reading directly from his display. "From Captain Mondragon to any Pact command staff." He spoke clearly and deliberately. "I am reporting enemy forces approaching from deeper in the X3 system. As we have not yet been able to map the deep system or discover any egress warp gates, I cannot specify the point of origin. It is clearly an as yet unknown warp gate."

Jacobs sat silently, anxious for details on enemy strengths. You're not going to get that, he thought, not now…Mondragon would have sent this drone as soon as he picked up enemy activity. He wouldn't have had detailed data yet…the information Jacobs really wanted – needed – might not arrive for hours.

"Enemy task force is too far out for detailed analysis, however preliminary scans indicate a substantial concentration… significantly larger than any force yet encountered on this campaign." Carp paused, clearing his throat. "I have dispatched a line of 10 vessels to approach the enemy formation and conduct detailed scans."

Jacobs looked down at the floor and sighed. Mondragon did the right thing, what he had to do. But Jacobs knew they'd be lucky if any of those ships made it back. It wasn't a death sentence for those ten crews, not exactly, but it was something close.

"Enemy force is approaching at 0.06c, on a projected trajectory for the X2 warp gate." Carp hesitated again. There had been no reason not to assume the enemy was coming toward them, but now they had confirmation. "I will send any further information as soon as it is available. Mondragon out."

"Lieutenant Hooper, send a drone into X4. I want a report from Captain Cleret now." With two egress warp gates in X2, Mondragon had been forced to send Cleret through one of them. He was completely comfortable with Mondragon acting independently, but he didn't trust Cleret as far as he could kick the insufferable Europan boor. But he only had the resources he had. With the concentration of Europan ships in his fleet, Jacobs couldn't just relieve Cleret without risking significant dissension. Repeatedly picking Mondragon over Cleret had caused enough trouble, but with two simultaneous missions, he was backed into a corner.

"Yes, admiral." Hooper turned her attention to her controls, programming the drone and setting it for launch. "Drone ready, sir. Beginning launch sequence now."

The drone was a precaution. Jacobs didn't trust Cleret, but the fool would certainly send back word if he ran into an enemy force. Still, he thought, no harm in being careful.

He was definitely worried about Mondragon and his people, though. With an enemy force moving at 6% of lightspeed, he wasn't sure if any of the scouts would be able to escape back into X2. Jacobs didn't know the current velocities of Mondragon's ships, but he assumed they were all heading insystem, which only made their escape more problematic. And he knew Mondragon wasn't going to turn and run until he had all the intel he needed on the enemy force.

"Commander Carp, bring the fleet to status yellow." A sustained alert would wear down the crews, but Jacobs decided it was more important to maintain increased readiness. His people were close to the warp gate, and he had sketchy data on what was coming.

"Yes, sir."

Jacobs looked down at his display and reviewed Compton's updated strength report. The admiral had 5 full battlegroups in X2 now, moving insystem to take position to defend the captured enemy vessel. He knew there was a lot more strength on the way, some of it scheduled to arrive soon, but he didn't have the data to even guess whether the rest of Compton's people or the enemy would arrive first.

He switched over the display to his own dispositions. He only had 11 cruisers and 12 fast attack ships, plus his hastily-converted makeshift carriers. The rest of his forces were in X3 and X4. "Commander Carp, plot a fleet course toward the X3 warp gate." His small force didn't have much of a chance against a large enemy fleet, but he figured they might have to buy time for Compton's forces to assemble. If that was what they had to do, he thought, then so be it.

"Yes, admiral." Carp's voice was tentative. He knew what Jacobs was thinking.

"And prepare all remaining laser buoys for launch." He turned toward Hooper. "Lieutenant, prepare a maximum efficiency deployment plan to cover the warp gate." The laser buoys were the one thing Jacobs had that packed a big punch. The bomb-pumped x-ray lasers could damage even heavy First Imperium vessels.

"Yes, sir."

Jacobs leaned back and looked straight ahead thinking quietly to himself...at least I'm going to prepare a warm welcome for these SOBs.

Terrance Compton read the incoming reports with growing consternation. The enemy force approaching X2 was a full-fledged battle fleet. Mondragon's people had confirmed its strength at 2 Leviathans and 40 Gargoyles, preceded by a screen of 24 Gremlins. Based on the enemy forces encountered on the campaign so far, Compton had to assume they were all antimatter armed.

That intel hadn't been cheap. Mondragon's task force had been unable to change vectors back to the warp gate and escape to X2. The enemy fleet's velocity was simply too high. Half his ships had apparently been destroyed, and the rest had scattered into the depths of the system.

The enemy was strong, but Compton had a considerable concentration of power himself. There were now 11 battlegroups in X2, each built around one of the newest and most powerful battleships possessed by the Powers. He had another four making their way through the X1 system, with ETAs ranging from 11 hours to 2 ½ days. He'd left his most damaged units in Sigma 4, positioned around the planet to support Cain's ground forces.

If he'd had no consideration beyond defeating the enemy fleet he would have stayed where he was, close to the X1 warp gate and his approaching reinforcements. But he had to protect the captured enemy ship. Sparks' people were working around the clock, trying to attach a towing cradle to the mysterious dark matter infused hull, but progress had been slow. It was going to take days, possibly weeks to get that vessel out of the system. And that meant Compton had to fight this enemy fleet...fight it and defeat it.

Compton was usually extremely decisive, but now he sat quietly considering his options, not sure which was best. If he moved deeper into the system and met the enemy near their entry warp gate, he could coordinate with Jacob's forces and Scouting Fleet's laser buoys. But that would rush the battle, making the engagement occur sooner. His own approaching units, not to mention Garret and the rest of the fleet, would have that much less time to approach.

On the other hand, if he remained where he was, the captured ship would be in the battle zone, at considerable risk of being destroyed. He'd have to stop Sparks' work on the vessel until the fighting was over. That was a risk he couldn't take. The enemy vessel was too important.

Whatever choice he made, with the enemy moving at high velocity, they would pass quickly through his own fleet...and then they would be between him and the captured ship. They could continue through the X1 warp gate all the way to Sigma 4, with Compton chasing behind, trying to catch up. Garret might arrive in time to face them, but Compton had no way of knowing where or when.

He pulled up a map of the system on his display. The warp gate was a white star in one corner, with the string of laser buoys positioned slightly insystem. He touched the display behind the lasers and just insystem from Jacobs' ships. "Designate intercept zone A, Joker." He was speaking softly, instructing his AI to mark the display accordingly.

"Done, Admiral Compton."

A line of orange light appeared where Compton had pointed. He was going to hit them there with Duke's attack ships and half of Greta's squadrons. He knew a synchronized attack of bombers and suicide boats would be tough to coordinate, but he had tremendous confidence in his two commanders. He believed they could pull it off.

He drew a second line behind the first. "Designate as fleet deployment area." That was where his battleline would make its stand.

Another line appeared at the specified location. "Done, admiral."

He took a breath and looked down at the display. He was going to send orders to the approaching forces in X1 to consolidate and transit into X2 as a cohesive force. With any luck, they'd hit whatever enemy forces were left after the main fleets passed each other...hopefully before the captured ship was exposed to attack.

He sat silently, mentally troubleshooting his plan. There were more holes in it than he cared to consider, but he couldn't come up with anything he thought was a better option. He turned toward Carp. "Commander, prepare to transmit a fleet battle order."

Chapter 23

"Dead Man's Ridge"
12 Kilometers South of Enemy Base
Planet Sigma 4 II

"Where the hell are those Obliterators?" Jake Carlson was talking to himself, his comlink mic switched off. His people had gotten the retreat order twenty minutes before, but by then they were already falling back. The enemy had launched a Reaper attack across the line, throwing their heavy units against the exhausted and depleted Marines and Janissaries. The lines didn't break – at least not yet – but that was only because they were all veteran units. They did retreat, giving up the ground they had fought so hard to occupy only a few hours before.

Carlson's carefully reorganized battalion was a shattered mess again, his survivors hopelessly intermixed. They'd lost all unit integrity, and he now commanded a mob fighting in scattered groups and as individuals. He was trying to form at least an ersatz reserve unit, but mostly he was just shouting encouragement, trying to keep his men and women in the line past the point of human endurance.

"Jake, what's your status?" It was Brown and, from the tone of his voice, things weren't any better on his end.

"Status? Fucked, that's my status." Carlson was a stone cold veteran, but he was near the end of his rope. Two-thirds of his Marines were down. They weren't all dead, but the wounded had pretty bleak prospects for recovery with his units in headlong retreat. Marines didn't abandon their wounded, no matter what. He was frantically trying to figure a way to get to his injured people, but he had no idea how he was going to manage it. A few makeshift squads had fought their way back to retrieve wounded comrades, but most of the Marines who were down were trapped behind the sudden enemy advance. He'd been planning to advance and grab the wounded when the Obliterators counterattacked, but the heavy units still hadn't come. Carlson kept looking back and checking his scanner, but there was still nothing. McDaniel's people were nowhere to be found.

"You have to hang on, Jake. We all have to."

Brown sounded better than he had any right to, Carlson thought...I guess this clusterfuck has made him forget his other demons for a while. Was fear easier to handle than guilt? Maybe, he thought. "Where are the Obliterators?" Carlson couldn't figure what was going on. He knew it would be a tough fight, but he'd never thought Erik Cain would let this happen.

"I don't know, Jake. I checked with HQ, and all they told me was assistance is on the way."

"What the hell does that mean?" Carlson was being insubordinate; he knew that. But after being trapped in the shelters on Adelaide with Brown for a couple years, the two had developed a close bond. Besides, Jake didn't give a shit for military propriety anymore. At least not right now.

"I don't know, Jake." Brown's tone was mildly scolding. He needed Carlson...he couldn't have the veteran captain losing it on him now. "I guess neither one of us is commanding this army."

"There isn't going to be an army in another couple hours."

"Jake, just do the best you can." Brown understood Carlson's anger, but it wasn't helping anything. "It's all any of us can..." Brown paused, then said, "Hold on, Jake."

He was gone half a minute, maybe 45 seconds. "Jake, hang on, you've got support on the way."

"Finally." There was a hint of relief in Carlson's voice. "We need those Obliterators now."

"You're not getting McDaniels' people, Jake. The Obliterators are committed elsewhere."

"Elsewhere? What the hell is going on?" Carlson was confused, and anger flared again in his voice.

"Colonel Sawyer is bringing up HVM teams. You're getting a dozen assigned to you. I need you to use them well...because they're all you're getting for a while."

Carlson stood where he was, stunned, silent. Hyper-velocity missiles were effective against Reapers, but a dozen launchers was no substitute for the Obliterators he'd been expecting. He wanted to argue, to complain, but he knew better. It wouldn't do any good, and he'd been a Marine long enough to understand his duty. No matter how much it sucked.

"Let's go people...speed is essential here." McDaniels was moving quickly toward the enemy base, careful to move side to side so she didn't take a huge leap into the air. She'd been in the rear, organizing the overall operation, but she intended to be in the front lines when they attacked. The entire army was essentially bait, drawing off the enemy Reapers and giving her this opportunity. There was no way to know how many of 1st Army's combatants were dying because her Obliterators were here attacking the enemy base instead of facing the Reapers assaulting their lines. She couldn't do anything about that, but she was going to make sure her people made it pay...that those on the battle lines were at least not dying in vain.

The energy readings from the base were off the charts. Cain and Hofstader had no idea what their scanners were detecting but, whatever it was, it was something they'd never seen before. They couldn't get any real details...the shell of the fort blocked most scanning activity. Maybe it was what they'd come for... some technology they could use to face the enemy on closer to equal terms.

Everything about the enemy base was conjecture, but Cain and Hofstader had chosen this spot, so that was where her people went in. She had 3,000 Obliterators massed on a front barely 3 kilometers wide...her people ripped right through the First Imperium defenders, and now they were almost to the armored bastion itself.

The enemy base was a massive construct, built into the side

of a mountainous ridge. Cain had asked Hofstader for his best guess on where to enter, and the German scientist had given it to him. It was wild conjecture, but it was all they had. They had no idea how big the facility was, or how far underground it stretched.

McDaniels' people had bombarded the area heavily with hyper-velocity missiles and plasma bombardment modules. She'd done everything she could to knock out the weapon emplacements that could fire on her units. Now it was time to storm the wall and plant the heavy charges. If they were lucky, the plasma mines would breach the armor. In case they didn't, her teams had nuclear charges as well. The atomic weapons would be harder on the inside and pose a greater risk of causing damage Cain wanted to avoid. But they were getting into that base one way or another.

"Assault team A, advance." She'd barely finished issuing the order when 400 of her most experienced troopers moved forward. They swept toward the wall, gradually fanning out, forming two lines perpendicular to the fort, covering the flanks of the breaching team. The area in front of the fortress walls was a relatively flat plain, though it had been torn up by bombardments during the initial fighting. There was the detritus of battle everywhere, mostly shattered First Imperium bots, but also her own dead, lying in the twisted wreckage of their heavy suits.

There was sporadic fire on each side, a few surviving enemy bots continuing to engage her advancing troopers. Her people returned the fire, hosing down the flanks with heavy autoguns, quickly silencing any pockets of enemy strength as soon as they exposed themselves. A few of her people went down, but they had overwhelming local superiority, at least for the time being. They'd hit the enemy forces hard and fast here, but she knew the gains wouldn't last. Enemy reinforcements would already be heading toward the area…and those counterattacking forces would probably be Reapers. She had over 2,000 of her people in reserve, ready to march out and block any enemy advance to the area, but she wanted to get Colonel Storm and his team inside the base before she had to worry about fresh enemy attacks.

Then it would be Storm's problem to take the facility…and hers to defend the breach against the enemy's attempts to seal it off.

"Breaching team forward now!" She shouted into the com, speaking slowly, clearly. Sixty Marines in their hulking Obliterator suits ran forward in small groups. To any but a trained eye they would have looked bizarre, waddling ahead in their massive suits, crouched low. There were six 4-man teams, each carrying a large plasma charge and escorted by another 6 Marines, weapons at the ready.

They closed the distance to the wall in less than two minutes. There was no fire from the fortress itself…the bombardment had taken out the gun emplacements along this sector. A few enemy cluster bombs came in, fired from mobile launchers off to the flank. Most of them went wide, but one spread came down around one of the breaching teams, taking out five Marines and destroying the charge they were carrying.

The rest of McDaniel's people made it to the wall without further losses. They knew what they were there to do, and they sprang into action immediately, setting the massive plasma charges and priming them for detonation. In a minute, perhaps 90 seconds, everything was ready.

"Charges in place, General McDaniels." Major Travers was the commander of the breaching group. "We are withdrawing now."

"Well done, major." McDaniels was standing upright, watching the action on her monitors. "Now get the hell out of there. I'm blowing these things in one minute."

"Yes, sir."

McDaniels watched the group withdraw. She was proud of her people, even more than normally. She had some of the pick of the Corps in her Obliterator brigade, and they had put everything they had into mastering the powerful new suits. Now she watched Traver's group move back in perfect order, pausing only to pick up their wounded.

She waited, watching the retreating Marines struggling to move quickly while carrying several wounded comrades. The Obliterator suits were massive and enormously heavy. It was extremely difficult to carry one…even for other Obliterators.

She glanced at the chronometer. It had been 55 seconds, but the breaching teams were still too close. She knew she couldn't wait long…she had to get Colonel Storm's people inside before enemy reserves arrived. But she stood still and watched the seconds click off. One minute fifteen…one minute thirty. She took a deep breath and pressed the button.

There was a flash of blinding white light along the fortress wall as the charges released their compressed gasses and super-heated them into plasmas. No physical substance could withstand the heat of those charges…by every law and theory of human science, when the plasmas cooled, they should leave a massive breach in the wall.

"I've got two more teams moving over there to back you up." Carlson's voice was ragged, hoarse. Things were hot on the line…very hot. The enemy was pushing hard, and the Reapers were driving through 1st Army's lines in several places. Carlson's section of front wasn't one of those, not yet…but it was damned close. "Still, it's gonna take at least ten minutes to get them set. Until then, it's all you guys."

The HVM teams were the only reason Carlson and his people were still there. The hyper-velocity missiles were really just projectiles that broke into a dozen pieces near the target, each delivering a massive blast of kinetic energy to anything it impacted. An HVM shot could take down a Reaper, but only with a direct hit.

"All units, focus your fire on the standard bots supporting the Reapers. Let the HVMs handle the bigs." Carlson was trying to think of orders to give his troopers every couple minutes…just to give him a reason to talk to them. He knew his lines were shaky. They weren't even lines anymore, just a bunch of shattered remnants clustering together. He doubted he had a squad with even half its strength still in one place.

He zigzagged forward, trying to keep the rising elevation between him and the Reapers he could see moving forward. There were three more HVM teams coming up, and he was going to place them personally. Every shot counted if they were going to stop the Reapers. Every shot.

"Captain!" Carlson's eyes focused on his visor projection, his AI automatically displaying the name and location of the Marine on the com. Sergeant Packer...up on the extreme left of the forward firing line. "They're pulling back! They're breaking off."

"Get a grip, Packer." Carlson snapped his response. "Give me a real report. Now!"

"Sorry, sir." The veteran sergeant sounded exhausted, and distracted. "Sir, the enemy was attacking us aggressively until just a minute ago. They abruptly stopped, and now they are retiring." There was a short pause. "It's a miracle, sir. I can't explain it. They had us. There was no way we were gonna hold out."

Carlson was just as surprised as Packer. Then the rest of the reports started coming in. All across the line...the enemy was abandoning its attack and pulling back. Pulling back, Carlson thought...what the hell is going on?

He called up Brown on his com. "Colonel, I have to report..."

Brown didn't let him finish. "You have to report the enemy ceasing its advance and commencing a withdrawal." There was confusion in Brown's voice as well. "I can't explain it, Jake, but it's happening all across the line." He took a quick breath. "And not just our front...the same thing's happening in front of Farooq's people. Everywhere, from what I'm hearing."

Nearly a kilometer away from each other they had the same thought...Erik Cain...what the hell did he pull off now?

"Hang on, Jake. I've got incoming orders."

"Yes, sir." Carlson's stomach tensed, and the relief he'd been feeling drained away. He wasn't sure why...he just had a bad feeling.

Brown was only gone a few seconds. "Jake, I'm back." There was a pause, a long one. "I've got orders for you..."

Carlson listened quietly, but he knew what was coming. He could tell from Brown's voice. His stomach clenched the rest of the way, and he could feel the sweat building up around his neck. He could hear the words before Brown even uttered them.

"Pursue the enemy. Attack."

Chapter 24

Alliance Intelligence HQ
Washbalt Metroplex
US Region, Western Alliance, Earth

Alex sat quietly at the conference table, seething with anger but hiding it well. She was alone, but she knew that meant virtually nothing. A hundred people could be monitoring her, and she'd never know it. Alliance Intelligence could spy on virtually anyone anywhere...but deep in their own building there almost nothing they couldn't be monitoring.

She was wearing a pair of silk pants and a tunic...hers, though she still hadn't been back to her apartment yet. She'd been a guest of Alliance Intelligence since Stark's men had pulled her out of the Washbalt slums. At least, she thought, they put me in one of the VIP housing units. They could just as easily have thrown her into Sub-Sector C, she supposed. The maximum security detention and interrogation unit of Alliance Intelligence was one of the most feared places on Earth. It wasn't someplace she wanted to end up...death was a far better option if it came to that.

She ran her fingers over the soft material of her tunic. The outfit had cost more than a Cog family earned in a year. It was one of several appropriate articles of clothing she'd found waiting in her new quarters. It was hardly surprising that Stark's people had been in her flat ransacking her closets, but she found it unnerving nevertheless. It had been many years since Alex Linden was on receiving end of that kind of treatment. Normally, she was the one violating someone's privacy, and she didn't like being back on the other side. Not one bit.

I suppose that's the point, she thought, tamping down on her rage as she did...this is all about showing me my alternatives. Stark was nothing if not a master of manipulation, something Alex knew better than anyone. If he wanted me dead, she thought, I'd be in a ditch somewhere already.

She moved around in her chair, unable to get completely comfortable. She was restless and itchy, and she found it hard to sit still. It was the Mindblast; she hadn't realized how addicted she'd gotten. The best she could figure, it had been two weeks since she'd had a hit, and the edginess had already peaked. The withdrawal from the drug was fairly moderate, certainly nothing she couldn't handle. But it was unpleasant nonetheless, and a distraction when she needed to be at her best and sharpest.

They'd treated her wounds, at least. The bites were already completely gone; she couldn't even see where they'd been. The cut had been deeper; it was mostly healed, but her leg was still a little tender.

Her mind was sharp, at least...clearer than it had been in months. She'd been confused and uncertain for a long time, but her field reflexes had snapped back into shape. Seeing Sarah had shattered her single-minded resolve and challenged everything she'd believed for so long. She still wasn't sure how she felt about her sister...the hatred and anger were still there, mixed now with affection she'd thought long dead. But that was something she'd have to face later. Right now she knew she was in a fight for her life. A twisted contest of some sort, no doubt, but she didn't kid herself. Garret Stark had the upper hand right now, and she knew he was trying to decide whether he should keep her alive or not. All the personal uncertainty and pain was still there, but Alex Linden was a survivor above all else, and she needed her wits now.

She heard the door slide open, but she resisted the urge to turn. She'd been careless on Armstrong, but now she was focused, ready. "Hello, Gavin. How have you been?" Her voice was neutral, non-committal...she might have been greeting an acquaintance at a cocktail party.

"I am well, my dear Alex." That voice...she hadn't heard it for two years. Charming, polite...but something else too. Something that sent a chill through her body. "Happy to see you still have those eyes in the back of your head."

She turned, slowly, with no sense of urgency. "It takes more than eyes, Gavin. You should know that." She'd almost called him Number One, but she wanted to draw at least somewhat on her closeness with him. The two had been sexual partners for quite some time, though she wasn't foolish enough to think that would stop him from having her terminated. She couldn't take familiarity too far or expect too much from it; she knew that. An appeal to friendship or affection would be weak and ineffectual...and an attempted seduction would be obvious, clumsy. No...casual familiarity was the way to go. She glanced at him with a friendly smile. She almost suggested they get right to the point, but she decided to stay silent and let him move the conversation.

He walked across the room, pulling out the chair at the head of the table. The Directorate's meeting room was palatial, a wood-paneled bastion of power and privilege, its wall of floor-to-ceiling windows providing a kilometer high view of the Washbalt skyline. To the northeast was a cluster of similarly majestic skyscrapers, the government buildings that housed the Politicians and their staffs...the people who ran the Alliance. Who thought they ran the Alliance, at least.

"Alex, my dear. I am so pleased that we were able to find you and extricate you from those terrible circumstances." Stark's voice was impossible to read, as usual. To anyone listening, he was expressing genuine concern. Alex knew better, yet she still couldn't get a feeling for what was truly going on in his sociopathic mind. "You must be more careful in the future."

Alex almost sighed, but she caught herself. Be patient, she thought to herself...play along with his little farce. "Indeed, Gavin. I am most happy to be back inside the Core." She paused, then added, "It has been quite some time since I frequented neighborhoods of that sort."

Stark leaned back in his chair, eyes focused on her. He wasn't leering, and there was no sign of anger in his expression. He just stared over with a moderately concerned look on his face. "Perhaps we should discuss the future." He paused, his glance unchanging. "I must say, I am a bit confused about your visit to Armstrong and some of the…shall we say, decisions, that you made there." His voice changed slowly, almost imperceptibly. He was getting serious…there was a tone there…pointed, almost threatening.

"Gavin, I know I performed poorly on Armstrong." She knew she had to express some sort of remorse or regret. It had to be just right. Too much and he wouldn't buy it…or he'd take it as weakness and assume she was beyond salvation. That would be a ticket to Sub-Sector C or, more likely, just a quick disposal. "I was not adequately prepared to handle my sister. I experienced some vestigial feelings I hadn't realized were there, and it threw me off-balance." She spoke calmly and coolly, her tone not changing at all. "And the First Imperium incursion and Erik Cain's resulting absence made it impossible for me to execute my mission."

Stark didn't respond immediately…he just leaned back in his chair watching her closely. "Number Three…you are very aware of this organization's policies on matters such as this. Indeed, you have been instrumental in carrying them out on more than one occasion."

Number Three, she thought…he's giving me a ray of hope, suggesting I can maintain my position. But the threat was obvious too. Alliance Intelligence tended to deal harshly with agents who'd strayed far less than she had. "Yes, Gavin, I am." She'd almost called him Number One, but she decided taking his lead so obviously would be pandering, weak. She considered elaborating, offering a further explanation for her behavior, but she stayed silent. It was better to hold back, to give out information slowly.

Stark sat quietly, his eyes boring into hers. Finally he stirred, shifting slightly in his seat. "Alex, I never ordered you to harm your sister." His tone was different, not apologetic certainly, but the tiniest bit softer. "Sarah Linden is of no interest to me or this agency. You may deal with your sister in whatever manner you deem appropriate. Forgive her or terminate her…I do not care."

Alex was quiet, considering Stark's words. He sounded sincere but, of course, that mean nothing where the head of Alliance Intelligence was concerned. Gavin Stark was a true sociopath and a pathological liar. But it was all she had to go with. "I understand."

"However…" His voice became darker, more ominous. "… your affection, if any, for your sister can never again interfere with your duties." He took a deep breath and paused. "Never." The word was dripping with menace. "Do we understand each other, Alex?"

"Yes, Gavin." She let her tone soften slightly. It was dangerous to play mind games with Stark…he was better at them than everyone else. But she needed him to think he'd gotten to her, at least a little.

"So I can count on you?"

She paused, just for a second or two. "Yes, Gavin." She almost told him he could depend on her, but that seemed fake, transparent. "I am ready to get back to work. With no distractions." Better. More professional, less pandering.

Stark watched her as she spoke and for a considerable period after. "OK, Alex." He smiled and stood up slowly. "Then I need you back on Armstrong…and wherever else your mission takes you. General Cain is currently battling on the surface of Planet Sigma 4 II. If the campaign to defeat the First Imperium is successful, the war will be over." Stark stood with his hand on the backrest of his chair, his eyes glinting coldly. "In that eventuality, you may do whatever you choose with your sister… but you must kill Erik Cain. He is a grave danger to our future plans."

She didn't look away, didn't move at all. "Of course, Gavin. I assure you, nothing will interfere with me this time."

He stood quietly for a few seconds then he nodded and walked toward her. "Very well, Alex." He reached into his pocket and pulled out a small leather folder. "Here are your documents and credentials." He gently laid the small pouch on the table. "Welcome back." He turned and started walking toward the door.

"It is good to be back, Number One." Her voice was cold, focused…just what she knew he wanted to hear. She leaned back, watching him leave the room. Her thoughts were racing… should I move against him now? She had hidden resources, assets and tools Stark knew nothing about. For a few seconds she seriously considered making a play for the top spot.

No, she scolded herself…don't be a fool. Stark would be watching for that now; she knew that much. And he had hidden resources too, probably many more than she did. No, she thought grimly…I have to pass my test first, win back some of his trust. "I'm going to have to kill Erik Cain."

Stark walked slowly down the almost dark corridor, the echo of his quiet footsteps the only sound breaking the eerie silence. The building above housed an import-export business selling rarities from the colonies to Washbalt's privileged elite. Though ostensibly owned by one of the larger megacorporations it was, in fact, nothing but a cover for Gavin Stark's most secretive operation.

No one working above even knew these subterranean levels existed. They were accessible only through a series of AI-controlled checkpoints. It would be easier to sneak into the Presidential Palace than to penetrate Stark's heavily defended lair.

He turned and stood in front of a non-descript plasti-steel door, waiting quietly while the AI conducted a DNA scan. "Number One, confirmed." The door slid to the side, revealing a drab room with a small table and 4 chairs.

Stark stepped slowly inside, extending his hand to the small, gray-haired man standing next to the table. "Dr. Zenta, welcome to Washbalt. I hope your trip was comfortable."

Zenta reached out and took Stark's hand. "Yes, it was fine. But I fail to see why it was necessary for me to come here at all. You know we are at a critical stage in the plan. I have much work to do." His tone was annoyed, impatient.

Stark caught the anger he felt welling up inside him. This pompous fool scientist, he thought…he has no idea to whom he is speaking. Stark imagined throwing the arrogant ass into Sub-Sector C for a while. It was an appealing idea, but not realistic. Not yet, at least. Zenta was crucial to his plans and, for now, he was irreplaceable. "I regret taking you from your work, doctor. However, I felt it would be too conspicuous right now for me to travel to Facility Q." Stark pulled out a chair and sat, gesturing for Zenta to do the same. "But I have important issues to discuss with you. Matters that cannot wait, I am afraid."

Zenta sat across from Stark, an expectant expression on his face. "Then you mean to launch Operation Shadow soon?"

"Immediately, Dr. Zenta." Stark sat totally still, staring into the scientist's eyes as he spoke. "That is why I summoned you here." He'd chosen the word 'summoned' very deliberately. It had an imperious sound to it, a subtle reminder of who was the master here.

Zenta's eyes widened with excitement. "My life's work… about to come to fruition."

"Indeed, doctor." Stark had to acknowledge that Zenta was a genius. He'd achieved something that had eluded Earth science for two centuries…something Gavin Stark was going to put to stunningly practical use. "I believe the time is right."

In truth, Stark knew he had no choice. Implementing Plan C, and the subsequent Shadow Project, had been enormously expensive. He'd managed to hide the unauthorized expenditures, mostly with a massive campaign of fraud, cover ups, and assassinations. But even he was running out of ways to disguise the massive costs. If he didn't launch the project now, it was going to be discovered. And the consequences of that would be catastrophic to Gavin Stark and his ambitions.

"What about the war? Shouldn't we wait until that is over?"

Zenta's question was a reasonable one. Stark paused for a few seconds, deciding just how much he wanted to share with his scientist ally. "I am privy to intelligence from the front, doctor. As we speak, General Cain and his ground forces are mopping up on the enemy planet. Admiral Compton has already defeated the First Imperium fleet in the system. Although it is not yet general knowledge, I believe the war will be over very shortly."

Stark's explanation was pure fiction, based only passingly on the actual facts of the campaign. But outside the highest levels of government, the First Imperium threat had been downplayed enormously. The elites were scared to death already...the last thing they needed was panic-stricken masses rioting in the streets. Zenta could believe Stark's words because the scientist had never been privy to just how serious the danger truly was.

"I will be meeting with General Samuels this evening, at which time I will instruct him to activate his portion of the plan." He slid his chair out and slowly rose. "You may return to Q and commence full activation, doctor. It is time."

"Yes, I will return at once." Zenta's excitement was obvious. He'd been working on the components of Shadow for 30 years. Now, finally, he would see his work in action.

Stark walked toward the door and out into the hall, his mind deep in thought. His actual reasoning for launching Shadow was considerably different from what he had told Zenta, something only another cold-blooded psychopath could truly understand. He had no idea whether Garret and Holm and the military would find a way to defeat the First Imperium. But if they failed, he was certain the navy and Marines would be virtually destroyed in the effort. There would be no second chances, no fallback lines of defense. If Garret was defeated, it wouldn't matter what Stark did...there would be no consequences to his launching Shadow if civilization was going to be destroyed anyway. Indeed, the Shadow project would be the only hope of defeating the enemy if Garret's people failed. And if the military succeeded...they would come home to find they were too late to stop Shadow. The game would be over, and Gavin Stark would be the only winner.

Chapter 25

First Imperium Sector Base
Planet Sigma 4 II

"Let's move it, people." Colonel Eliot Storm was watching his tactical display as he barked out orders to his Marines. They'd had no intel at all about the size or layout of the enemy base...the outer hull was impervious to scanners, just like First Imperium ships. But now his scanning units were feeding him a flood of data, and his AI was constructing a schematic of the place on the fly.

They hadn't run into any resistance yet. Their entry point seemed to be an out of way spot. All they'd found so far were vast empty storage areas with huge rack systems along the walls. It wasn't Storm's place to speculate on the design of the enemy base, but he was pretty sure these were the storage units for the battlebots and Reapers they'd been facing since the war began...the First Imperium equivalent of barracks. Other than subtle differences, racks rather than bunks, for example, the base didn't seem all that different from an Alliance facility.

His group came to an intersection, the third they'd found. "Sergeant Jamison, take your section down the south corridor. Reiger, take yours north." He wasn't going to be able to detach half a platoon down every hallway they found, but he didn't know what else to do. The scanning results were still incomplete, and they had no idea where any of these corridors led... or which ones might have enemy forces lurking in them.

"Colonel Storm, we've got the high-powered scanners set up now. We're getting good readings. You can ignore those lateral corridors. They just lead to more troop storage areas, all empty. Post a pair of guards down each just in case, but you can recall the sections."

Cain, Storm thought…what the hell is he doing here? There was no way the commander-in-chief should be in here exposing himself to God knows what, at least not until his people had established some kind of secure zone. "Yes, sir." He paused. "Sir, I really think you should hold back until we can get this place scouted out better."

"Noted, colonel. And ignored." Cain's voice was firm, but not scolding. Storm was only doing his job. "There's no place for normal procedures now. We need to get this place scouted out, and we need to do it now."

"Yes, general." Storm still disagreed, but he kept his mouth shut.

"I'm sending you the revised tactical map. You should be receiving it now."

"Yes, sir." Storm was watching the map on his display change subtly, as his AI added the information Cain was sending, expanding on what was already there. "It's coming in now, sir."

"Good, now keep moving. Our units are catching hell out there on the surface, trying to keep the enemy forces from breaking through and trapping us in here. So I need your people to haul ass!"

"Yes, sir." Cain had already cut the line. Storm could only imagine what the commander was dealing with on the surface. He flipped his com to the unit-wide line. "Alright, I'm feeding updated tactical maps to all squad leaders. We're going to pick up the pace." All of the Marines down in these corridors had ten years or more service, and most of them had served in Cain's special action teams during the Third Frontier War. Fighting men and women just didn't get any better. They would do whatever they were ordered to do if it was humanly possible. Storm wondered if they could do a bit of the impossible as well. They might just get their chance, he thought as he jogged forward, deeper into the seemingly endless depths of the tunnel.

"Fourth Company...advance to the left...now!" McDaniels had just watched 3 of her Obliterators blown to bits right in front of her. The enemy pressure on the flanks had been getting steadily stronger. They must have pulled everything back, all across the line and thrown it at us, she thought. She wasn't surprised. She'd expected some sort of panicked reaction once the enemy got word that forces had penetrated their base.

Expecting it and being able to handle it were different things, however. She'd had 2,000 Obliterators in reserve, ready to face anything that moved against the breach, but now, after the 4th moved out, she'd be down to her last uncommitted company.

"McDaniels, how's it going out there?" Cain's voice was softer than usual, warmer. He knew what she was facing."

"It's bad, sir." She was trying to sound as firm as she could, but the strain was wearing her down. She wanted to scream at him, tell him he'd promoted her too fast, that she wasn't good enough to handle a situation like this. But he didn't give her the chance.

"Erin, keep it together. I have complete confidence in you." His voice was reassuring, supportive. "If I didn't, trust me...I'd be out there in a flash."

In spite of the crushing tension, he almost managed to get a laugh out of her. "Thank you, sir." She wondered how long she'd have to serve with Cain before he stopped surprising her. He was such an ice cold automaton on the battlefield...unflappable, irresistible. Now he spoke to her and the empathy was almost overpowering. She knew he understood what she was feeling...he'd been in her place many times, and he'd always managed to prevail. He was telling her she could too, and somehow, through some connection she couldn't even fathom, she believed him.

"Just do the work, General McDaniels. You're exactly the person we need there right now."

"Yes, sir." She could feel the adrenalin, her own body responding to Cain's words. She wasn't sure what she thought of Erik Cain personally, but failing him when he'd placed his confidence in her…that was unthinkable.

She looked at the tactical display. The forces on the left were really taking it hard. There were columns of enemy Reapers moving up, and the entire area was getting pounded by cluster bombs. This is the enemy's big push…if we can stop them here, we can hold out. "Let's go, 4th Company, move your asses!"

She checked her display; there was heavy action on the right too, but nothing like the left. She turned her head, looking off toward the position the 4th was on the way to bolster. She was two klicks from the front line, but she could see the inferno of the battle. "Time for me to get over there." She muttered softly to herself and started jogging toward the hottest part of the line.

"Are you sure, Friederich?" Cain's question was genuine. Hofstader carried a colonel's commission, but that was just a convenience. The German scientist was a brilliant man, and well on his way to becoming one of Cain's few real friends, but he wasn't a soldier.

"Yes, general. As I've heard you remind your subordinates, time is not on our side. And if we are going to discover anything immediately usable in this facility, I suggest that I am more likely to identify it than any of your Marines." He stumbled forward clumsily. The armor was a special-purpose AI-assisted unit. They were used mostly to accommodate dignitaries or other non-combatant officials who visited a battlefield. You couldn't do much but stagger around in one, but there was no way Cain was letting Hofstader into the base unprotected. Not until it was a damned sight more secure than it was at the moment.

Cain admired the scientist, and his respect grew each time they worked together. He demanded a tremendous commitment from his Marines, but they were trained, veteran warriors. Friederich Hofstader had spent his entire life in a lab until the First Imperium invasion hurled him into the front lines. Cain was continually surprised at the physicist's courage and perseverance. Without Hofstader's research and the resulting weapons flowing from Tom Sparks' labs, Cain knew his Marines would all be dead now…and the war lost.

"OK, Friederich. Come up and meet me. Your escort knows the way…and you are to remain with them at all times. Agreed?" Cain had assigned two veterans to escort Hofstader while he was in the combat zone. He was genuinely concerned for his friend, but it was more than that. Losing Hofstader would be an incalculable disaster for the Pact. A mind like his was simply irreplaceable…and there was no other human alive who better understood First Imperium technology.

"Yes, general." The scientist's voice betrayed fear…but also excitement. The equivalent of thousands of years of human advancement was laid out before him. Now he was looking for anything that could be adapted quickly enough to aid in the war effort. But if the victory was won, he could properly research the facility. He could only imagine the scientific advancements he might make given time. "We are on the way."

Cain glanced back at the tactical map Hector was projecting inside his visor. It was growing as new data came in from the scanners his forces were setting up at various points in the facility. The immense scale of the structure was slowly becoming apparent. There were hundreds of empty storage areas, cavernous rooms that once held tens of thousands of battlebots and Reapers. It was becoming clear that all or most of the ground forces his Marines had fought had come from here. He tried to imagine attacking a base like this if most of its ground units hadn't already been expended…if a quarter of a million robotic warriors were formed up to face any assault.

He drew his mind from such pointless conjecture. Besides, he thought, we faced those bots…we fought them on a dozen planets, and we have the dead to prove it. "If we have an easier time here, it's only because of the sacrifices Jax and Kyle Warren and a hundred thousand others made."

"Are you addressing me, general?"

Cain hadn't even realized he was speaking out loud. "No, Hector. Just indulging myself with pointless thoughts."

"Very well." The old Hector would almost certainly have delivered a more sarcastic reply. "General, I have Colonel Storm on the line."

"Eliot, what's up?" Cain got right to the point. Storm wouldn't be calling now if there wasn't a problem.

"We've run into resistance. They appear to be some type of security bots. They're not all that hard to kill, but they're armed with close range particle accelerators…and the damned things slice right through our armor." Energy weapons were rarely used during ground battles. Atmospheres quickly diffused the power of lasers – or particle accelerators – greatly reducing the effective range of such ordnance. But for short range security - where the fighting would be at close quarters in the corridors of a base – they could be extremely dangerous.

"I'm sending you the reserves. They should be there in a couple minutes. I need you to push ahead, no matter what the cost. McDaniels' people are catching hell out there keeping the enemy off our backs."

"Yes, sir." Storm sounded surprised. Getting reserves out of Cain was generally considered the next closest thing to impossible, especially on the first request. Not even request…Storm hadn't even asked. Erik Cain liked to have the last uncommitted forces in a battle, but there wasn't time for that now.

"I know you're all exhausted and hurting, but we've got to hit them again. The battle is not over, and victory has not been won." Jake Carlson was up in the front lines, doing everything he could to rally the shattered remnants of his battalion. He could feel his heart pounding in his chest…the tension, the fear…the feeling in the pit of his stomach. But there was no time now for his weaknesses. Carlson the warrior, the Marine, was firmly in control now. He knew what he had to do. "General McDaniels and her people are facing everything the enemy has, fighting and dying, but not giving a centimeter. They need us, and there's no way we're leaving fellow Marines to fight alone!"

He started walking forward, slowly at first, just a step at a time. "I am tired and hurt and mourning friends too. But I know what I am doing now. I am attacking the enemy; I'm going to aid my fellow Marines, and I will do it if I must stand alone and battle all the enemy has to face me. Anything else

would be a disgrace to our brothers and sisters who died today."
His voice was hoarse and he couldn't hide the fatigue, but he
forced the words out with raw force. "Who's coming with me?"
He accelerated, working up to a jog, zigzagging from boulder to
boulder, grabbing what cover he could as he lurched forward.
The ground was rough…rocky and chopped up from the bombardments, slowing his pace.

He glanced at his tactical display. No one else moved…not
for a second or two. Then, almost as one, the entire mass surged
forward, the previously silent com assaulted with a cacophony
of screaming voices. The battalion – what was left of it – was
with him. To a man.

The enemy forces were heavily engaged with McDaniels'
Obliterators, and Carlson's forces were moving against the First
Imperium rear. They advanced against light fire, sweeping away
the scattered enemy units in their path until they linked up with
Commander Farooq and his Janissaries. The combined force
continued forward, charging the small enemy rearguard and,
after a quick, bloody fight, seizing the heights that overlooked
the main fighting.

"HVM teams, deploy along the ridgeline. Target enemy
Reapers." Carlson was shouting his commands. His blood was
up, his earlier doubts and complaints forgotten. If he had to
die, what better place than here, surrounded by his brethren…
by Marines.

He watched as the HVM teams swarmed up onto the hillside and began deploying their heavy launchers. "Squad leaders, advance to the nearest HVM team and deploy." There was
no point in issuing more specific orders. The battalion was a
wreck, scattered survivors from a dozen units hopelessly inter-
mingled. Now it was the sergeants and corporals who mattered.
"All Marines, rally to the nearest squad leader. Cover the HVM
teams."

The enemy was sandwiched between the remnants of the
former battle line and McDaniels' Obliterators. The ridge was
an ideal firing position, and all along the line the HVM-armed
groups hastily set up their weapons. Carlson's people and the

rest of Brown's Marines were positioned right next to Farooq's Janissaries. And across the whole front, Colonel Sawyer's hyper-velocity missile teams were ready...ready to open fire and rain death down on the enemy Reapers. "Now is the time," Carlson yelled into his com. They would either win here or die.

Cain moved quickly down the corridor, followed by Hof-stader and a dozen Marines. He'd almost taken off at a dead run when he got Storm's last message. His people had found something...deep in the center of the base and a dozen levels below ground. They had no idea what it was, but they knew immediately it was something. This could be why we're here, Cain thought as he rounded the corner, a bit too quickly for Hofstader to follow. The scientist tried to keep up, but he stumbled. He would have fallen, but the AI running his armor corrected his balance.

"Sorry, Friederich." Cain slowed and looked behind. "I'm just anxious to see what they found."

"No more than me, general." The scientist was out of breath, but he was moving forward again. "Don't worry. I will keep up."

Storm's people were scattered throughout the facility. The security bots had turned out to be only a minor danger. Their weapons were deadly, but there weren't many of them, and they were easily tracked down and destroyed. They were clearly intended to address small incursions, not a full-fledged invasion of the base. Presumably, enemy doctrine called for the thousands of stored bots to deal with that kind of occurrence. But the robotic defenders of the base had been largely expended in invasions of human space...and the rest were outside, engaged in a death struggle with McDaniels' forces.

Once they'd eliminated the security bots, Cain had ordered Storm and his people to scatter and explore as much of the base as possible. It was a risk, certainly, but one he felt was worthwhile.

They reached what looked like a core area. The center was open, surrounded by a wide catwalk. Cain walked slowly to the edge and looked over. The shaft descended into darkness, farther than he could see, even with his helmet lamp on full power. There were concentric rings every 10 meters or so, all the way down. He couldn't even guess how deep the lower levels of the facility were.

He looked around. Storm had said there were ramps around the outside of the circle that would lead his people down. His eye caught an opening in the floor about ten meters around the circle. "That looks like the ramp," he said, pointing.

Two Marines of the escort immediately rushed to the spot Cain indicated, clearly wanting to go down before they allowed the commanding general to do the same. Cain sighed softly, but he let his bodyguards have their way. They were good Marines, and he appreciated their loyalty.

Cain followed the guards down. Storm had told them to come ten levels. It took about fifteen minutes for them to reach the designated spot. When they got to the tenth level they discovered that Storm had left a group of Marines there to lead them to his location.

"Colonel Storm sends his greetings, sir." The hulking Marine snapped to attention, his armored boots slapping loudly against the metal floor.

"Thank you, sergeant." Cain was looking around as he spoke. The facility didn't look all that different than an Alliance base, not really. Still, there was an eerie feel to it...something strange, alien. "At ease."

"Thank you, sir. Colonel Storm requests your presence. I am to lead your party there." The sergeant was a huge man, well over two meters tall. His voice was loud and deep, though there was something else there too. Cain recognized it immediately...intimidation. He never ceased to be amazed at how these grizzled killing machines quaked in his presence. He knew it came from respect, but he sometimes wished they knew how uncomfortable it made him. The hero worship stripped him of what little of his humanity remained.

Cain pointed, though it was more a gesture than anything. He had no idea which way they had to go. "Lead on, sergeant."

"We're losing it, general. There are just too many of them."
The voice on the other end of the com was ragged, cracking.
Major Sorenson was a veteran of 20 battles, but he sounded
close to the end of his rope. Very close.

"Pull back, maintaining fire." McDaniels was trying to hold
it together herself. She was just realizing she had paid more for
those stars on her collar than she'd thought. Her people could
have doubts, they could call her on the com looking for reassur-
ance, confidence. But she had no one. She was the top of that
chain, and she'd given up the right to be afraid or unsure...even
human.

She did have Cain...he was the one who truly had no one to
turn to. But she knew the commanding general was busy, and
she'd rather die here on this alien world than tell Erik Cain she
couldn't handle the job he'd given her. No...she'd rather face
anything than that.

"Sorenson, I'm sending you some backup, but you need
to keep your people together. Fall back 500 meters and, by
God, you hold there no matter what comes at you. Do you
understand?"

"Yes, general." He didn't sound solid, not exactly. But she
was pretty sure he'd hold. At least for a while. She had no idea
where she was going to get the reserves she'd promised him.
She paused for a few seconds, thinking. "Captain Claren, I need
you to organize the staff and lead them to support Major Sorenson. Immediately."

"Yes, general." The reply came back almost instantly. Claren
was a good aide, but a little young and inexperienced – at least
compared to most of her other officers.

She didn't have much of a staff to begin with, but right now
she needed them in the line more than she did attending to her.
She didn't know if 30-odd Obliterators would make the difference for Sorenson's people, but it was the best she could do.

McDaniels sighed. So close, she thought. We almost pulled
it off. She'd hoped the forces attacking the enemy rear would
be enough, but she knew in her gut they were too battered, too

exhausted. Against a human enemy, yes. But the First Imperium warriors weren't scared or shaken by the rear attack. They simply reordered their formations to face to both sides. It was still a tactical disadvantage to them, certainly. But the crippling morale effect simply wasn't there.

Now Cain and Storm's people would end up trapped in the enemy base and exterminated. No one was going to leave this planet. There were just too many of the enemy. She took a deep breath and pulled her rifle out of the harness. If her people were all going to die in the line, by God, she was going to be with them. She turned and followed the path her staff had taken. She'd gone 5 or 6 steps when her com erupted.

"Attention General McDaniels." The voice was female, vaguely familiar. "This is General Gilson. Hold your position. I have two brigades inbound now, landing 3 klicks from your position."

She felt a surge of relief through her body, and she let out a deep breath. Garret and the rest of the fleet were here. McDaniels stood quietly for a few seconds before responding. "Acknowledged, General Gilson." She didn't know what to say next. A million things poured into her mind, but finally she just said, "Welcome to Sigma 4 II, general."

Chapter 26

Bridge – AS Indianapolis
System X2
40,000,000 Kilometers from X3 Gate

Jacobs watched silently on his screen as the First Imperium task force transited. He had all his remaining laser buoys deployed and connected into an extensive scanner network. If everything went well, the enemy would get quite a hot welcome when they transited into X2. His ships were deployed behind the laser screen, at the edge of missile range. Every vessel was on red alert, ready to launch all their missiles at his command and then run for their lives. The enemy ships were coming in fast, and Jacobs' tiny force was no match for them. Still, he'd initially planned to put up more of a sustained fight, ignoring the mismatched odds. Admiral Compton had put an end to that plan. The fleet admiral OK'd the missile attack, but he'd explicitly ordered Jacobs to button everyone into the couches immediately after launching and blast away at full thrust.

Jacobs had ordered all ships and laser buoys to concentrate fire on the enemy Leviathans. The monster battleships were over twice the size of an Alliance Yorktown and vastly more powerful. They could absorb a lot of damage, and their defense arrays were extremely powerful. Catching them as they came through the warp gate would be the best chance to inflict heavy damage…before they could close with Compton's fleet and unleash their own fearsome weapons.

But things weren't going as planned. Jacobs felt his heart sink as Gremlin after Gremlin passed through the warp gate and into the X2 system. They're sending the screen through first, he thought with frustration…by God, they're learning their tactics from us!

"Fourteen enemy Gremlins have transited, admiral." It was as if Carp was reading his mind. "No sign of heavier units yet." Carp turned his head and looked expectantly at Jacobs.

The admiral knew he had to make a decision. The laser buoys packed a tremendous punch…they had more than enough firepower to take out the Gremlins, especially with Jacobs' missile barrage to finish off any survivors. But the x-ray lasers were wasted on the smaller ships. They were one of the Pact's few weapons powerful enough to seriously damage a large enemy vessel.

"Enemy ships are moving at a slower velocity than projected sir." Carp's voice cut through his concentration. "And decelerating at 60g."

Jacobs' head snapped up. That was a surprise, though maybe, he thought, it shouldn't be. "They don't want to just whip past us." His words started as a whisper, but the volume increased as he continued. "That fleet is here to engage and destroy our forces." His mind was racing. As big as the enemy fleet was, it wasn't strong enough to wipe out both Compton's and Garret's fleets…and the enemy had to have a rough idea of the total human strength from the Line battles. "Prepare a message for Admiral Compton."

Carp paused for a second, a confused look on his face. Then he spun around and worked his controls. "You may begin when ready, admiral."

"Admiral Compton, it is my opinion that the enemy fleet reported by Captain Mondragon is not the only force en route to this system." He paused…he was taking a massive leap here, one he had no evidence to support. But he'd never felt as sure of anything in his life. "As Captain Cleret has reported no activity in X4, I believe there may be a second force behind this one, deeper in the X3 system." Of course Captain Cleret still hadn't even managed to find another warp gate in X4, at least as of his last report. The scouting effort in X4 was going much more slowly than Mondragon's had in X3. Which didn't surprise Jacobs a bit. "Captain Mondragon's forces may be unable to report at this time." *Assuming any of them are still alive,* he thought...*though he kept that to himself.*

He took a quick breath and continued. "I must note that I have no substantial evidence to back up this assertion, except that the enemy appears to be decelerating to give sustained battle." He paused again, thinking of what else he wanted to add. But finally he just said, "Jacobs out." He looked over at Carp. "Send that immediately, commander."

"Yes, admiral."

Jacobs sat for a few seconds, just staring forward. "Lieutenant Hooper, order all ships to commence missile attacks at once."

"Yes, sir."

"And order Major Bogdan to launch his squadrons immediately." A vessel couldn't launch missiles and fighters simultaneously. A battleship would normally have to launch its fighters before firing missiles or else wait until it had ejected its external racks and restored its bearing. But Jacob's squadrons were on his 3 makeshift carriers, and they didn't carry any missiles.

Without the laser buoys, his fleet was completely outmatched by the enemy task force. But he was going to try to take them out anyway. Without the buoys. Maybe, just maybe...if he could coordinate the missiles and bombers to hit at the same time. Perhaps there was a chance to defeat this advanced force. And even if there wasn't...it was worth his whole fleet to save those laser buoys for the heavier targets.

"The fleet will execute 30g thrust in 60 seconds." Compton was lying down, completely cocooned in his acceleration couch. He hadn't planned to thrust hard enough to force his crews into the couches, but Jacobs' message changed his mind. It was a baseless speculation, a wild guess from an officer who'd been at flag rank for less than half a year. And Compton was completely convinced by it.

It made perfect sense...at least to the fleet admiral. The

enemy wasn't trying to break through to Sigma 4; they were here to destroy as many human ships as they could. The enemy didn't think like a human commander did. They didn't care if a fleet was completely destroyed if it did enough damage to serve the strategic purpose.

If this fight was going to be a battle of annihilation, Compton wanted to fight deeper in the system. With any luck, after the first round he could sandwich the decelerating enemy between his force and the newly arriving units...possibly even Garret's entire command. Then the united human fleet could turn to face any new enemy forces that arrived.

If they were able to hold off the First Imperium attacks here, Compton figured they could fortify Sigma 4 or one of the planets in X1, and mount a Line-like defense across the single system bottleneck between human space and the First Imperium. Maybe, just maybe, they could hold that position long enough for Sparks and Hofstader and their people to pull some game changing tech out of the captured enemy ship and base.

Compton felt the breath pushed from his lungs as Midway's massive engines fired. The fleet would accelerate halfway to the location Compton had designated. They would go into freefall while Hurley's squadrons launched, and then they would decelerate, reducing their velocity before entering range of the enemy. Compton needed his fleet at a dead halt to effectively deploy the x-ray laser buoys, and without those powerful weapons he didn't have a chance in the energy duel.

He was thinking about Mike Jacobs, too...and all the people on his ships. He'd ordered Jacobs to retreat after he fired his missiles, but now Scouting Fleet's commander was planning to face the enemy vanguard without using his laser buoys. He was still following the original plan, more or less. But now his fighters would be deployed, which meant he had to retrieve them somehow. Jacobs insisted he could scatter his fleet and work around the enemy task force, landing his fighters and getting out of range before he got hurt too badly. Compton wasn't too sure, it sounded like a lot of conjecture to him. But it didn't matter. He agreed with Jacobs – they had to hold those laser buoys to hit the heavy enemy ships when they were transiting, and he was willing to risk Jacobs' fleet to do it. He wasn't sure he'd have ordered Jacobs to do it, but the erstwhile admiral had asked for the go ahead. Compton didn't like it, but he'd given the OK anyway. If Jacob's laser buoys could target the enemy heavy units rather than the Gremlins, it would make a big difference in the battle. The main enemy line would have damage before the battle lines even exchanged fire. Those first shots could be enormously important.

His eyes had been watching the chronometer count down…5 seconds…4, 3, 2, 1. Now he felt the massive gee forces slamming into him, and he struggled to force breath into his lungs. He felt partial relief almost immediately, as his system increased the air pressure in his helmet, adjusting to partially offset the acceleration. He was trying to stay focused, but he knew his mind would begin to wander and the line between fantasy and reality would blur. Once again, he thought before lucidity retreated…once more into battle.

"All units, maximum deceleration now." Bogdan was in his acceleration couch, held firmly in place. The verbal order to the squadrons was more for the benefit of his crews – and himself – than any real need. With everyone buttoned up in the couches, the AIs were flying the bombers…and the machines already knew what they were doing.

Bogdan's craft had accelerated full more than halfway to their projected attack point; now they were reducing their speed, allowing the missile volley from Jacobs' fleet to pass them. If all went according to plan, they'd ride in on the coattails of the missiles, avoiding most of the enemy defensive fire.

He had 31 bombers, each one with a veteran crew…and every one of them double loaded with plasma torpedoes. They'd be going in right behind the missiles, trying to target the ships worst damaged by the nuclear detonations. Then they'd have to get out…and do it quickly. Jacobs had launched a second spread of missiles, flushing his ships' magazines. Bogdan wanted his craft well out of the combat zone before those nukes started blowing.

Bogdan couldn't help by admire Jacobs' battle plan. A first wave of missiles, screening his bombers and causing enough damage to create vulnerable targets for the plasma torpedoes. Then a second missile attack, which would be crossing the point defense zone while the enemy was fighting off Bogdan's attack. It's just possible, Bogdan thought...maybe Jacobs can really take out this whole force without using the laser buoys. But his optimism didn't last. Even with a strong plan, the mathematics of war in space were inescapable. Without a miracle, some of these Gremlins were going to survive the long-ranged attacks...and then they'd tear Jacobs' cruisers apart with particle accelerators before he got a chance to close to laser range. The buoys had been designed to offset that mismatch, but Jacobs had forgone using his.

"Approaching link up zone." The bomber's AI made the announcement. Bogdan was startled at first; the meeting point was over an hour from where they'd begun deceleration, and it seemed that only a few minutes had passed. But as the AI-administered stimulant cleared his head, he realized an hour had indeed passed while he was in his drug-induced state.

He sat up in his chair, twisting his head, working the kinks out. "Pilot taking over." He reached out, grabbing the controls as the AI relinquished the flying duties to him. "Attention all craft." He was speaking into the com, transmitting on the force-wide line. "I want everyone at 150% for this attack. If you think you need another stim, take one now." He looked down, checking the tactical display. He smiled broadly. The strike force was in perfect formation.

"All units. Perform final weapon system diagnostics and arm plasma torpedoes." It was almost time.

Jacobs was sitting on the bridge, watching the scanning report from his missile barrage. The enemy point defense had been effective, knocking out two-thirds of the incoming warheads, but the surviving missiles were performing far beyond his expectations. One Gremlin had already been destroyed, caught between two 500 megaton explosions each less than a kilometer away. Another four enemy vessels had taken significant damage, and half the others suffered minor hits.

Now it was his turn. The enemy barrage was almost through his own defensive zone. At least half the approaching missiles had been destroyed, and his shotguns were still firing full, whittling down the incoming volley. Still, his ships were going to take a lot of damage…that was basic math. They should survive it, most of them at least, as long as none of those warheads were antimatter-armed. As far as Jacobs knew, no Gremlin the Pact had yet faced had been antimatter-equipped, but he also realized that guaranteed exactly nothing.

"Lead missiles entering detonation zone." Carp knew Jacobs was completely aware of the enemy missiles' location, but it was his job to advise him anyway.

Both the First Imperium and the human powers utilized missiles in the same basic manner. The goal was to get the warheads as close as possible to an enemy vessel and then detonate them. Missiles were intended to score near misses, not direct hits. It was almost impossible to accurately target something as small as a spaceship from hundreds of thousands of kilometers away, especially when the target was exerting random thrust in an evasive pattern.

Nuclear explosions in space were obviously dangerous to anything nearby, though the effective zone was far smaller than it would be in an atmosphere. A weapon that would carry deadly shockwaves and heat 10 kilometers on a planetary surface might be truly dangerous only out 1-2 klicks in space.

The First Imperium had better targeting systems, but they were susceptible to human ECM and more easily confused by truly random maneuvering. Overall, the two sides were fairly evenly matched in missile duels. Unless the enemy had antimatter warheads.

"Detonations, captain." Carp was bent over his workstation, as usual. "All standard nuclear warheads so far."

Jacobs sighed softly. He hadn't really expected antimatter weapons from the Gremlins, but it was good to be sure. "Very well, commander. All damage reports as they come in." He knew there would be a lot of them.

"Kooshi govno ee oomree!" Bogdan's shouted with a laugh, wondering how much indigestion he'd just given the translation AI. The shot had been perfect, a bullseye. The Gremlin had been hit hard by Jacobs' missiles, and a secondary explosion had blown a ten meter-wide hole in the hull. Hitting a 10-meter target in space combat was like splitting an arrow, but Bogdan had landed his torpedo dead center. The stricken enemy ship was bursting open like a hatching egg. There were massive internal explosions and vast plumes of internal gasses blasting into space. "That's one fucker down!"

Pavel Bogdan was a hardened veteran, calm and professional in the face of the enemy. But he was a true fighter pilot at heart…a tracker, a hunter. There was nothing more exhilarating to him than the kill, and that went double when fighting these scum-sucking robot ships. In his wars against other humans, he'd been just as driven, but victory was always tempered with respect for those who fell under his guns. But fighting this enemy felt more like exterminating vermin. There was no pity, no mercy, no hesitation.

His crew was cheering too, watching the enemy ship's death struggle on the monitor. The strike force was ripping through the enemy fleet, blasting straight at their targets and firing at point blank range. They paid a price for their aggressiveness…10 bombers were destroyed by close in point defense. But 19 of the remaining 21 scored solid hits. Six Gremlins had been completely destroyed, and all the rest had at least some damage. Bogdan counted four cripples among the survivors, ships so badly damaged he doubted they could have much offensive capacity to hurt Jacobs' fleet.

"Well done. We earned our pay today, my comrades." Bogdan's voice roared on the force-wide com line. There were only 63 of them left, on 21 surviving ships, but they had done their duty. "Now it's time to get back to base before these bastards pull themselves together and start shooting at us again. All craft, prepare for full thrust."

Yes, he thought...we earned our pay today, he thought with
satisfaction. But he knew the day wasn't over yet.

Compton took a deep breath, then another, enjoying the
absence of crushing pressure. The fleet had been at 30g for
almost eight hours, with just a short break to launch Hurley's
strike force. He pulled himself upright. His muscles were stiff
and sore, but his mind was clear. He owed that to the double
dose of stims.

"Status report, Commodore Harmon."

His aide was already bolt upright and working furiously at his
controls. Well, Compton thought, he's a lot younger than me.

"The main enemy force has completed transit, sir. They
have continued decelerating. Current estimate is they will enter
missile range in approximately 45 minutes." Harmon paused,
checking his other readouts. "Admiral Jacobs' ships have withdrawn away from the enemy approach vector and are conducting emergency repairs."

Compton allowed himself a fleeting smile. Admiral Jacobs
had earned his stars and then some. His combined missile and
bomber attack had savaged the enemy vanguard, and a second
sortie by his battered bomber wings had taken out all the survivors. Compton hadn't been sure Jacobs' people could handle the entire enemy force, not without using their laser buoys.
They'd done it, though...and Jacobs still had 3 or 4 cruisers in
good enough shape to get back in the fight if they were needed.

Scouting Fleet's bomber force had given its all. Only 13 of
its 42 original craft were still functional. Pavel Bogdan's wasn't
one of them. He'd taken a hit on the second sortie, and the
cockpit erupted in flames. Somehow he'd managed to give first
aid to his two crew members and engage the AI before passing out from the pain. He was in Borodino's sickbay, horribly
burned, with no better than a 50/50 chance of survival.

Compton had never met Bogdan, but from what he'd heard,
the Russian was one hell of a pilot and officer. He hoped he'd get
the chance to congratulate him when the fighting was through.

But he had other things to do now. "Commodore Harmon, all vessels are to prepare for missile launch. We'll be clearing the external racks and then firing an immediate barrage from internal magazines."

Harmon paused for an instant. Firing from the magazines right after launching externally mounted missiles was tricky. Ejecting the empty mounts was a complex operation, and ships had to fire their positioning engines to realign themselves afterward. Hurrying the process vastly increased the risk of problems. But Harmon knew Compton was well aware of the difficulties. "Yes, sir. Advising all task forces now."

Even without the other half of Grand Fleet, the force under Compton's command was the largest fleet any human being had ever led into battle. On the journey to the frontier, Compton had wondered how it would feel to be sitting in his chair commanding such an awesome force, how he would handle the pressure. Now that he was there, it didn't seem very different from any other battle. He was cold, focused...everything he had to be during a fight. Later he would second guess his decisions, and then the regret would come, and the grief for those lost. But there was no place for that in the heat of battle, and Compton had locked it away...as he always did.

Jacob's laser buoys had attacked almost immediately after the enemy fleet entered the system. Scanning data was still incomplete, but it looked like at least 4 Gargoyles had been destroyed and one of the Leviathans was heavily damaged. Compton was grateful. Jacobs' heroism in holding back the buoys would make a big difference when the main lines clashed.

John Duke's attack ships would be going in next. Then Greta Hurley's people would attack right behind Compton's first missile volley. With any luck, the enemy fleet would suffer serious losses before they even engaged Compton's main force.

"Commodore Harmon, all ships are to prepare to deploy laser buoys after missile launch." He was going to place his own x-ray lasers right here. "Targeting programs will prioritize the enemy Leviathans." Compton really wanted those monsters destroyed as quickly as possible.

"Yes, admiral."

"And prepare a thrust plan. The fleet will be pulling back 1,500,000 kilometers after laser deployment." He wanted his laser buoys engaging the enemy before his own ships were within energy weapons range.

"Yes, sir."

Compton leaned back and stared at the display. He was silent. His thoughts were with John Duke and Greta Hurley.

"Group A, begin deceleration in three zero seconds." Hurley was speaking loudly, almost shouting. She didn't want any slipups on this mission. Her A group was assigned to missile defense, their sole focus taking out as many antimatter missiles as possible before they could reach the fleet.

"Group B, prepare for acceleration in six zero seconds." B Group – along with Hurley herself – was going at the enemy fleet, coordinating its assault with Compton's first missile barrage. With missiles and bombers coming in at once, the enemy would have to split their point defense fire. Hurley had no idea if they'd concentrate on one threat or divide their resources, but either way, more attacks were going to get through to the enemy line.

Her plan was complicated, and she'd drilled it into her squadron leaders' heads. They were going to be attacking as the missiles were seeking targets and detonating. She and Compton had worked out specific attack corridors for her wings...designated locations the missiles would be programmed to avoid. If her pilots got crazy, if they flew out of their specified zones, they could easily find themselves on top of a 500 megaton warhead about to blow.

One thing would be different about this attack than the last. Hurley's ship would be in the middle of the action. Commander Wilder had put up a good fight, invoking Garret's name at least three times. But Hurley wouldn't take no for an answer. She came close to bringing her sidearm into the debate, but Wilder finally relented. He didn't like hanging back from the fight any more than she did.

"A Leader to command…A group breaking off now." Hurley had handpicked Captain Akira to lead the anti-missile group. He was the PRC's most accomplished pilot, and she trusted him to direct the pinpoint flying it would take to effectively intercept the enemy's antimatter missiles. She'd given him the PRC squadrons and a good portion of her own Alliance flyers. She kept the less experienced Europan and CAC bomber wings in her B Group. They were more accustomed to executing attack runs at capital ships, and she knew she'd be there to keep them on a tight leash.

"Initiating thrust in 10 seconds, admiral." The AIs on every ship were making the same announcement. The acceleration couches were partially deployed, which would provide enough support against the 10g maximum she expected from her thrust plan. It wouldn't be pleasant, but she wanted to avoid having her crews under the influence of the drug cocktail a full burn would require. She didn't think anyone could be 100% right after coming out of that, even with the stims…and she wanted everyone in her group focused like razors.

She leaned back and closed her eyes, listening to the AI count down the final few seconds to the burn. She'd gotten knocked out of the last fight early, but this time she was going right down their throats.

Chapter 27

First Imperium Sector Base
Planet Sigma 4 II

Cain had been standing and staring for at least ten minutes. The room itself was enough to inspire awe. It was perfectly round, 300 meters in diameter, rising 80 meters from where he stood. He was on the edge of a circular catwalk looking down. The space was impressive enough, but the giant dish below was truly extraordinary. It looked like some type of antenna or projector, but Cain was just guessing. Hector told him it was exactly 240 meters in diameter, constructed of a material similar to that in the First Imperium warship hulls.

"Confirm that energy reading, Hector." Cain heard what his AI said, but he simply didn't believe it.

"The object appears be powered by a total of 3.17 terawatts of power. This is, without question, a major component of the power output we detected from the exterior of the facility."

Cain stood on the catwalk silently, staring at the alien mechanism. Hofstader was standing next to him, working with a small scanning device. "Can you detect the power source, Friederich? I can't imagine what could be producing so much energy."

"I believe I can offer you an answer to that question...if you do not mind my filling in the gaps with conjecture." The scientist's eyes didn't move from the device in his hands.

"Not at all. I'd appreciate any thoughts you have."

Hofstader finally looked up from his scanner, turning to face Cain. "It appears that the entire facility is powered by the internal energy generated by this planet. There are a number of significant similarities with the energy sources in the antimatter factory on Epsilon Eridani IV."

"I would have expected it to take some type of massive reactor to generate that kind of power." Cain's eyes had drifted back to the giant dish.

"Our studies on Epsilon Eridani IV have been quite illuminating, general. We have known for centuries the vast amount of energy that could theoretically be tapped from the geothermal and tectonic properties of a planet." He paused, catching himself before he launched into a full blown lecture. You're not in a classroom, he reminded himself. "Simply put, our exploitation of this energy source has always been limited by engineering constraints. We've been compelled to locate geothermal power plants near points where tectonic plates meet, for example, and our conversion efficiencies are therefore very low." His eyes moved toward the alien structure. "But the First Imperium has far more advanced technology. On Carson's World, there are multiple shafts drilled directly to the planet's core." He paused again. "The First Imperium is able to harness virtually all of a planet's energy, a power source equal to thousands, if not millions, of fusion reactors. It is the secret to their ability to mass produce antimatter."

"So the ability to power this device is not even extraordinary to them?" Cain's question didn't really demand a response... he knew the answer already. "Do you have any ideas on the purpose of thing?"

"I am speculating wildly, General Cain, but it appears to be some sort of jamming mechanism utilizing a form of dark energy we do not completely understand, one that is difficult even to detect. It may very well be projecting a field that would make an object in nearby space invisible and otherwise undetectable." Hofstader was walking slowly along the catwalk, his eyes fixed on the object. "That might explain why we detected nothing from orbit. I'm afraid our scanning devices are nearly useless with these types of emissions."

Cain stood facing Hofstader. "Are you saying you believe there is something hidden somewhere near this planet? Something we have not picked up on our scanners?"

"That is exactly what I am saying, General Cain. Though the entire supposition is pure guesswork." There was doubt in Hofstader's voice, but only a touch. He sounded fairly confident.

"I have to warn Admiral Garret." Cain's voice had become more urgent. "There could be some type of fortress or battleship hiding up there."

"Indeed, general. That is a very real possibility." Hofstader paused. "But I would guess that it is something different, more singular. Though I am at a loss to offer a suggestion as to what that may be."

Cain glanced down at his display, confirming what he already knew. His com didn't have the power to reach the fleet from this deep in the enemy base. The First Imperium metals interfered enormously with transmissions. He turned to face his aides. "Captain Haney, get up to the surface immediately and contact Admiral Garret. Tell him what we found, and advise him that we suspect there is some type of enemy construct either in orbit or nearby that is currently being hidden by a jamming device."

"Yes, sir." Haney snapped to attention before turning and walking quickly back the way they had come.

Cain turned to face Hofstader, a deliberative scowl on his face. "So what happens if we destroy this thing?"

"This is appalling." Sarah Linden had been running around snapping out orders since she'd stepped out of the shuttle. She turned to one of her aides. "Get on the com. I want two mobile field hospitals down here...and I mean now!"

"Yes, colonel." Captain Roan was Sarah's newest assistant and, so far, she'd been the best of them all. She quickly relayed the orders to the orbiting hospital fleet.

The plain was covered with wounded, thousands of them. They were being tended by a bunch of medics and six overwhelmed surgeons. Half of them were still in the wreckage of their armor, waiting to be extracted by the single overworked plasma torch crew. At least, she thought, looking out over the twisted heaps of humanity intertwined with machinery, some of their trauma control systems were probably functioning…at least partially.

Sarah had still been assembling Grand Fleet's medical task force when Compton and Erik and the rest of their people had taken off for the frontier. They may have had the newest and strongest warships with them, but their medical services were woefully inadequate, especially to support a major ground campaign.

Thank God these suits are so good at keeping wounded men and women alive, she thought, or we'd have nothing but a plain full of corpses by now. "Tricia, I need triage teams down here too. At least thirty."

"Yes, colonel." Her voice was sharp and crisp. Tricia Roan was proving to be as tireless as her boss. Sarah went through aides quickly, generally burning them out with the workload before moving on to the next. Sarah Linden was calm and pleasant in normal settings, but when there were wounded to care for she was a brutal taskmaster, and she didn't hesitate to employ her iron fist on anyone who didn't keep up with her relentless standards. She was as intense in her own way as Cain was in his. Those who knew both of them considered it some kind of bizarre fate they found each other.

It looked like the casualties in the battle had been enormously high. She was shocked to see so many wounded, and stunned to encounter the terrible conditions in the makeshift field hospitals. She'd been able to confirm that Erik hadn't been killed or wounded, which at least let her put that worry out of her mind. She didn't want any distractions right now, not even Erik…she was going to give 100% to these wounded Marines. And the Janissaries too. Sarah Linden would treat any wounded soldier, but she made a note to try to assign male doctors to the Caliphate casualties whenever possible. She didn't approve of the gender roles in the Caliphate, but that wasn't an argument she intended to have with wounded and dying men on the battlefield.

She wondered briefly about the cultural differences between the Superpowers, how much of it was real…and how much was manufactured, designed to keep soldiers loyal to the state and hating their enemies.

She'd spent weeks working on Commander Farooq after the fighting on Sandoval. The Janissary commander had been horrifically wounded...even Sarah had been sure he was going to die. But she pulled him through somehow, and he expressed nothing but gratitude and kindness to the female doctor who'd saved his life. Ali Khaled, Farooq's superior, had been equally gracious, sending her a personal note of thanks...as well as an official communique to General Holm, praising her work and awarding her the formal gratitude of the Janissary Corps. Fighting alongside old enemies had taught them all a great deal, she thought...maybe we'll get the time to figure it all out one day.

"Stop your daydreaming, Linden," she said to herself. "There's work to do." She tapped her comlink. "Tricia...we need plasma torches down here too. I want those on the first shuttle."

"Get General McDaniels to Colonel Linden." Catherine Gilson's voice was firm, commanding. "Immediately."

McDaniels had taken a pretty bad hit, but Gilson didn't think it was too dangerous. The Obliterator suit was very tough, and its trauma control system was top notch. Still, she wasn't taking any chances.

"Yes, general." Tim Karantz snapped to attention and ran over a small hill to the west. McDaniels' people had carried her back from the line to a relatively safe spot in a protected ravine. Word had spread quickly through the ranks, the story escalating as it did. First, it simply was news that the general was down... then the reports of her death began to spread. Her Marines were shaken, heartbroken at the word their beloved general had been killed. But there was more than sadness...they were enraged too, and the lust for revenge pushed away the fatigue and the fear. Her lines stopped their retreat and surged back at the enemy, attacking savagely, ignoring their losses. The enemy was momentarily stunned by the ferocity of the advance...and then Gilson's people hit them on the flank. An imminent First

Imperium victory turned rapidly into an ignominious defeat. In less than an hour it evolved from a battle to a hunting expedition, Gilson's newly arrived forces tracking down the last enemy survivors among the rocks and gullies. There were still a few rogue enemy bots holding out here and there, but Gilson had declared the planet secure.

She'd tried to reach Cain half a dozen times, but it was impossible to force a signal into the depths of the enemy base. Finally, she sent a party inside with orders to find Cain and report. Cain knew the fleet had arrived, but he probably had no idea how the fighting had gone. She knew he had to be sweating what was happening on the surface, especially since he was out of touch. He'd put McDaniels' brigade – the whole army, really – on the spot so his lighting attack could penetrate into the base. Gilson smiled. It was another brilliant plan…but risky as all hell. No one, she thought, could say Erik Cain didn't have balls. Though this time, she thought, he might have pushed it too far. Her people had arrived in a nick of time…if they hadn't…she didn't want to think of what might have happened to Cain and his forces.

"General Gilson…" Major Horace had been one of the heroes of the campaign on Garrison. He'd been a captain who found himself in command of a brigade before the fighting was done. After the battle, Gilson had promoted him and made him her top aide. "…I have one of General Cain's people with me."

She turned. Horace was walking down the hillside to her with a heavyset Marine following him. She read the small nameplate on the aide's helmet. "Captain Haney, I am glad to see you in one piece." She walked slowly toward the approaching figures. "How is your boss?"

Haney walked the last few steps toward Gilson and snapped to attention, always a clumsy affair in armor. "He is well, General Gilson."

"Can you get word to him that we have secured the surface?" She paused, then added, "It will be one less thing for him to worry about."

"Yes, general. Certainly." Haney's tone was distracted,

uncomfortable. "But first I have orders from General Cain.
I need to report to Admiral Garret and General Holm.
Immediately."

"Admiral, I didn't expect you to come down here." Cain
was surprised to see Augustus Garret walk into the room. The
admiral got around fairly well in powered armor, especially for
someone who wasn't a regular ground pounder. "Don't you
have a fleet to run or something?" It was highly irregular for
the fleet admiral to leave his flagship and go down to a planet's
surface. But Cain's shock quickly faded. He knew Garret well…
well enough to realize he shouldn't have been surprised at all.
"Or you, general." Elias Holm had come in right behind Garret.

"How could I not get a look at this thing you found?" Garret was standing on the edge of the catwalk, staring at the massive dish. "I've got the fleet on full alert, but we're going to have
to figure out what this dish is hiding. Soon."

"Yes, Dr. Hofstader and I were just discussing ways to…
um…disable the device."

"Well, knowing you, Erik, disable is probably code for chuck-
ing a fusion bomb in there." Holm took a quick glance at his
protégé then turned to face Hofstader. "What does the good
doctor think?"

Hofstader cleared his throat. "First, general, if I may ask…
is General Sparks coming down, sir? I believe his insight would
be extremely useful. His experience runs more to practical
application than my own."

"No, Friederich." Garret answered before Holm did. He
turned and looked at the scientist. "Admiral Jacobs has apparently captured an enemy vessel in System X2, and Admiral
Compton sent General Sparks to investigate."

Hofstader took a deep breath and looked over at the alien
structure for perhaps half a minute. Finally, he turned back
toward his companions. "If I must reach my own determina-
tion then I believe my thoughts are very similar to those you
ascribe to General Cain, though I might suggest we stop short
of a nuclear detonation." He took another breath before con-

tinuing. "We do not have time to analyze this device, seek a way to deactivate it." Another pause, longer this time. "We have to disable or destroy it. Immediately."

Garret nodded. "Unless there is another way to determine what this thing is screening, I am in full agreement." He looked over at Holm, then Cain. "It's just too big of a risk to leave it hidden." He turned to face Hofstader. "Do you think you can disable the dish, Friederich? Without nuking it, I mean."

Hofstader didn't answer right away. He turned back toward the edge of the catwalk and stared at the massive structure. "Yes, I think so." He continued looking out over the room. "Actually destroying it would be quite difficult...at least without employing weapons of power very close to a nuclear warhead." He turned back to face his companions. "But the power leads must be located underneath...and it is likely we can sever those far more easily than we could wreck the actual structure."

Garret stood still, staring at the ground for a few seconds before he looked up at Hofstader. "Do it." He glanced over at Holm, who was nodding his agreement. "Erik, can you see that Dr. Hofstader has everything he needs? I know your people are in rough shape and low on supplies, but General Gilson has two fresh brigades onplanet now. They are at your disposal."

"Yes, sir." Cain looked over at Hofstader. "Friederich and I will see it done, admiral."

Chapter 28

Bridge – AS Midway
System X2
75,000,000 Kilometers from X3 Gate

"All laser buoys fire!" Compton's voice reverberated across the flag bridge. He'd been waiting, watching for just the right moment. The enemy had been in range for several minutes, but he wanted them to get closer. The x-ray lasers were hard-hitting even at long range, but they were extremely powerful against close in targets.

Compton had followed the enemy closely on his scanners, looking for any indication they'd detected his buoys. He was ready to fire immediately at the slightest indication of evasive maneuvers, but the First Imperium fleet maintained its course straight for his ships. Directly toward the waiting laser buoys.

"Issuing fire order now, sir." Max Harmon sounded relieved. He was an experienced officer and a strong tactician, but he didn't have Compton's cool patience under fire. He'd have fired already if he'd been in command.

The signal took 5 seconds to reach the buoys. Their tracking systems had been constantly updating data feeds, maintaining fire locks on the optimum targets. Now, as one, 250 atomic bombs exploded. The immense energy released by each of them was contained, for a brief fraction of a second, by strong magnetic fields that directed it into the lasing mechanisms. Enormously powerful beams of focused x-rays lanced out, invisible fingers of death traveling at lightspeed, reaching their targets in a fraction of a second.

The two Leviathans were heavily targeted, and each one was buffeted with multiple blasts. The dark-matter infused hulls were highly resistant to normal laser fire, but the bomb-pumped x-rays tore into them and penetrated deeply into their interiors. The actual damage caused by each shot varied with the systems that were hit. Some ripped into non-critical areas of the ships, inflicting only minor damage. Others tore into vital sectors, causing secondary explosions and rupturing internal conduits and systems. Gasses and liquids spewed into space from the worst hit areas, freezing almost instantaneously as they hit the frigid vacuum.

The buoys had been programmed to prioritize the Leviathans, but the algorithms directing the AIs were complex. A platform with a significantly better shot at a Gargoyle targeted the smaller vessel instead, and a dozen of the mid-sized enemy ships were bracketed with fire. Five were hit by multiple shots and destroyed outright, and the rest suffered varying degrees of damage.

Compton leaned back in the chair, watching the damage reports scroll across his screen. Max Harmon was giving him verbal updates, but he wasn't really listening. His mind was calculating, adding up the damage inflicted and comparing it to his expectations. He was silent except for a quiet sigh. The buoys had done fairly well, but they hadn't been quite as effective as he'd hoped. He had really expected to take out one of the Leviathans completely, but they were both there, damaged certainly, but still moving toward his waiting ships.

"We've got to stop underestimating these guys." He was whispering, his voice barely audible. "We have to remember how far ahead of us they are, how tough their ships can be." His people had done an extraordinary job so far...but there was still a hell of a fight ahead.

"Let's go." Greta Hurley was terrorizing the flight deck. "I want those plasma torpedoes double loaded. All of them."

The maintenance crews were frantically refueling and reloading her bombers. The same scene was being repeated on every capital ship of the fleet. Hurley was harassing the crews of the other vessels over the com, which would have been marginally less intimidating if her promise to fly over to any ship that lagged and shoot the crew chief hadn't been so convincing.

"Sorry, admiral." Commander Simmons was the flight deck leader. "We can't move too quickly with these double shotted torpedoes. They're too volatile."

The overpowered plasma torpedoes were something she'd invented, or at least a modification she'd asked her tech crew to make. The gas that would be superheated into plasma was compressed at much higher pressure. More gas produced a larger, more damaging plasma. But the gasses were under so much pressure, the containment vessels bordered on unstable. Dropping one could easily cause an explosion. The nuke wouldn't detonate, and there would be no plasma, but it could still put a large section of the launch bay out of commission.

"Would you prefer to wait until the enemy particle accelerators tear this flight deck into scrap metal…along with the rest of Midway?" Hurley knew the deck commander was right, but she wasn't in the mood for excuses. She'd lost a quarter of her people in the first strike, and now she was taking them right back out. The least the support crews could do was load these damned torpedoes.

Midway had a fair amount of damage, but at least both flight decks were more or less intact. If she kicked a few asses she might get her birds back out in another 15 minutes. That required ignoring virtually every safety protocol, but she'd always been convinced those directives were written by desk jockeys anyway, fools who'd never been within ten lightyears of a real battle. Her people were the best, she'd always felt that way. Now they'd get a chance to prove it.

Hurley had reorganized her wings. She left any squadron over half strength the way it was. But she had a good number weaker than that, and three that were down to their last bomber. She combined those to make functional formations, trying to disrupt her chains of command as little as possible.

"Greta, can you give me an estimate on your readiness?"

She'd been leaning over a workstation reviewing her revised OB, but she straightened up and tapped the com. "Yes, Admiral Compton." She paused, just for an instant, trying to decide if her timing was realistic. "We'll be ready to launch in 15 minutes, sir."

Compton's first response was barely above a whisper, and she pretended not to hear it. "I have a pretty good idea how many complaints I'm going to be getting from the flight crews." He didn't laugh, not exactly. There wasn't time for that. But he was clearly amused...and pleased. "Greta, I'd say I'm surprised, but I shouldn't be by now, should I?" He took a quick breath and added, "Good job, Admiral Hurley."

"Thank you, sir." Hurley wasn't an officer who cared much for medals or honors, but the approval of a leader like Compton meant more to her than any other rewards. "We'll do our best for you, sir."

"I know you will, Greta. Don't let me keep you. Carry on."

She turned and looked out over the deck, panning her eyes from ship to ship. Her mood was still foul and impatient, but she was having trouble forcing the smile off her face. Praise from Compton was a rare and precious thing. Not quite as rare as a pat on the back from Admiral Garret, perhaps, but close.

"Let's get moving." She shouted across the deck instead of using the com. "We're launching in 14 minutes." There was no way Greta Hurley was going to let Admiral Garret down...no matter how hard she had to push her people.

Jaguar shook hard, rolling and pitching wildly until her maneuvering thrusters righted the ship. The particle accelerator had barely clipped her aft. The damage wasn't severe, but she'd lost some of her oxygen, and the blowout into space had given her the roll.

"Get us back on vector, Lieutenant Barrat." Duke's voice was worn and raw from the smoke permeating the ventilation system. The AI would have cleared the impurities from Jaguar's life support, but the scrubbers were damaged and operating on sharply reduced power.

"Yes, captain." Barrat sounded worse…just as hoarse, but rattled as well. Not many officers were as cool under fire as John Duke.

Barrat worked his controls, feeding instructions to the navigational AI. Jaguar's attack vector had been carefully plotted, but any release of pressurized gas or liquid into space imparted a velocity, skewing the ship's 3 dimensional vector. The automated system had stopped the rolling, but it hadn't fully corrected the primary thrust to restore the previous heading. That vector was straight at a wounded Leviathan…and Duke was planning to plant two plasma torpedoes in its gut.

"Correcting course now, sir."

The ship lurched, softly as the positioning thrusters fired and then harder when the main engines pulsed. The whole thing took less than a minute.

"We're back on our initial vector, captain." Barrat coughed again. The smoke was getting thicker. It wasn't really dangerous, at least not yet, but it was getting more annoying. "Range to target, 155,000 kilometers and closing at 9,000 kilometers per second."

Duke was in command of the entire task force, but he'd released his captains to seek out and attack their optimum targets. Right now he was wearing his hat as Jaguar's skipper, and his only concern was the Leviathan his ship was racing toward.

"Range to target, 120,000 kilometers."

Duke stared at the targeting scope. His gunners were good, and the closer he could get them, the better chance they had of landing the torpedoes right on the bullseye. They were well within firing range already, but he was going closer. Much closer.

"Passing 100,000 kilometers." Barrat knew Duke was planning on taking a good shot, but they were getting close. The enemy defensive fire was lighter than expected, but it was still dangerous. Jaguar had taken a couple hits already. They were both minor, but her luck would run out eventually.

Duke just sat still, his eyes focused on the scope. If Jaguar could score two direct hits here maybe, just maybe, they could finish off the immense enemy battleship. The First Imperium monster was badly damaged; that was obvious from the low rate of interdictive fire she was putting out. Scanners confirmed internal explosions and large areas of the ship without power. Duke's targeting was focused directly on the hardest hit area, the weak spot.

"We're under 80,000 kilometers, sir." Barrat's tone was getting edgier with each announcement. He looked over, but Duke's eyes didn't move from the scope. "Captain…"

"As you were, lieutenant." Duke sat rigidly as he addressed his nervous subordinate.

"We're at 55,000 kilometers, sir." The tactical officer's face was glistening with sweat. They were beyond point blank range now, closer than Barrat had ever seen a ship come to an enemy vessel.

Duke turned his head slightly, holding the mic from his com in front of his lips. "Fire."

"I want that Leviathan." Hurley's voice was loud, determined…almost bloodthirsty. "Duke got the other one, and by God, this one is ours."

In the end, her flight crews hadn't had her ships ready to go on time. But even with the extra five minutes, they'd done a monster job, and she knew it. She wondered offhand if that was the fastest turnaround on record. It had to be close.

"We've got six squadrons coming in on it, admiral." Wilder's job was piloting the command fighter, but he'd also been serving as an ersatz tactical officer for her. "They're stacked up in waves, and I've assigned them each an attack quadrant."

"Excellent, commander." She sat quietly for a few seconds. "And bring us around. We're going in with that attack."

Wilder paused, conflicted. He wanted to attack as badly as Hurley did, but he'd been instructed to keep her away from the fighting. He'd relented and agreed to fly up with the squadrons, but going on a close-range attack run would make a mockery out of Garret's orders. It wouldn't have been an issue – the original command fighter didn't have any weapons. But after he'd crash landed that ship on Midway, they'd been forced to change to another bomber, a fully armed one.

"No arguments, commander." Hurley knew she was putting him in a bad spot, but she didn't care. At least not enough to sit out the attack.

Wilder let out a deep breath. "Yes, admiral." He closed his eyes for a few seconds. I'm sorry, Admiral Garret, he thought... but she's right...we have to be part of this. "Prepare for 8g thrust."

The bomber shook as the thrusters fired, and Hurley and her crew were slammed back into their seats. The burst would be short, only 30 seconds or so...not worth dealing with the acceleration couches.

The "Lightning" fighter-bomber was a long sleek craft, though there was no need for aerodynamic efficiencies on a vessel built to fight in space. Most likely, it was simply the result of subconscious prejudices by the designers. Whatever the reason, the Lightning was one of the more attractive ships Hurley had ever seen. She often imagined a whole wing of them together, and they looked majestic and fearsome in her mind. In reality, of course, even the ships of a single squadron were spaced so far apart they were invisible to each other with the naked eye.

"Approaching final attack run." Wilder's voice pulled her out of her daydreaming. "We're going in with the third wave."

She glanced at her display, watching the reports of the first wave's assault as they came in. They'd lost half a dozen bombers on the approach. The Leviathan was badly hurt, but its point defense systems were still filling space with hyper-velocity projectiles. Her survivors came in fast and closed to point blank range. She saw hit after hit reported as the damage assessments poured in. The overpowered plasma torpedoes packed a hell of a punch, especially if they hit near an existing breach and didn't have to expend most of their strength blasting through the hull.

The second wave attacked on the heels of the first. The point defense fire was weakening, and only two ships were hit. Hurley was watching again as her people flew in close and unloaded their torpedoes into the guts of the wounded enemy giant. She was amazed how many hits the gargantuan vessel could take. Her people had scored enough hits to destroy five Yorktowns…and the Leviathan had been damaged already.

"Third wave going in." Wilder was excited now too, totally focused on the attack. His coerced violation of Garret's orders was forgotten, at least for now, and all he cared about was taking down the beast. "Would you care to take the shot, admiral?"

Hurley looked over at Wilder. She did want it…more than she could express. But it was poor conduct, she thought, to supersede an officer as capable as Wilder. "Thank you, commander, but it is your shot."

"I'd be honored, admiral, if you'd care to take it." He sounded sincere.

She knew he was full of it, that he was just being respectful. But she wanted it too badly to say no again. "Thank you, commander. Your gesture is greatly appreciated."

She pulled up the firing scope, staring into it as Wilder fired the engines to line the fighter up for the shot. There were numbers and symbols running up the screen on one side of the scope…data from the firing computer. The AI would actually provide most of the targeting data. Hurley would just inject a bit of gut feel, firing a bit early or late…or adjusting the trajectory a touch.

"The ship is yours, admiral."

She took over flight control as her workstation became live. The pilot was usually the gunner as well, and she couldn't take a proper shot unless she was flying the ship too. Her eyes were focused, her finger half-tensed on the trigger. She was going to wait another few seconds, but then she jerked her finger and fired almost immediately. It was a feeling, the instincts of a veteran.

Her torpedo launched and quickly closed the distance, slamming into the Leviathan dead center. She blasted the engine at 3g to change the vector slightly allowing the bomber to clear the immediate area of the enemy ship.

At least five other torpedoes hit the giant First Imperium vessel within 3 or 4 seconds. It stood there, drifting along in space, spinning wildly as internal explosions and material leaks impacted its previous vector. Hurley watched intently on the monitor, waiting, wondering if her people had done it.

Then the screen went bright white, answering her question immediately. The scanners were almost overloaded...and the massive enemy vessel was nothing but a rapidly expanding ball of plasma.

"Scratch one battlewagon." Her raw voice cracked as she screamed. She turned and looked over at Wilder. "Take us home, commander." She paused, a wicked grin on her face. "We're done here."

"Prepare the fleet for full forward thrust." Compton sat upright in his chair, a barely perceptible smile on his lips. Duke's and Hurley's people had performed phenomenally. Both Leviathan's were gone...the attack ships and the bombers each got one, so the battle honors were pretty even. "We will be accelerating at 30g in ten minutes."

"Yes, admiral." Harmon sounded surprised. He'd expected Compton to remain where he was and fight it out in place.

The enemy fleet was badly damaged...even critically wounded. But it was still dangerous. His fighters had flown two sorties and suffered 50% combined losses. John Duke was down to 28 attack ships still in operating condition. The fleet had expended all its missiles and laser buoys. There was nothing left but to finish off the enemy with an energy weapons duel. And Compton had no intention of sitting in place while the enemy raked his ships with their particle accelerators. He was going to close as quickly as possible to get his lasers in range too. Then, he thought, at least we'll have an honest fight.

Accelerating now would mean getting everyone in the couches. He didn't like having his people strapped in and drugged up in the middle of a battle, but this time there was no way out of it. Every kilometer he closed with the enemy was that much less time for them to ravage his ships before his people could return fire.

"All ships perform diagnostics on laser batteries and targeting systems." He snapped out the order. "I want every vessel ready to fire at full the second we're in range."

"Yes, admiral." Harmon's voice was crisp and confident. It had taken him a few seconds, but he understood what Compton was doing. He was amazed at how Compton's mind worked through each detail, every angle…trying to find any advantage he could gain. That's what makes him a legendary commander, he thought…and if the legends are true, such a good card player too.

Compton sat quietly for a few minutes before lying back as his chair converted itself to the acceleration couch that would keep him alive. Midway's massive engines would soon be blasting at over 30g, and that would create serious problems for anyone onboard who wasn't buttoned up.

This is it, he thought, lying back, eyes shut as the couch closed up around him…this is the death struggle. His layered attack had ravaged the enemy. There wasn't an undamaged ship in the force still heading for his fleet. But that didn't mean they weren't dangerous. The battle's won, he thought…as long as you don't make any mistakes and give it away.

Now go do the work, he thought, as he felt the massive kick of Midway's engine burn. He felt his consciousness slipping, his focus weakening…the drugs kicking in, their effect exacerbated by the intense pressure. He drifted off, his mind hanging onto that one thought…just do the work.

Chapter 29

Bridge – AS Pershing
Sigma 4 System
3,000,000 kilometers from Sigma 4 II

Garret sat in his command chair, staring impatiently at the main display while he waited for word from the planet. He'd pulled his ships out of orbit, and he wasn't going to move them back until he knew for damned sure what was hidden there. The fleet was in a dispersed formation, several hundred thousand kilometers from Sigma 4 II...just in case they uncloaked some type of fortress or superweapon and it came out blasting.

He hadn't withdrawn every vessel...Sarah Linden had demanded he leave three of her medical support ships in orbit, insisting that moving them would be tantamount to murdering several thousand of 1st Army's most seriously wounded troopers. He suspected she was exaggerating, but he wasn't going to argue with her...he trusted her judgment completely. And she was as stubborn as Erik Cain. However, the rest of the fleet was as safe as he could make it...at least until they knew what was important enough for the enemy to hide.

"Still nothing, sir." Commander Tara Rourke was new to Garret's staff. So far he was extremely pleased with her performance. He'd picked her to replace Max Harmon when he'd reluctantly given the recuperated Compton his tactical officer back.

Rourke had reprogrammed the scanners three times, sweeping the area for anything, even the slightest anomaly or trace of a signal. There was nothing. Whatever the enemy was hiding, their jammer was proof against human scanning technology. "Perhaps if I increase the probe overlaps to 100%?"

Garret sat for a few seconds, thinking silently. "Negative, commander." He paused, looking like he might change his mind, but then he shook his head. "There's no point wasting so many drones. We're not going to find anything until they knock out that jammer." He glanced at the chronometer. "Which should be just about any time now." He looked back at the glowing blue numerals of the clock. At least I hope it won't be much longer, he thought...what is taking you guys so long?

Garret had expected the signal by now, but there had been nothing but silence. He'd almost called down to the planet twice, but he stopped himself. Be patient, he thought...this is a huge job, and they'll get it done as quickly as they can.

"We're getting a signal, admiral." Rourke turned to look over at Garret. "It's from General Holm." Pershing was about 7 light seconds from planet, making conversations possible but annoying. But it didn't matter...Holm had just sent a one way message. "Transferring it to your com, sir."

"Very well, commander." Garret flipped a switch on his workstation and the familiar voice of Elias Holm was piped into his helmet.

"Augustus, sorry this took so long. This enemy equipment is amazingly complex." Holm's voice sounded a bit odd...edgy. Being around First Imperium technology tended to make people nervous, even when it wasn't actively trying to kill them. It was humbling to be surrounded by machinery built by a race that had been there thousands of years before.

"We're all set. Send a signal when you're ready, and we'll cut this thing's power. Hopefully." Holm chuckled softly. "Actually, Friederich is pretty sure he's located all the power conduits, so we expect this to work." Holm paused briefly. "Good luck up there, Augustus."

Garret looked over at Rourke. "Bring the fleet to red alert, commander."

Rourke acknowledged the order and relayed it to the rest of the fleet. Garret sat quietly, waiting until every vessel had responded. Grand Fleet, his half of it anyway, was ready for whatever was about to happen. As ready as he could make it, at least.

"Send a response to General Holm, commander." He took a deep breath. "We are ready. You are authorized to proceed as soon as you are able."

"Yes sir." Rourke sounded a little nervous herself. No one knew what was going to happen when the crews on the surface blew those power lines, and imaginations were running wild. "Message sent sir."

Garret leaned back and looked out over the flag bridge. Fighting and maneuvering in space require enormous patience, something he'd learned from 40 years at war. But now it was failing him…he was anxious, nervous.

"I have a confirmation from the planet, sir. They are cutting the power immediately."

"All ships…scanners on full power. Anybody falls asleep at their post, they're going to be scraping the inside of a fusion core." Garret was watching his own display as he spoke, waiting to see what happened when the enemy jamming was cut.

"Yes, sir. All vessels confirm…" Rourke stopped abruptly and snapped her head around. "We have a contact, admiral."

Garret was already staring at his screen. There it was, orbiting the planet's moon. It was fairly small, a sphere about 100 meters in diameter. "I see it, commander." The data was just starting to come in. It didn't appear to mount any weapons or engines, but there was a significant energy output. "Now if we can just figure out what it is."

The AIs were analyzing the data too, streaming updated information to the workstations. Garret was reading, ignoring most of what passed by his eyes, looking for something that might give a clue as to what the thing was. He finally focused on a small block of numbers followed by a few lines of text. He read it three times, unable to turn his eyes away. "Oh my God."

The admiral's conference room on Pershing was large. Located just off the flag bridge, it bore a superficial resemblance to the board room any large company might possess. On closer inspection it was quite different, and considerable concessions had been made to the needs of space travel and combat. The seats were plush but also designed for stability. Far bulkier than a terrestrial office chair, they had heavy straps and small med units built into them. The meeting chairs didn't convert into acceleration couches, but they did offer considerable protection to occupants at anything up to around 10g...and they could deliver a quick stim or anti-rad shot if it was needed.

Garret sat at the head of the table. The admiral's chair was bigger and more complicated than the others, connected to a sophisticated communications network tied into the fleetcom system. In theory, the admiral could direct the entire fleet, even fight a battle, from his chair. But Garret wasn't monitoring anything; he wasn't reading any reports. He was completely focused on the presentation he was watching. Friederich Hofstader was trying to explain the incredible device they'd just found.

"The object contains not just antimatter, but some previously unknown manifestation of highly concentrated antimatter." Hofstader couldn't hide the amazement in his voice. What he was describing was as far ahead of Earth science as a spaceship was over a canoe. "I have run several estimates, utilizing the data from our scans. The density of that material is approximately equal to that of Uranium 235. I cannot, as of now, even guess if we are dealing with actual anti-uranium or if it is some other form of antimatter entirely unknown to us." He took a deep breath before continuing. "It is theoretically possible, of course, to form any element on the periodic table from antimatter, however we have only been able to produce five of the smallest...and those only in trace quantities. The processes and energies required to produce large quantities of anti-elements with high atomic numbers are simply incalculable to us."

Hofstader was standing to the side of the table, his eyes moving from one occupant to the next. The sizable room was mostly empty, just a small cluster of occupied chairs at one end of the table. The gathering was small, but the subject matter was extremely important. They were discussing the most amazing artifact ever discovered by man...and trying to figure if there was a way to use it to defeat the enemy. Hofstader was nervous, and he didn't like trying to explain something so complex on so little research. He wished he had a year to study the alien device. Ten years.

General Holm was watching silently. He hadn't offered any comments or asked any questions. Holm was usually silent when the topic became highly technical. His leadership skills were beyond question, but Elias Holm had never been strong in the sciences, and he followed the discussion only with great difficulty. Though he'd never admitted it, he tended to be embarrassed by his lack of knowledge on the subject, which was one reason he kept his mouth shut.

Erik Cain was watching too. He had remained quiet as well, though his reasons were different from Holm's. Cain was able to follow Hofstader quite well. He'd enjoyed the sciences in training and at the Academy, and he was more knowledgeable than even his close comrades would have guessed. But Cain tended to be guarded, keeping what he knew to himself unless there was a compelling reason to do otherwise. It was habit, an offshoot of his suspicious, cynical personality.

Cameron Francis was Thomas Sparks' protégé, second in command of the Corps' research division. An accomplished and capable engineer, he'd always been overshadowed by his brilliant boss. He was sliding around uncomfortably in his chair. He understood Hofstader better than anyone else present, but he still felt inadequate to the task of filling Sparks' shoes. And he'd had even less time than Hofstader to examine the alien device.

"We already knew the enemy was well ahead of us, Friederich. Especially regarding antimatter." Garret was twirling a small stylus nervously as he spoke. He was concentrating on Hofstader, but his mind was also wandering to Compton and the rest of the fleet. He'd been surprised not to find them at Sigma 4, and he was concerned about what was going on in X1…or X2 or wherever Compton had gone.

"Yes, admiral, you are correct. However, this device and its contents are far beyond any other enemy technology we have seen to date." Hofstader glanced down at the 'pad he'd laid on the table. "Let me quote some figures to give a clearer insight into this device and its power. There is an inner sphere of antimatter held within the mechanism's magnetic fields. This…" He paused, fishing around for the right word. "…payload, for lack of a better term…is 48 meters in diameter, and it is 1.3 million tons in mass." He stopped, letting that sink in. "If that amount of antimatter is allowed to annihilate, the resulting explosion will measure approximately 50 petatons." Another pause. "Fifty million gigatons."

There was a long silence. Everyone in the room was staring at Hofstader, but no one spoke. Finally, Garret took a deep breath and said, "So, this is a bomb then. A very big one." There were a few very brief chuckles around the room. No one was in much of a mood for humor.

"Indeed, admiral, I believe you are correct. I cannot think of any alternative reason to go to the expense and risk of producing such dense antimatter unless the purpose was to make an astonishingly powerful, yet highly portable weapon."

Garret looked down at the table, his forehead wrinkled in thought. "I can't imagine it would be cost-effective for space combat. Certainly, it could destroy an individual ship of any size within a wide area. But I can't believe it would be worth this concentration of resources to accomplish that." He looked up at Hofstader. "And while I don't have a ready conception of the area of effect of a weapon like this, I still find it unlikely that more than one ship would be within its kill zone. Certainly no more than two." Navy ships were deployed at considerable distances from each other. Even a dense formation allowed at least a thousand kilometers between vessels.

"You are correct, admiral." Hofstader had already considered everything Garret was now going through…and in roughly the same order. "I have taken into consideration every permutation I could devise…and I cannot conceive of any purpose for this weapon. Save one." He panned around the room quickly before focusing on Garret. "I believe it is intended for use against enemy planets."

A ripple of soft whispers and deep breaths worked its way

around the table. Most of those present were nodding, having found their way to the same conclusion. Garret broke the near-silence. "So it's a planet destroyer?" It was half statement, half question.

Hofstader let out a deep breath. "Not technically, admiral. At least not in the sense of physically destroying an Earth-sized world. As large as this weapon is, vastly more energy would be required to accomplish that." Hofstader walked slowly along the edge of the table. "Although as a practical matter, I believe your statement to be correct. A detonation of that size would almost certainly destroy all life on a planet and render it perma-nently uninhabitable. Depending on specifics, it might also be sufficient to destabilize a world's orbit, with obvious cataclysmic consequences."

"Sowing the ground with salt." Cain's voice was soft, barely a whisper.

"What?" Garret turned and looked at Cain, just as everyone else was doing.

Erik looked up, startled from his musing. "Sorry. I didn't mean to say that out loud. I was just thinking."

"What were you thinking, Erik?" It was Holm this time. He'd been silent until now, but he wanted to hear Cain's thoughts.

"I was just thinking of the legend of Rome salting the ground where Carthage stood."

Everyone was staring at Cain, with varying levels of confu-sion. Garret was the first one to speak. "I think we're all famil-iar with the story, Erik. What does it have to do with our current situation or this new weapon?"

Cain shifted uncomfortably in his seat. He hadn't intended to get this involved in the discussion. "I was just thinking that this device may tell us something about the enemy. About what to expect going forward." He paused for a few seconds, but the expectant expressions all around pushed him on. "Destroying your enemy is one thing. I have to imagine…" He turned to face Hofstader. "…and tell me if I'm wrong Friederich…that it would be far more cost effective to build enough conventional nukes to lay waste to a planet and destroy all life on it."

"Yes, General Cain." Hofstader was nodding vigorously. "We can safely say that. By several orders of magnitude."

"So why build this thing?" Cain's voice was getting louder, more authoritative as he spoke. "I can think of only two reasons…and neither is good news with regard to our long term prospects of communicating or coexisting with them." Not that Cain had any desire to coexist with the First Imperium. He wanted to destroy them, exterminate every trace that they had ever existed. He knew that was likely impossible, but it was what he craved. Maybe in a thousand years, mankind would have the power…but first they had to find a way to survive the current war.

The room was silent, everyone focusing on what Cain was saying. "The first possibility is pure megalomania…a feeling of superiority so profound that they have a compulsion not only to defeat or destroy an enemy, but to do so in a spectacular manner. To display their might for all the universe to see." Cain took a deep breath and held it for a few seconds before exhaling. "The second possibility that occurs to me is paranoia. True, uncontrollable paranoia. A world that is saturation bombed with nuclear weapons can be rehabilitated, at least theoretically. But one that has been stripped of its atmosphere, massively irradiated, and probably seismically damaged…that is an enemy planet that will never again threaten you." Cain slid around uncomfortably in his chair as he finished speaking. He knew paranoia well. He controlled his own, kept it reasonably hidden…but Erik Cain agreed whole-heartedly with the concept of so completely destroying your enemies they could never again threaten you. He'd never had that power, but he knew if he ever did, he would use it.

The room was silent. Cain's points had been tangential to the primary topic, but they served to remind everyone present of the overall context…of what they were truly fighting.

"I believe I can add on more bit of analysis with regard to what we can derive from this device." Hofstader had broken the silence. His voice was soft, somber. "I think we need to realize that its existence supports one other extremely unpleasant assumption. This represents a level of technology well beyond anything else we have seen. I now believe it is highly unlikely that the vessels we have encountered to date represent the best the enemy has available…or even anything close to it. I would speculate that there are far stronger forces that we have not yet seen. If they possess a weapon of this power, I hesitate to even guess at what else they might have."

Hofstader's point hit everyone in the room. They'd been resigned to a fight against long odds, but the thought of even more advanced enemy forces was extremely demoralizing.

Garret broke the silence. He didn't really have anything to say, but he wanted to interrupt the somber musing. "Well, we will cross that bridge when we come to it." He shifted his glance down the table. "For now let's…"

"Admiral Garret, you have an urgent message coming in." Garret had removed his earpiece, so the AI was speaking on the open com.

"Yes, Nelson…what is it?" Garret answered in the open as well. There was nothing classified from the people in the room with him.

"We have received word from Admiral Compton. He has engaged enemy forces in System X2."

"Very well, Nelson. Transfer all available data to my command console." He looked up at his companions. "And issue a fleet order, Condition Yellow." He stood up and glanced down the table. "Gentlemen, I'm afraid we're going to have to cut this meeting short." He turned and walked quickly from the room.

"Admiral Garret, may I have a moment?" Hofstader stood in the open doorway, looking meekly into the admiral's office. "I know you are busy getting the fleet ready to move out."

"Of course, Friederich." Garret was motioning for the scientist to come in. "Have a seat. I always have time for anything you consider important." He pointed toward the two guest chairs facing his desk.

"Thank you, admiral." Hofstader walked from the door and sat down. The office was small, utilitarian. In a starship, especially a warship, space was always at a premium. Even the fleet admiral's office was small and cramped.

"What can I do for you, Friederich?" Hofstader had been sitting silently, apparently hesitant to begin what he'd come to say. "Is there a problem?"

"No, admiral." His voice was slow, tentative. "I have a plan...more of an idea than a plan, really." He paused, trying to decide how to proceed. "My plan...idea...whatever...is based on some of my former work. Former theories, actually. I have no real evidence to support it. But if it works, it could end the war immediately."

Garret had been half-gazing at his 'pad as he listened to Hofstader, but his head snapped up, and he stared right at the physicist. "Friederich, I don't care if something came to you in a dream last night after you ate a big dinner. If you have something in mind that can end this war I want to know about it...fact, theory, or wild guess." His eyes bored right into Hofstader's. "Immediately."

"It has to do with an extensive body of theoretical work I did some years ago regarding warp gates and their physical properties." He paused. "Without going into detail, it is my belief that the release of an extraordinary amount of energy inside a warp gate would cause a disruption that would..." He was looking for the right word. "...disable the gate."

"By disable, do you mean the gate would no longer facilitate transits? That the warp gate would be non-functional?" Garret couldn't keep the excitement out of his voice.

"Admiral, please remember that this is the wildest speculation on my part. I was never able to test any of these theories because we didn't have access to a sufficiently large energy source." He had been looking down toward the desk, avoiding the admiral's stare. But now he looked up, directly into Garret's eyes. "Until now."

"You are suggesting that we detonate the enemy device inside a warp gate?" It was a question, but Garret already sounded convinced.

"I wouldn't go so far as to suggest we actually do it, admiral. I just wanted to share my thoughts with you." His eyes dropped down again, and he continued nervously. "That device is of incalculable value, and I can offer no proof whatsoever that such a course of action would work. First, my theories may be utterly incorrect. Beyond that, we would need the time of detonation accurate to within a microsecond." He paused then added, "Even in the best of circumstances, it would be a considerable longshot, Admiral Garret."

Garret sat quietly for a minute, considering Hofstader's words. He knew the German scientist was a genius, considered brilliant even among his peers. He'd never been wrong about anything in the time Garret had been working closely with him. Hofstader seemed to have considerable doubts about his plan, but Garret began to realize he himself was convinced. "Is the disruption permanent?"

"Please understand, admiral. I cannot even guarantee there would be disruption. However, my theory is indeterminate on the duration of the effect. It could be permanent but, more likely, it would be temporary. There would be some degree of leakage from the gate. The trapped energy will dissipate over time. Nevertheless, I believe the period of complete disruption would last at least several centuries. Possibly longer."

"So if we detonate that thing in the gate between X1 and X2 we would cut the First Imperium off from human space for at least a few centuries?" Garret knew Hofstader would come back with another protestation about the untested nature of his plan, so he beat him to it. "Assuming your theories are correct?"

"Yes, admiral. And assuming they do not find an alternate route through space that is still uncharted by us." The tension in Hofstader's voice was obvious. "I was extremely reluctant to suggest this course of action but, as you have noted, if it does work we will have effectively ended the war. Or at least forced a hiatus of several hundred years. By then, perhaps our civilization will have gleaned sufficient technology from the enemy artifacts to face them on even terms." He left unspoken the selfish thought that it would also be someone else's problem.

Garret leaned back rubbing his face with his hand as he considered the options. He thought about calling another meeting, but he decided that wasn't necessary. He was in command, and he realized he'd already made a decision…one he wasn't going to change. There was too much upside not to try. They'd come here looking for some type of miracle…and Hofstader had just dropped in on his desk.

"Friederich…" Garret stared right at Hofstader as he spoke. "…well done. Do it." Another pause. "What do you need from me?"

Chapter 30

Alliance Primary Shipyards
Orbiting Wolf 359 V
Wolf 359 System

The Alliance's great shipyard at Wolf 359 was a series of orbital structures, majestic and immense, that dwarfed any other construct in space. The nearly endless series of factories, storage facilities, workshops, and space docks extended in a line over 180 kilometers in geosynchronous orbit, 110,000 kilometers above the system's fifth planet.

A gas giant, larger by a third than Jupiter, Wolf 359 V was a vibrant blue globe, the most distant of the worlds orbiting the red primary. Uninhabitable, and useful only for its gravitational hold on the shipyard facilities, it had long been unnamed, referred to only as planet 5. Eventually, the name Poseidon came into informal use, and some years later it was made official. Whether the name was motivated by the presence of the shipyard or the fact that the blue of the planet resembled the color of Earth's oceans is unclear.

The system's third planet was Arcadia, one of the Alliance's largest and most important colonies. A flash point of the colonial rebellions, Arcadia remained one of the most fiercely independent of the Alliance worlds. It had a diversified economy, but it had become more dependent on its proximity to the shipyards in the years since the rebellion. The Confederation Agreement that ended the insurrections also provided for control of the shipyards to pass to the colonies, and more and more workers from Arcadia had taken positions on the various production lines.

Before the First Imperium invasion, the shipyards had been garrisoned by a full battlegroup, but now, with all humanity allied against the enemy, those defensive forces had been redeployed to the front lines. There were only a few patrol ships on duty now, and those were second line units, not the veteran forces that had historically protected the complex.

"Attention Faulkner, this is Convoy Gamma Epsilon, inbound for Wolf 359 shipyard central docking…answering your query." The challenge by the patrol ship had been an automated one. Standard procedure.

Faulkner was a small vessel, an old suicide boat too obsolete to maintain its place in a front line fleet. Ensign Jon Cleon glanced at his scanner, then at the manifest on his workstation display. Convoy Gamma Epsilon…there it was…27 ships, just as expected. And right on schedule too.

"Convoy Gamma Epsilon, you are cleared for final approach to Wolf 359 central docking." Cleon make a cursory effort to hide the boredom in his voice. "You guys are right on time," he added. "Almost to the minute. Can't remember the last time that happened."

"Authorization received and acknowledged." The reply was quick, concise…and exactly what regulations specified.

Wow, Cleon thought, whoever's in charge of that convoy must be one hell of a nutbuster. He leaned back in his chair, glad he wasn't part of that crew.

The red light switched to green. The docking connection with the freighter was secure. "Open the hatch." The deck chief had a sleepy sound to his voice. It was late, at least simulated late. Orbiting a gas giant didn't offer much frame of reference for time of day, so the shipyards ran on an Earth normal clock. For an Alliance facility, that meant Eastern Standard Time.

The hatch was big…ten meters across by four high, and it made a heavy scraping sound as it slid open. "Let's go, you lazy sacks. We got a lot of unloading to do. They've been waiting for these reactor control units on the line." He dragged himself to his feet, turning and checking on the progress of his crew. "Hey! Let's go."

He heard footsteps coming from inside the freighter. They made an odd sound, like metal on metal. He was still trying to figure it out when a dozen hyper-velocity rounds ripped the top half of his body to shreds.

Armored soldiers poured out of the freighter, firing at the dock crew as they did. There were only 20 or so crew, and they were unarmed. It only took a few seconds for the attackers to wipe them out.

"Force A leader reporting. Dock Beta secured." The officer spoke clearly, sharply, with the relaxed confidence of a veteran.

"Very well, A Leader." The voice on the com was similar, almost eerily so. "You are to proceed to secondary objective and secure the area." There was a short pause. "Personnel at secondary objective are considered essential, so you are to utilize non-lethal ordnance in taking control of the area." Another pause. "Any maintenance or security personnel encountered en route are to be terminated."

"Yes, Control. Orders received and understood." He turned and walked across the open bay. "Force A Leader, out."

"All security forces, Condition Red. I repeat, Condition Red."

"What the hell?" Ian Jones leapt off his bunk, almost tripping in the process. He hadn't been asleep, just relaxing. His team was scheduled to go on duty in a little over an hour. He hopped through the door on one foot, pulling his boot on as he did.

His team was in the outer barracks doing much the same. They were in uniform, mostly, but they were standing around raggedly, confused expressions on their faces. "What's up, Cap?" Hank Young was the first to ask, but they were all looking at him expectantly.

"I don't know anything you boys don't." They all knew what Condition Red meant. It was an all-hands call to duty. It meant the complex had been boarded by hostile forces. "Just get your asses in gear, and we'll all know soon enough." He walked over to a large cabinet on the wall and punched a combination into the keypad. His people were normally armed with stun pistols, but not during a Condition Red alert. The cabinet slid open, revealing a long row of neatly stacked assault rifles.

Jones grabbed the first rifle and started toward the door. "Let's go. You guys waiting for a written invite?" He tapped the pad to open the door and looked back over his shoulder. His people were lining up at the weapons locker, grabbing their rifles and moving up behind him.

Jones had no idea what could be going on. The Powers weren't at war; they were allied against the First Imperium. And that fight was almost 200 lightyears away. Who could be invading the shipyard complex? He was still wondering that when he jogged through the door and out into the corridor.

"Control, this is Force A Leader." He was standing on a wide catwalk, looking out over the massive bay. A 600 meter long hull stretched almost out of sight into the distance. It was a Boise-class cruiser, undergoing heavy repairs. Most of the work at the shipyards was done in the outer spacedocks, but some tasks were more easily completed in a pressurized environment. "All Sector A primary objectives secured."

"Very well, A Leader. Continue report."

"All engineering and skilled technical personnel we have encountered have been confined in one of the empty bays. We have penetrated the main AI's security and are identifying all confined individuals. I have search parties out looking for unaccounted essential personnel." He looked out over the docked cruiser. His people were still searching the ship...a stubborn group of security troopers had retreated this way, and he wasn't about to move forward if they were hidden behind his force.

"Excellent, A Leader. Report on armed resistance."

"In general, the security forces have been easily destroyed with minimal losses to our units." He paused. He had to report something that had been unexpected. "There is one security team that has been considerably more difficult to destroy than the others. My forces are currently in pursuit."

"Understood A Leader." There was a pause...possibly a discussion taking place on the other end. "You are to prioritize the
neutralization of enemy security forces. All such personnel are
to be terminated on sight."

"Yes, Control. Understood."

"These guys are pros." Ian Jones was out of breath, his
shoulder drenched with his own blood. The hyper-velocity
round had only clipped his shoulder, but it almost took off his
arm. "If I didn't know better, I'd swear they were Marines."

Jones knew the Marines well. They'd plucked him out of
the slums of Bristol, and offered him a chance at making their
grade. He did five years of Marine training, but he washed out
because he suffered from extreme claustrophobia. He simply
couldn't handle being entombed in a suit of powered armor,
and none of the counseling had solved the problem. The Corps
had reluctantly sent him packing with an honorable discharge as
a private and a letter of recommendation. That had opened the
door to virtually any security job in occupied space.

"You've got to get word to Arcadia. They've got control
of this place already. I'm pinned down with half a dozen of
my people, but I can't raise any other security teams." He was
speaking to the only admin office he could still reach, trying to
get word out about what was happening. He was propped up
against the wall, holding his rifle with his good hand. The pain
in his shoulder was unbearable. Every word he spoke was a
torment.

Jones had been a guard captain for a little over a year. He'd
been hired to do two years on the job and then take over the top
security position in the shipyards. Now it looked like he was
going to die in this cargo hold.

He could hear the sound of metal pounding on metal.
"They're coming." He spat the words into the comlink. "You
have to reach Arcadia."

There was a large explosion, and the door blasted inward,
hanging loosely, still connected at one corner. He could see the

shadowy shapes outside, moving closer. Then the fire, rounds zipping into the room...his people going down, one by one.

Finally it was just him, leaning behind the desk, trying desperately to hold the rifle up so he could fire. Then more pain, then none. Just wetness on his chest, his gut. Then haziness, floating...darkness.

Chapter 31

Bridge – AS Pershing
System X2
3,000,000 miles from the X1 Gate

"General Cain and Dr. Hofstader will be in position with the device in approximately eleven hours, admiral." Tara Rourke was turned around, facing Garret. "They will advise when they are prepared and then await your further orders."

Hofstader had hastily constructed an attachment to the First Imperium device. It was a small explosive that would destroy the power source keeping the magnetic fields in place. When the fields dropped, the antimatter would instantaneously begin annihilating with any matter it encountered. Hofstader had jury-rigged a shell of high density matter, mostly highly radioactive elements, around the exterior of the alien device, providing a sufficient mass to pair off with the antimatter and insure a rapid release of the full energy potential. It was a rushed effort, and one he hoped to have time to improve upon before it was needed.

"Very well, commander." Garret had been quiet and thoughtful since his half of Grand Fleet transited into X2. Compton's ships were far across the system, near one of the two egress warp gates. The two forces were almost 2 lighthours apart, which was doing nothing to facilitate communication. "Nelson, estimated time for a response from Admiral Compton?" Garret had sent Compton an extensive communique, filling him in on the plan, and directing him to move his fleet back toward the X1 gate. That had been about 3 ½ hours before.

"Assuming Admiral Compton received your message and responded immediately, the transmission should reach us within a range of 8 to 18 minutes, the margin provided to account for the unpredictability of human response times."

Garret sighed softly. He'd worked closely with his AI for many years, and the personality module had been uniquely attuned to him...at least until Alliance Intelligence had sabotaged the system, destroying the persona that had been Nelson. The AI managed to save a portion of its personality kernel, but Garret had always felt the reconstituted system had lost something. He tended to use it far less frequently than he once had.

"Admiral Garret, we're getting a transmission from Admiral Jacobs on Indianapolis." The remains of Scouting Fleet had been pulling back toward the X1 warp gate. Jacobs had wanted to rejoin the main fleet, but Compton ordered him to withdraw instead. His force had the highest casualty rate of any formation in the campaign, and Compton wasn't going to ask any more of his men and women...unless he had no choice. They'd done their part.

"Very well, Commander Rourke." Garret's voice was still vaguely distracted; he'd been reviewing the latest message from Hofstader in X1. But his focus snapped back instantly. "On my com, commander."

Garret listened to the message, and Rourke could tell from his expression it wasn't good news. He turned his head toward his workstation screen and pulled up the system map.

"Commander, bring the fleet to Condition Yellow. All ships are to prepare for maximum thrust within 15 minutes." He looked back down at the workstation for a few seconds then lifted his head, flipping on his com as he did. "Attention all personnel. Admiral Jacobs is reporting enemy forces inbound from the X4 warp gate. The First Imperium force is inbound at 0.08c and decelerating rapidly. We will be moving to meet them. I know each of you will do you very best...as you always have. Garret out."

He turned to Rourke. "Advise all captains to perform a complete program of weapons diagnostics and to prepare a full spread of x-ray laser buoys for deployment. All battleships are to perform pre-flight checks and hold all bomber squadrons at Status Yellow."

"Yes, sir." She'd turned to her workstation and started forwarding Garret's orders as he was still firing them off. "Admiral..." She turned back toward Garret. "I have Admiral Compton's message incoming. Forward it to your com, sir?"

"Yes, commander. By all means." Then softer, a whisper to himself. "Let's see what Terrance has to say. I haven't spoken with him since he grabbed half my fleet and took off." There was a tiny smile on his face. He was looking forward to seeing his old friend once the fight here was over.

"Motherfucker." Compton immediately realized his voice had been a lot louder than intended. Fucking Cleret, he thought, making certain to keep it to himself this time. Not a God-damned message from X4...not a drone, not a ship returning. Nothing...except enemy forces transiting into the system.

Mike Jacobs warned me, he thought bitterly...he told me Cleret couldn't be trusted. The diplomacy we need to keep the Pact together may end up being the reason we lose this war, he thought.

Compton had just listened to Jacobs' message. He knew Scouting Fleet's commander would have advised Garret as well. Indianapolis and the battered remnants of the advance force were roughly equidistant between the two main Pact fleets. There wasn't a question in his mind that Augustus Garret was already moving to fight the new arrivals. He was going to do the same. The First Imperium forces would be sandwiched between his and Garret's forces. For once we've got the advantage, he thought with grim satisfaction.

Augustus should have my confirmation by now. He'd gotten Garret's message a couple hours before. He'd had to read it four times before it sunk in. The possibility of disrupting a warp gate seemed impossible, unreal. But if Friederich Hofstader said it could be done, that was enough for Compton. He knew there were a lot of uncertainties, but it was hard not to get excited. If

Hofstader was right, all they had to do was defeat this new force, and both fleets could withdraw, blowing the gate behind them. The First Imperium would be cut off from human space. The war would be over…not won, exactly, but survival seemed as good as victory considering the circumstances.

Max Harmon's voice pulled him from his thoughts. "Admiral Compton, we have vessels transiting through the X3 warp gate." A pause. "Three ships, working on IDs now." He snapped his head toward Compton. "It's Captain Mondragon, sir. Incoming message." He forwarded the transmission to Compton's com without asking.

"Admiral Compton, Captain Mondragon reporting." He sounded haggard, out of breath. "I have to report another enemy task force approaching the warp gate roughly 15 minutes behind us. Approximately 20 Gargoyles."

"Understood, Francisco." Fuck, Compton thought. He knew his ships could never outrun a First Imperium fleet, and he wasn't about to let these enemy ships end up on his rear. We'll have to stand here and engage that force, he thought… Augustus will have to handle the X4 fleet himself.

"Captain, maintain velocity and rejoin Scouting Fleet. Once you are there, advise Admiral Jacobs that the combined force is to withdraw toward the X1 warp gate." Mondragon's 3 survivors all had damage. His battered force had already done their part, and they had nothing left to give. Compton was impressed with the Europan captain, especially considering everything Jacobs had already told him. He was damned sure going to pin a few medals on Mondragon and Jacobs. If they both survived, that is.

"Yes, Admiral Compton." Mondragon's reply sounded sharp, but he couldn't hide his fatigue. "Mondragon out."

Compton turned toward Harmon's station. "OK, Commodore Harmon. We don't have much time." He was glad he'd brought up the transports and rearmed the fleet right after the last battle. He'd hate to face any First Imperium force with only his standard lasers. "I want all ships ready to deploy laser buoys in five minutes." It wasn't enough time…Compton knew that.

He also knew it was going to have to be…that was all they had.

Francisco Mondragon looked like hell. Most of his task-force was gone, and the survivors had been trapped deep in the X3 system. They'd tried to hide for a while, but when new forces moved into the system bound for the X2 gate, he knew he had to get word to Compton. He tried to launch a spread of drones – his last – but none of them got through. So he buttoned his people in the couches, fired up the reactors to 120%, and made a run for the gate. He started with 8 ships…3 made it.

He wasn't sure if any of his other ships had survived. He'd scattered the task force, giving each captain orders to hide in the deep outer system. He'd reassembled everyone he could find, but it was possible there were others out there somewhere, now trapped behind the lines. There was nothing he could do about that, not now. All he could do at the moment was follow orders and rejoin the remnants of Jacobs' fleet.

He'd gotten through the warp gate just ahead of the enemy task force, but before his ships transited he picked up some intermittent contacts from probes deeper in the system. He couldn't be sure, but his gut told him there were more enemy ships behind the ones transiting now. He had no idea if the contact was real…or how large a force might be there. But he'd reported all he knew to Compton. It was the fleet admiral's problem now, he thought. There wasn't much Mondragon could do with 3 battered suicide boats.

"Captain, I've got Admiral Jacobs on the com." Carp sounded as tired as Mondragon felt.

"Put it through, commander." Mondragon put his earpiece in. It made his earlobe sore if he left it in for too long, so he tended to remove it from time to time.

"Captain Mondragon, you have done an outstanding job, and I know what you and your people have been through." Jacobs sounded exhausted too. All of Scouting Fleet had earned its pay…no one could doubt that. All except Pierre Cleret, whom Jacobs fully intended to stand in front of a firing squad if, through some miracle he made it back.

"We've been ordered to reposition to the captured enemy vessel and provide any support General Sparks may require. I am sending you revised coordinates. Revector your approach and join us there as soon as you are able. Jacobs out."

Mondragon looked over at Tomasino. "Confirm receipt of orders, lieutenant." Jacobs' ships were still almost 30 light minutes away, much too far to allow for a normal verbal exchange. "And forward incoming coordinates to the other ships. We will be executing course change in five minutes."

Camille Harmon sat in her command chair, leaning heavily to her left, trying, as always, to get comfortable. Ever since she'd been shot on her own bridge in an Alliance Intelligence assassination attempt, the pain in her back had been constant. The med team pulled her through, though she'd come very close to not making it. But they hadn't been able to regenerate everything the explosive bullet had destroyed. Her spine was a combination of regrown organic tissue and machinery. It worked well, but it hurt like hell most of the time. It was the integration of the mechanical parts with her central nervous system, they told her. The painkillers made it bearable, more or less. They'd offered her stronger meds, but she wouldn't take anything that might impair her judgment. She preferred to put up with the pain than allow that.

"The taskforce is in position, admiral." Clyde Dawes had proven to be an excellent tactical officer for her. He'd been a bomber pilot, one of the best. But his vessel had suffered a critical malfunction in a training mission. He'd brought the crippled bomber in for a hard landing, but he'd lost his arm in the crash. At the hospital they found a genetic anomaly, a rare disorder that precluded regeneration or even sophisticated nerve graft prosthetics.

Harmon wasn't sure whether she'd picked Dawes for his record or because she sympathized with another broken toy. But whatever the motivation, it had proven to be the right choice. Even with a mechanical arm 150 years out of date, Clyde Dawes was one hell of a capable officer.

"Very well, commander." Garret had divided his fleet into two waves and put Harmon in charge of the forward units. Her orders had been to advance, drop a line of laser buoys, then pull back and prepare to launch fighters. Garret was doing the same, 500,000 kilometers back. They were creating a deep layered defense. The enemy would be under constant attack as they advanced. "Advise Commodore Kessel that I will be issuing the launch order in five minutes." Garret had kept Captain Al'Sabat to command his wings, giving Harmon the CEL's top pilot to lead hers. The crews were already on alert, manning their ships and waiting for the order to go.

"Yes, admiral." There was a short pause then: "Commodore Kessel reports all squadrons ready to launch."

She glanced down at the tactical screen. My God, she thought...Garret really is a genius. Harmon was considered an excellent tactician, but Augustus Garret in an admiral's chair was like Mozart at a keyboard. There was a natural comprehension, a visualization that others lacked...that they could never understand. Genius was an overused word, but it was the only way to describe Garret.

The enemy would enter the range of her laser buoys in about fifteen minutes. Then Kessel's fighters would go in...just before the enemy hit Garret's line of x-ray lasers. By the time the First Imperium ships had gotten through Garret's fighters, and both force's missile barrages, Compton's fleet would be hitting them from the rear with its own fighters and missiles. If everything went according to plan, they would never have to withstand the enemy particle accelerators. There wouldn't be a First Imperium ship left to fire one.

Still, something was troubling her. When, she thought to herself, was the last time you saw anything go according to plan?

"Sir, Commodore Al'Sabat is requesting permission to launch another sortie. His ships will be rearmed and ready in ten minutes." Rourke had really proven herself to Garret. She'd been a rock during the battle, one of the best tactical officers he'd ever had. A fitting replacement for Max Harmon.

Garret was still distracted. He'd had a scare a few minutes before when Harmon's flagship was blasted with radiation from an antimatter warhead...one that had come way too close. Yorktown had taken considerable damage, but she was still in the fight...and Camille Harmon was still in her command chair.

Garret frowned. He hated sending Al'Sabat's people right back out there. He hadn't expected it to be necessary. But then he'd planned on Compton hitting the enemy rear by now... instead of being stuck out at the X3 warp gate fighting yet another enemy task force. "Authorize the commodore to prep another attack." He glanced at the tactical display. "And prepare the fleet to pull back 500,000 kilometers."

It was a clear choice. Send the fighters in or expose the capital ships to a lopsided energy weapons duel. Garret felt bad, but the cold truth was the squadrons were more expendable than the battleships. The bomber crews knew that better than anyone.

"Order Admiral Harmon to launch a second sortie with her fighter wings as well."

"Yes, sir."

Garret stared at the display. His forces had done well so far. The enemy was badly battered. Even without Compton's fleet, he knew he could probably take them out before they closed and raked his ships with particle accelerator fire. It would cost him in fighters and missiles, but he knew it was the right choice.

"Admiral Harmon has already launched a second attack, sir."

Garret smiled. He'd known Camille Harmon for a long time, ever since she was a captain commanding one of the ships of his task force. She had a reputation as a savage fighter, one he knew was well deserved.

Now, he thought, let's see if we can finish this...then Terry's people can get back here and we can get the hell out of this system...and blow that damned warp gate behind us.

"Launch bombers."

Chapter 32

Bridge – AS Midway
System X2
1,500,000 Kilometers from X3 Gate

"Joker, give me another stim." Terrance Compton sat quietly in his command chair, trying to fight the urge to slump forward. "Make it a double dose."

He felt the injection, as his AI instructed the med system to give him the stimulants he'd requested. Joker would normally have at least reminded the admiral that he was well over the safe dosage, but now wasn't the time. Compton was under enormous pressure, and Joker understood that and acted accordingly.

"Max, get those transport shuttles launched. I want the laser buoys loaded first. We don't have much time." Fatigue was wearing away formality.

The fleet had destroyed the Gargoyles, but his ships had drawn heavily on their ordnance to do it. The support task force had reloads, but it took time to transfer to the warships. Time they didn't have.

"Yes, sir." Harmon had already been coordinating the rearming. He was as tired as Compton, his mind fighting hard to drive away the cloudiness. He'd just taken his own dose of stims. Without them he wouldn't have been able to stay sharp… and now was no time to let efficiency slide.

"And I want every ship ready for full thrust in 60 minutes." There was a sharp edge to his voice that hadn't been there before. "I need no-bullshit assessments. Any ship that can't be ready is to be evacuated."

"Yes, sir." Harmon had already advised all ship captains that they were to abandon ship if they couldn't be ready for 30g thrust on time. But he knew someone would inevitably over-estimate what could be repaired in an hour. He wondered if Compton would make good on his threat to leave them behind.

Grand Fleet was bugging out. Once everyone had transited into X1, Hofstader would blow the warp gate...and if his theories held, disable the thing for at least a few centuries. The war would be effectively over, with no known route remaining between human and First Imperium space.

It would take about 44 hours for Compton's fleet to reach X1 and transit. In two days the war would be over. At least that was the plan.

"Sir, we're receiving orders from Admiral Garret." Harmon was reading from his display. "He is confirming our scheduled course and timing."

Way ahead of you, Augustus, Compton thought, a tiny smile on his face...no one wants to get out of here more than me. "Confirm that we will begin initiated thrust plan as scheduled."

"Signal dispatched, admiral." Harmon's eyes were focused on his screens. "First wave of supply shuttles launched."

"The first wave is going to be the only one, I'm afraid. I want those laser buoys offloaded and secured in half an hour, I don't care if it takes every man and woman on those ships to do it." He wanted his fleet as ready for action as possible...but nothing was stopping them from blasting for the X1 warp gate in an hour. He looked at the chronometer. No, 58 minutes.

"What the hell is that?" Mike Jacobs stared at his screen in horror. "Is this some sort of malfunction?" It had already been a nightmare. He'd been watching First Imperium ships exit the X4 warp gate for the last 20 minutes...hundreds of them. But this...this was like nothing he'd ever seen before.

"Scanners are functioning properly, sir." Carp didn't sound any better than Jacobs. He was staring at the readouts on the gargantuan vessel just as Jacobs was. "Estimated length, 18.7 kilometers, mass 4,650,000 kilograms."

"Have you confirmed that data, commander?" Jacobs sounded incredulous. He understood what he was being told, but he couldn't quite absorb it all. A battleship with twenty times the mass of a Yorktown B? He'd never conceived of such a thing. He couldn't begin to guess at the weaponry a ship like that mounted, especially considering the overall level of First Imperium technology.

"Forward all incoming data to Admirals Garret and Compton." He glared over at Carp. "I mean the instant it comes in, commander!"

"Yes, sir. Understood." Carp's voice was raspy. The young officer sounded like he had to struggle to draw a deep breath. It was tension, fear. This enemy vessel was like something out of his darkest nightmares.

The remnants of Scouting Fleet were en route to the X1 warp gate, but they were still the closest formation to the X4 gate, the first to pick up the new enemy force pouring through.

Jacobs stared at the display. Fucking Cleret, he thought, not a word...not a bit of warning...stupid bastard probably got his entire command blown away without even getting a drone back to report. He felt the rage coursing through his body, his hands balled in pointless fists as he sat and watched doom rush into the system. He'd have cut the Europan captain's throat if he'd been standing there, just for the sheer pleasure of watching the useless fuck bleed to death.

The enemy fleet was moving at 0.08c. That was fast...too fast. Jacobs did a quick calculation. His ships were close enough to the X1 gate to escape...and Garret's too. But there was no way Compton's fleet could accelerate enough to get through the system before they were cut off. And even the combined Grand Fleet was no match for the enemy forces already in the system... and there were more still transiting. Jacobs thought of Garret and Compton, wondering what they would do, grateful that he wasn't in command, that the decision wasn't his to make. He couldn't even guess at what decisions he would make in that situation.

"Sir, Captain Mondragon requests permission to change his

vector to get a close in scanner sweep of the enemy battleship. Carp's voice sounded strange. He knew Mondragon was asking permission for a suicide mission, and he was wondering what Jacobs would say.

Jacobs sat silently. He wanted more data...he knew Garret and Compton needed all the info he could get them. But he realized Mondragon would just throw his life and the lives of his crews away. They'd never get close enough to get useful data. Jacobs knew in his gut he would have said yes if they had any chance at all to succeed. He might have even ordered Mondragon to go. But it would be a senseless waste.

"Advise Captain Mondragon permission is denied. He is to continue on his present bearing toward the X1 warp gate." We've lost enough lives in this war, Jacobs thought...no need to throw away more for no gain.

Jacobs knew there was nothing he could do other than report his findings up the line. This was Garret's and Compton's problem. He had a bad feeling about what they would be forced to do, but it was out of his hands. Michael Jacobs had never been more grateful to be powerless in his life.

"Admiral Compton's fleet will never make it to the X1 gate before the enemy is in range."

Rourke was speaking to Garret, but he was only half listening. He'd already come to that conclusion. His mind was racing, trying to think of what to do...but he knew it was fruitless. He'd already realized the only way the thing could end. He didn't know how he could possibly bring himself to actually do what he knew had to be done.

The forces advancing through the system were almost beyond conception. Over a thousand ships had transited, including 20 of the massive new behemoths. Now it was all clear to Garret. Their earlier victories, the successful defenses on the Line...they had awakened the wrath of a vengeful giant. Now they were looking at the true might of the First Imperium. And it was as grim as death incarnate.

The enemy fleet was a vastly stronger force than his fleet

could face...orders of magnitude beyond anything all the might
of humanity could stand against. Against this vast array of
First Imperium power, all the force mankind had ever mustered
would be little more than a forlorn hope. It was pure mathematics...and no amount of courage, no stroke of luck, no brilliant
tactic...would make the slightest difference. If that fleet transited into X1, all would be lost. His ships couldn't outrun a First
Imperium fleet...there would be no second chance to disrupt a
warp gate and block off human space. And that was now the
only hope.

"Instruct Dr. Hofstader and General Cain to position the
device for insertion into the X1-X2 warp gate."

"Yes, admiral." Rourke's voice was strained, somber. She
didn't envy Garret the crushing responsibility of command. She
was an ambitious officer, but she never wanted to sit in Garret's
chair. She couldn't imagine how a single man could bear so
much burden.

"The fleet will prepare to withdraw toward the warp gate."
There was no emotion in Garret's voice. Just fatigue as deep and
black as space itself.

It was time. He could end the war in the next few hours. All
he had to do was sacrifice his best friend...run and leave behind
the man he'd called brother for forty years. Abandon him and
his 40,000 crew to certain death.

Garret felt cold inside, lifeless. He was on autopilot, issuing
the commands, prepping the fleet for the unthinkable. Everything would be ready. But Garret had no idea how he'd bring
himself to issue that final order.

Terrance Compton sat quietly in his command chair, staring
at the incoming data, but not really absorbing it. None of it
mattered. Not anymore. He knew what they had to do. What
Garret had to do.

He looked around the flag bridge, watching his staff working
at their stations. A few of them had figured it out for themselves. Max Harmon certainly had. His expression was somber,
but he was still focused on his duties. Still, Compton could

tell he knew they were doomed. Harmon was a good officer, one of the best Compton had ever seen. Most of the others were still trying to grasp the scale of the enemy fleet they faced, wondering what miracle Garret and Compton would produce to salvage things.

Compton laughed bitterly. There is a miracle, he thought, but this one carries a high cost...one we will have to pay ourselves.

He tried to imagine what Garret was thinking. He knew how difficult this was for his friend. In some ways, he thought, it is easier to face death than to send someone else to do it. Terrance Compton wanted to go home...he wanted to survive the war. He wanted to walk the green hills of the Academy again, looking up at the massive domes...and the beauty of space beyond. But he knew it was not to be. He'd been prepared to face death in battle for most of his life. If now is the time, he thought, I am ready...and saving all of humanity isn't such a bad reason to die.

There was one last thing he could do for Garret, though. He could send a message, tell his friend he understood. Try to take some of the burden off of his shoulders...deflect some of the guilt he knew would torment Garret.

"Commander Harmon, all ships are to perform complete engine and weapons diagnostics immediately. And I want all vessels fully rearmed. I expect Admiral Garson to do wonders with the transport task force. I want this fleet 100% ready for action in two hours. Understood?"

"Yes, sir." Harmon felt a surge of pride. He knew very well if Terrance Compton was going down, he was going down fighting. And he felt the same way.

Now, Compton thought, closing his helmet and activating the com...it's time to say goodbye to Augustus.

"Please, General Sparks." Jacob's voice was raw, pleading. "You have to board the shuttle now. There's no time left." Jacobs' people had evacuated the engineering crews working on the captured enemy vessel. They'd made a mighty effort to rig the ship for towing, but there just hadn't been time. They'd have to abandon it. That was something that seemed unthinkable a few days before, but Jacobs found it hard to give a shit in light of what was happening with Admiral Compton and his people.

The rest of Scouting Fleet's survivors had blasted off toward the warp gate already. In another 20 minutes, they'd all be in the X1 System. But Indianapolis had stayed behind, waiting for General Sparks and the last of his crew.

"Ten more minutes, admiral." Sparks was onboard the enemy ship, scavenging every portable instrument and recording anything he could for future research. Even if they managed to end the war by disrupting the warp gate, the ship offered centuries of scientific progress. Sparks wanted to salvage anything he could. It was killing him to leave it behind.

"No, general." Jacobs understood the engineer's devotion to his work. But they were out of time. "We have to leave. I need you on that shuttle immediately."

Jacobs was close to sending his Marines to drag Thomas Sparks to the shuttle. He and Sparks were of equivalent rank, and they were in space, which made him the superior…but he wasn't sure his Marine detachments would follow an admiral's order to arrest a Corps general.

There was a pause. "Very well, admiral." Sparks' voice was distracted. "We will be in the shuttle in 3 minutes. Is that satisfactory?"

"Yes, general. That will be perfectly fine." He turned toward Carp. "Prepare a thrust plan to take us directly through the gate. We'll be accelerating at full thrust." That meant being stuck in the couches, but Jacobs wanted to get the hell out of this accursed system as quickly as possible. "We'll be executing as soon as General Sparks' people are secured aboard."

"Incoming message from Admiral Compton. It's marked for your eyes only, sir." Rourke's voice was shaky. Everyone knew what was happening, and just the thought of Compton was enough to bring a veteran spacer to tears.

The rest of the fleet had already transited. Pershing was alone, 200,000 kilometers from the warp gate. They'd been sitting there for 20 minutes, waiting for Garret's orders. But the fleet admiral had been silent, sitting rigidly in his chair, a stony, unmoving expression on his face.

"Send it to my com, commander." His voice was dead, lifeless.

"Yes, sir. Transferring now."

Garret flipped the com switch, closing his eyes as Compton's voice filled his headset. "Hello, Augustus." The transmission had visual as well as audio. Compton was sitting there, a weak smile on his face.

"You have to go, Augustus." Compton's voice was firm, remarkably so considering the circumstances. "Get your fleet through the warp gate and blow that thing."

Garret heard the words coming through the com, he saw his old friend's face on the monitor. Compton sounded rational, reasonable. He could have been discussing an exercise. But Garret saw the facts behind his friend's words, stark and naked. Compton was telling Garret to leave him behind...him and over half of Grand Fleet...to strand them here with the massive First Imperium force.

Garret stared into the screen, his eyes a plea for salvation. For the first time in his long and storied career, Augustus Garret would have gratefully dumped his responsibilities on someone else. Anyone.

"I wish we could have a conversation about this, my old friend. One last talk...a few minutes to chat about the old days, maybe." The calm rationality of Compton's voice was cutting into Garret like a dull knife. "But space is a harsh mistress, and two light hours might as well be the other side of the universe."

Compton's smile slowly faded, and he stared intently from the screen. "I'm asking you to go. I'm begging you. If you don't, my people and I will just die in defeat rather than in victory. We will die for nothing instead of something." His smiled again, briefly. "Besides, don't give up on me so easily. I just may get out of here and find another way back home."

Garret knew it was bravado. Even if Compton got his people out of this system somehow, they'd be lost, refugees. Comp-

ton would never try to find an alternate route to human space…
Garret was sure of that. He'd never risk leading the First Imperium back with him.

"Go, my friend. It's what I would do. It's our duty. We have
lived lives of duty, my old friend. Now is no time for either of
us to stop."

He's worried about me, Garret thought, he's trying to make
this easier for me…God damn you, Terrance. Garret was
watching the screen, fighting to hold back his tears.

"You have been more than a friend, Augustus…more than a
brother. I had no idea, when I left home for the Naval Academy
all those years ago, that I would find a friend like you. We had
quite a run, Admiral Garret. It's been my great honor and pleasure to be at your side…to watch your back." Garret stared into
the screen, feeling like his insides were being torn out.

"Go now. You will have to move forward without me, bear
the burdens alone that we would have shared. I'm sorry I won't
be there to help you face the next battle. Because we both know
there will be a new one. Eventually." Compton paused, his own
carefully checked emotions threatening to burst through his
mask. "You are the best, most honorable man I've ever known,
Augustus Garret." Another pause, longer this time. "Goodbye,
my friend." Compton's face remained for a few seconds…then
the screen went dark.

"No." Garret whispered to himself, his resolve weakening.
"We'll hold them back. Somehow. I'll bring the fleet back…
we'll make a stand." He could feel how empty his words were,
even as they escaped his mouth. His lips parted again, but there
was nothing else to say. Compton was right. Garret couldn't
save his friend. There was nothing he could do…and even trying would condemn billions of people to almost certain death.

Terrance Compton had won the war. If he hadn't moved
up the timetable and rushed to the front with half the Pact's
ships, the combined Grand Fleet would have arrived to find
all the enemy task forces assembled and drawn up to defend
Sigma 4. There would have been no invasion of the planet,
no capture of the enemy base, no discovery of the device that

was likely to save mankind...the Armageddon weapon that was likely intended for Earth. Compton is the hero, Garret thought bitterly...and his reward is to be left behind. Abandoned.

"Commander Rourke, we will be withdrawing through the warp gate in ten minutes." He stood slowly. "Advise General Cain that we will be activating the device as soon as Midway is clear of the gate." There...he'd said it. He'd still have to order the device detonated, but he'd done what had to be done now.

"Yes, sir."

Garret walked slowly, silently toward his office. He had 10 minutes, 600 seconds, to record a message...his own farewell to a friend.

Chapter 33

Main Corridor
"Officer's Country" – AS Pershing
Sigma 4 System

Erik Cain walked slowly down the corridor. He was quiet, somber...like almost everyone in the fleet. They'd done what they had come to do. They had found their miracle and shut the enemy out of human space. Hofstader's plan had worked. They'd tested the warp gate a dozen times...it was completely non-functional. There was only a faint blue aura where it floated in space...50 million petatons of trapped energy slowly escaping, as it would do for the next several centuries.

The war was over. But the cost had been beyond reckoning, and dealing with the aftermath would be brutally difficult. Death in battle would have been far easier, much more merciful. Leaving comrades behind, trapping them and condemning them to almost certain death....Cain couldn't imagine anything worse for an honorable fighting man. And there were few more honorable than the man who'd had to give the order...Augustus Garret.

Cain had become close to Compton, and he mourned his new friend and the thousands who'd served with him, but he knew it was different for Garret. He and Compton had been like brothers for more than 40 years. Erik Cain was no stranger to difficult decisions and the consequences of giving fateful orders...but he couldn't imagine what this one had cost Garret. He knew, better than almost anyone else, what it took, how deeply it hurt to accept the responsibility for such commands.

There had been no choice. Compton's fleet had about 40,000 Marines and naval personnel aboard. If those enormous First Imperium dreadnoughts had gotten through the X2 warp gate, the billions of people in human occupied space would have been as good as dead. No, Garret hadn't had any choice. But Cain knew that didn't make it any easier. Not even a little.

He stopped at a wide hatch with a small wallpad next to it. "Admiral Garret?" Cain touched the pad and spoke softly. "It's Erik Cain, sir." No one had dared disturb Garret. The admiral had calmly remained at his station after Hofstader blew the warp gate, ordering test after test to confirm the operation had been a success. Then he issued orders for the fleet to regroup and begin the journey home. After that, he left the bridge without a word. That had been two days before, and no one had seen him since.

There was no response, but after a few seconds, the door slid open. Cain hesitated. He always hated when people disturbed him in situations like this. He knew they meant well, which, perversely, seemed to make things worse. Friends always felt the need to try and help…and they never seemed to understand what Cain was sure he knew. There was no making things better…there was only surviving them. And that was something you had to do alone. But now he felt obligated to pay this visit…not just for Garret, but for Compton too. Terrance Compton would have been the one to disturb Garret's isolation, to make the futile effort to succor his friend and relieve his pain. But Compton was gone, unable to sit with Garret, to offer his friend absolution. Since Compton couldn't do it, Cain decided he had to do it for him…he would stand in for the fallen hero.

He stepped slowly into the room. It was dark, just a small bank of dim lights on. "Admiral?"

"Yes, Erik. I'm over here." Garret was lying on the sofa, eyes closed. "What can I do for you?"

"Nothing, sir." Cain found it hard to continue. He'd tried to think of what he wanted to say on the way to Garret's cabin, but he'd come up blank. Now he was winging it. "I just thought we could talk." God that sounds stupid, he thought…you hate it when people say shit like that to you.

"Sit." Garret's arm flopped up, pointing sloppily toward a pair of chairs. "Did you draw the short straw?"

"No, sir." Cain sat gently in the closer chair. "Actually, no one knows I'm here. I think the rest of them will leave you alone, at least for another day or two."

Garret let out a short, bitter laugh. "It's going to be more than a day or two, my friend." Garret's voice was toneless...not sad, not angry...just dead, without any emotion. "Let me tell you a little something, Erik. I've made a lot of command decisions in my career...but only two I felt I couldn't live with. The first one was a long time ago, and it almost finished me. I came this close to leaving the service." He held up a hand, two fingers almost touching. "You know who pulled me through that?"

Cain sat quietly, listening. Garret's question didn't require an answer. They both knew it already.

"Well, now he's gone...because of another command decision I made." He was motionless, eyes still closed. "What is that? Irony? Symmetry? I'm not sure." He was quiet for a few seconds. "But this is the one that did it. I'm out. As soon as I get the rest of the fleet safely home, the navy can have my stars back."

"Admiral..."

"Fucking Christ, Erik, I'll give you half a dozen more platinum stars if you cut out the admiral and sir bullshit."

"Yes, si...Augustus." Cain took a breath before continuing. "I didn't come here to give you a pep talk or assure you that you did the right thing. You know perfectly well you didn't have any choice." Another pause. "And you also know that means exactly nothing to how you feel...to the price it rips from your soul."

Garret finally stirred, turning his head to face Cain. "You're really not good at this at all, are you Erik?" Garret almost let out a short laugh, but it died on his lips.

"Like I said, Augustus...I didn't come here to bullshit you and to tell you the world's all warm and fuzzy. We both know better." Cain's own voice was strained, emotional. "But this war has cost each of us our best friends." He paused to gather himself. "I thought maybe we could talk about them for a little while. About Terrance and Darius."

Garret pulled himself upright, sitting on the couch looking over at Cain. "I'd like that, Erik."

Tara Rourke was sitting quietly at her post. She was worried about Garret, as virtually everyone in the fleet was. She was mourning as well. Those were her comrades too that they'd left behind...and more than one friend. She'd imagined many sorts of danger and sacrifice would be part of her military career, but in all of those thoughts she'd never considered being forced to abandon her comrades. She knew there had been no other choice, but it still felt wrong. Dirty. Cowardly. And yet somehow it was also the bravest command decision she'd ever seen. Not for the first time, she gave silent thanks that Augustus Garret was the supreme commander. There wasn't a doubt in her mind the First Imperium would have destroyed mankind if Garret hadn't been the supreme commander.

Despite the sadness, she could hardly believe the war was over. The fleet, and the Marines too, had worked themselves up for the fight, convincing themselves they'd find a way to win. But she wasn't sure she'd ever really believed it...she didn't know if any of them had. Now the war was really over. Perhaps it hadn't been a victory in conventional terms, but the invasion had been stopped, and human space saved from destruction. Their comrades had not been lost in vain.

One of her console's indicator lights flashed green...a message coming in from the Commnet station in the system. She pressed a small button, and the contents were displayed on her screen. She wasn't expecting anything important, but as soon as she started reading she felt her stomach shrivel. My God, she thought. Admiral Garret has to know this immediately!

Cain and Garret were both silent. They'd talked for over two hours, about things neither man had discussed with anyone before. They were too drained to continue, but both knew they had done what had to be done. They had said their farewells to lost friends…fallen brothers.

They hadn't showered each other with platitudes and point-less feel good nonsense. They both knew they would carry the pain of their losses as long as they lived, that time would per-haps dull the edge a bit, but nothing more. Garret hadn't told Cain that Jax's death wasn't his fault, as everyone else insisted on doing. It had been, at least partially, and both men knew it. Instead, Garret had told him they all make mistakes, that Jax would have understood, would have told him the same thing. He tried to offer him the forgiveness he knew Jax would if he'd been able. Then he told a story, an old story, of how his own foolishness and recklessness had cost him someone very dear to him. It was something Garret had spoken of only once before… and never again in the almost 40 years since it happened.

"What is that?" Cain finally spoke, gesturing toward a 'pad lying on the table between the sofa and the chairs. "If I may ask."

"It's from Terry." Garret's voice was heavy with exhaus-tion. "He attached a personal message to his last communique." There was a body of text – a normal note – and below there were several columns.

"It looks like a list of planets with numbers following." Cain had a quizzical expression on his face.

Garret's eyes moved to the 'pad. "They're bank account numbers, Erik." His voice was soft, shaky. "The legendary poker winnings of Terrance Compton. He didn't want it to go to waste." Garret closed his eyes tightly, breathing deeply as he sat still as a statue. "Damn you, Terry," he whispered, his barely audible voice cracking with emotion. It was just like Compton, he thought, feeling his control slipping. He gritted his teeth and held his eyes closed tightly, but a tear still forced its way out and ran down the side of his face.

Cain started to get up. "I guess I should be leaving, Augus-tus." He was sure the talk had done them both some good, but he also knew Garret's loss was only two days old…he'd had two years to adjust to Jax being gone. He needed to give the admiral time to grieve alone. "But if you want to talk again, just com me. Anytime."

"I will Erik." He started to rise himself. "And Erik... thanks."

"Like I said, admiral. Anytime." He turned toward the door.

"I'm going to do something I should have done two days ago...something you just shamed me into doing." Garret looked down at his rumpled uniform. I'm going to change into fresh clothes and shuttle over to Camille Harmon's ship." He paused. "We lost our best friends, Erik. But she lost her son."

Cain had a pained expression on his face. He'd forgotten that Max Harmon was Compton's tactical officer. "Do you want me to come along, admiral?"

"No Erik, I think this is my job to do. Alone." He started walking toward the bathroom, then he stopped and turned back. "But thank you, Erik."

"Yes, si...Augustus. All you ever have to do is ask." Cain started walking to the door.

Garret was going to make one more stop after seeing Harmon. Elizabeth Arlington loved Compton...he was sure of that. And he knew his friend had felt the same way. They'd never had their chance together...duty had always intervened... and now they never would. Garret knew Elizabeth would be devastated, but he was just as sure she'd never let it show, not while she was in command of one of the fleet's task forces. She might talk to him, though. And he owed it to Compton, his lost brother, to see that Arlington got through this. He still wasn't sure how he was going to deal with it all himself, but that wasn't going to stop him from doing his duty to Compton. No, by God...he wasn't going to fail Compton again.

"Admiral Garret...Commander Rourke wishes to speak with you." Garret shook himself out of his deep thoughts. It was Nelson...Garret had put a block on his com, meaning anyone had to convince the AI to disturb him in order to get through. "It is extremely urgent."

"Put it on speaker, Nelson." He looked over at Cain. "You better stay and see what fresh disaster this is."

"Admiral Garret, I'm sorry to disturb you." Rourke's voice was uncomfortable, apologetic. It was clear she'd rather be cleaning the fusion core with her toothbrush than disturbing Garret now."

"It's fine, commander. What is it?" Garret tried to keep his voice even, professional.

"We just received a message on the Commnet, sir." She paused to clear her throat. "It's from Wolf 359 III, admiral...a Gregory Sanders. He says he is the prime minster of Arcadia."

Cain and Garret looked at each other with stunned expressions, listening intently. They remembered Greg Sanders well. He had been one of the prime movers in the rebellion on Arcadia.

"It is a text message only...no audio or video. And it's staticky. It sounds like someone was trying to jam the initial signal."

"Read the message, commander."

"It says, Wolf 359 V shipyards under armed attack by forces unknown. We are scanning a group of unidentified vessels approaching Arcadia. I have placed all planetary military forces on high alert. Will report further, if possible. Sanders, Prime Minister, out."

Garret and Cain stared at each other in stunned silence. Finally it was Cain who spoke first. "It's time to get home, sir."

The Shadow Legions
Crimson Worlds VII

The war with the First Imperium is over, and Grand Fleet is limping home from the frontier. Erik Cain, Augustus Garret, and the rest of the high command are grimly satisfied that humanity has been saved from the First Imperium menace. There is no joy, however…no elation at the "victory." The losses this time were too heavy…too personal…to bear. They had done what had to be done to drive back the enemy and save the human worlds from certain destruction. Now they were left to find a way to live with the gut wrenching decisions that victory had required.

Augustus Garret needed time. Time for repairs, time to replace losses, time to learn how to go on in the aftermath of what he'd done. But the fleet wasn't heading for a well-deserved rest…they were moving into another firestorm. A new menace, one as deadly as the First Imperium, was waiting for them, and it threatened to shatter the fragile alliance of the Earth powers and throw all of human space into another desperate war…one that might truly be the final confrontation.

On world after world, mysterious forces are invading, taking control of the most vital colonies. The invaders are well-drilled powered infantry, veteran forces that quickly shattered the planetary militias and established brutal occupation regimes.

Garret, Cain, and the leaders of the Pact's forces must rally themselves once again to face this new threat…an unknown force that is as well trained, experienced, and equipped as the Marines themselves. Indeed, on some colony worlds rumors are already spreading that the invader are the Marines, that they have come to conquer, to rule.

December 2013

By Jay Allan

Tombstone (A Crimson Worlds Prequel)
Bitter Glory (A Crimson Worlds Prequel)
Marines (Crimson Worlds I)
The Cost of Victory (Crimson Worlds II)
A Little Rebellion (Crimson Worlds III)
The First Imperium (Crimson Worlds IV)
The Line Must Hold (Crimson Worlds V)
To Hell's Heart (Crimson Worlds VI)
The Last Veteran (Shattered States I)
The Dragon's Banner (Pendragon Chronicles I)

Upcoming

The Gates of Hell (A Crimson Worlds Prequel)
(October 2013)
The Shadow Legions (Crimson Worlds VII)
(December 2013)
Even Legends Die (Crimson Worlds VIII)
(March 2014)

www.crimsonworlds.com